EXCITING, ISN'T IT?

Counterpoint
Volume One

by

David O'Neil

Argus Enterprises International
New Jersey**North Carolina

A-Argus Better Book Publishers, LLC

For information:
A-Argus Better Book Publishers, LLC
9001 Ridge Hill Street
Kernersville, North Carolina 27285
www.a-argusbooks.com

ISBN: 978-0-615744858
ISBN: 0-6157448-5-0

Book Cover designed by Dubya

Printed in the United States of America

Preface

The people at the funeral stood around as they always do, nobody quite sure when, or whether, they should move off to the house, or wait uncomfortably while John Murray stood saying a final farewell to his wife, his friend and lover of the last 21 years.

John had always regarded the graveyard as a pretty, restful place, backed by the Norman Church in the sunlight. Today, in the rain, it had the feel of graveyards everywhere, damp and depressing. A place for regrets, lost hopes and sad farewells. He stood for a while with his two daughters beside the grave. Then he moved them over to the car, the girls holding hands, still sniffing.

There were plenty of people milling around at the house but most were acquaintances.

The close friends stayed until the others had left. Kelly Martin, Deputy Director of MI6 and one time colleague of John's, came over and gave him a hug. "Anything I can do to help, just let me know." She left, kissing the girls on the way out. The last few, close friends kept the family company and helped to clear up the mess left by the departing guests.

Chapter One

Six feet tall, fairish hair, steady hazel eyes, and completely lost, John Murray at forty-six years felt quite empty and alone.

Always having to think of others, never really of just himself, being alone was a strange alien feeling. He shrugged telling himself he'd better get used to it. The girls had their own lives and he had his. For what it was worth. Get on with it!

He thought that returning to work would help him get over his loss. Over the next few months he buried himself in commissions, taking on several different projects. The work actually caused him sleepless nights and made him a lot of money. He also began to feel guilty that he was not spending the time on the work that he felt it really deserved, and that the money he was making was not earned.

He did not cut himself off from life, but also did not go out of his way to socialise. His clean cut, good looks and slightly melancholic manner drew interested glances from many of the women he was in contact with through business. Though he did not really connect with anyone at that time, he was, bluntly, not interested.

One way and another, there was a deep dissatisfaction in his life that work could not fulfil. It seemed nothing short of the return of his wife could make the difference. Over time, he realised that he would have to decide what to do with the rest of his life.

He started running again, every morning, rain or shine, building up to three miles at least each day, while meanwhile carrying on working, just to create more capital.

Eventually, after considerable thought on the subject, he decided he needed a complete change from his way of life.

The *Altair*, his ketch, was laid up at Grasse in the south of France. On impulse he contacted the yard and gave instructions to have her re-fitted and prepared for launch in the Med. He made no decision about whether to keep her or not. Still unsure he was prepared to leave the decision, for the moment at least, until he had sorted out just where his life was going.

After a meeting with his accountant he arranged to settle all his affairs within the next six months, arranging to sell the business and cash-in his life insurances, savings plans etc.

It was then that he discovered that his wife had taken out several long term bonds and saving plans that were now coming to term. All had been funded from their joint account and based on joint names. There had been no payment problems, so had been just part of the mess of papers and documents involved in her death.

The full significance of much of the information his lawyer and accountant had passed on was only now becoming significant. It did mean there was a lot more cash than John had anticipated. Added to the value of the house, which he felt was far too big for himself alone, his capital value, after giving the girls a tidy sum each, was in the region of £1million.

It was difficult to take in at first. Though they had always been comfortably off, he had never considered the possibility of being a millionaire.

The day John finally walked out of the bank in Lombard Street he realised he was a rich man, for the moment at least.

As he walked down to Cannon Street he felt himself shedding the pressures of working for a living. For the first time in over two years he was looking ahead. With a sense of restrained excitement, he took a taxi to Waterloo. There he collected his bags from the left-luggage and boarded the train to Portsmouth.

At ten thirty that evening he took his drink out to the open deck of the ferry to watch the port slip astern.

He took a deep breath. He wanted to shout at the moon, poking its face through the breaking clouds. *"The first day of the rest of my life,"* he breathed to himself. He looked about, feeling foolish, in case he had spoken aloud.

Handling the holiday barge along the waterways of Northern France was easier than John had imagined. Certainly the thought was more daunting than the deed. During the first day it really seemed that he should have accepted the offer of a crew for a day or so. On several occasions, he felt his lack of experience at handling such a long unwieldy craft. But by the second day he felt a little more at ease, and the third day proved that he had mastered the complexities of steering and engine management to a level of, if not expert, certainly inspired amateur.

The ever changing scene, passing at an even 5 miles each hour, allowed plenty of time for relaxation and winding down. For someone whose life had been full of events, wife, children, work and travel, the sheer joy of life at such a leisurely pace was a tonic. For the moment, John was prepared to live from day to day.

Paris within the week was not the joy it had once been. Moored in the river near Notre Dame may have been convenient for eating out, but re-visiting the scenes of his younger days, reminded him of the odd, fun weekends of another time. It was in a sombre mood that he departed Paris early, for the long haul south through the heartland of France, en-route to the distant Mediterranean.

At Villeneuve St George he stopped for coffee, and started to regain his earlier mood of relaxed enjoyment. The weather helped. The summer sun shone in a blue sky with odd white puffs of cloud scattered loosely across the northern horizon.

The river lay like a sheet of glass, dappled blue and grey where the shadows of trees lay across the water. The barge lay alongside the north bank facing up river. He stretched and strolled along the cabin top from bow to stern. Looking down into the water he paused and a shadow passed over his face. He stood there for several seconds, and then walked back along the boat to the wheelhouse and went below to get changed into his running gear.

He set off along the tow path easing into the loping gait that would allow him to cover several miles without particular strain. There were few people on the tow path and John found he was beginning to enjoy the day.

The sun stippled the track beside the river with light and shadow, and the level ground made running easy underfoot. He passed other boats moored to the banks on both sides of the river and waved back to several people who waved to him and called as he passed.

The river Seine forms part of the system of rivers and canals throughout France that have become a popular means of holiday travel during the summer months. He ran for about three miles before turning back on the return journey. At a small riverside shop he stopped for coffee, and managed to buy bread, cheese and fresh butter before setting off on the last short stretch back to the boat.

Boarding the *Aimee Bretonne* he put his purchases down on the cabin table. After a shower he dressed in casual shirt and fawn chinos, slipped on his rope-soled deck shoes and went up on deck.

He had already adopted the routine of travel on the waterways of France, and had relaxed easily into the slower pace of life that the river imposed. The unhurried journey down the waterway made it possible to observe nature as it passed at the steady speed, dictated by the rules of navigation for rivers and canals in France. Having left Paris that morning, he planned on staying at St. Mammas or Montereau that night.

Jumping ashore he removed the bow rope from the bollard on the bank of the river.

As he turned to jog back to clear the stern rope, he noticed the youth who was already removing the mooring rope and looping the coils to throw on to the after deck. Becoming accustomed to the casual friendliness of the people using the waterway, he waved thanks to the boy and stepped back on board. The river barge, all of 45 feet from bow to stern, was just beginning to drift away from the bank.

His programme, of sailing by river and canal to the south of France throughout the next three weeks, would give him plenty of time to adjust his progress more or less as he pleased.

The provisions he had just purchased should keep him for the next day or so, especially if he stopped for lunch at one of the many riverside restaurants on the way.

The engine started at the press of the button and glancing around before engaging gear, he noticed the lad by the stern was standing with a leather satchel in one hand waving his other hand with thumb in the air, in the time-honoured request for a lift. With a shrug, why not, he gestured for him to come aboard and concentrated on swinging the long hull out into the fairway of the river, slipping past the stern of one of the many cabin cruisers still moored to the bank.

On the deck of the moving barge his passenger coiled the stern rope neatly before trotting up to the bow to tidy the rope tossed onto the fore deck by John. Then having come to the bridge, deposited the satchel and the small backpack on deck, and removing the hooded jacket, revealed a slim, decidedly feminine figure, dressed in tee shirt and jeans.

Shaking her blond ponytail free, she held out her hand in the continental manner, and said in French,

"I am Gabrielle MacLean, from Paris, and I appreciate the lift".

He took in the open serious face, with the big grey eyes framed by the blonde hair, looking expectantly at him and couldn't suppress the smile that came in response to her formal introduction. He replied equally formally.

"I am John Murray, from Newbury, England. Welcome aboard the *Aimee Bretonne*." His French was fluent, but slightly accented. "Where are you heading for?"

"I am hoping to crew on a boat in the Med in June, and since I have time to spare, I thought I would hitch my way south enjoying the country and the weather on the way," she replied in perfect English. But what of yourself, M'sieu? This is a big boat for one person."

"I'm in no rush, so I manage quite well," he replied.

Waving at the hatch, he said, "Down below, there is coffee, cheese and bread. If you put it together we can talk whilst we eat."

For the next twenty minutes the boat cruised quietly along the waterway, the sun glinting off the water, the flash of the occasional Kingfisher making slashes of blue fire against the green banks.

He had been a little taken aback when he realised that he was giving a lift to a pretty woman rather than a boy. How old? Late twenties perhaps? On an earlier occasion he might have thought twice, but today? He shrugged and grinned wryly. Why not? She seemed bright and cheerful and obviously knew her way about boats. He would just wait and see how it worked out.

The murmur of the engine had become part of the background of birdsong and the chuckle of the water. With the burble of the occasional passing boat, it all combined to become the sound of summer.

John was able to lose himself in the peace of the afternoon, just happy to be cruising without a care in the world on the placid river. It was an adventure he had often promised himself without any real expectation of achieving it.

In other circumstances he might have done it accompanied by Mary, his wife. But they had seemed never really to have time. Then it was too late. Though he had learned to deal with the memories now, they still hurt.

Gabrielle found the bread and cheese. Rather than the coffee she found a bottle of chilled white wine in the fridge and opened it.

While she worked she thought about her host, and decided she liked the look of the man. His hazel eyes were friendly and he looked trim, possibly late forties early fifties, but showing little sign of the passing years, really quite good looking. She shook herself and gathered the food and drinks together and returned to the deck.

John's daydream was interrupted by the arrival of the bread and cheese, accompanied by the wine in the hands of his new passenger/crew.

"I thought the wine more appropriate at this time of day," she said hesitantly.

With a smile of appreciation, he agreed. "I am still becoming accustomed to the way of life on the river, so you'll have to forgive any lapses into the habits of my past!"

She edged onto the opposite seat, and the two sat companionably in the sun eating the fresh bread and soft cheese, sipping the wine and watching the rolling countryside slide past. John controlled the boat with just the occasional touch of the wheel. Their conversation occurred naturally, progressing with increasing ease as the couple got to know each other.

Gabrielle's English was without accent, for which John was grateful. His French was fluent but he was a little diffident about expressing himself, still not quite adjusted to conversing regularly in a foreign language.

He found himself telling her about the death of his wife and friend of over twenty-one years: how only now, after nearly two years had he come to terms with living alone. He was surprised at how easy it was to talk of these things to this woman that he hardly knew. And for the first time in the last two years he was completely at ease talking about himself.

Though his daughters had done their best, he had not been able to open up like this with them. They of course had their own lives to lead, and realising that, he had, finally at 49, set out on this journey through France.

"So here I am," he concluded. "I chartered the *Aimee Bretonne* and left Le Havre just over a week ago. I am on my way to Grasse where my boat is waiting. I thought, while I was on the way, I could sort out what to do with the rest of my life. So far I've been so busy just enjoying being here, I keep putting off tomorrow until it comes, then I put it off again. I'm sure I'll have thought of something by the time we reach Avignon."

When he stopped speaking they both sat quietly, comfortably enjoying the mild air in companionable silence. At Montereau he steered to the bank, and they moored for the night. The easy conversation resumed over another glass of wine, the setting sun cast shadows across the river, patterning the water and giving cover for the fish rising to catch the low flying insects that chanced the crossing.

After a period of quiet contemplation, Gabrielle spoke. "I have a confession to make. I am not expecting to join a boat in the Mediterranean. I am just hoping! I needed to get away from my life in Paris." She stopped for a moment, and John noticed that her face looked quite sad. She carried on.

"The life I was leading was beginning to make me feel hemmed in. My closest friends moved to Lille and my landlady died, leaving the apartment to her son, who was a pig. You know the sort. Despite being married he began pestering me to become his 'friend', offering to let me stay rent free if I 'looked after him' when he was visiting Paris.

For the last four years I have been trying to get established as a writer, and while I lived in Paris I wrote my first book. I'm told it's quite good.

Problems arose when I looked for a publisher. All my attempts to find someone interested in the book ended in failure.

Most of the men I encountered seemed-more interested in my body than my book. Getting into the publishing world has never been easy. The people I encountered were apparently on the fringes of the industry. I doubt if they even bothered to open the manuscript."

John looked at the elfin face across the cockpit and felt his heart miss a beat. He cleared his throat and concentrated on what she was saying.

"Sorry, John. I was running away from my past when you happened along. You appeared in the right place at the right time. I feel I'm guilty of using you in the same way that those horrible men were trying to use me."

John grinned, "Are you saying you are after my body?"

She looked swiftly up at him with alarm. Then seeing his grin, she realised he was kidding and relaxed.

"At least you don't stink of garlic and Gitaines."

They sat on in silence for some time before John rose, stretched and turned to her with a smile.

"After that heavy session of truth or consequences, how about a stroll in the moonlight along the river? I promise not to harass you. I do enjoy company when I take an evening stroll, but it's entirely up to you."

She rose to her feet immediately smiling back at him, and stepped ashore, taking his hand to steady herself as the boat moved slightly with the current.

They walked close together but, without touching, in silence. The warm, soft night and silent company seemed to be enough for both of them, occupied as they were with their own thoughts.

When they returned, John thanked her for her company. On impulse Gabrielle reached up and kissed him on the cheek. "Thank you," she said. He stood and looked at her for a moment, then turned, starting to descend the companionway.

"I'm off to bed. It's been a long day." As he went down the steps he called back

"Take the forward cabin. I'm in the aft cabin. You'll find the key in the door and towels in the seat locker. The shower is electric. Sleep well. I'll see you in the morning."

He eased down the companion way and was soon courting sleep on the bunk in the after cabin. It had been an interesting day. What was it his daughter, Sally, said? *"Go to new places, do new things, and meet new people."* Well, he was certainly doing as he was told. He wondered what Sally would make of Gabrielle, and he drifted off to sleep with that thought in mind.

Gabrielle lingered a little longer, watching the moonlight on the water. For her also the day had been good. The meeting with John had been fortuitous. He seemed a nice man, still troubled over the death of his wife but naturally open and friendly, and, incidentally, quite unconsciously attractive.

She gave a little shiver, suddenly aware that the night air was cooling fast after the heat of the day, and went below to find the shower and her cabin. Before falling asleep, she thought perhaps her luck was changing.

Chapter Two

It was the scent of frying bacon drifted through the boat, accompanied by the clatter of crockery that woke her in the morning. She got up and poked her head round the fore cabin door.

Seeing her, John called, "Come on, lazybones. Breakfast is served! Stir yourself. We have some miles to make today."

She withdrew hurriedly and a few minutes later her tousled, but fully awakened, figure came into the main cabin.

"What's the rush?" Gabrielle asked. "I thought this was supposed to be a relaxed summer cruise."

"Relaxed maybe, but I still want to see some of the country before I hand the boat back. I hope you're hungry."

He served up two plates of bacon and eggs, setting them on the table where the basket of bread was already in place. They sat and ate in silence, both busy with their own thoughts.

John broke the silence first, looking at Gabrielle across the table.

"So, what made you choose *Aimee Bretonne* in particular?"

"What do you mean, choose? I did not really choose you. You just happened along at the right moment. You needed a hand, and I was there. I think that's what they call serendipity. It was just as simple as that." She looked up at him with big grey eyes, suddenly anxious.

"Would you rather I left?"

"Do you want to leave?"

"No...no, if it is all right, I would like to stay." She looked at him, trying to see if he was serious and wanted her to leave.

His face relaxed into a broad grin,

"That's alright then. You are now an official member of the crew of the *Aimee Bretonne,* expected to do all those jobs that the Captain, that's me, designates."

After eating, they unmoored the boat and resumed the journey along the wide river, at a sedate speed.

The hum of the engine was a gentle murmur against the sound

of the waking countryside and the swish of the passing water. Once again the sun climbed high in the sky and the temperature climbed with it. Gabrielle went below, returning within a few minutes in a minute bikini.

Unselfconsciously, she walked round to the foredeck, and lay down on a towel in the sun.

John looked on in silent appreciation. There was nothing boyish about the reclining figure. He thought ruefully..... *Perhaps, if I were 10 years younger? He* sat back and resumed his contemplation of the program for the next two to three weeks, and the sheer pleasure of being alive, steering the long boat in the sunlight, in France, without a care in the world!

At noon near Sens, he spotted one of the many riverside restaurants to be found on both banks. He eased the wheel to bring the long boat into the bank, where the tables were laid on a terrace, with a sun shade casting a welcome shadow over the seated diners already enjoying their meals. On the bank bollards were placed for the convenience of passing boats.

"Wake up, crew!" he called. "Get onto the bow line. Time for lunch."

The figure on the foredeck was already on her feet, and she leaped into action, jumping ashore with the line and wrapping it around the nearest bollard. John strolled aft to the stern, and stepped ashore in a more leisurely fashion to secure the aft line. Gabrielle slipped below and emerged within a few minutes dressed in a pale blue summer dress that showed off her slim shapely figure to perfection. The sandals completed her outfit and she stepped ashore quite unconscious of the effect she was having, while John stood on the towpath looking on in approval.

The food was good and lunch lasted over two hours. When they finally rose to return to the boat, most of the other diners had left and the river bank was deserted. Both felt relaxed and they lazily discussed whether to take a siesta before moving on, or perhaps to move on straight away. They were rudely interrupted by an angry young man with a shock of black hair, who came striding down on the towpath towards the boat.

Gabrielle put her hand to her mouth, and said resignedly, "Oh, no!"

Reaching them, the young man sprang forward and grabbed Gabrielle's arm, breaking into an angry tirade in French shaking his fist, demanding that she explain why she had left Paris without telling him and obviously hurting her where he was gripping her. She cried out in pain, and tried to pull her arm away from his grip. John stepped forward and grabbed the young man by the scruff of his neck and his wrist, freeing Gabrielle. The man kicked out at John, who evaded the wild feet, and dragged the man to the river bank where he dropped him into the water.

"You know him?" He queried.

Gabrielle nodded. "His name is Pierre. He appointed himself as my boyfriend in Paris, though I did nothing to encourage him. He would keep turning up wherever I went, always refusing to take no for an answer. He has continued to pester me ever since and was one of my reasons for leaving Paris."

She looked depressed and carried on. "Needless to say, when I departed I didn't bother to tell him. Nor did I say where I was going. I've really no idea how he found me."

John chuckled. "He did seem a bit hot and bothered. That's why I thought he needed to cool off."

Gabrielle grinned back. "I suppose we had better get him out again!"

They went over to the river bank and after a moment Pierre held up his hand. John bent over and grabbed the upheld hand. With a smooth jerk he yanked the bedraggled man from the river, depositing him on the bank in a pool of water.

Gabrielle couldn't help noticing how smoothly and easily John lifted the stocky young man out of the river.

"Apologise to the lady, and explain yourself." he said.

The young man raised his head and looked at Gabrielle.

"You left without a word," he said. "Why did you not tell me you were leaving?"

"Why should I? You mean nothing to me. Why are you following me? I've told you I do not want to be with you or your creepy friends. Just leave me alone."

"Mathieu was furious and has blamed me. If I do not take you back he will be very angry!"

Gabrielle went pale at the mention of Mathieu. "What does he want from me? I owe him nothing. Just because I refused to sleep with him to get my book published. This is quite stupid!"

"No, no. It is because when you left you took some papers

from his office, very important papers according to him. He has ordered that you be brought back with his papers, no matter what!"

John leaned forward taking the abusive young man by his hair. He looked into his eyes and said very quietly. "If you come near this young lady again, I will personally make life very difficult for you. By near, I mean don't even think of following us, if you value your personal comfort."

The man shrank back from John. "You don't know what you are saying. Mathieu cannot be crossed. He'll kill us both."

"Your choice. It's him or me!" John threw him back in the water, and picking up the stern line threw it onto the deck and called Gabrielle to handle the bow line. He stepped back on board and started the engine.

They pulled out into the stream once more, leaving the bedraggled figure dragging himself out of the river for the second time.

"Should cool him off. Perhaps he'll think twice before he approaches you again! By the way, what did he mean about papers?"

"I've no idea? I don't know what he means? I know nothing of any papers other than my manuscript. I was furious when I left Mathieu's office. He gave me the creeps. His eyes always seemed to be undressing me, following me whenever I was near him. I picked up my manuscript from his desk and shoved it into my satchel, and got out of there as fast as I could. Outside I went straight back to the flat. It was then that I decided that I had enough of Paris for a while, so I packed my bag and left. I used to come to Villeneuve from Paris just to relax and enjoy the river and the peace. That's why I was there when I met you. The sight of the river reminded me that it was a good place to thumb a lift on a boat.

"Quite often people find they would rather pay someone to do the work, while they enjoy the scenery, so it's possible to get a lift where you picked me up. It's just far enough from Paris for people to realise there is more to cruising than lying on the deck sipping sundowners. If you hadn't come along, hopefully someone else would have. Otherwise.....?"

"Otherwise what?"

"Otherwise I would have got on the train to the south and looked for a berth on one of the boats in the Med! You see I had really got sick of Paris, of the sleazy types I kept bumping into in the area where I was living. Pierre was a pest." She indicated the bedraggled figure on the bank of the river. "But Mathieu frightened me."

The boat progressed along the river, and soon a bend hid the waterlogged figure standing on the bank.

John thought about things for a moment, then said, "Get your bag. We'd better look for these papers before we get into something we could regret."

Gabrielle went below and returned carrying her satchel. As she drew the manuscript from the bag, a slim wedge of papers, held together by paper clip, became detached from the rear of the manuscript.

"What's this?" John caught the slim package as it came away and glanced down the first page. There were six pages altogether, six sheets of A4 paper clipped together with a simple paper clip. John flipped through them. All typed in headed paragraphs, neatly collated into a formal report.

John looked at Gabrielle. She looked back at him, frowned and shrugged her shoulders.

"They must have attached themselves when I grabbed my book from his desk on the way out!"

John re-scanned the papers carefully passing the pages to Gabrielle as he read each one without comment. She read, flushed, and reached for the next page. By the time they had finished reading, John looked very grave.

The Report was addressed to M. Mathieu Ormande, Managing Director, Mathieu Enterprises, and it was addressed to him in Paris. Dated for the current month it was a review of current operations for the organisation:-

Operations Underway.

Movement of Goods (a) Pharmaceutical (b) Human, (here were named location of stocks in transit, and destinations.)

. Materials (a) Weaponry (b) Explosives (c) Drugs

Income.(a) Gambling (b) Protection (c) Ransom*

Miscellaneous (a) Shares and contributions from delegated work.(b) any other contributions.

Current informant and dedicated sources of information, and pressure sensitive contacts.

* The only current ransom operation is based at Auxerre at the

Chateau Maronne. It is not anticipated that the subject will be released as she has seen both of her captors.

The headings were all followed by dissertations on the state of play of each section listed. It mentioned places names and statistics, and included recommendations, just as if this was a legitimate operation.

Whoever had produced the documents obviously intended them for confidential distribution only.

The reference to current informants and pressure contacts listed a worrying number of police in the French, UK and German police forces. It also included members of the Armed Forces of four European countries. There was a note indicating that the list for USA was under separate cover, it not being relevant to Europe.

"From what I've seen so far, the place for this information is with the police. He refers here to a woman who has been kidnapped and held in the Chateau Maronne at Auxerre. Your M. Mathieu is more than a sleazy publisher. From what I can see, he runs a pretty big operation covering drugs, weapons, and traffic in women. I don't think we should give the papers back. On second thoughts, nor from the looks of things, can we go to the police. There are too many names of police and government figures here. It all hints at influence in high places.

Since he threatened you through his puppy, Pierre, I would rather we hang on to them just now, and decide how to deal with them when we have had time to think things through."

"But," asked Gabrielle. "Who can we go to, if we cannot go to the police?"

"I don't know just now," said John. After considering for a few minutes more, he decided that he should give the matter some thought without distractions.

"I'm going for a run along the tow-path so that I can concentrate on this. You can take the boat and pick me up further along the river. Stop for no one and keep clear of the riverbank. You should be alright, and I won't be far away"

"But, John," Gabrielle said. "This is my fault. You need not get involved. Perhaps if I talk to Mathieu and give his papers back?"

John looked keenly at her. She blushed and dropped her eyes. "He won't listen, will he? This is too critical. I would be playing into his hands."

"And you know what that would mean. A very unpleasant time, followed by a painful and lengthy death."

"But why should you get involved. You've had enough trouble, without adding my problems to the list!"

"Gabrielle, what would you suggest I do? Your little friend, Pierre, already knows who I am. He is not likely to forget me after I dumped him in the river twice, and threatened him with bodily harm if he came near you."

He grinned. "Anyway, how can I resist the chance to assist a damsel in distress? I'll admit when I started out on this trip I really thought that the rest would do me good. I was wrong and I can see now that I would soon have been bored to death. I had no real plans, just a vague urge to go somewhere and do something, anything. I have never been inclined to drift around aimlessly. I always preferred to have some purpose. Well, now I have. So, let me take a little time out and think things over. After all, we can go to the police tomorrow, if that's the best answer ...or not! I'll go for a run and do some thinking and we'll make plans when I get back aboard."

He went below and put on his sweatshirt and trainers, then, as Gabrielle steered the boat into the bank, he jumped ashore and limbered up. As the boat moved off he called, "Don't stop for anything until you see me. O.K?"

She waved and steered back into the mainstream once more.

Chapter Three

John watched the *Aimee Bretonne* approaching steadily along the river, Gabrielle at the wheel. He was just about to call her over, when he noticed something odd about the appearance of the barge. As an experienced sailor it was an instinct that often dictated the difference between life and death. Looking at the boat he was aware something was wrong. Then he noticed that the wake was spread far wider across the river than it should be. So he hung back in the concealment of the bushes and waited until the boat passed. The wide wake was caused by an outboard dinghy tied alongside the barge, hidden by the bulk of the boat from the South bank.

"Damn." John thought for a moment. Ahead the river ran through a small town where there were two bridges, the second of which would give him the chance to board without being seen.

Luckily the river made a long bend at this point. If he crossed the bend, he could be at the bridges before the boat. He stood and looked at the retreating boat. Then he stretched his stiffening legs and started running, leaving the tow-path and striking cross-country, over the broad fields towards the distant group of lights that marked the location of the town. Dusk was falling and he was panting by the time he reached his destination. But he was ahead of the boat once more. He could see it coming into sight around the long bend before the bridges.

At the second bridge he climbed up into the girder framework where it was in dark shadow, and prepared to drop onto the deck as the boat passed beneath him.

In the dim light of the control panel he could make out a shadowy figure crouched behind Gabrielle as she stood at the helm inside the cabin.

The boat slid under the arch of the bridge beneath him. When the aft deck was below he hung down and dropped the last few inches on to the deck. The sound of his trainers was covered by the grumble of the engine echoing under the bridge.

Dropping to his knees he peered over the cabin top.

Below, seated on the side deck, was a brutish looking man in a tight suit jacket, cleaning his nails with an evil looking knife.

Jean, for that was his name, was contemplating what he would do when he had his turn with the girl, Gabrielle. She was quite a dish and he was looking forward to sampling the goods. Pierre would want to be first since he was in charge. Anyway, ever since his term in prison, Jean had learned that he would always be second. As he daydreamed, his thoughts were interrupted by the most shocking pain in his ears, followed by a sharp pain in his neck, followed by nothing!

John, having considered for a moment, had decided what he would do. He had positioned himself immediately above Jean's head, then let his arms drop past each of Jean's ears. Jean was completely unaware of his danger. With a grunt, John slammed his cupped hands simultaneously over both ears. Shocked and stunned, Jean made no immediate reaction. Gripping the head between his hands, John twisted sharply, feeling the neck crack and the figure slump down, with his head at an odd angle, no longer a threat. Right or wrong, he was committed now.

The aft cabin was screened from the main cabin by a curtain across the open doorway. John parted the curtain slightly and saw the back view of Pierre, the young man he had thrown into the river. Pierre held a knife which he was stroking along Gabrielle's calf. He was looking at her legs.

Pierre was speaking. "You should have stayed in Paris with us, girl." He grinned lewdly. "You should not have turned me down in Paris. You'll find out what you were missing, as soon as we dispose of the old man."

Gabrielle stirred, moving her leg away from the knife blade.

"Don't move! I am looking forward to taking what you should have offered when you had the chance. My friend, Jean, is also interested, after I have finished, of course. Perhaps I should mention he has peculiar tastes. It's the prison you know. Survival there requires the cultivation of a strong stomach, and interesting sexual habits."

Gabrielle's voice was deeply contemptuous.

"I presume you've been looking after him with his strange habits. Obviously no woman would want a girly type like you!"

Pierre's reaction was to grab Gabrielle's ankle pulling her back towards him with the knife raised.

David O'Neil

John, who had heard enough, moved quietly through the cabin. He reached round the young man, plucking the knife from his hand. Pierre looked round startled still furious but puzzled, his reactions slow. John's arm wrapped round his throat and squeezed. Pierre struggled, but he could not move the arm. John squeezed tighter.

"I warned you!" He said. "I don't make idle threats." With a wrench of his arm Pierre slumped. Dropping him, John turned to Gabrielle. "Are you all right? Did he hurt you?" She turned with a glad cry and flung herself in his arms.

"I knew you would come. No. Yes. I'm alright. They were saving me for later. That horrible Pierre was describing what they intended doing to me. But there is another man with him!" She said in alarm.

"It's alright. He's no longer a problem." He stroked her hair and whispered softly into her ear. "You're safe now. I'm here and they can't touch or harm you anymore." Enjoying the relief that she was unharmed, at that moment he felt a great flood of warmth for this woman, whom he'd only known just over 36 hours. "Thank god, they didn't hurt you. I should never have left you on the boat alone like that."

Gabrielle looked at him strangely, put her hands either side of his face, and kissed him firmly on the lips. "I never doubted you would come." She looked at the body of Pierre lying on the deck, "He's dead, isn't he?" She shuddered then said, "I'm glad." Then ever practical. "Let us clear up, have a drink and sort out what we are going to do now!"

Full darkness had now fallen and the boat was still chugging along the river. John went on deck and emptied the pockets of Jean, the thug, and rolled the body into the small boat tied alongside. He went below once more, collected the body of Pierre, and dragged it on deck depositing it with other in the small boat. Gabrielle had emptied Pierre's pockets, and piled the contents, plus the flick knife and 9mm automatic, on the bunk, with the contents of Jean's pockets.

There was a considerable amount of money, about 5,000 euros between them: an address book, two sets of I.D., cigarettes, two lighters, two automatics and a note, signed by Mathieu.

The note was interesting. It removed any doubts they may have had about removing the two men. It stated quite explicitly what their job was. Recover the documents at all cost, and eliminate the woman and any companion who may be with her. Two thousand euros, in payment, with a further two thousand on delivery of the papers.

"They haven't mentioned you to Mathieu," she said. "Plus the note is addressed to Pierre at his Paris address."

"Before we go any further." John held up one of the 9mm automatics. He dropped the magazine from the butt and working the slide action ejected the round in the chamber. He then stripped the gun and showed her how to assemble it. He made her do it several times until she could do it easily. He then showed her how to load and cock the gun, stressing the position of the safety catch. "I can't let you fire it here, but I can tell you that to shoot, squeeze the whole butt closing the trigger at the same time. If you align the gun with your forearm, wherever you point, the bullet will go. Hopefully you will never have to, but its best you know anyway."

Gabrielle dropped the magazine and checked the chamber was empty, and then practiced lining the gun up with her forearm, as John had instructed. "Shouldn't I use two hands like they do on the movies?"

"That's creating the maximum target for anyone shooting at you. Better to turn sideways making the slimmest target and shooting one-handed, just as they did when duelling in the past. If you have to shoot, you often don't get time for anything fancy, so better aim and fire using the eye line along your arm if you can." He watched her load the gun and put the safety on. "Keep it with you all the time now. Put it in your bag, and don't forget it's there."

They moored the barge for the night and ate quietly by lamplight, not surprisingly neither was very hungry. They shared a bottle of wine before going to bed. John locked the boat up for the first time since he had collected it.

In the morning the mist was still lying over the water as they set off, towing the small boat behind them. Neither said much, and they concentrated on getting under way without fuss. It was Sunday and the early morning on the river was quiet with nobody stirring at this time.

Gabrielle spotted a building site, just over a mile after starting off along the river. The site was deserted. A partly-filled hole and a certain amount of hard work and both bodies lay together, covered with earth, ready to form part of the foundations of the new building.

They trailed the boat behind the barge, until an opportunity came to dispose of it.

The atmosphere was more relaxed after the grisly chore had been accomplished. They did not stop at lunchtime, preferring to put as much distance as possible behind them. Gabrielle produced the last of the bread with the cheese and coffee, and by evening they made the outskirts of Auxerre.

With the boat tied up alongside, they dined at a bistro in the town. It was a quiet meal and John was conscious of the growing tension between them. There wasn't much said, but the silences were uncomfortable. He had thought their relationship had developed to the point where they had become friends and was upset by the coolness that she was displaying. The more he got to know this girl, the more he wanted to know. So, rather than beat around the bush, he plunged straight in. "Okay, Gabrielle. What's bothering you?"

She stopped and looked steadily at him. "You killed both those men without mercy, on my say-so. Why?"

"You were in danger. I did not want to tackle both together. The first man had to be disabled quietly to clear my back without warning the other man. The second, Pierre, was touching and threatening you with a knife. I take no chances when someone I care about is in danger."

The words, quietly spoken, expressed without particular emphasis, were chilling but thrilling to Gabrielle, who was finding her feelings for this man extended way beyond the instinctive liking she had felt, when they had first met such a short time ago.

Though nothing was said at the time the atmosphere improved and it was in a much more relaxed frame of mind that they walked back to the boat.

John mentioned something which had concerned him.

"Whilst Mathieu doesn't know where we are at present, and France is a big place, I think it would be a good idea if we changed your appearance: maybe dye your hair, change the style and add glasses. With the sort of influence he obviously has, we should try to make it as difficult as possible for him. Travelling together as we are it would make sense if you became my daughter or niece, and gave you another name to go with the change?"

Gabrielle considered for a while, then......

"I agree, except I think it would make more sense if I was your wife! Nowadays couples of our relative ages are quite common, and it makes it more realistic for us to tend to keep ourselves to ourselves. Recently married lovebirds, if you see what I mean." She grinned and tucked her arm through his, and leant against his shoulder as they walked along, He smiled and tipped her head back with a finger under her chin, as she looked up she smiled, and winked. "Do you think I make a convincing bride?"

"You convinced me," said John. "Though we need to pick a name we can both remember. Can you think of any offhand?"

She thought for a while, her brow wrinkled, then her face cleared. "When I was at school we had another Gabrielle who was a little older than me, so they called me Gabby, probably because I talked too much. I thought perhaps because they couldn't think of anything else. Gabby.... Murray', Mrs Murray, how does that sound?"

"Gabby, where did we meet?" He thought for a moment." Ah, yes! In the Tate Gallery at the Turner exhibition, last summer, and married this year. 1st May. The Kensington Registry office. O.K.?"

Laughing, they boarded the boat.

"From now on we must play the part. You get some hair colour tomorrow, and from now we'll start our married life."

They went to their separate beds that night. John lay there with his thoughts for a long time not quite believing how his quiet tour through Europe had included killing two people. He felt no guilt over the killing, as he had already told Gabrielle. When someone he cared about was in trouble, he did whatever was necessary to protect them. The actions of the two men dictated that neither man deserved to live.

They spent much of the next day in Auxerre, Gabrielle having her hair restyled cut close to her head and dyed dark chestnut, the blonde ponytail gone. With narrow black-rimmed designer glasses and darker make- up, when she met John at a café in the square, he hardly recognised her.

He rose from his chair as she came to the table. It seemed the most natural thing in the world to kiss the raised lips and take her hand as she seated herself. He would have removed his hand, but she gripped him tight. He stayed holding her hand like the lover he was supposed to be.

"Well, Mrs Murray, you look absolutely stunning. What can I get you?"

"Why, thank you, kind sir. White wine would be great, darling." Both slipped into the part of newlyweds comfortably.

He took her left hand in his and discretely slid a ring on her third finger. "I hope it fits. I nearly forgot!" He said.

After lunch they shopped for supplies, but once back on the boat the reaction set in. The strangeness of the situation made both feel awkward at first. Then Gabrielle burst out laughing,

"Excuse me, Mr Murray. As your wife, do I have to iron your pyjamas?" Startled, John looked up.

"I don't wear pyjamas," he said. The silliness of the situation hit him all at once and he burst out laughing too, and the growing tension eased.

Over coffee they sat and Gabrielle mentioned something which had been bothering her.

"John, you dealt with two murderous thugs quickly and efficiently, and you know all about guns. Who are you? How did you know what to do?"

John was slow to reply at first then. "I was a Police Officer for 8 years. I graduated to Special Branch. I was seconded and later joined MI6. There I learned all sorts of antisocial skills. I served with them for 10 years. My wife became fed up with the continual upset caused by the demands of the job, so I resigned. I've always kept fit, and I belonged to a martial arts club for years, as a way of keeping in shape. Then my wife died. That was nearly two years ago. I concentrated on running from then on just to keep fit. Happily old habits die hard, and it seems the skills I learned haven't deserted me.

"Now it's your turn." He smiled and drained his coffee cup.

"Nothing much to tell, I'm afraid. I was born in Falmouth. Father was a professional yachtsman who delivered boats all over the world. Mother was the French au pair of one of his clients who lived in the area. When they married she joined him in the delivery business and became as good as Dad at boat handling. I was educated in England and France, and sailed every holiday. I found that I enjoyed writing, studied in the Sorbonne for a while and wrote articles for the college magazine and some of the local Parisian magazines. I nearly got married two years ago, but Mom and Dad were lost at sea when delivering a 60ft ketch to the Bahamas. They found the boat, but neither they nor Jack the third crewman was ever found.

"I went home to clear up their effects, sell the house etc. It took nearly three months. When I got back to Paris, my fiancé was living with the girl he has since married.

"I carried on writing and trying to get published. That's where I encountered Mathieu and our late lamented friend." She looked John in the eye.

"You're enjoying this situation, aren't you?"

"Yes," he replied. "As I said before, I think I knew that I was not cut out to drift as I had planned. Oh, I would be quite happy to relax and enjoy the good life for a holiday, but spending the rest of my life doing nothing more than bumming about, is not really my scene. You, appearing as you did, scared the hell out of me. I realised that I had been only half alive for the last two years and it was a painful awakening. Oh, by the way you need a new bikini!" He grinned. She chuckled.

"I didn't think you had noticed. I bought a new one today to go with my new hair."

"Seriously though," John said. "Before we leave Auxerre, I would like to take a look at the Chateau Maronne. I am concerned for the prisoner being kept there, if she is still alive, especially after reading the notes and hearing the comments of the late Pierre referring to you."

"Good idea. Perhaps we can find out about the Chateau here," Gabrielle suggested.

He caught the eye of the waiter and asked him about the Chateau Maronne.

The waiter, a man of about forty, said that, though it was picturesque, it was no longer open to the public. When M. Latour died it had been bought by an American. He didn't quite spit in disdain, but the message was obvious. Apparently the new owner was away at present, but the two 'caretakers' were still there to look after the place. Once again the expression said it all. John thanked him and gave him a healthy tip as they left the restaurant.

Before John could say anything, Gabrielle said "I'm coming to the Chateau with you. I am the reason we are here. This is a partnership or nothing, so where you go I go." She looked into his eyes and he could see that there was no middle way, together or nothing.

John shrugged. "All right. But we go armed and prepared to act if the chance arises, agreed? And, partnership or not, this is my territory. You do what I tell you. Understood?"

She nodded meekly, and they returned to the boat to prepare. Later in town John hired a car. They loaded it with a picnic and a travel rug and set off, the guns concealed, the flick-knife in John's pocket.

The Chateau was as beautiful as described. The tall gates at the entrance to the drive were closed though not locked. On impulse John got out and opened the gates and they drove up the drive to the impressive front door. They got out of the car, walked over to the door and rang the bell.

A man came round the corner of the house and, seeing them, ran up to them gesticulating angrily.

"Who the hell are you? How did you get in? This is private property. You must leave immediately."

When he stopped in front of them, red faced from his efforts, John said evenly,

"We were invited by M. Latour last summer. Please inform him that we are here!"

The front door opened and a smooth looking man in a black jacket stood in the doorway and took in the scene.

He said, "Get back to your work, Maurice. I will deal with this." He looked enquiringly at the visitors. John repeated the story of the invitation from the deceased M. Latour. The man nodded and stood aside.

"Please come in, Sir, Madam. My name is Bertrand. I am the butler." When they entered he led them to a drawing room to the right of the door, and invited them to sit. He then explained that M. Latour had sadly died last year, and the house had been sold to an American gentleman in the computer business. The house was closed for renovations, though it was hoped that it would be reopened later in the year, when Mr McCord would be back from California.

It was beautifully done. Were John and Gabrielle not already aware that the story was merely a cover, they would have been taken in.

As it was John rose from the settee and faced the man and casually asked to see Madam. Bertrand's face changed.

"Madam?" He queried.

"Yes. The lady who is currently a guest in this house."

"But there is no lady here," said Bertrand tautly. "Now I must ask you to leave. I will let M. McCord know you called." He waved a hand at the door. "If you please."

John grabbed his lapels and thrust him down into a chair. The door opened and Maurice appeared with a shotgun in his hands. For a moment everything seemed to start going wrong, until Gabrielle put her automatic to Maurice's head.

"Please put the gun down slowly and carefully, on the table in front of you.....Good man. Now sit down and be quiet."

John returned his attention to Bernard.

"The lady?"

Bertrand bared his teeth.

"Fuck off," he said.

John took out the flick knife and pressed the blade release. The blade snapped open and glinted evilly in the light from the window.

"Let's go over that again shall we. Now where is the lady?"

Bertrand looked at the knife that was weaving in front of his face, approaching his left eye, getting nearer and nearer. He tried to move back from the knife, but was stopped by the chair back.

"She is in the cellar." He jerked his head to one side away from the knife. John stood back and gestured him to his feet.

"Wait," he ordered, and frisked him down for weapons, The Berretta was tucked down the back of his trousers under the jacket. He then checked Maurice, and collected another automatic which he gave to Gabrielle to put in her handbag. She put the gun away then, taking two cable ties from her bag, proceeded to tie the hands of both men behind their backs.

The cellar door was locked. The key hung on a hook next to it. Stairs led down to a large vaulted area, with wine racks in rows on both walls and down the centre. The cellar was empty apart from the wine. The group moved through to the far corner, where another door opened into a small room with a naked light hanging from the middle of the ceiling. In the corner was a bed where a woman was laying facing the wall. As they all trooped in, she spoke.

"Leave me alone, pigs." The cultured American voice was defiant, but resigned, as if she knew they would not leave her alone until they were ready to.

"Madam?" John asked quietly. She turned swiftly and saw the two bound men, Gabrielle and John. When she turned it was apparent from the torn state of her clothing, the bruised face and arms, that the men had taken their pleasures violently. Gabrielle gasped when she saw the damage.

"Can you walk?" John asked.

"Give me the chance," she said, and held up her bound hands. The flick knife made short work of the rope round her wrists which had been tied to a pipe that was against the wall by the bed. With a sigh of relief, she rose to her feet and stretched, ignoring the fact that by so doing, her torn clothing revealed her breasts unfettered by the tattered remains of her underwear. She then turned to Maurice and kicked him hard in the groin, sending him moaning and writhing to the floor.

"Animal," she spat. She kicked him again in the throat and, ignoring the frantic wheezing as he tried to breathe, turned to Bertrand. He cowered back and fell onto the bed on his back shaking his head. John and Gabrielle were stunned by the speed of her reaction, and, before he could prevent it she snatched the flick knife from where it lay on the bed and plunged into Bertrand's stomach. He screamed.

"Bastard," she said. "Fuck me to death would you. Fuck this." She withdrew the knife and plunged it between his legs. He screamed once more and fainted. The pool of blood from the wounds rapidly grew on the floor below the bed. She turned to Gabrielle and collapsed in her arms. Maurice was still trying to breathe through a smashed windpipe, and Bertrand was dying possibly already dead, of shock from the terrible wounds that he had suffered. John ignored them both and gathered the slight figure of the lady into his arms and carried her upstairs, going directly to the first floor where Gabrielle found a bathroom. She took over, stripping the lady and seating her in the shower, where she washed her, gently cleaning the dirt of several days of privation and abuse from her bruised body.

In one of the bedrooms John found an expensive set of suitcases containing woman's clothing, which he guessed belonged to the hostage. He called to Gabrielle and told her, then continued searching. He found where the men had been sleeping and searched their possessions. Apart from ammunition and nearly 10,000 euro's stuffed in a small cupboard in the kitchen, he found nothing of real use.

The keys of a Mercedes 230 were lying on the hall table. After a look around the outbuildings, he found the car in one of the garages behind the house. It was apparently the car being used by the lady when she was kidnapped.

Before leaving the Chateau, John cleaned everything they had touched, including the front gates where he had opened and later closed them. The two men, Bertrand and Maurice were both dead in the cellar, Maurice having suffocated from his smashed throat and Bertrand from his terrible wounds

John followed Gabrielle, who drove the Mercedes and the lady whom they now knew as Jeanne Ascher back to the boat. There she collapsed on the bed in the fore cabin with a sigh of relief.

John spoke to a profoundly relieved Michael Ascher, who was at his Company's Paris Headquarters, and arranged to meet at Auxerre. He established that Michael Ascher had been contacted by Mathieu. He stressed to Michael that under no circumstances should Mathieu be told that Jeanne had been rescued, better he find out the hard way.

Michael agreed.

When he arrived John brought him to the boat to a tearful and loving reunion with his wife. No ransom demand had been made, only an assurance that payment would be expected for services in the future and no reassurance that Jeanne would be returned. From the comments in the documents and from the signs at the Chateau, it appeared that there was no intention of either.

"So far, I've told him nothing, but I have demanded proof that he has Jeanne."

"Have you told the police?" John asked.

"No. I was told that if the police were brought in, Jeanne would be dismembered, and the pieces returned to me by letter post."

"It's just as well, as he has contacts in the police forces of several of the European countries, and appears to be able to exert pressure in many government areas."

Whilst Jeanne slept, John and Michael sat with Gabrielle and compared notes. Michael's immediate reaction was to offer John and Gabrielle an enormous amount of money, as a reward for returning his wife. They refused, and John explained their situation in relation to Mathieu. He pointed out that the only reason they were in a position to help Jeanne was because of their accidental possession of the documents from the Mathieu's desk. For this reason alone, they were now targets for Mathieu and his men. In essence, they were both living on borrowed time.

"So you see, for Gabrielle and I, the only way out of this, the only way to escape the attention of Mathieu, is to take the war to him, to destroy him."

Michael's reaction was as expected. "You must be joking. From what you say this man has the resources of an international criminal organisation behind him. What do you think two people can do against a set up like Mathieu's?"

"Don't you see? If we don't do something, who will?" John was serious. "The only real advantage we have at this time is the fact that they are a large organisation. To them we are small fish and regarded as a nuisance. After all how could we dare oppose the might of the Organisation.

"As I see it, that is our greatest advantage. We don't wish to spend the rest of our lives running. The option is to accept whatever Mathieu cares to dish out, and frankly, I will not allow Gabrielle or myself to suffer without a fight." He stopped and took a swig of his drink.

Michael sat back stunned. He did not know what to say. They had already discussed the fact that this gang supplies weapons and explosives to terrorists and drugs to the distributers.

John continued, "They have already tried to recover the documents and kill us both. They may still be unaware that your wife has been recovered, but you can bet, when they find out, we will be suspected, because the kidnapping is mentioned in the documents." He paused once more, then, "So far we have been funded by the crooks. He produced the 10,000 euro's he had found that day and the remains of the money found on Pierre and his friend. As things stand we could do with help, but, with or without help, we will carry on hurting the organisation wherever and whenever we can.

"How we do that? I don't know. Perhaps we will need to recruit people who think like us, to infiltrate and sabotage any way we can, starting with the enemy we know: In this case, Mathieu."

It was a thoughtful man who went off to join his wife that night, and it was a long time before he finally slept.

John and Gabrielle got down to the business of planning for the next few days, deciding their route and what arrangements they needed for security. Finally Gabrielle brought up the subject of the arrangements within the boat.

"I will have to move into the aft cabin with you. People would consider it odd if newlyweds did not share sleeping arrangements. I will make up the other bunk, and we can undress in the dark, if that's alright?"

"O.K. We should be able to manage," said John. "I'll pack my gear away now. We'd be as well moving the boat before we do anything else, just in case anyone sees what's happening and wonders what's going on."

The following morning Michael and Jeanne left for America. They took his private jet from Dijon. A helicopter collected them from the airfield on the west side of Auxerre. Before they left, Jeanne hugged them both with tears in her eyes, and thanked them for saving her life. Michael shook hands. He took John aside. "About our conversation last night. I'll be in touch!" He said simply.

The Mercedes was a hire car and would be collected later that day. They locked the keys inside the car and left it on the quay for collection.

That evening they moored the *Aimee* beside a tree fringed meadow.

John had tethered the boat to two substantial trees, using a slip hitch and bringing the loose ends back to the boat. "Just in case," he remarked later.

They cooked spaghetti for dinner and John produced Chianti to accompany the meal. They had managed the sleeping arrangements without any problems, though John found it difficult to sleep, disturbed by the sound of Gabrielle's soft breathing from the bunk opposite.

Mathieu was angry. Things were going wrong. He had not heard from that idiot, Pierre and his partner, Jean. No phone calls, nothing since they last spoke three days ago. Enough was enough, he picked up the phone and dialled a number in Marseille, he gave his instructions in a terse clipped voice. "Check Dijon. Try the Post Office first. There's a girl and some Englishman. Send your best. I want them to ambush their boat *Aimee Bretonne* somewhere quiet on the river. I want it searched thoroughly then torched. It's a holiday barge en route to the south of France. Collect all the papers on board and kill all the people you find. Have you got that? Good. Do it!"

He slapped the phone down. Things had started going wrong ever since that girl had walked into his office. He had decided to have her from the moment he first saw her, and he had allowed her to get away with a lot since they had first met. Had he really agreed to publish her novel? He shrugged and sighed. Well it was too late now. If they brought her in he would have her anyway, and he would enjoy playing some of his games with her body before he was finished. If they had to kill her to get the papers it would be a pity, but at least he would not need to worry about the documents anymore.

Now he had made proper arrangements he felt much better. The real problem was that he had to depend on people he didn't know, and this man travelling with Gabrielle was also an unknown quantity. He was obviously no pushover. He hesitated, perhaps he should send one of his own men perhaps Cruz, or Barat? With a shrug he decided to leave things as he had arranged. If it went wrong again, he would send his own men to deal with things. Feeling a little more settled he called for one of the girls held in the basement to be brought to him. He felt he needed a little diversion to take his mind off things. As the girl was thrust through the door to his room, he observed her fear-filled eyes with pleasure. "Come, little one," he called to her. "Show me your smile........"

Chapter Four

It is always difficult to decide why the noise of the dawn chorus and the glint of early morning sun can be so normal one day, but so exhilarating the next.

John awoke to the sounds of the stirring world around them. As he opened his eyes he realised he was gazing into the grey eyes of a beautiful, dark-haired girl. For an instant he had forgotten how different Gabrielle looked. It was as if he was seeing her for the first time. He wasn't the only one to get a shock, as she suddenly realised he was awake and looking back at her. She started, and then a grin spread across her face and she sat up. The T shirt she was wearing left little to the imagination, pulled tight against her body by the pressure of the blankets.

With the same impish grin, she pulled back the blanket and leapt out of the bunk. With a twitch of her briefs-clad bottom she dived into the shower and slammed the door. John hauled himself out of his bunk and stripped off his shorts, grabbing his swim trunks he pulled them on and went up on deck. The water was cold and clean. He swam across the river and back, pulled himself out of the water and, grabbing a towel, dried off.

Below, the sound of the shower still operating, gave him the opportunity to discard his trunks, and dress. He put the kettle on, extracted a baguette from the provisions cupboard and swiftly sliced it up into pieces. The kettle boiled and he waited, then poured the hot water into the coffee filter. It was only then he called through to Gabrielle.

"Breakfast, Mrs Murray."

"Coming, love," she replied, and stepped out of the shower wrapped in her towel. "Just give me a moment."

He turned his back and heard the swish of the towel as it dropped to the floor, followed by the breathy sounds of her dressing. "All clear" she said, sitting down at the table in T shirt and jeans and holding her cup out for the coffee. "I could get used to this marriage business, waking up with a man beside me, having my breakfast prepared and a smiling face opposite me at the table."

Looking across at Gabrielle, it was becoming more and more difficult for John to ignore the way he felt about this woman, who had entered his life so dramatically. He decided not to make an issue of it, just enjoy the situation while he could.

As they cruised south for the next two days, it was difficult to remember that there was a serious threat to the happy atmosphere that surrounded them. The summer weather and the lazy cruise down the calm waters of the centre of France conspired to lull them into a feeling of security, that John realised was extremely dangerous. As they sat on deck on the evening of the third day after their 'wedding day' he raised the subject.

"These last two days have been wonderful."

"But...."

John held up his hand to stop the interruption

"But, as you probably realise, we cannot just carry on like this without making some plans to deal with our little problem. Having examined the papers thoroughly, it's clear that Mathieu will stop at nothing to recover them and prevent them falling into the wrong hands. I've thought about it and I think it would be best if we got rid of the papers for just now. If they find and search the boat, it will give us something to bargain with."

"What do you suggest?" Gabrielle asked.

"If I post them to myself at Grasse, where the boat is being prepared, we can pick them up when we arrive." John had obviously given the matter some thought.

"Why don't we try sending them to the police? They can arrest Mathieu and get him off our back."

"Great idea. Who do we know in the police who is not on Mathieu's payroll?"

"Right.... I forgot," she said. "Your boat in Grasse?"

"Yes, as I told you I had planned to travel to the south of France in the *Aimee*. On the way I would consider either cruising in the Med and deciding what to do about the rest of my life, or selling the boat, and deciding what to do at that time. Then you came along."

"If you want me to leave I..," her eyes started to fill with tears." I'll get my thi...."

He stopped her in mid word, grabbed her hand and looked

fiercely into her eyes.

"I thought you realised. You've become part of my life. We have shared danger, adventure and a great deal of pleasure in the few days since we met. Why would you think I would ever want you to leave?"

"But I've brought trouble and the chance of serious injury, even death!" Her eyes grew bigger and she spoke through her tears.

He got up and walked over to the thwart and stood there for a moment looking out over the water. Then he turned and said. "When you walked into my life, I was a lonely man stuffed full of self pity. I met you, a hitchhiker who needed a lift. Now we are involved together. You're no longer a stranger. What has happened to us has made us think and work as a team. To me you're more like family than friend, and I could never let you to come to harm. At this moment I can't envisage life without you"

He stepped ashore and wandered along the bank. After a few moments there was the patter of running feet and a hand clasped his. He squeezed her hand, and released it to put his arm round her shoulder as they strolled in companionable silence alongside the river.

Sending the papers to Grasse would lift a burden from their shoulders. In addition John made sure that concealed around the boat were various weapons. In the pocket beside the steering wheel was the flick-knife taken from the Parisian, Pierre. His companion's knife was under the coil of rope ready to moor at the stern. The bow rope concealed a large sabatier knife from the galley. Elsewhere, the brass rule was lying in the recessed shelf above the starboard bunk. Two guns were hidden below the deck in the bilge space. The other two were in Gabrielle's bag and the pocket of John's windcheater, hanging ready on the back of the cabin door.

Though John did not anticipate being attacked on the boat, it was best to be prepared. He was more worried about the big towns en route. He had arranged to pick up mail at the post office in Dijon, and later in Lyon. Both were important centres and he was not sure if their attackers had passed on any information before they were silenced.

When they reached the outskirts of Dijon he put Gabrielle ashore, arranging to meet opposite the Hotel de Ville at 1.00 pm. He then sailed on to the town moorings and tied up, making sure the concealed weapons were in place. At the Post Office he adjusted a beret donned for the day and drifted up to the post restante counter where he requested, and received, a bundle of mail. He then posted the documents to himself at Grasse.

Casually scanning the crowd in the Post Office, he noticed two hard-looking characters who seemed interested in him. They had reacted when he had given his name to the postal clerk.

He left through the side door and stopped immediately at the bottom of the three steps down to the pavement, bracing himself for the expected, and received, impact of the first of the hard men from the Post Office. As the man came through the door John bumped into him and straightened his head, catching the man under the chin with a crack. Stunned the man started to fall. John caught him and propped him against the railing, hooking his collar over the top prong of the ironwork.

He swung round towards the corner of the building and waited. As the other man turned the corner, John's elbow caught him in the midriff, causing him to fold over like a closing book. John completed the move with a vicious chop to the back of the neck and, straightening up, hooked the second man to the railing next to his friend. The pedestrian passing, at the time flinched, unsure of what he had seen because of the speed of the action. John's comment, "drunks", seemed to satisfy him. No one else stopped or cried out. Unsurprised, he relieved them of their guns which seemed to be standard issue for the villains of the area. There were also two wallets stuffed with notes, which he retrieved to add to the kitty of ill-gotten gains, to be used in the current dispute.

Later, a bareheaded John met Gabrielle outside the Hotel de Ville, and brought her up to date.

"I think we should leave town as soon as possible. We don't need them to find the boat or you. Make your way back to the dock. But don't board until I get there, please!" He looked her in the eye. "No heroics this time."

She returned his look, and nodded.

"Okay. I'll be good. I presume we must not be seen together?"

"Exactly. See you later." He left her there and got a taxi to the river port.

Stopping the cab before he reached the port entrance, he

wandered into the mooring area as if he hadn't a care in the world. There was no one to be seen near the *Aimee* and there was no sign of movement on board. John wandered up to the boat moored ahead of his, where the occupants were sitting drinking wine in the shade of an awning spread over the centre deck.

The couple were English and John introduced himself as their neighbour at the quay. They invited him aboard to join them for a glass of wine. Seated, he steered the conversation round to their holiday, and Dijon, and established that no-one had been nosing around the boats since he had gone to town earlier. He excused himself, promising to meet later in Lyon. On board, he was relieved to find there had been no intrusion. When Gabrielle returned, they left the mooring and carried on downstream through the fields of vineyards on either side of the river.

They moored in the quiet of the evening. The water rippled down the side of the barge as she lay at anchor in the holding pond above the lock. John and Gabrielle sat enjoying the evening air with the last of the wine from dinner.

John passed Gabrielle a letter

"Michael left this for us at the Post Office." He said.

"What do you think?" Gabrielle read the note,

"What does he mean? Contact Bank of Cayman, account 700689?"

"I can ring the phone number and find out!"

"Oh, leave it until tomorrow." Her voice was drowsy as she sat back in the lounger enjoying the evening.

After a while John spoke,

"You know we have to split up, don't you! The enemy are getting close. If they get you, they'll have me, and if they have me they'll have the documents."

Gabrielle sighed "But what will I do? I don't want to leave now, things are just getting interesting." She looked at John, thinking of his comments earlier about not imagining life without her. She shivered and twitched her shoulders, and admitted to herself that it was difficult to envisage life without him.

"It will only be a temporary separation. This boat is too conspicuous. It will not take long for them to find out that I am on it, and I don't want them to find you. What I want you to do is to make your way to Lyon by hire car. There I want you to contact an old friend of mine in London."

"An old friend?"

"Yes. A lady named Kelly Martin. She is the Deputy Director of M.I.6. I will ring from here and explain. She will want you to speak on the nearest secure telephone. That will be in Lyon, I hope she can bring in some assistance to help take the pressure off. I'll just try her number now" He punched a number in on the mobile phone and held it to his ear. After a few moments, he spoke.

"Kelly? It's John Murray. Where can we get a secure line, between Dijon and Lyon? Is that the closest? How do we access it? I'm with someone. Gabby Murray. Yes. My wife. She will tell you all about it when she gets to Lyon. Hey, Kelly….thanks."

"My wife?" He grinned. "What can I say? I could not give your real name over an open line. There may be a tag out for it, through Mathieu's police contacts."

They planned their strategy for the next few days, arranging to meet in Lyon in four days.

By the time John got into his bunk, he was tired but satisfied that they had done all they could to keep Gabrielle safe. He admitted privately that she meant a lot more to him than she should. He lay back in the bunk with a sigh, only to realise that Gabrielle was standing by the bunk.

"I couldn't sleep. I'm frightened. Can I come in with you?"

He said nothing, just held out his arms and held her close, burying his face in her hair, hardly believing this was happening to him.

Morning came all too soon. John made a hasty breakfast and passed the boat through the lock with the first group. He pulled over to shore by the small town of Thorey-en-Pleine. Gabrielle took the stern rope and looped it loosely round the bollard. She then looked round to see if there were any watchers. Seeing nothing, she waved to John and walked into town. In her bag was one of the guns retrieved from his two attackers in Dijon.

As she walked down the street, she became aware she was being followed. To identify her follower, she stopped suddenly and looked in a shop window, as she turned she saw a tall man step into a shop doorway. He was a slim figure in a trilby hat, and a grey shirt, and white shorts with slip-on shoes. She walked to the next café-bar and sat at a pavement table.

Trilby hat approached and sat down nearby. Gabrielle took out her compact and studied the man, who had taken out a paper and was reading it. She noticed the shirt was not tucked in and suspected that there was a gun tucked into the waist band of his shorts. She thought for a moment, then called the waiter and asked for the toilet. She rose and went into the café to the toilets at the rear. After a moment, trilby got up and followed.

The toilets were typical of French country towns throughout France. A room with urinals against one wall with two cabinets against the opposite wall. A wash basin was beside the door. The toilet was empty. Gabrielle drew her gun and waited beside the door. As it opened she caught a glimpse of her shadow. Then she slammed the door behind him and ground the gun against his temple.

"Give me your gun. Use two fingers only." Her voice was cold and hard. The man did not argue he lifted his shirt and removed the gun carefully and dropped it into her open bag.

"Now. Both hands behind you." He lowered his hands and stood with them crossed behind him. Gabrielle dropped a looped cable- tie over one hand. "You know what to do," she said, and stepped back, holding her gun steadily aimed at the man's head. He slipped the loop over his other hand and presented his hands to the girl who grabbed the end of the tie and yanked it tight. She kicked open a stall and indicated for him to sit.

"Who are you?" She said. He sat for a moment, amazed that he been taken so easily by this little woman. The gun waved in his face.

"My name is Paul Cadet. I was told to look for a girl from a boat on the Canal de Bourgogne. I saw you and thought I should follow you and see if you were the target."

"Target?" she prompted.

"We were all told to look out for a girl called Gabrielle MacLean."

"What were you supposed to do with this girl?"

"I don't know. I was just told to shadow her and call in."

"You can do better than that." The gun lowered and she hit him deliberately on the kneecap.

He yelped with pain,

"Hey. I'm telling the truth."

"Who were you going to call?"

"Some guy in Paris, the number is in my pocket." He indicated the breast pocket of his shirt.

She found the note and recognised the telephone number.

"Do you know this man?" she waved the paper at Cadet.

"As I said, I was told to call the number if I found you, that's all. I don't even know the man who gave me my instructions!"

She looked at him and decided he was probably telling the truth.

"Where is your car? Quickly now. I'm in a hurry.

"I'm parked just over the road, in the square."

"This is what we are going to do. You turn round now. Cadet struggled to his feet and, with difficulty, managed to turn facing the wall.

"Please don't shoot me," he said. To his surprise, he felt a blade cut the cable tie releasing his hands.

"Turn around," the voice behind him was icy and he turned quickly. She held out another cable tie. "Round your neck." He slipped the loop over his head. Gabrielle gripped the end of the tie and tightened it enough to grip his neck so that he could just breathe. If she pulled her end he would choke to death: no way to undo it without a cutter.

"We are going to walk over to your car and we are going to get in and drive off. But before we go, have you got any friends in town? Please don't lie to me. I would have no compunction about pulling this tight."

He shook his head.

"No. I come from Pouilly-en-Auxois, back up the canal. I know no one here."

"O.K. let's go. Nice and friendly." They walked out from the toilet and the café, her arm round his shoulder affectionately. Across the road the blue Peugeot 406 stood parked in the square. They approached the nearside and both entered through the passenger door, Cadet in the driving seat. "Right. Drive to St Jean-de-Losne!"

Without another word, Cadet drove out of Thorey-en-Pleine, on the D road south to St Jean - 18 Kilometres down the road.

When they arrived, she produced more cable ties. He groaned and held up his hands to receive the loop which she slipped on and tightened. With a second tie, she attached his hands to the steering wheel.

Taking the keys from the ignition, she got out of the car and locked it. With her hand bag slung over her shoulder, her hand comfortably gripping her gun inside, she set off up the tow path. Out of view of the car, she stopped and sat on a seat by the canal, for the next few minutes she sat and shivered in reaction. She could not believe that she had just captured a man at gunpoint. Her breathing slowed and she calmed down. She had the irresistible urge to laugh. The thought of her banging the man on the knee with the gun to get his attention struck her as very funny. She calmed down and keeping an eye on the car, and the canal waited for the *Aimee Bretonne* to reach the junction with the River Saone

Chapter Five

The boat came round the long curve John standing by the wheel, scanning both banks of the canal.

Taking a last look at the car, Gabrielle stood and waved to John. He steered to the bank and she leapt on board.

"Pull over to the bank by that car." She said.

Without a word John swung the wheel, slid alongside the bank and stopped.

Gabrielle explained what happened, and indicated the car with its occupant.

"He called himself Paul Cadet. I think he was telling the truth about just being told to trail and report. I don't think he called anyone, as he wasn't sure if I was the right person. The number he was to call was Mathieu's."

They stepped ashore and went to the car. Cadet was asleep. Gabrielle took cutters from her bag and cut the three ties securing Cadet.

"Out," John said crisply. "Get onto the boat."

Without a murmur, Cadet stepped onto the deck of the *Aimee* and preceded John below, where he was tied once more and stowed in the fore cabin.

Gabrielle went down to the car once more and climbed in. Putting it in gear, she set out for Lyon.

Back on board, John put together sandwiches and coffee, and, pushed Cadet through to the main cabin.

"I'm going to cut you loose so that you can eat. Make a move and you can save yourself the trouble of eating. Do I make myself clear?" Cadet nodded.

"One more thing; Mathieu, the man in Paris, will have written you off. To him you are already dead." He released the loop round Cadet's wrist, and watched whilst he ate a sandwich and drank a cup of coffee. Then he renewed Cadet's bonds, and sandwich and coffee in hand, he returned to the wheel and started the engine. He strolled down the bank and threw off the ropes and jumped back on board.

The big barge nosed out from the bank and cruised down to the junction with the River Saone. He anticipated spending the night at Chalon-sur-Saone, leaving the final run to Lyon over the next two days. The weather was still fine and the soft air heavy with the scent of flowers and hint of the vintner on the west bank of the river. As the day wore on his thoughts, never far from Gabrielle, were concerned with how she was managing in Lyon.

Gabrielle threaded her way through the outskirts of Lyon, searching for a secluded parking place to leave the car. Eventually she settled for a small square with a church on the East side and small shops around the other three sides. Having parked the car, she ate at a small restaurant on the west side opposite the church. When she paid her bill she got directions to the city centre from the waiter.

By 3 o'clock she stood outside the office of the Commercial Attaché for the United Kingdom. Whilst she watched, the door opened. A man dressed in waistcoat and black striped trousers hooked the door back to allow entry through a second door into the main reception area.

Taking a deep breath she crossed the road and stepped through the door. Inside the building she enquired for the Commercial Attaché. After a few minutes wait, she was shown in to a large office, carpeted with a deep pile rug at the end of which stood a large, rather ornate, desk located in the bay window. The man seated at the desk looked up and rose to his feet when he saw her.

"I'm Robert Fuller. Mrs Murray, I presume?"

"I am expected?" She said quizzically.

"I had a call from friends in London to expect you and make some arrangements for you. May I see some identification, your passport perhaps?"

She passed over her passport in her real name, expecting to have to explain about the assumed name. To her surprise Fuller examined the passport under an ultra violet scanner, checked her photograph and returned her passport without comment.

"This way, please." He indicated a door into the adjoining room. In the next room there was a table, chair and a telephone.

"Pick up the phone and ask for your contact. I will leave you to it. By the way the room is soundproof and the door locks on this side. Please lock it when I go, and knock when you are ready to leave." With a brief smile he returned to his office and closed the door. She walked over to the desk, remembered the door and went to lock it.

It wasn't quite shut and she heard Fuller speak.

"She's here now. What shall I do?" Whoever he was speaking to said something. Fuller replied, obviously repeating his instructions.

"Right. Keep her here until 3.40 then send her out. Okay, will do."

Gabrielle closed the door quietly and slid the bolt over. She picked up the phone, it was answered immediately. She asked the operator for Kelly Martin.

"Martin here," the voice was crisp but feminine.

"It's Gabby Murray and I have to hurry. Robert Fuller, the Commercial Attaché here, has been in contact with someone who has asked him to detain me, until, I presume, an ambush can be arranged. He also was not surprised to see my passport with my own name on it He didn't query it."

Kelly pressed a button on her desk and answered her. "Get out of there as soon as you can. I will send someone to you."

Gabrielle broke in, "John said the papers will be copied and sent to you during the next four days. If you can arrange some help, it should meet us at the dock at Vienne on the Rhone in two days time. If Fuller is suspect, will this phone be safe?"

Kelly reassured her. "The phone is checked by my staff every day, nothing to do with Fuller. You can talk freely."

"Tell your man to carry a copy of Nussbaum's Map of the Waterways of France. By the way my real name is Gabrielle MacLean. I must go. We will be in touch."

Replacing the phone, she glanced at her watch. It was 3.24.

She knocked at the door, then walked through. "I wonder if I could use the toilet?" She dropped her eyes as if she were embarrassed. Fuller leapt to his feet.

"Of course, it is just through here." He indicated a door across the corridor. She thanked him and went through the door.

Fuller looked relieved as she passed.

"Please stop in before you go. I have some things for you."

She nodded and shut the door.

She waited a moment until she heard his door shut. Then, clutching the grip of the automatic in her handbag, she opened the door walked down the empty corridor and slipped out of the building. Looking around she could see nothing out of the ordinary, so she crossed to the car and got in. Crouching down, out of view, she waited.

After a few minutes Fuller ran out of the building looking frantically around the area. Whilst he was there a green Citroen screeched to a halt beside him. There was a rapid exchange of words between the men in the car and Fuller, who was now looking scared. Then the car raced off in the direction of Avignon to the south.

When the excitement died down, Gabrielle calmly started the Peugeot and drove off north to Villefranche.

The call to Mathieu was not a happy one. The man from Marseille was apologetic, but as he explained, he had not realised that the Englishman was a professional.

"What do you mean professional?" Mathieu was furious. "I told you to use your best men, a simple thing for two good operators. They could not manage a simple task like that?"

"They will not make the same mistake again!"

"I certainly hope not." Mathieu's tone was biting. "I expect better results than this. I suggest you get your act in order, or I will need to find a replacement for the Marseille operation. Do you understand?"

"I get the message. We will take the boat and deal with it as you have ordered!"

Putting the phone down Mathieu pulled another phone from the desk drawer and pressed a speed dial button. In Chicago the phone at the other end was lifted and a voice said

"Yes?" The voice was smooth, the accent mid-Atlantic, and as cold as Mathieu's own.

The conversation was not long, neither man bothering to defer to the other. Politesse was lacking and they spoke as equals. Mathieu told him there were no problems with the expansion plans, and that the people concerned were all in place. The American said that the group would be prepared to finance the establishment of a proper headquarters in Paris, as it seemed the potential business would merit it. His last words on the subject contained a menace that was not lost on Mathieu. If he allowed things to get screwed up, his future would be part of the payment exacted.

The car was tucked away behind the 'Petite Auberge' where she had booked in for the night. Gabrielle found she was exhausted from the activities of the day. She was amazed at the lengths she had taken to cover her tracks, and hoped she had done enough. When she asked for a parking place out of sight of the road, she had indicated that she was running away from her violent husband. When she showed the bruises on her arm, received some days ago, Madame Bonnard, the widowed owner of the Auberge, was immediately supportive. She insisted the car be parked behind the building turned and ready for a swift getaway if necessary. Gabrielle described her so-called husband. Paul Cadet conveniently came to mind, but said that his friends, people she did not know, might be helping.

That night she slept safe under the protective roof of the formidable Madame Bonnard. As she drifted off, she wished dreamily that she had the comfort of John's arms around her.

At Chalon-sur-Saone the *Aimee* was moored to the east bank of the river. Having eaten, John was quizzing Cadet. He had already established that he was involved in small time crime. Collecting debts, occasionally helping punish people who upset the local bosses, though he said he was not into the violence and avoided getting involved if he could.

"Why," John asked, "Did you get involved?"

"I suppose it was the usual things. Girlfriend wanted more than I could afford on my pay, the chance of this little job here and that little job there, nothing serious but paying more than I made in a month. Suddenly I wasn't working anymore. The girlfriend got scared and left. But for me, it was just too easy to carry on. I have arranged to get out, and having saved quite a bit, I put my nest egg into a fishing boat in Marseille. My partner was a former friend from the army. He needed finance. I wanted to get away from of all this. I got called whilst I was packing up."

"So why did you agree to join this circus?"

"I didn't dare not to. When these guys say jump you say, 'how high?' I haven't called in so far. So you are probably right when you said that I'm dead, as far as they are concerned."

"Just who are 'they'?" John was really curious to find out who the opposition was, and apart from the mysterious Mathieu, he knew very little so far.

"Locally, the firm is known as 'Union'. The boss came from Marseille one day. He held a meeting with the three local gang leaders at a farm outside town. When the meeting was over, he was the boss. One of the locals is his second in command, but he follows orders from Marseille."

"Have you ever heard of Mathieu?" John asked. Cadet thought for a few minutes, "It doesn't ring any bells," he said. "But then, I was always contracted, never actually part of the mob. Do you think we could get rid of these ropes?" He asked plaintively.

John just looked at him and said nothing.

Paul lay thinking in the fore cabin, no longer worried about what John and Gabrielle would do with him. He was actually reviewing his life. John had posed the question about what he was doing here. He recalled all the excuses he had made over the years, the girlfriend he had been trying to impress? That was a joke. She had dumped him soon after he had done his first job for the Union.

He was happy that he was doing the right thing, getting out at last. So far he had done nothing really bad. But if he stayed, he guessed he would be forced to do more and more.

His friend from the army, where they had served in Africa and Bosnia together, was even now waiting for him to join him as partner in his fishing boat.

In the army, he had risen to the rank of Sergeant within the year and was selected for Officer training. He left the army because his so-called preferential treatment caused a lot of resentment and he decided that he didn't need it. He realised his mistake as soon as he returned to civilian life. But it was too late to turn back. Things had gone downhill from then on. Now, if he had packed and moved a little sooner, this job would have gone to someone else. He would be fishing with his friend in the Mediterranean.

He lay there thinking and was still awake when John appeared at the cabin door.

John hushed him finger to his lips, and pointed to the stern of the boat, and indicated the noises coming from the rear of the boat. Someone was boarding.

He went off to investigate.

The intruder came into the cabin next door. After several cautious steps the communicating door swung open and a gun appeared, followed by the man holding it. The bulbous silencer made it loom even more menacingly in the semi-dark of the unlit cabin. Paul recognised the face behind the gun. The man smiled and fired. Paul felt his head explode and collapsed with his legs half in and half out of the cabin door. Blood ran from a wound in his head.

With a laugh, the gunman went back into the main cabin and started rummaging about. A few moments later Paul opened his eyes. His head felt as if it had split in two and someone was using it as a anvil. The noise of the man searching came through the open door. At the far end of the cabin, Paul saw a movement. It was John. Entering the cabin he tripped on something stumbling to his knees. Legs appeared in the doorway in front of Paul, and the voice of the gunman made a sneering remark. Paul drew back his legs and kicked the legs of the gunman. The gun went off. The bullet missed John, whose hand came into sight carrying a knife that swept out of sight. There was a cry of pain and the gun fell to the floor. The next thing Paul was aware of, was John untying the ropes and examining the wound on the side of his head.

They had come at 3.00 am. The murmur of the outboard engine had been what had awakened John, who was bedded down in the main cabin. The slight rocking of the barge told him that they had come aboard.

John had slid out of his bunk and pulled on his jeans and a sweatshirt. He opened the door to the forward berth and tapped Cadet's leg holding his hand over Cadet's mouth. He put his finger up to his lips as Cadet woke, and pointed to the deck above where the odd slight bump and scrape could be heard. Cadet nodded and relaxed. John picked up the brass rule, and crept up through the fore hatch.

On deck he made out two shadowy figures in process of lifting a container from the motor boat. It was awkward to handle and they were having trouble keeping it from bumping against the deck.

A third man was just opening the after hatch to go below. John waited until he was below the level of the cabin roof and then rose to his feet.

He crept aft towards the two men who had just managed to place the container quietly on deck. Coming up behind the first figure, he heard sound from below, Pfutt! The two on deck still unaware of his presence laughed quietly. They had obviously heard the sound of a silenced pistol before. At that point John hit the first man behind the right ear with the brass rule.

There was the sound like a bar striking a bag of sand. The man sank to the deck already dead. The second man cursed and reached to his belt. The rule was already on its way thrown by John at point blank range straight at the man's face. He raised his hand far too late to stop it, but just deflected it slightly so that it caught him on the cheek bone. Following the missile was John, who struck the man squarely on the chest and flattened him with a thud on the deck, with John on top. The man was not moving. When John got up there was no sign of him recovering for some time, his cheek bone shattered and swelling up. He was breathing torturously as he lay on the deck. Below John could hear the sound of drawers opening and being slammed shut. So collecting the rule once more he made his way to the after hatch, no longer bothering to keep quiet.

In the centre cabin the intruder was searching, without worrying too much about wrecking the place. John could see the legs of Cadet on the deck half in half out of the fore cabin. As he watched, he saw the legs move. So Cadet was still alive.

He went through the curtain into the main cabin and promptly tripped over a drawer lying on the deck. The searcher grinned and snatched up a silenced automatic and raised it. John looked down the barrel at death. The gun fired and the bullet went through the roof as the would-be killer collapsed onto the deck from the kick behind his knee, by the recumbent Cadet.

John recovered and, having lost the rule when he fell, grabbed the big kitchen knife lying where it had been flung in the search of the cabin. The gunman swung round to shoot once more, but his arm met the finely-honed blade of the knife. He screamed as the gun fell from his suddenly nerveless fingers onto the deck. His arm spurted blood. He frantically tried to stem the flow with his other hand, with little success.

"Help me," he cried. "I'm bleeding to death." John ignored him and went through to Cadet who was lying in a pool of blood on the deck. He looked up at John as he undid his bonds, and tried a grin.

"Did we get them all?" he said.

"Yes," said John. "You seem to have a new parting." He indicated a groove in the side of Cadet's head. He undid the rope binding Cadet's wrists, and helped him to his feet, steadying him as he swayed.

"Here. Sit down and I'll get a bandage and stop the bleeding. By the way, thanks. You saved my life."

"Well, I had to do something. You were right. That bastard, Perrot, knew who I was, and shot me anyway."

"Was he local?" John asked.

"Yes, from my own village. Is he dead?"

"I'm afraid so," he said, looking at the silent figure on the floor beside the cabin table.. He pumped up some water, and with a cloth, cleaned the wound.

"It's not too bad." He produced the first aid kit and took out a dressing which he taped over the gash.

Cadet indicated the dead man. "Don't waste your pity on him. I know of three girls who disappeared after a date with that pig. He is no loss to humanity."

"I'll have to clear up the deck and dispose of these bodies before dawn." John said.

"I'll give you a hand if you like. If you'll have me, I would like to stick around. It seems I'm already on the shit list. I think I'd rather take my chances with you two, than run on my own."

John looked at Paul intently. He stuck out his hand.

"Welcome to the club."

Chapter Six

The noise of the returning motor boat heralded Paul Cadet's return from his self-appointed task of disposing of the intruders bodies. John put the kettle on and made coffee. There were no other boats moored nearby. It was one of the reasons for John choosing to stop there. But it was getting light and, with daylight, the river came to life once more.

With the boat tied alongside, Paul and John between them wrestled the container the intruders had brought on board last night, back into the motor boat. The tank, full of petrol sat in the centre of the boat securely tied to the thwarts. Hauling the rowing dinghy onto the deck, they tied it down and trailed the motor boat behind on a long painter.

"Everything go all right?" John asked Paul.

"Yes. Last year I followed Perrot on a little excursion into the country. Perrot had been rather nasty to a friend of mine, and I was looking for a way of getting a little payback on my friend's behalf. Perrot had two friends with him so there was no chance to do anything on my own. But I was there, so I followed them anyway.

That is when I watched them dispose of a body, taken from the boot of their car. The old mine shaft had a rusty metal door, and the shaft cover was well rotted. I'm convinced that the three girls I mentioned finished up down that hole. I am delighted to tell you that there was room for three more, and I just hope that rotten bastard is somehow aware that he has finished up alongside those three poor girls. Sorry I took so long. I had to drag all three across a field to get to the shaft. I had forgotten that when I was there last they were able to drive up to the entrance in the car."

The *Aimee Bretonne* cruised onwards down the Saone, towards the junction with the Rhone at Lyon. On the way they dropped their tow in a small overgrown creek. It was hardly visible from the river.

At Villefranche-sur-Saone, Gabrielle sat beside the car on the riverbank the sun was warm, and she had just finished the packed lunch provided by her friendly hostess, Mme Bonnard. There were several family groups scattered along the river bank, with children knee deep in the river fishing for anything that moved.

She took out the new cell phone purchased that morning and called John's number. When he answered she told him briefly what had happened, and where she was at present.

"Come north along the river towards Thoissy. We'll get together as soon as possible for a council of war. By the way we've found a new ally. See you soon, love." He rang off.

'Love', he called me, 'love', she thought recalling the warmth of his voice. She climbed into the car with a light heart and, for the first time dared, to think that perhaps this big warm protective man liked her as much as she liked him. She laughed, what was she thinking about..... Liked, whatever her feelings might be, it wasn't just liking. She was pretty sure she had fallen in love with him, and she really hoped that he felt the same way about her.

With this thought in mind she set off to the north following the Saone, keeping her eye out for the *Aimee* as she threaded her way through the country lanes in the sunshine.

There are worse ways to live, she thought. She tried to remember when she had actually felt more alive or happier than she was now. There was something to be said for the mixture of excitement, fear, and sheer exhilaration of the last few days. She was honest enough to admit to herself that things may not have been quite so interesting had John not been involved. A shiver ran down her spine at the thought of going through the past few days events without his reassuring presence at her side. She concentrated on her driving and soon the barge came into view, solidly butting its way along the river.

Parking the car in a gap in the trees beside the river, she took the bow rope from Paul, who was on the fore deck ready. She made no sign that she recognised her prisoner of the previous day. She stepped aboard into John's open arms and returned his comforting embrace. As she squeezed his arm, she felt him wince and was immediately concerned.

"What has happened?" she asked. "You have been hurt. Tell me what's been going on?"

"I'm all right," John said, "It's just that we had another run in with Mathieu's men during the night. It gets a little wearing at my age!" John's grin belied his words. Since Paul had now joined them he used the opportunity to cover an awkward moment.

"Gabrielle MacLean, also known as Mrs Gabby Murray, meet Paul Cadet."

"We've already met," Gabrielle said dryly.

"Last night he saved my life." John said quietly. In addition, he nearly died himself." He indicated the plaster on the side of Paul's head. "Bullet wound. Sit down have a drink and we'll tell all."

Over a cup of coffee, he related the events of the night before. Paul mentioned that he had known the leader of the group. He warned about the type of people that were involved in the operation, a warning hardly necessary in view of their experiences up to now. The fact, that there were already seven dead men, had impressed them all with the seriousness of the situation.

"Mathieu must have realised that we haven't been to the police. He would have expected some reaction by now if we had. I also think he suspects that we are frightened of his organisation. We have been lucky so far. I don't think he regards us as a physical threat at all. After all, we are just two people on the run. Since we're bound to be picked up sooner or later, he can deal with us at his leisure."

The three sat around the table in the main cabin, deep in thought.

"We should contact Kelly's man in Vienne tomorrow at lunchtime!" Gabrielle said at last. "Provided she decides to support us!"

"I think we can assume she will," John said. "I think now is the time to start taking the war to the opposition. As it is, we have no control over events. We can't expect to be lucky all the time!" John's comment caused the others to look up expectantly.

"We know from the documents that there are three collection points in the Marseille area, for drugs, guns and money. I don't think they will anticipate an attack on their resources. As far as they know, we are only two. Paul is an unknown quantity and they cannot know of Kelly's involvement. Accustomed as they are to having their own way, they own Marseille. Nobody would dare interfere with the affairs of the 'Union' there, would they?"

Paul interjected, "With Kelly's man, four of us could cause quite a mess of the operation with the right pressure." He paused and thought for a moment. "Did you say one of the locations mentioned in the documents is in the Old Port area?"

John thought for a moment,

"I believe it is," he said. "Estes Romande et Cie."

"I know the place. I was sent there to collect someone when I was living in Marseille. It is one of those places visitors avoid, narrow streets and old buildings, no shops. It's strictly a business area for warehousing and so on. I didn't know it was part of the Union empire."

"It isn't," replied John. "It's owned, I believe, by Mathieu. If Union is involved, it will be as agent for Mathieu. Knowing where it is helps. What is the place like?"

"It's old Marseille, down on the waterfront, a warehouse built when Marseille was one of the great trading ports for the Mediterranean. I think it was originally used in the wool trade, but not for the last 20 years. It's location in the Old Port could be useful. The place becomes deserted by the normal working staff every night. There are people about after that, but they tend to mind their own business. It could certainly work for us, if we choose the right time to go in!"

The three sat in companionable silence, while they drank wine and ate the sandwiches that Gabrielle made.

Eventually John commented. "The boat has to go. They obviously know about it and, whilst we carry on using it we are tied to the waterways. They can find us whenever they want. We'll leave it at Lyon. If we carry on straight away, we should be there before dark. We can slip off after dark and quietly fade into the night. He indicated Gabrielle.

"If you go to Vienne and meet Kelly's man. I will take the documents, and fax copies to Kelly. Paul, you meet us with the car at Lyon tonight. Park away from the quays, in the city square. We'll find you. Gabrielle can take the car to Vienne. Find another car discretely. Hire if necessary. It will save time. We all meet at Cabries tomorrow evening at the La Villa Viche. Any questions? Or suggestions perhaps?"

There was nothing else to discuss. Gabrielle tossed the keys to Paul, who led the others up on deck. Paul leaped ashore and walked over to his car. He was gone within a few moments,

"Will we see him again?" Gabrielle asked.

"Yes, we will," John said confidently. "That man has rejoined the human race and he is on our side. Wait and see."

They unmoored the barge and set off once more down the river.

The weather continued to be warm and sunny. It was difficult to imagine that death and mayhem could happen in these peaceful surroundings. The warmth between them did not go away and the pleasure each found in the other's company was becoming more apparent as the hours passed. Neither seemed anxious for this time together to end.

The boat moved easily through the traffic on the last stretch to Lyon. John and Gabrielle sat side by side, John with one hand on the wheel the other resting on Gabrielle's shoulder, while she sat resting her head contentedly against him. Drowsily John turned to Gabrielle tilted up her chin and kissed her,

"I presume you are aware that I am in love with you!" He said quietly.

"I was rather hoping you were," Gabrielle answered in a small voice.

"Does that mean you feel the same way about me?" There was a catch in John's voice.

"Of course, you idiot." There was a short silence. "Does this mean I can come and crew for you when this is all over?"

"You would probably be my first choice, if you still want to after all the excitement. Though I think we should get this business behind us first, don't you?"

They arrived at Lyon in daylight, and tidied up the boat, ready to leave later. They went below and before John realised what was happening, Gabrielle was in his arms. They parted reluctantly as darkness fell. As they dressed, John wondered when or rather if, they would ever get the chance to make love again.

Darkness had fallen by the time they slipped ashore, leaving the cabin lights on as they made their way into Lyon to meet Paul.

The car was parked in the square next to a nearly new Audi A4. Paul was sitting in the Audi reading the paper. Seeing them approach, he opened the driver's window of the Audi and passed the keys to the Peugeot to Gabrielle.

"I've refuelled and she is all ready to go," he said. "There is a room booked for you across the square," he indicated the hotel opposite.

John tipped up Gabrielle's face and kissed her,

"Look after yourself. These guys are very bad news. We will see you at the La Villa Viche tomorrow night." Paul started the engine of the Audi and John got in. He was carrying the bag containing the spare guns which he put on the floor. With a quick wave, they drove off with a throaty roar, to Grasse nearly 700 kilometres to the south-east.

John contacted the boat hire company from his mobile phone as they raced down the A43 leaving a message on their answer phone, 'an emergency, the boat was safe at Lyon. Could it be collected there rather than at Port St Louis as arranged? Apologies for inconvenience, would contact them later.'

The two men settled themselves for a long hard drive through the night.

In the hotel Gabrielle found her room. She had dinner in the small dining room and after a coffee in the lounge took a stroll around the square. The streets were busy in the soft summer evening and she was able to get her hair trimmed and re-tinted in a salon down one of the streets off the main square. With some of the money given her by John, she bought a smart grey suit, with a pencil skirt to the knee, white cotton blouse with a high neck and a black, bootlace tie, court shoes and hold-up nylon stockings, to complete the outfit. Back in her room she tried the outfit on and, examining herself in the wardrobe mirror, was satisfied that she looked like a lawyer perhaps, or maybe a business woman, but nothing like the blond, pony-tailed writer in blue jeans, who had started off from Paris such a short time ago.

The following morning Gabrielle set out confidently to meet Kelly's agent in Vienne.

The Audi drove into Grasse at 7.00 am. Both men had been able to sleep, albeit in snatches through the night. On the journey John had heard the full story from Paul, and, what was important, decided, that he had been right to accept his help in the forthcoming fight. Paul's training as a paratrooper with the Foreign Legion had equipped him well for the sort of action he anticipated. They had eaten at an all-night service area, where they stopped for fuel. So they drove direct to the boatyard where John's boat was waiting, loaded ready to be transported, either to auction or to be launched at Antibes. With Marseille in mind, John altered his instruction, asking for the ketch to be launched at Toulon rather than Antibes.

There was activity at the yard even at that time of the morning, as John had anticipated. So the two men were able to use the shower and toilet facilities in the yard before arranging with the boss to have the boat launched, and the masts stepped ready to sail. A temporary berth was booked for the next seven days at Toulon.

Once all the arrangements had been made he went to the Post Office where he collected his mail. Then, with the documents in hand, John went into an office services shop that advertised fax facilities, where he faxed the papers to Kelly at MI6 in London. He bought a large envelope from the shop and slipped the original papers inside then returned to the car. By 10.00am they were on the A8 bound for Cabries.

At Vienne Gabrielle bought a smart slim leather briefcase, to complete the image of the lady professional.

Vienne was a small village with the church, a square and the usual local shops. The market was in full swing when she parked the car outside a waterside restaurant and ordered coffee from the young waitress. "You seem to be very busy this morning." She commented.

"Always when we have the market we are very busy," The girl replied and rushed off to fetch the coffee. Gabrielle spotted the contact ten minutes later. He opened a copy of the Waterways map and spread it across the table. The young man studying it was fair haired, pale blue eyes, about six feet tall with broad shoulders and a narrow waist. He was dressed casually in sweatshirt and jeans; there was a soft Nike bag on the ground beside him. On the chest of the sweatshirt there was a message, 'Say, hello Mike.' When he stood and strolled over to one of the market stalls she saw on his back another message, 'Say, goodbye Mike'.

Gabrielle smiled and rose, collecting her briefcase and handbag and walked over to the man. He looked up and saw her coming. She smiled and ran the last two paces.

"Hullo. Mike," she put her hands on his shoulders and kissed him on both cheeks in the French manner. "What a surprise to see you here? Are you with a boat?"

He grinned. "Fancy meeting you too, and to answer your question, I was. I've just been dumped by the boat manager. He found out I couldn't cook anything but ham and eggs, so here I am now looking for a lift to Marseille."

"Fancy him firing you for not being able to cook. Why would he expect you to?"

"Possibly because I was hired as cook in the first place?"

Gabrielle laughed. "I see. Well, this is your lucky day. I was just leaving for Marseille in the car. Do you want a lift?"

"That would be great. I'll just get my bag. He picked up the Nike bag, gave it to Gabrielle, and said, "I have my suitcase at the moorings. It will just take a moment."

"Right. I'll get the car. You get your case."

Mike nodded and hurried off. Gabrielle followed him until she saw him pick up a big case from the quay. She then turned to the car and opened the door, dumped the Nike bag on the back seat and drove over to pick him up.

Mike put the case into the boot and slid into the car beside Gabrielle.

Once out of earshot of the passersby he introduced himself properly.

"I'm Michael Ross. Kelly sent me. We should be able to collect my colleague at Avignon with luck. What do I call you?"

"Gabby Murray will do for now. Mrs. Gabby Murray. Who is your friend in Avignon?"

"Patricia O'Hara; known as 'Paddy' to her friends."

They opened the sun-roof of the car and set off for Avignon en-route to Cabries and La Villa Viche.

The A7 Auto route was 'peage' all the way to Marseille. The Peugeot cruised effortlessly mainly at 110 Kph. At Valence they stopped to refuel and eat, and changing places Michael drove for the next stretch. They exchanged stories. It seemed that Michael had been undercover, following the trail of arms imports, with Paddy as backup and handler. He was armed. He indicated his bag on the back seat. So far, he had been unable to connect with anyone further up the chain in the organization. When Gabrielle told her story, she mentioned the information contained in the papers she had acquired, and the source of the information, some of which tied in with what Michael had discovered so far.

"So, why are we going to Marseille?" he said.

"In Marseille is a company called Estes Romande et Cie. We think it is a depot used by the group. It's probably operated by 'Union', the local mob, though it seems to be owned by the Paris connection, Mathieu. We are planning to cause a little mayhem for them for a change. They have been targeting John and I for the last week. Although it's cost them seven dead men, there is no sign of them letting up.

"It's for that reason we decided to take control of matters ourselves. We both felt that it would be only a matter of time before they got one or both of us. Paul Cadet joined us. He was one of the opposition, until they shot him too. By the way, he was able to confirm our information about Estes Romande et Cie."

Michael thought about things for a few minutes. Then "Take over driving for a while. I need to contact Paddy."

They swapped places at the next service area, and when they were travelling once more Mike got on the phone. He brought Paddy up to date with their progress and asked her to see what she knew about Estes Romande et Cie. As an afterthought, he also suggested she bring everything to the rendezvous in Avignon. "We'll need everything!" he repeated and rang off.

"What was that all about?" Gabrielle asked. He explained that they had a supply of weapons and explosives stored in their temporary base.

"I have the feeling we might need everything we can muster. If we're going to war, I like to be prepared."

They collected Paddy, a beautiful, raven-haired lady, possibly thirty-something, with blue eyes and, Gabrielle observed, a figure to envy. Dressed in a pair of battered jeans and a tee shirt she was stunning. She was also nearly staggering under the weight of the two holdalls she was carrying.

In a throaty voice she said, "Fetch the rest down, Mike" and to Gabrielle. "I'm Patricia O'Hara, Paddy to my friends. Hi."

"Hi, yourself. I'm Gabby Murray, sometimes known as Gabrielle. What is this? 'A bring and buy' sale." She indicated the growing heap of bags on the pavement.

"Mike asked for it all and this is it!" Paddy said, laconically. Mike reappeared with another two bags and loaded the lot, mostly in the boot of the car. The final bag sat on the back seat next to Mike as Paddy took the other front seat.

Chapter Seven

John and Paul were sitting at the back of the room when Gabrielle, Mike and Paddy walked in. Both John and Paul had to look twice to recognize the smart figure of Gabrielle. They rose to their feet when she came to the table. Hesitantly John held his hand out to Gabrielle, who, without stopping, slipped straight into his arms and kissed him. Reassured he responded enthusiastically, until Paul coughed. They reluctantly broke apart, and turned to the others still holding hands.

Introductions were made and the group settled down to eat, drink and get to know each other.

Though the restaurant was quiet that evening John insisted they save plans for later.

They were booked into the Ibis Hotel, La Valentine in Marseille. There they could discuss matters without worrying about eavesdroppers.

At the hotel they assembled in the room booked for John and Gabrielle. She had insisted that she was still unhappy staying on her own. Besides, they were supposed to be married, weren't they?

They gathered round the map of Marseille which was taped to the wall. Pins identified their current location and the premises of Estes Romande et Cie.

Paddy briefed them on what she had found out about the company. There was little enough, except from the fact that they were an import/export company, owned two small freighters, and no record or apparent association with any criminal activity. There was nothing to show that they were other than an ordinary shipping company dealing in general merchandise, to and from, the eastern Mediterranean.

The two small freighters, owned by the company, were kept busy most of the time.

The fact that there was nothing known publicly of any shady dealing, was suspicious in itself. Their record with the local customs and port police was immaculate. Probably indicating that they pay well, and wisely, to the right people.

Paul came next. Although he had not been inside, he was able to describe the approaches and indicate where the guards were likely to be located: certainly in the front of the building.

John said, "We decided to attack this particular building, as we know it is owned by Mathieu. In addition we guessed that, given all the muscle they have in Marseille, they will not expect a raid. I think it fair to say only a fool would attempt it.

Since we are already targets we decided that we have everything to gain and nothing to lose, though I must say I am pleased that we now have reinforcements. By the way, how do we justify M1-6 getting involved with the French Mafia"

"M1-6? Who said anything about M1-6? Did you, Paddy?"

Paddy shook her head and grinned. "Some people do have a vivid imagination," she said. "Too much James Bond, I think. That'll be what causes these flights of fancy. Anyway, M1-6 is not permitted to work in this area!"

They discussed splitting into teams and what each team would concentrate on. The two girls would look after the office and paperwork. The safe was Paul's province and he buried himself in the supply boxes provided by Paddy.

The set the raid for two days later, John and Mike would form the hit squad. They would cover security for the group. They would in addition, set explosives to destroy as much of the contraband goods as possible. The intention was to hurt Mathieu.

John rang Kelly on her private number, verified that she had received the fax, and that the team would cooperate fully with his plans. She spoke briefly with Paddy, confirming her instructions. They finalised their plans and decided on a 3.00 am start.

Later as Gabrielle lay in John's arms, she returned to the subject closest to her heart.

"Have you decided about the boat? And are you happy with your crew?" she queried.

"All things being equal, I think I might just decide to chance keeping it, providing the crew is up to scratch."

She jabbed him in the ribs with her elbow, turned over and, with a contented sigh snuggled as close as possible to him, and was soon asleep.

At 3.00 am it was cold and still very dark. In the Peugeot, loaded with all the gear they thought would be needed, and with Paul driving, they threaded their way through the streets of the city, keeping strictly to the speed limit. One street away from the target, Paul stopped the car. Gathering their gear they walked quietly round to the tall warehouse building.

The sign Estes Romande et Cie was visible in the reflected light from a lamp in the neighbouring street. The building was silent and looked deserted. Paul walked straight up to the front door and tried the handle. Drawing the silenced Glock pistol provided by Paddy, he carefully turned the handle and opened the door. He stepped swiftly inside and allowed the door to close behind him. Outside the others waited, the tension only shown by a tightening of the lips and the firmer grip of the weapons held.

The door opened once more and Paul beckoned them in closing the door behind them and locking it. There was a man on the floor by the wall behind the door. He looked, and in fact was, dead.

"He recognized me," Paul said and waved them through the next door which led to a lobby. There were four doorways and a staircase. He indicated the two right-hand doors and mimed "Office". He pointed to the centre door, "The warehouse." The fourth door was marked basement, and was obviously access to the waterside."Down there is the quay, and the customs bond area." He whispered.

John glanced round swiftly. "Mike, upstairs and clear the floors." Mike armed with a silenced HK smg, courtesy of the British Government, nodded and trotted up the stairs to the upper floor. They didn't anticipate finding anyone there at this time, but they weren't taking chances.

The girls went through the door to the empty office and began sifting through the papers on the desks, prior to going through the file cabinets.

Paul followed and went through the communicating door to the inner office, where he located the safe. As he checked it he realised that it was old and had not had much use lately. There was dust on the hinges and even the handle didn't feel as if it was smooth with use. He turned the handle and was not surprised that it opened immediately to reveal empty shelves. Careless he thought. Should have locked the door and wasted my time. He sat back and examined the safe, by torchlight. Then looked up at the windows and realized that they were all blacked out with paint. The street light that shone on the sign outside was not visible. He switched on the desk light and examined the safe carefully. At the back of the safe by the wall there were finger marks. When he ran his fingers along the edge of the metal he found there was a ridge that he could hook his fingers into.

He pulled and the old safe slid easily round, away from the wall, revealing a safe door built into the wall behind the old safe. This had a more modern, keypad locking device and it was not open. A formidable proposition, but by no means impossible.

Paul reached for the little electronic box, especially designed for number crunching in these circumstances. Looking at the lock, he guessed 20 minutes maximum. He shook his head at the arrogance of these people.

Outside John made a quick survey of the warehouse through the centre door. The lights within were not switched on. Though, as he circled round, he noticed a door down steps with a light above it. He guessed it led to the lower reception area by the quay. He went down the steps and put his ear to the door. He heard rumbling noises, and guessed there was some cargo being moved. There was a swivel, drop bar upright against the door jamb. When dropped, it slotted into two metal clamps, effectively locking the door from this side. Putting it in place, he returned to the floor of the warehouse and verified that there was no one there.

He then returned to the lobby and quietly opened the door to the waterfront and quay. There were steps down and another door at the bottom, with a light above it. He closed the lobby door and, as he went down the steps, pulled the cocking handle of the silenced HK, provided by Paddy.

The door opened easily and quietly. A cool breeze brushed his cheek and a whiff of smoke from a cigarette warned him that there was someone close by. He peered round the door, and saw the broad back of a man with a shotgun on a sling over his shoulder. The man was watching the unloading of a small coaster, maybe 200 tonnes burden, lying alongside the quay.

On the quay three men were guiding the crane load of goods on to a pallet truck. While John watched, they loosed the hook and the crane swung back. The driver got out and hooked the sling to the upright securing it from use. The truck was pulled through the warehouse door, and the men came out accompanied by a fourth, who slammed and locked the door. The group walked over to join the shotgun guard. John ducked back through the door and ran up the stairs. In the lobby he closed the upper door and ducked into the office. The girls looked up at him in surprise. He put a finger to his lips. He waited by the door until all the men had reached the hall, as they stood talking he opened the door and stepped through.

The men were stunned and as John lifted the HK they raised their hands. The man with the shotgun tried to lift it and shoot John, but he was far too slow.

As he raised the gun John fired a short burst that threw him back against the closed door. Two of the others reached and started to draw guns. John crouched and swept the spitting barrel across the entire group still standing, the action was brief and brutal. A single survivor had his hands in the air and was shaking with fear. John relieved him of a Browning automatic and motioned him to his feet. He prodded the man ahead of him through the door into the lobby. Paddy appeared at the office door. She raised her eyebrows with an unasked question. John nodded that all was O.K. and made his prisoner sit on the floor. Paddy produced a plastic cuff and locked his hands together.

"Let's find out how much time we have. I'll leave him with you if you don't mind."

"You'll soon know if we have problems." Paddy replied drawing her gun. John went into the office. Gabrielle was studying some papers intently. Through in the inner office Paul swore "Merde!"

Look at this!" He called. "There's more money here than in Credit Agricole."

John and Gabrielle went through to the open safe door. They both gasped in amazement. Through the door was a walk-in safe lined with shelves. On the left hand side the shelves were covered in stacks of paper money, euros, dollars and sterling. On the right were stacks of small plastic sacks of white powder, boxes of cards of tablets, and brown paper wrapped packets which Paul identified as untreated opium. The smell was heady, and they were all relieved when Paul found the switch to the extractor fan. In the corner of the room was a two drawer cabinet, which on examination contained the sort of files the customs never saw.

Whilst they were taking all this in, Mike appeared.

"All clear upstairs." He spotted the money. "Drinks are on Mathieu, I presume!" As he realised what he was seeing, his voice faltered, "Is that what I think it is?"

John's answer was succinct. "It is and we'll need some sacks….. Anyone?"

"Upstairs, tons of them." said Mike," and turned and ran up to fetch them.

"Paul, we will leave a little money in the safe but blow it with all the drugs. I would rather nobody realised that we had taken it away." Mike returned with an armful of bags, and they started packing the money, tying the sacks with cable ties. Paddy came through to see what the excitement was all about.

"We'll never get that lot into the car," she said. "We'll have to use their van." She jingled some keys obtained from the prisoner. "It's parked on the other side of the warehouse. My new friend and I will bring it round to the quay." She left with her prisoner.

They carried the files and the account books out to the car, and sent Gabrielle back to find the boat at Toulon, while the others waited to help load the van.

John went into the warehouse, dragged the bar up and opened the door. He passed through and watched the van come round and reverse up to warehouse.

Paddy went to the double doors where the cargo had been stored. She unlocked them and flung them open. She called, and her prisoner climbed awkwardly out of the van and came over. They spoke in a local argot that John could not follow. Then she went to the nearest package and, with her knife, slashed the wrapping. She performed the same function on the other packages scattered round the floor: 14 pallets of weapons and ammunition, smg's, shoulder fired missiles, A.A. and anti-tank. AK 47's and boxes of ammunition; cartons of explosives, and boxes of grenades, stun, smoke and fragmentation. John surveyed the booty with some consternation. He had anticipated the drugs and possibly tobacco, but this? Mike staggered down with the first of the bags of money. He saw the weapon boxes and let out a low whistle.

"We could use some of this for the other raids," he suggested. "The rest should add a little interest to the bonfire."

He heaved the sacks into the van and returned for more: 8 sacks of money, a box of grenades assorted, 3 cartons of plastique with timers and fuses, 4 anti-tank missiles with launchers, and a box of claymore mines found under the cartons of explosive as an afterthought.

The van was well down on its springs as it drew away with Mike driving. Paul had come up with the solution to the problem of the safe. When the charges had been laid throughout the whole complex, ready to fire, he took a launcher and an anti-tank missile up to the office. Then carefully closing and locking the safe, he withdrew through the open inner door to the furthest wall from the safe. He then fired the missile at the safe door. The initial impact of the missile punched a small hole through the door. The secondary effect was to hose flaming metal through the hole obliterating everything within the safe. The safe's own integrity worked for the missile. Its devastation was contained. Paul then dumped the launcher and ran out of the front door slamming it, on the same principle of containing the blast of the various explosions within.

The rendezvous was at the Marina at Toulon. On the way Mike dumped the van, having transferred the money and weapons to a hired vehicle. The stolen van was sent to rest on the bottom of the harbour. Their hired van fitted into the scene, alongside several other hired vans in use for deliveries to boats in the marina. They loaded the money and weapons into the boat as she lay alongside.

The *Altair* was a 58 ft overall, Bermuda-rigged ketch, the wheelhouse set aft of the mainmast and with seating around the area. Three double cabins provided plenty of accommodation for the group, and the central saloon was roomy enough for the group to hold a council of war in comfort.

The mooring had been booked by the boatyard in the yards' name. There was nothing else to connect the boat with John Murray. Paddy had strolled down to the town centre to see what the reaction was to the events of the night. So far there was nothing, rumours indicated accident, possibly gas explosion.

The papers had the story. Only by now the bodies had been discovered at the warehouse of Estes Romande et Cie. The police were looking for the seventh man, who was known to have been present at the time of the explosions. Their prisoner on hearing the report was terrified.

"Oh God, I am a dead man. If they suspect me, they will kill me. I can't hide from them?" he was sweating and almost crying.

"You help us and we'll help you," suggested Mike. "In fact, it could save you a long holiday in prison if you were really helpful. Possibly even get you a ticket to U.S.A." When Paddy returned, she had a man with her, whom she introduced as Remy, a member of the Ministry of the Interior. To John and the others he looked more like a paratrooper than a Civil Servant. They accepted him into the group on Paddy's recommendation.

The prisoner, a man called Baron, was able to confirm the information on the other two sites in Marseille. He was also able to pinpoint the headquarters used by 'Union'.

John sent Paddy, Remy and Mike off to watch things in Marseille.

The lunchtime papers were suggesting that the warehouse fire may have been the work of rival gangs in the Marseille area.

The group, now six strong, regrouped at the mooring in Toulon. They decided to take out both of the remaining establishments mentioned in Mathieu's papers at once.

Paddy, Mike and Remy, taking Baron with them would tackle the Marignane depot, and John, Gabrielle and Paul would take the depot at Carry-le-Rouet. They chose an earlier time, though still after dark.

Over the following two days John and Gabrielle sailed the *Altair* on around the coast to Cassis. The coastal village was linked to Marseille by road. The half-hour drive would make it easier for the getaway following the next two raids.

At Carry-le-Rouet John and his party linked up with Remy, who was able to report no activity for the last three hours. He then left to join Paddy and Mike at Marignane.

The three friends armed, and carrying explosives and tools in tote bags, went round to the warehouse doors, where Paul went to work on the lock of the entry. After a nerve stretching wait he signalled that he was in, and they all slipped through the door.

Inside the door the warehouse floor was piled up with boxes in rows, with corridors between them, to allow a fork lift truck access to stack and extract as required. It all looked innocent enough, like any other warehouse in fact. They split up and searched the area, finishing up together again by the door at the rear of the store. Paul worked his magic once more and the door opened to reveal a passage with a glassed-in office to the right and two other doors on the left. Gabrielle went into the office, whilst the two men tried the other doors. One was a toilet and washroom. The other was a storage cupboard containing cleaning materials and stationery. The scent of air freshener was strong and penetrating, causing Paul to sneeze.

In the office Gabrielle drew a complete blank except for the records of vehicle collections and deliveries. The excessive orders for cleaner's materials, including large quantities of air freshener, raised a question that nagged at John. There was something about the whole setup? Then it came to him.

This was a warehouse staffed by men, almost exclusively. It had the freshest smelling toilets he had ever encountered in France, so fresh smelling that it had caused Paul to sneeze. Why?

He called Paul back to the toilet and washroom and began to search for signs of a doorway. It was Paul who spotted it. Of the four stalls, three had battered and in two cases broken seats. In the fourth despite a dirty and foot-marked floor, the seat was intact and comparatively clean. The toilets had old fashioned, high-level cisterns, the badly used ones with broken chains or string used to flush. The suspect toilet had a smooth polished rod attached to the lever and, when the rod was pulled, the side wall of the toilet slid to one side revealing another door, with an electronic key pad.

Even with his wonder electronic device it took Paul 15 minutes to get the door open, to reveal a plastic curtain draped room.

"A clean room," he said. "This is a lab." He pushed the curtain to one side and they realised immediately why the use of the air freshener was so important. The raw opium smell hung heavily on the air.

The lab had workstations for 40 people. There were chemicals and stacks of raw opium in several places along the walls of the room. The room had no windows and air conditioners were set in the walls at intervals along its length.

Through the door at the other end was an office where Gabrielle was able to find schedules of production and delivery, naming consignees and carriers, payments, and bulk shipments of money and product, to other distribution points.

"Jackpot!" She said. "This is just what the Doctor ordered."

"Shhhh," Paul said. He was standing by the door at the other side of the office. "Someone is coming. Go quickly." He urged them through into the lab shutting the door behind them. They ran down the lab to the far end and Paul switched off the lights. Before closing the door, he took out a pre-fused piece of explosive. Pressing the set button; he hid it under a bench and slid the door shut behind him. "Run," he said quietly. "Get out, fast."

They ran and nearly didn't make it. As they came through the outside door there was a bang followed by a huge explosion that threw them flat on the ground. The men in the car that had just drawn up were also knocked down, but they were slower to recover than Paul, who recognised them. His gun stuttered the silenced rounds, stitching a pattern across the four figures, starting to get up. None of them made it. The three raced round the corner to their car and made off at a sedate speed, still high on adrenaline, Gabrielle, still clutching the bunch of papers taken from the office.

The warehouse surrounded by fire appliances was the subject of a special news bulletin on the car radio as they drove back to Cassis.

Chapter Eight

The discovery of the dead men reinforced the theory that there was a gang war in progress. There was also the mystery of the enormous explosion at an ordinary warehouse. By law they could not store fuel or other low flashpoint material. The reporter theorised that perhaps an excessive amount of explosive had been used to drive the point home. No mention was made of drugs.

At Marignane, when Paddy and her team arrived, the thoroughly frightened Baron cowered down in the back of the car to avoid being seen. The area was still quiet though there were two cars parked outside the building. The Jaguar with the British number plate looked out of place beside the battered Citroen parked beside it.

"I wonder who that belongs to?" queried Paddy. "You don't think Gabrielle's friend from Lyon is here. do you?"

"Could be, or even an international customer for all we know. Shall we find out?" Mike seemed to think the whole idea was a joke.

Edouard Chamaise looked across the desk at his visitor with ill-concealed distaste. Charles Wilson was the type of Englishman that that he hated on sight. The air of superiority, the Jaguar car, the languid expectation that all would be done to ensure his needs would be satisfied, whatever he wanted. As a regular customer, it was necessary for Edouard to be polite to him and keep the trade between France and England running to their mutual benefit, but he didn't have to like it.

The man was being irritating once more, asking that deliveries be speeded up, though prices should remain the same. Surely the idiot knew that there would be extra work involved. Things didn't happen by themselves!

Barat, Mathieu's enforcer, standing watching the proceedings, suddenly looked up.

A knock came at the door......

The team walked into the lobby of the building to be met by a stocky, brutish looking man in overalls, "What do you want?" he said aggressively.

"To speak to your boss," Mike replied.

"The boss is not here." He answered aggressively. "So, push off, the lot of you." He suddenly noticed Baron trying to hide behind Remy.

"Hey. I know you. Aren't you from the warehouse that got blown up? The boss'll want to talk to you." He tried to grab Baron, but found himself struggling for breath as Mike's arm tightened round his neck. His efforts became weaker as the stranglehold took effect. Finally he collapsed onto the floor taking Mike with him. Remy tied his hands together and slapped a strip of duck tape across his mouth. They laid him in a corner out of the way. Paddy went to the door marked Office, knocked and walked in.

The three men seated round the desk looked up in surprise. Behind the desk sat Chamaise. He was a well-dressed man in a grey Armani suit, dark hair pulled back in a ponytail from a strong tanned face, a powerful man who was aware of his power?

Across from him sat a quintessential English gentleman, navy blue, Saville Row suit, white shirt, club tie and black oxford shoes highly polished.

The third man was standing very still, wearing a black roll-neck sweater and black slacks. His moccasins were also black His face was sharply handsome with flashing black eyes. The hair cut short and evenly across his head, was white. His whole attitude was of controlled menace. Mike raised the gun he was carrying and covered him personally, leaving the others for his companions.

"What is all this? What are you doing here? Why the gun?" Chamaise spat out the words, one after another in rapid succession.

"Who are you?" Paddy shot back equally quickly.

"My name is Edouard Chamaise. I own this building. Now, who are you?"

"Your worst nightmare," Paddy said. "What is your name?" She swung round to the Englishman.

He jumped in surprise.

"Oh. I'm Director of Wilson's we import North African cotton goods through this company. My name is Charles Wilson. Who, may I ask, are you?" Paddy did not answer, just nodded to Mike who produced a cable tie and looped it round the hands of the man in black pulling it tight he pushed him down to the floor. He then did the same for Charles Wilson to Wilson's extreme discomfort. Paddy waved Chamaise to his feet and nodded to the door.

"Out" she said, and helped him on his way with a push. Mike followed Paddy, whilst Remy and Baron stayed in the office, keeping an eye on the others.

In the warehouse, pushing a protesting Chamaise in front, Paddy and Mike searched the premises as completely as possible.

They found nothing at first. Then, as Mike examined the bales of cotton goods consigned to Wilson Ltd, he was intrigued to notice that they were stacked in two distinct lots separated by a wide passageway. The first stack was in Egyptian wrapping, consigned to Wilson's. The second stack had been repacked and re-labelled to Wilson's in French packing.

Whilst Chamaise watched fuming, Mike unpacked a French consignment pack. In the centre of the cotton material bale was a plastic wrapped parcel of white powder, about two kilos in weight. Chamaise had become more and more agitated as the bale had been unpacked. When the package was disclosed, he dived behind the other bales, drew a pistol from an ankle holster, shot at and missed Paddy. She did not, she fired twice

The first took him in the chest, the second through his right eye.

"Bring the explosives, Mike. We'll give this place the treatment, like the others."

Mike went out of the warehouse, calling to Remy in passing, as he returned from the car with the explosives. Remy came out of the building with the other two men and Baron. He seated Wilson and the white haired man in the Citroen, tying them together with yet another cable tie. Paddy and Mike came out on the run and jumped into their car, to get away from the area before the place blew.

They were nearly half a mile away when they heard the blast. Baron and Remy saw the cloud of smoke through the rear window as they continued to put distance behind them.

John spoke to Kelly that night, using a public telephone. She was concerned for them stirring up a hornets' nest with no real backup. The loss of millions in drugs and equipment, not to mention the buildings, must have hurt Mathieu considerably. Even worse, the loss of face could result in other gangs trying to take over his territory, causing even more mayhem. She told him that the diplomat at Lyon, Fuller, was still in place, but under surveillance. They should leave Marseille as soon as possible. Without telling her how, John re-assured her that they were leaving that night. Of the two men left in the Citroen, only the white haired man survived, Wilson had a heart attack. He was dead when the services arrived.

Baron was on the Air France flight to Miami, comforted by the healthy bundle of currency packed into his bag. It was with considerable relief that John steered the ketch out of the marina at Toulon, on a reported course to Malta. Gabrielle sat beside him at the wheel. Paddy was below lying down, unhappy at the motion of the boat. Mike, Paul and Remy were stripping and cleaning the extended arsenal of weapons, acquired during the last two days.

John, having set the course, went below, leaving Gabrielle in charge. He prepared food for those who could eat. That only excluded Paddy as she alone could not face food. He poked his head up through the hatch and spoke to Gabrielle.

"Excuse me, Mrs Murray, could you manage a little sustenance?" Setting the self-steering she slid down into the galley put her arms round John's neck and kissed his ear.

"What do you mean by sustenance?"

"Food, woman, food," John grinned and threatened her with the omelette pan.

"Oh, very well. I suppose I could manage something." Kissing his other ear, she returned to her post at the wheel. At 3 am they changed course for Spain.

The weather did not improve as they sailed north of west to clear the Balearic Islands, but the winds which came from the North African coast pushed them at speed on their way. Paddy never did recover sufficiently to eat, though the others managed to make up for her, in the boisterous breeze that kept them on their toes, keeping the boat trimmed.

By the time they slipped into the yacht harbour at Barcelona, they were all happy to take advantage of the calm waters alongside the pontoon and enjoy seven solid hours sleep.

The sun was up when John peered out from the hatch at the acres of quietly nodding boats. They were tied up at the seaward end of a pontoon.

Checking in with the harbour master and customs had required considerable effort at 8.00pm yesterday. He had been miffed to find the rest of the company fast asleep when he returned from logging in the necessary paperwork.

Since he believed the boat was not known to the opposition, he took the risk of doing without a lookout and joined Gabrielle in their bunk and slept himself.

Now with the mid-morning sun blazing in the cloudless sky, the sense of urgency returned.

John looked around the peaceful scene. The Marina was buzzing with activity, but it was all associated with the boats moored there. With a last rueful look around he ducked down into the cabin once more, and woke Gabrielle, whom he put to making coffee and starting breakfast. He then woke Paddy who had at last been able to sleep, now the boat had stopped tossing about. She came through and took the coffee and the bacon sandwich Gabrielle held out.

"What's up?" she said.

"I want you to contact London and get all you can on Mathieu: address, contacts, business, everything. I don't want him tipped off, so this must be kept in the family. Use the consulate, but don't tell them that we are here. Mathieu has too many contacts for my liking, and that may include some of the members of your club, if you take my meaning."

Paddy nodded round her sandwich, and went through to the forward cabin to dress for Barcelona. When she returned, John whistled silently, as she sidled past him looking stunning in a modish skirt and top that would not have been out of place at Cannes. Gabrielle jabbed him in the back with her elbow. He protested.

"Credit where it's due. Paddy, you look gorgeous." Ignoring Gabrielle, he said "Go for it."

Paddy blushed.

"Thank you, kind sir. I have to look my best for the diplomats, otherwise they may take me for a spook. That would never do."

She mounted the stair to the deck carrying her shoes. On the pontoon she put the high heels on and with the toss of her head strutted down the pontoon towards the city, like a Prada model. As

Mike observed, having been roused from his bunk by the noise, "You could hear every male eyeball click as she passed."

When Remy joined them and all had eaten, they discussed their next move. As John pointed out, the money, sitting in the plastic bags, could not remain where it was. They had no real idea how much was there to start with. Apart from the cash given to Baron, both John and Gabrielle would need a certain amount of operating expenses. Their gleanings from the various thugs they had encountered were now just about exhausted. They were still deciding what to do, when Gabrielle went ashore and fetched the local and French papers.

On her return, she interrupted the discussion, and showed them an item in the French national daily. The hire barge *Aimee Bretonne* had suffered an explosion believed to be from a faulty gas cylinder. The boat was completely destroyed and the two people aboard killed instantly. The condition of the bodies made them difficult to identify. Though, since it was a man and a woman, they were assumed to be the British couple, a Mr John Murray and friend.

John's immediate reaction was to ring the boat owners and tell them that it must have been the collection crew who were killed. Then Gabrielle found a footnote. The owners of the boat had received a message from Mr Murray, saying that he would be cutting short his hire and leaving the boat for collection, by the owners. Since the collection crew had not left the yard, he presumed Mr Murray had not left the boat by the time the accident occurred. In the circumstances he decided it would be better to say nothing at present. But they did wonder who the dead couple were.

The explosion on the barge at Lyon had been unfortunate for Candice and Maurice Bonnard. Both had an extensive and varied career in theft and murder. Admittedly, the murder was always for one reason only, survival. The discreet disposal of witnesses had become a talent that they had both, over the years, perfected.

They had been staying in Lyons for the last three months, conducting a quiet and efficient series of break-ins among the local empty houses of quality. The area was popular with the middle class of Paris, many of whom had bought local houses as holiday retreats.

Unfortunately the last collection made by the couple had been interrupted by the arrival of a suspicious dog walker who had paid for his intrusion with his life. The disposal of the dog caused Candice more sorrow than the death of its owner.

The *Aimee Bretonne* was a lucky accident. The goods, acquired over the last few months had been despatched to their agent in Paris by hired van, but the latest killing had made it necessary for a discreet withdrawal from the area. The idea of using the river had occurred as they watched John and Gabrielle leave the barge. Maurice had followed them into Lyon and watched the woman receive the keys of a car and go to the hotel, and the man disappear in a car with another man.

He wandered into the hotel, and discovered that the lady had been booked in for the night.

Maurice and Candice moved into the *Aimee* and quietly settled down for the night.

It was after midnight when the couple were disturbed by someone boarding the boat. Whoever it was, made the effort to keep quiet. Maurice wakened Candice and picked up his pistol from the shelf by the berth. Candice armed herself also, rose naked from the bed and, with gun poised, opened the door of the fore cabin. She saw a man, gun poised turning towards her. Obviously he had heard the slight sound of the door opening. She fired at him and realised she had missed, as she saw the muzzle flash from his gun. As she fell dead, Maurice gave a cry of anguish and fired several times at the shadowy figure, without effect. The stranger fired twice, the successful partnership of Maurice and Candice had been dissolved, finally. The intruder turned to his companion, "What the fuck?"

His companion shrugged, "Get on with it, search the boat. Mathieu may be pissed because we killed them, but, if we find the papers, it should be alright."

The pair searched without success for the next hour. They then opened the gas taps on the stove and for good measure, emptied the can of petrol they had brought in with them around the cabin floor. As they left, they threw a lighted firework through the cabin door and slammed it shut.

After a breathless few seconds, there was a bright flash from the firework, followed by an enormous explosion. The *Aimee Bretonne* disintegrated.

Mathieu still had a nagging worry about the papers, but was pleased that the annoying matter of Gabrielle and her friend had been disposed of, finally.

"Count the money. Let's see just what we have liberated here!"

John went into the fore cabin, pulled the first sack through to the main cabin and dumped it on the table. They drew the curtains, and he tipped the contents of the sack onto the table. There were so many packages that half of them spilled onto the floor. This sack contained dollars in plastic packs of $10,000, in one hundred dollar bills. Since they were mainly unbroken, the count was quite easy. There were 98 packs, and the loose bills brought the total to $988,000. They were stunned. Eventually, Mike spoke, "I thought these packets were one thousand. I didn't realise they were ten thousand. No wonder Baron was pleased. I gave him $20,000 to set himself up with in the States!"

Refilling the sack they brought in the next, which was euros, the third which was sterling and the fourth and fifth, which were assorted, and took more time to count that the rest put together. The total was a mind-boggling $8,700,000 in value, at the current rate of exchange.

The count over, all four sat back silenced by the sheer scale of their windfall.

Finally, Mike observed, "Of course, getting rid of cash is the biggest problem the criminal element face in this day and age. Of necessity, most of the business in drugs is cash trade. Banks all over the world are now on the lookout for excessive cash amounts that can't be accounted for by normal trade. They must advise the police of anything that comes to notice. That's what money laundering is all about. That will be the reason for the huge amount of cash."

Whilst they were sitting drinking coffee still trying to take in the result of the count, Paddy knocked on the hatch and stepped daintily down into the cabin. She looked at their faces, and said, "Who died?" John gave her the piece of paper on which he had totalled the various sums of money.

"Wow!" She said. "That's impressive. Is that was what was in the bags?"

John nodded. They sat in stunned silence, trying to take in the enormity of this event. Paddy broke the silence.

"Before making any decisions about all this, you had better hear my news." They all looked at her expectantly.

"First the bad news, Kelly has been sacked and we are ordered not to get involved. That is, Mike and I are so ordered. We therefore carry on as we were before. Remy, of course, is not under London control. You, indicating John and Gabrielle, if we find you, are to be brought in to Police H.Q. in Marseille and handed over to the local police to be charged with murder, arson and general mayhem. Paul was not even mentioned.

"O.K. What's the good news?" Gabrielle asked.

"The good news is that they don't know about this," she indicated the money.

"Who did you speak to?" John asked.

"Arthur Wilson." They were all absorbing this piece of news when John said,

"Where has Kelly gone? Do you know?"

Paddy said, "The operator started to say the Home Office, when she checked and said she was no longer in the section."

"Mike, get onto the Home Office and see if we can find Kelly," John said. "Do we all agree we say nothing about our finance at the moment? The reason I prefer to keep the money to ourselves is, if we hand it in to government, it will disappear straight into the kitty, and none of it will be used to fight crime. I'm sure you have all seen the way promises of action are made but seldom kept. Well, this is a time when we can do something about it, without the interference of political hacks that treat the rest of us as idiots."

He looked around, and they all nodded agreement in turn.

"I've had an idea about this that I'll discuss when we know what Kelly has to say. First, I am going to cover expenses and payment. We have all taken part in recovering this money. We will all have a share in compensation. I'll establish a petty cash account for all our out-of-pocket expenses in future, and salary payments for all involved. Since our opponents have been so generous, I think it only fair that they fund the expenses involved in putting them out of business."

The weather continued fair, but a little boisterous, so the party planned to move to a shore base. This particularly suited Paddy, who was still not fully recovered from her uncomfortable voyage.

Michael Ascher spoke to John by satellite from California, indicating he would be flying into Barcelona for a business meeting tomorrow, and requested a meeting with John in the evening.

Chapter Nine

The shadows were lengthening, when John switched off his mobile phone and settled back in the open cockpit of the big ketch. The others were already sprawled around the cockpit with glasses of wine.

John spoke, "Paddy, I'm sure you'll be delighted to know. We will be moving into a hotel tomorrow, and if you like you can go and book us all in tonight. Since you'll be there already, why not just stay rather than coming all the way back to the boat. Now, you all heard my side of the conversation with Kelly. I know that you all guessed that there was something going wrong with the investigations into organized drug trafficking, arms dealing and terrorism.

"Interference, at high level across several National and the European Governments in particular, has been severely hampering efforts of the police and security services to get on terms with the crime terrorist machine creating mayhem throughout the western world.

"The cynical use of religion, to drive a wedge between different communities, is just one of the many aspects of this unholy alliance fogging the boundaries. We have apparently upset the apple cart of one of the biggest organizations in the business. Mathieu is the link man for the mainland Europe group, dealing in drugs, arms and explosives.

"Because of his criminal origins, his own business includes, in addition, the importation of young girls and boys from the ex-eastern bloc countries to service his brothels and prostitution operations.

"Here, on this boat, we have gathered a large part of the war chest for Mathieu's operation.

"Kelly has been shifted sideways into a Home Office post, because she is not part of the cabal that is currently profiting from the system. What is most important, is that they don't know who we are. Both Paddy and Mike are on independent undercover operations. They only report when necessary. Remy?"

"I have been attached to Paddy's team from French Security. I report to Paddy."

"Any comments so far?" Receiving no replies he carried on.

"This is where you make your choice. If you decide to stay with us, there will be no going back. The chances of being hurt or killed are pretty good. However you could be in a position to make a difference to the people who, at the moment, are at the mercy of this scum. The choice is yours."

He sat back and waited for their reaction. It was not long in coming.

"I'm in," said Gabrielle.

"Me too," Mike followed. One by one they all chose to continue.

"Right," said John. "We don't have any financial problems to start with." He indicated the money in the fore cabin. "We will need to set up a secure base and administration, but we will also need to keep the pressure on Mathieu. I can make a call and get the services of one of the best controllers I know. Shall I make the call?"

At the meeting between Michael Ascher and John in the early evening the following day, the disposal of the cash windfall was arranged. Because of the huge amount of money involved in the trade of computer software and hardware, large sums came in and out of Michael's account regularly.

The kidnapping of his wife, he had realised was to force him to use those resources, on Mathieu's behalf, for money laundering. It was particularly ironic that money he might have been forced to launder, would in fact be processed through the system with his complete cooperation. With the agreement of the others John arranged for Michael to take the money to the Cayman Islands on his way back to California. The numbered account, for one million dollars already established from Michael Ascher's own pocket, could be used to deposit the money. Once deposited, drawing facilities would be arranged here in Spain.

Michael had one request only. "Jeanne wants to do something positive with the organization here in Europe. Could you find a role for her that would not be too dangerous, but would be of real value?"

As they shook hands, watching the last sack of money being

pushed into Michael's jet, John promised. "I'll do my best for Jeanne!"

Kelly took leave of absence, pending her resignation. No one was surprised in the circumstances. Being sidetracked from her high profile job in MI6 provided ample excuse for her resignation. By evening she was on the plane to Spain, and by midnight she was sitting having a drink in the Hotel Paradis in Barcelona.

Seated at a corner table, she was observing the noisy groups of holidaymakers scattered through the area, drinking sangria. She sipped a G and T and wondered what she was doing in Barcelona. She was still stunned by the speed of events over the last three days. The call from Gabrielle, followed by the action to cover Robert Fuller the attaché in Lyon. The subsequent interview with the Director of M16, who accused her of misuse of department staff in France. This was used as an excuse to have her replaced by the odious Arthur Wilson, a person who had dogged her steps for years trying to get into her pants, as her staff so delicately put it. Followed by the final indignity of being evicted from M1-6.

She was sitting, lost in her own thoughts when she became aware of a presence, hovering beside her. A familiar voice spoke.

"Fancy a night on the town, darlin'?"

"Not with you, you cheeky bugger!" She couldn't help smiling as she said it. Mike had always been a favourite of hers'.

He sat down across from her, swiftly joined by the others. She knew them all, except for the pretty brunette, who stayed close to John Murray.

"Kelly, this is Gabrielle. She started this whole thing off!"

Gabrielle held out her hand, Kelly looked at her then at John, and with a faint smile said, "Mrs Murray, I presume?"

Gabrielle blushed, "A 'ruse de guerre' that was necessary at the time."

Kelly smiled openly and looked up as Paul approached the table. John noticed Kelly's face flush faintly and she caught her breath as Paul dragged a chair up to join them. He looked at Paul as the introductions were made, and was not slow to observe the reaction from him. He sat, seeming unable to take his eyes off Kelly. To John, this was not so surprising. Despite her exalted position in M16, Kelly was only 46 years old, and as many had observed, a very trim 46 years old at that. Dark hair, cut in a short bob: soft brown eyes set in an elfin face with a clear skin a body, the envy of many of the younger staff at the Thames-side building. Kelly was a package well worth a second look.

On the other hand, Paul was one of those Frenchmen that Englishwomen cannot seem to resist, with that slightly world-weary expression that invites a sympathetic bosom to rest on. The fact, that he had shown no sign of interest in any of the other beautiful women in the group, made his interest in Kelly obvious, at least to John, and intriguing.

John had insisted that the gathering be social rather than business, as Kelly had had no chance to relax after her flight. Having arranged a meeting time of 10 00 the following day, John invited Gabrielle to dance. They left the party and joined the other dancers on the floor. Paddy turned to Kelly

"They fit together well, don't they?"

Kelly smiled. "I am happy for John. He really suffered when his wife died. It seemed he would never really recover. I do hope she doesn't let him down."

Paddy was quiet for a few minutes "And how about you? It's been seven years since he died. Is there no one on the horizon?"

"No one so far, though now I have a little more freedom. Who knows?" The ever-perceptive Paddy didn't fail to notice how Kelly's eyes went to the figure of Paul, currently dancing with a hotel guest. Interesting, she thought, if that's the way the wind blows.

The following morning the group assembled in one of the hotel meeting rooms, settling down around the long table provided. John sat at the head of the table, for once and once only, was the way he put it. He spoke briefly and succinctly.

"Gabrielle and I were dragged into a situation that caused us a few problems, from time to time." A chuckle went round the table. "The origin of the problems was a man called Mathieu. A Parisian mobster who dabbled in many things, or at least that's what we thought. In fact he was no dabbler. His operation is concerned with drugs, terrorism, gun running, and political manipulation: plus the usual range of things such as money laundering, flesh trading, robbery, murder and general mayhem. Gabrielle and I are anxious to resume a normal life. With Mathieu still around,, we are going to have to do something about him, if we ever wish to stop looking over our shoulders.

"In the course of our journey through France, we came across papers that landed us into a heap of trouble, and we were able to help a lady back to her husband.

"As you are all aware, the way we chose to get out of our trouble may have seemed drastic, but it has gained us a friend. He nodded at Paul. And what I can only describe as wealth beyond our wildest dreams.

"The return of Jeanne Ascher caused Michael, her husband, to set up a fund in the Cayman Islands to be used, however we wished. I know Gabrielle agrees that the fund be best used to set up an anti-crime organisation, dedicated to the protection of the public at large. Crime, terrorism and more serious problems, have risen from self-serving politicians and criminal elements. Combined they have made mockery of the welfare of the people.

"That fund is one million dollars, with the promise of more if needed.

"Michael Ascher is a computer billionaire. His resources are immense, and his cooperation both financial and otherwise practical, is guaranteed. In addition, we have the money recovered from the Marseille raids, over $9,000,000 in cash. You are all professionals. Neither Gabrielle nor I can be considered in that class. While we will happily continue to support and help in any way we can, neither of us wishes to interfere in what we consider to be a most professional business.

"As we have already discussed, the best way to establish our operation is by the establishment of respectable operating company, to be used as cover for the covert operation of the anti-crime force. To that end I have been in touch with friends in the shipping business, who have suggested that international freight and shipping, would be the most suitable for our purposes. Gabrielle and I will form Trans-Ocean Trading, which is a legitimate trading company with us as directors. This will permit international travel, money and personnel movements with little interference from commercial agencies. We have also proposed a sister company to be created to provide security, as well as private enquiries. A suggestion, made by Michael, was to call it Secure (International) Incorporated. It will simplify the concealment of the covert agency.

"For Gabrielle and I, our last effort in the field will be dealing with the problem of Mathieu and then we will bow out." The chuckle, which ran round the table at his suggestion of 'last operation' was instant and sympathetic. He continued with a wry smile.

"The reason you are all here, is to give you the chance to do what you know is right." He turned to Kelly.

"I could not think of a better qualified leader than you, and since every one of you has proved yourself time and again, I obviously could not have found a better team for the job in hand. We have the money and the nucleus of the personnel. Now, all that's needed is to get the show on the road." John rose from his chair and waved for Kelly to take over the meeting.

"Kelly is some lady," John said, as he returned from the Charles de Gaulle airport, to the apartment in Paris, three days later.

"Everything went well then. She did the business?" Gabrielle asked.

"She certainly did. She has a base for operations that is available and she will take it over tomorrow. She has a friend in Spanish security who she reckons will be useful in getting set up.

"I contacted Cayman. The numbered account for one million dollars, given as a first instalment towards the 'vigilantes', has been enhanced by the cash input from here.

"Michael Ascher, incidentally, suggested the site, a former NATO base in Spain near Rosas, close to the border with France. It is being refitted as we speak."

They went to bed and he collapsed, exhausted.

Over the next three months, they registered the company in the Bahamas as Trans-Ocean Trading funded by the finance in the Cayman Islands. They set up the centre in the former NATO base at Rosas. The site had been abandoned in the '80's. The team of workers to make the place habitable had been recruited in North Africa and accommodated on site. When the work was completed they were delivered back to their homes in Southern Morocco. The existing airstrip was long enough for a B52, so the Gulfstream V/550 would be easily accommodated. The large hanger provided ample accommodation for the three helicopters, and the twin Cherokee turboprop, since it had been built to accommodate a B52.

It was not surprising that in a partitioned section there was room for most of the ground transport as well.

The Headquarters building was situated away from the hanger on the other side of the runway. Here, in her admin offices, Kelly's office was located, on the corner of the upper floor, overlooking the runway and the surrounding country. The snow-capped Pyrenees were in view through the west facing windows. As an office, it was comfortable without being opulent. A desk and leather chair occupied the corner facing the windows, On the other side of the office was a state-of-the-art boardroom table, with twelve chairs and inset computer screens for each place. A second door led into the secretaries' office, shared by Paul's secretary as well as her own.

Paul had been dragooned into remaining within the base, temporarily at least. It was agreed, that the possibility of his being recognised on the street in France was not worth the risk, for the present.

He had been asked to work beside Kelly, to take some of her workload while the base was being established. In his own words, it was the first real work he had done since he left the army. Rather to his surprise he was enjoying it, though, how much of that was due to being in close contact with Kelly, was the subject of considerable interest to the other staff.

Paul had established his office on the other side of the secretaries. Less elaborate than Kelly's he had a desk, chair and a settee against the wall beside a drinks cabinet. His window only overlooked the runway.

Below their offices, were the general offices of the company which operated a legitimate trading business. The warehouse next to the office was used for both open goods, and those under Customs bond. Below the warehouse, a concealed ramp and lift gave access to the covert side of the business.

There was an accommodation block beside the offices that contained several suites for visiting directors.

The covert section of the operation had been expanded to include in essence two platoons of Special Forces personnel. The obvious shortcomings of the limited number of the original group had become apparent. Remy had identified two storage and resource centres, one in Versailles, the other in the immediate vicinity of the Disney complex on the outskirts of Paris at Montry for their first operation. Both centres were manned twenty four hours of the day, guarded by what appeared to be armed men, many of whom were identified as ex Foreign Legion Paratroopers. They had managed to upset the Versailles centre by inserting a time bomb into a delivery of material to the depot.

Sadly, it only appeared to get the guards on their toes. As a result, action had been suspended temporarily, until reinforcements could be recruited.

Because of the private nature of the organization, everything had to be done discreetly. Through her position in MI6 Kelly had previously established good relations with the S.A.S at Hereford. At a secret meeting with a trusted friend who was a senior officer, Kelly managed to enlist his aid in recruiting suitable candidates to join the Security International team. The first recruits recommended others until the two platoons had reached full strength of 40 men and women, including N.C.O.'s and three Officers. The C.O. was Major Alan Gilmore. The other two officers were former Captains: Peter Maddox, ex-Marine S.B.S. and David Cameron an ex-Para who had served in the S.A.S.

The four female recruits were all specialists. Two were Medics, and the others were Comms and Computer experts. All four were also trained soldiers, who were said to scare the hell out of the others in their platoon. The standard armament provided was the H&K silenced smg's, Glock 9.mm automatic, Fairburn knife and, a personal preferred weapon, ranging from garrotte to knuckleduster.

As trained soldiers, despite lack of training together, the unit was quite ready to undertake these first jobs, given the intelligence gathered and the expertise of their officers. The enemy seemed to have had time to get over the last attack. The return to Paris had been planned: staggered hits on both depots led by two teams Paddy and Remy, and Mike Ross and John Murray.

Kelly had been working, organizing and sourcing equipment, and recruiting staff over the last three months. Despite the efforts and assistance of her deputy Paul, it showed in the dark rings round her eyes, and the droop to her shoulders. John noticed when he visited in his capacity as Chairman of the board. The directors, who consisted of the original five person covert team, were reinforced by two specialists, an international lawyer, Mark Harris, and an accountant, David Levy. The other addition was the company marketing director, Bill Hamilton. These specialists were aware of the current operation being conducted under the Secure Inc banner, but played no part in the operations.

Kelly promised to take time off when the Paris operations were over. Until then, she refused to take a break.

The operation to remove the threat of Mathieu from the Paris scene was a compound one, involving the disposal of not only Mathieu himself by John and Gabrielle, but also the neutralisation of the two depots located in the Paris area.

One of the puzzles that had intrigued both of them had been finding a name on the list of police officers apparently under the control of the organisation, which stood out from all the others. The man in question was famous throughout the western world for his forthright attitude to crime. His no-nonsense approach was respected everywhere. Commissioner Aristide Ferat ran the Special Investigation Department of the Ministry of the Interior: effectively, the French version of Special Branch in the UK. Known as the Ferret, he was feared and revered, depending on your viewpoint. As a member of the Security Service, he had had several major successes throughout his career.

Neither John nor Gabrielle could recall any reason why he should be on the list. So, based on Kelly's acquaintance with him, John met him by appointment at a discreet location, armed only with a copy of Mathieu's papers with the name and address removed

Ferat was not easy to read. He sat opposite John across the café table, coffee still untasted while he read the documents provided by John. Eventually he raised his eyes and studied John. "Why have you shown me this?"

"These documents were obtained, by accident, from the desk of a man known as Mathieu Ormande." At the name Ferat looked up sharply. "Mathieu Ormande?"

John nodded and continued. "You know him, of course! What is he holding over you? I am aware of your reputation and I know it was earned honestly. So tell me - why are you on that list?"

Aristide Ferat's eyes blazed briefly at John, then they dropped and he spoke quietly.

"These documents were not given to the police. They should have been handed in when you first obtained them."

"Don't treat me like a fool. Look at the list. Who could I trust?

Even you are there. Handing those documents to the police, would have been signing not only my death warrant, but my friends as well."

Ferat said quietly, "Mathieu captured my niece three months ago. She has spoken to me on the phone several times since, to prove that she was alright. Her life was held against my cooperation in certain matters. She has not yet been returned, though I am told she will return soon…"

John looked at Ferat sadly. "You don't believe that any more than I do! I am sorry, but I believe that your niece is dead. Mathieu holds life very cheaply. Whatever act or acts you performed for Mathieu, will be all he needs now to keep you in his hands. Holding the proof of that, he can tie your hands by threatening your exposure at any time."

John rose, "I'll leave these papers with you. Hopefully Mathieu will soon no longer be a problem, and this conversation will never have happened. I leave it to you to deal with this information as you will. Please don't disappoint me." John left the café, with Ferat still sitting there in front of his cold, untouched coffee.

Chapter Ten

The research had begun a week ago in the Latin Quarter of the city. The office of Mathieu's enterprise was situated above a shop selling travel goods, luggage etc. The offices consisted of a suite of three individual rooms, an ante room with chairs and a settee, a reception room where the secretary sat with a computer. The lady herself was a formidable woman of some fifty years with a waspish temperament. She defended her boss from all comers.

The main office, occupied by Mathieu himself, contained a large desk, with chair, settee and a safe.

The chair was special with a control panel in the arm that allowed him to open and shut the doors and shut down the office suite with steel shutters at the press of a button. In the basement beneath the shop below was a cellar mainly used for holding prisoners when needed. Otherwise it was used as a barracks for the accommodation of any men he may require from time to time. There was always a crew of three men on call, regardless of time or day.

There were certain regular events in the life of Mathieu. On Mondays he visited the nightclubs he controlled, collecting the takings from the weekend. These were brought in and counted, placed in the safe for temporary safekeeping. Tuesday was the judgement day, any event requiring punishment or reward was kept for judgement until Tuesday, unless immediate response was needed. Wednesday was spent at the chateau just outside Paris, a peaceful time with his long term mistress in the comfort of his own home. Thursday was time for a circuit round the city, visiting other enterprises and co-ordinating business with rivals and competitors.

Friday was entertainment day and that was the day he entertained any female visitor he took a fancy to. To this end he used whatever means necessary to manoeuvre them into the office. Once there they could not escape. One of the reasons for his irritation with Gabrielle was that somehow she had slipped through his fingers. Mathieu was not accustomed to failure!

However this did not mean that he was tied to the routine

every week. If an opportunity offered, or even if he just felt like it, he varied the programme.

The steel shutter came into use when unwilling people needed to be persuaded to submit to Mathieu's will, on the occasions when ladies were not prepared to be compliant, or perhaps men needed his personal discipline. Once the shutters dropped, there was no way of escape. Mathieu was quite ruthless and he took his pleasures regardless of whether permission was given or not.

The local people of the area made sure that, if they had daughters, they kept them well clear of anything to do with Mathieu and his men.

The block behind the office was taken up with the warehouse where several different enterprises were centred. The basement below the storage facility was converted into a holding area for the consignments of girls regularly shipped in from Romania, Bulgaria and the other Balkan countries. Here they were groomed for a future career in a brothel, or if they had the right qualifications, high class call girls. This, of course was a ready source of light relief for Mathieu, as well as his employees. It must be said his personal preference was for respectable, well brought up girls, who had 'morals'. They satisfied his particular tastes. The knowledge that he was making them break the taboos of their upbringing, especially when he was forcing them, added a fillip to his sexual appetite. Mathieu was not a nice man, and he made no real effort to be nice unless there was good reason, or money, to be made from it.

Mathieu's right hand man was a real piece of work. Albert Cruz was a product of the alleys of Marrakesh. He was the son to a Foreign Legion Officer, Capitaine Philippe Cruz, Croix de Guerre, and a hero of WW2. His mother was the daughter of a local goldsmith, whose bazaar shop provided a profitable income to the family. The union of the Franco-Spanish officer and the craftsman's daughter was frowned upon, and the resultant pregnancy caused her eviction from the family home, and the loss of future prospects from the business. It also caused the gallant Capitaine to lose interest and abandon the unfortunate girl to life in the gutter with her half-breed infant.

She did her best and managed to obtain the protection of the local crime boss that allowed her to get an education for her fatherless son, an education which included an intimate knowledge of the local criminal underworld. Having learned of his heritage, young Albert nurtured a deep and abiding hatred of his grandparents and his father.

Upon the death of his mother, he decided to leave Marrakesh for the fleshpots of France. Before his departure he took revenge for his abandonment, on his grandfather's family,. At the same time, incidentally, it financed his move over the water. In a carefully planned sequence of moves he looted the family shop, and then called in on the family at home armed with an AK47 and a stick of dynamite. Over the next two day period he strangled his grandmother and uncle, raped his aunt and two female cousins several times, and then sodomised his male cousin, before blowing the safe and removing the considerable sums of money and gold bullion within. He then blew up the house with the family inside killing all who had survived thus far.

Albert Cruz arrived in Paris dressed in Cardin suit, a tall, tanned, wickedly good-looking man. He was an immediate success with the ladies. When his money ran out, he found the ladies only too willing to provide him with a living.

He drifted into the area of influence controlled by Mathieu, an up and coming gangster, as ruthless as he. They had hit it off immediately and had been together ever since. Now after ten years his place was secure and his life style reflected that.

He lived in a smart flat overlooking the Seine. His current companion was a very elegant lady of impeccable antecedents, wife of a respected member of the Government. Her husband's mistress was one of Albert's call girls, a detail which he did not bother to mention. The lady was currently sprawled naked across the silk sheets of the king-sized bed. Albert was standing at the bar equally naked and pouring himself a drink.

The phone rang and the answerphone cut in. "Get over here, now!" The voice of Mathieu cracked over the line. Albert picked up the phone but Mathieu had rung off. With a muttered oath he slammed the drink down on the sideboard and grabbed his clothes. To the woman he said. "Wait. I'll be back!"

He drove the short distance between his flat and the warehouse. There he found Mathieu striding up and down, furiously,

"What's up boss?" he asked.

"I'll tell you what's up. That fool in Marseille has become too soft. After the series of raids on the storehouses that cost me millions in stock and money, I cannot even get hold of anyone. With the death of Edouard Chamaise there seems to be no one else in a position to take responsibility.

Those lost documents have cost a fortune one way and another. The destruction of the Marseille property seems to have frightened everyone off. Trying to get re-established seems to be beyond the capabilities of whoever is in charge down there. Barat is back in Paris, so there is no one I can trust to get things done."

"So, what do you want me to do, boss? Go to Marseille? Shoot someone? Or is there something else?"

"Don't you be cheeky to me, Cruz. I want you to do what I discussed three weeks ago. Find out what is going on in Marseille. If necessary, take charge yourself. If there is any sign or news of the MacLean woman, bring her to me or kill her."

"Have you any idea where I start looking now?"

"Try 'Yellow Pages'. How the hell would I know? Perhaps it might be worth looking in Marseille since that is where the raids took place."

When Albert returned to his flat, he eyed the woman still lying in his bed, he threw back the covers, exposing her naked body. Stripping off his clothes, he spread her legs apart and mounted her whilst she was still only half awake, savagely thrusting his way into her without concern for her cries of pain. He pumped away until he finished. He then withdrew and flung himself to the other side of the bed and fell asleep immediately. The woman curled up in pain, then left the bed quietly and went to the en-suite bathroom. She showered and cleaned herself up, dressed and left the apartment.

When she returned two days later the apartment was closed and locked. She entered with the key hidden for emergencies and noticed that the answer phone was flashing. Without thinking, she pressed the button to retrieve the messages. There were three waiting. The first detailed instructions for Albert to bring Gabrielle MacLean for punishment to Mathieu. If it's not possible, kill her. The message was given in a cold unemotional voice. The next message came up.

"Cruz, get rid of that woman you're sleeping with. Her husband is of no more use to us. I have arranged an accident for him. You'll need to eliminate his wife to make sure there are no loose ends. The third message was possibly a wrong number. There was the sound of breathing at the other end followed by the click of the phone being hung up.

She froze in panic hearing the messages. She rang her husband on his mobile, no answer! She rang his office next, but he had not come in today. He was not expected until tomorrow. She remembered he was at a conference in Abbeville. He would not leave the conference until tomorrow morning.

She rang his hotel and left a message for him to call her. Searching the desk to see if there was anything of interest, she was disappointed. Apart from a gun, she found nothing. In the bedroom she continued her search, and found a file under the bed in a concealed drawer. There was also money which she took as well. As she left, she replaced the hidden key.

Outside John and Gabrielle who were watching the apartment, collected the lady between them and bundled her into their car. She protested but was unable to get free from their grasp. In the car John slipped a cable tie over her wrists, and Gabrielle drove off to the car park underneath their apartment building.

Later, over a drink in the apartment, the lady calmed down. She had been shivering ever since she had been lifted. But now she began to relax, as she became aware that their interest was in Albert Cruz, not her.

"Where is Albert? Do you know?"

"Mathieu sent him to Marseille to find Gabrielle MacLean. He left last night."

"If, as you say, you wanted to leave him, why did you go back to the flat?"

"He had information on my husband and I wanted to find it. I found the papers I have with me, but no others!"

John looked through the papers quickly.

"This looks interesting," he said. "The file contains a rundown on the operations under the control of Mathieu. I reckon this is Albert's insurance policy, something he can use to blackmail Mathieu with, if things go wrong."

"The messages on the answer machine regarding you and your husband: do you believe them?"

Her voice was shaky still as she answered, "Yes, I believe them. That man's voice made my flesh creep. He was unconcerned. It meant nothing to him. I am scared."

John considered for a few moments. Then "Get hold of your husband and disappear for the next few days. Use whatever excuse you have to. Get away from Paris. You can call us next week. We'll let you know if it's safe to return. Better still, give us your mobile number and we will call you when it is safe to return!"

Gabrielle led the woman down to the lobby and put her in a cab. Back in the room they planned their next move.

Knowing what Mathieu looked like, she was able to recognise him as he entered his office at 9.00am the next morning. He was alone, carrying a briefcase like any other office worker in the city. His suit was crumpled and he looked worn and bad tempered.

Remy had joined them. Since this was his particular area of operation and expertise, he had entered the building during the previous night and, as he put it, manicured the electrical circuits, so the steel shutters and electronic locks were immobilised. A friend on the police force had contacted Mathieu's secretary, and detained her with a trumped up story about her car registration. She would not be in the office for at least an hour. Remy visited the basement just to make sure there would be no awkward interruptions to the proposed visit.

Gabrielle entered the building. Her bag, containing her Glock pistol, swung over her shoulder close to her hand. In the other hand she had the original papers that she had taken by mistake from Mathieu's office desk. At the door, she nodded to John who was standing to one side, and walked in. The inner door was open and Mathieu was bent over the office safe. He turned angrily as she went in, saw who it was and froze for a moment in shock. He recovered quickly and a sly smile lit his face.

"Gabrielle, how nice to see you. I've missed you these last weeks. Have you come to see me about your book?"

"No. Not that. This!" She held out the file with his papers. "They must have caught on the back of my manuscript when I left your office last. I thought I should return them!"

"Why, thank you, my dear." He spoke ingratiatingly. "I had missed them and wondered where they had gone."

His cheesy grin disgusted her.

"Don't bother lying to me." Gabrielle said cuttingly. "I've been avoiding your hoodlum friends over half of France for the last several months. Perhaps now you've got them back, you will leave me alone."

"My dear girl, what do you mean, hoodlums? I know nothing of this. Perhaps Albert has overreacted in trying to get the papers back. If so I am sorry. Tell me did you read the papers?"

"I tried, but I could not really understand them. Anyway, can I take it that you will leave me alone now?"

Mathieu had pressed the button below the desk top to call for men to come to the office.

"I'm afraid not, my dear. I would rather you stayed. In fact I insist that you do. It would have been better if you had taken my offer in the first place." He pressed the button again, angrily. Gabrielle had seated herself in the chair opposite the desk.

Puzzled he sat down himself, "What is going on here?"

"I was giving you the chance to redeem yourself. You failed the test, so I will need to punish you. Tell me does the safe contain all the details of your business?"

Mathieu sat back astonished.

"*You* are going to punish *me*......How?" He reached into his desk drawer for the gun he kept there. It was not there! He was becoming worried. Where were his men? They should have come in answer to the bell. Why was Gabrielle looking so unworried?

Something was terribly wrong! He started to get up from the chair. Gabrielle lifted the Glock and indicated for him to remain seated. He sank back into the seat, his mind in turmoil. Where was Albert? He remembered he had sent him to Marseille. A knock came at the door. Gabrielle swiftly moved over to the wall and wiggled the gun at Mathieu to answer,

"Yes. Come in!" He said hoping for a diversion. Albert came in.

"Sorry, boss. I heard that the girl was seen here in Paris yesterday, so I decided to stay here to see if I could fin..... " He stopped, becoming aware of the girl and the gun. His hand made a move towards his gun.

The silenced Glock spoke. The bullet hit his elbow and shattered it. He dropped to the floor in agony. Keeping Mathieu covered, Gabrielle rolled Albert over with her foot, and lifted the gun from the waistband of Albert's trousers. She tucked it into her handbag,

"The safe. Now!" her voice cracked out and Mathieu swung

round and opened the safe door wide.

"Out!" The gun waved him out from the desk and into the middle of the room. "Look after your friend." She said, and Mathieu obediently dropped to his knees beside Albert, who was rocking and moaning with his arm clutched in his other hand. Albert drew up his leg beside Mathieu, exposing his ankle holster and gun to Mathieu's view. Seeing it Mathieu grabbed it and turned it towards Gabrielle. The hair trigger caused the gun to fire early. The bullet missed Gabrielle, but hers didn't. Mathieu Ormande, super crook and villain extraordinaire departed life with a bullet between the eyes, as irrevocably dead as any of the many people killed on his orders.

Albert, his loyal henchman, scrabbling with his good hand for the gun, followed, with the help of a bullet from John's Glock that passed through his head from front to back.

"I heard the gun shot and guessed there was trouble." He took Gabrielle in his arms, "I would have left you to it as you asked, but I knew your gun was silenced."

"Oh, John. I shot him!" She sobbed.

"You did well," he said. "Now you clear and lock the safe, while I arrange the bodies." He took the gun from her hand, cleaned it carefully, and placed the gun in Albert's good hand. Then he took his gun, cleaned it also and placed in Mathieu's hand. The ankle gun went back into its holster having also been cleaned.

"There...that should do it!" He went over to Gabrielle and helped her clear the safe. Once they had emptied it, he closed and locked it, taking the key with him as they left the office. John wiped off the outer door knob, where he had touched it. They left the building quietly. No one seemed to have heard the single shot.

Across the street a figure stood in the doorway of the electrical shop, watching as the two people left Mathieu's building and drove away. He then strolled across the road, went through the door and climbed the stairs to Mathieu Ormande's office. The door opened under his gloved hand and he entered cautiously. The gun in his left hand seemed to be there without any conscious thought on his part. Through the empty outer office, the open door of the inner invited the intruder's attention. He crossed to the open door and looked through at the carefully arranged scene.

Nudging both bodies with his polished toe to make sure, he carefully vetted the scene, to make sure there was no obvious clue that could spoil the carefully arranged scene.

Below in the basement Ferat found the answer to the question of his niece's return. The furnace that heated the building was in the corner of the outer cellar. There was a wire basket next to the furnace containing rags, amongst which was a torn piece of cloth from the white dress patterned with roses worn by little Angelique when she was abducted. The bloodstains on the material told the story. Ferat stood and tears ran unheeded as he wept for his niece.

Next door the three gunmen that were Mathieu's bodyguards lay bound and gagged where Remy had left them. Ferat found them after he got over his immediate grief. He removed their gags and questioned them. He went swiftly upstairs to the office and removed the Glock from Mathieu's hand and returned to the basement. There he shot all three men several times. He returned the gun to the office, carefully rearranging the scene, and left as quietly as he came. The time delay on the explosives, planted by Remy within the warehouse premises, went off 21 minutes after the departure of Aristide Ferat. The three men reporting for duty in the basement were just entering the building as it collapsed, all three survived.

Gabrielle informed Albert Cruz's former mistress that it was safe to return. When they left Paris, Gabrielle was beginning to feel safe for the first time for what seemed years. In fact it was only a matter of months since she first met John and the nightmare had begun. Now it was impossible for her to imagine life without him. Just one more operation and he would be all hers'.

Chapter Eleven

The follow up operation commenced as soon as John and Gabrielle confirmed the demise of Mathieu and the clearing of his office and premises on the Left Bank.

Paddy and Remy walked down the road hand in hand, chatting and laughing like any of the other young couples wandering in the area. Despite the late hour, the sound of music and the almost continuous light show emanating from the Disney show grounds created a summery atmosphere that went with the bright red dress that Paddy wore and the blue t-shirt and jeans over grey moccasins worn by her companion. They walked entirely round the target compound, noting the gatehouse with three security guards, and the high chain link fence surmounted by a razor wire coil.

The buildings within the compound were close to the fence on the north side, with no windows. In front there was a concrete apron and there were open double doors leading to a loading dock.

In the middle of the eastern wall was a row of windows for what looked like offices, and below the windows there was a glass front door. The concrete apron extended round the side of the building and several cars were parked in white-lined spaces. To one side was a larger space in which was parked a left-hand-drive Bentley saloon, and behind it a black Porsche Carrera. Within the area several men in black overalls and berets, obvious security men, were wandering around.

Satisfied that there was nothing more to see, Paddy and Remy walked down the road and boarded the bus that sat among several others parked in the vicinity of Disneyworld. They both changed into grey coveralls. As she stripped off the dress Paddy drew several quiet wolf whistles from the waiting troopers. She grinned expecting, and appreciating the reaction, pleased that the men were relaxed and ready for action. Paddy and Remy held a final briefing. They updated John and Mike who were stationed in their vehicle with the second platoon in case they were needed.

The driver started the engine and prepared to move off.

On the street the advance party, beer cans in hand, were

strolling arm in arm past the gatehouse. It was difficult to see what happened next. Three cans went through the window, smoke billowed out, to be swiftly dispersed by the fresh breeze. No one else seemed to notice. Two drunks continued down the street, the third walked past the barrier and stood and raised it when the bus rolled up. The bus passed through and drew into the loading dock. The other two 'drunks' returned to take over control of the gate house,

Meanwhile, in the loading dock, two men who came to question the arrival of the bus were swiftly subdued. The doors were closed, hiding the group from view. The others debussed swiftly and began to disperse to their assigned goals. Three armed men swiftly rounded up the visible security men in the lighted area round the building. They assumed the role of the captured men. Two went along the corridor to the staircase to the offices. Paddy went along the other corridor in the front of the building, heading for the private suite located there. Her party of three men included Pete Maddox. The ex-Marine flanked her as she opened the double doors quietly. Inside there was a carpeted lobby with a reception desk currently unmanned. Behind the desk the door to the executive suite was half open, and the sound of voices could be heard

The two intruders moved over to the door and listened. Someone was instructing another to stack the bags neatly or there would not be room for them all.

At a nod from Paddy, Pete stepped through the door, gun up and ready. Paddy followed. There was a slim, well-dressed man sitting behind the desk. The white haired man, Barat, they recognised from Marseille, had been caught with his hands full of packages. A slender blond was leaning on the corner of the desk, her close-fitting silk dress clinging to every curve of her spectacular body. Pete's gun was covering the two men. Paddy shot the blonde who had swept a small automatic up from the desk top. The two bullets took her in the side throwing her across the desk to crumple against the wall with her head at an odd angle. The gun flew out of her hand. The white haired man dropped the packages and dive-rolled across the floor to pick up the weapon, he was still lining up to fire when Pete's gun spat fire and nailed him, wounded, to the floor. The man behind the desk was still sitting, looking up the barrel of Paddy's H&K.

"And who might you be?" She said sweetly.

"Marc Artois. This is my business. Who are you and what are you doing here?"

Paddy ignored him and waved for one of the troopers to secure him to his chair. The door on the side of the office, where the white haired man had been working, opened into a small room lined with shelves.

The shelves were stacked with a surprising variety of objects. Paddy surveyed the room with interest.

"We'll need boxes and packing for this lot." She indicated the shelves of objet-d'art. "The money can be bagged and the dope destroyed. I'll take two guys and send some boxes in Take great care of the artistic bits. My guess is that they are very valuable."

Elsewhere in the building the takeover had been comparatively smooth. There was a broken ankle where one of the troopers turned his foot on a floor tie bolt, no other casualties. The official files of the company were removed, including a second set found under the carpet in the executive office. Marc Artois was loaded into the bus with the other removable items. The rest of the staff had been assembled in the lobby of the building. The entire operation had been carried out either in complete silence or only by native French speakers.

By design, although the coveralls were unmarked, they were of the pattern and design of those issued to French special forces. That was the impression that they left with the witnesses. The goods in the warehouse appeared to be genuine. But following the scorched earth policy already established, charges were laid, and as the bus left the compound, the captives poured out of the building and were safely clear when the building blew up.

The second warehouse was attacked within one hour of the attack at Disneyland. The Versailles depot was the major point for the transfer of imported women from the eastern countries. A large part of the complex was devoted to the grooming of the product, as the women were called.

There was a wide range of facilities on the premises, the night club providing a cover for money laundering, and a brothel operated by a local manager of, using the recently groomed product as an introduction to their new career. The raid, led by the team of Mike and John, infiltrated several of the troops into the night club in plain clothes. At the warehouse premises behind the facade of the club, the lateness of the night, combined with the imminent closure of the premises, had introduced an element of sloppiness into the routine. This was a result of many quiet, untroubled, nights. The second team was thus able to get close enough to neutralise the gate guards before they could give warning.

There were several, short, brutal fire fights throughout the premises, but the complete takeover of the complex was accomplished before dawn. The final revellers were evicted without being aware of the takeover.

The Versailles operation cost the raiders two wounded and several cuts and bruises. The reward was $4.500.000 in cash, plus the release of 87 girls from the grooming facility. In addition several million euro's worth of drugs were destroyed when the buildings collapsed and burnt, apparently from the use of inferior building materials and consequently fractured gas mains.

After a thorough interrogation Marc Artois was released. For his own safety he disappeared into the hills of the Massif Central and retired from the public life of his past.

A letter appeared on the desk of Commissioner Ferat marked 'personal'. Within it there was another envelope also marked Personal. The document within explained the role of Aristide Ferat in facilitating the release of a person suspected of bombing the railway station at Gard du |Nord, Paris. The signatures on the document made it clearly genuine. The note attached was brief. *Only I have seen this. There are no copies. I suggest you burn it now!* It was signed with the initial J.

John made a full report of all three operations to Kelly. He passed over the papers and funds recovered from both Mathieu and Albert Cruz.

Paddy added to the collection of papers and funds swelling the fighting fund, with cash alone in excess of $3.000.000 and an, at present, unknown sum for the antiques recovered from the warehouse. Many of these were identifiable from records of burglaries. The custody of the identified 'objets d'art' was passed to Commissioner Ferat, for return to the owners.

When added to the results of the Versailles operation, the contribution to the fighting funds was considerable.

That evening in the company of their friends, John and Gabrielle formally retired from the front line activity with the embryonic organisation.

They spent the night enjoying their farewell party, boarded their boat the following day, and set sail eastward down the Mediterranean.

Chapter Twelve

The ketch *Altair* moved quietly through the waters of the Aegean Sea, The island of Andros was off to starboard. The boat left a white scar on the blue waters as they passed through the Cyclades on the way out to the Mirtoan Sea, and the Mediterranean.

John and Gabrielle had been cruising for over a month. The memories of the hectic times of the past few weeks since they first met, now faded by the therapy of the lazy days of sun, sea and the islands.

The tanned figure of Gabrielle relaxed in the cockpit her arm resting on the wheel. John, equally tanned, appeared from below with two cold drinks, one of which he passed to Gabrielle. She spoke.

"Who was on the satellite phone?

"Kelly, she was just checking that we were alright."

"How are things in...... Rosas?"

"Going well, apparently, as you know, she set the whole thing up using a genuine trading company as a cover. The company when purchased, had a client base that was largely redundant. At least that was what they thought. To the surprise of Bill Hamilton, the interim General Manager, two major former clients of the Trans-Ocean, were both dissatisfied with the alternative company they had turned to. Seeing the company had been placed under new management and knowing of Bill's reputation in the industry, they were only too willing to give Trans-Ocean another try. It has made the expansion of the company a priority. Extra funding had been put into TOT to help the company grow and maintain its credibility.

"COMCO, the company that was responsible for causing the collapse of the original Trans-Ocean has been upsetting clients in several areas. It seems that the international expansion of TOT has become an urgent priority.

"According to Bill Hamilton, with the market as it is at present, "If we move now we will be entering the market on the upsurge toward a forecasted boom in the industry.

"The need to establish branches elsewhere can now be justified to accommodate the increasing business. The security team is being expanded using mainly ex-Special forces and spooks, past employees of various Government agencies concerned in secret services. Under the cloak of Secure (International)Inc, they seem to be expanding equally fast in the uniformed security market, which has made the undercover activity of the company much easier to conceal.

"After several exercises Sinc (Secure Inc) has successfully recovered considerable booty and released over forty women, currently being looked after by Jeanne Ascher. Would you believe, her hostel, as she calls it, now has over 150 residents."

Happy that things were still going well they relaxed and enjoyed their drinks. However as they sailed into Piraeus, Gabrielle took another satellite call from Rosas.

Kelly was most apologetic, "Gabrielle, since you are already in the area we wondered if you could take a look at Lebanon. We have become aware of the possibility of a new training camp for specialists, run by an Iranian group of fundamentalists. It is located on the Lebanon coast north of Batrun. Rumour has it that it is linked to the so-called Al Qaeda group. Could you and John feel out the ground in the area; possibly sniff around; perhaps make a few enquiries? We do have a contact in East Beirut named Jacques Billeret. He runs a news agency there. He's a passive agent but reliable."

Gabrielle discussed Kelly's request with John.

"What do you think? Should we really follow this up?" She knew what he would say even as she spoke. He put the wheel hard over and the *Altair* came round to the new course, leaving their intended destination port at Piraeus behind.

With Gabrielle at the wheel, John went below and operated the panel behind the satnav. This panel folded forward on concealed hinges exposing the gun locker behind it. He removed the two suppressed H&K smg's, stripped them, and reassembled them, ensuring they had full magazines. Then removing two Glock automatics he performed a similar strip and check over, once again making sure the loaded magazines were to hand. The last thing he checked was the box of small explosive packages ready to use. He ensured the fuses were safe in their separate package.

Satisfied, he took two beers up to the wheel and joined

Gabrielle in the cockpit.

The journey across the eastern Mediterranean was made mostly under full sail. As they approached the Lebanon shore they shortened sail, took time to clean up the boat and prepare to clear customs at Beirut.

The customary social drink with Beirut authorities went off with the usual speed and efficiency. Once cleared, they moored for the night.

The morning light woke them, and John rowed ashore to get some fresh milk and bread. The city was quiet and showing signs of returning to a more relaxed state after the turmoil of the past few years.

However he did not want to linger, so he made his purchases and returned to the *Altair* as quickly as possible. Later that morning after a leisurely breakfast, they both went ashore to find Jacques Billeret.

The tall thin newsman had a tired, lived-in face and a world-weary look. He greeted them with a quiet smile and glasses of thick coffee.

While they drank their coffee he confirmed that the camp at Batrun did exist. It was linked to several, different training programmes though he had not heard of anything specific. The local people were leaving the camp strictly alone, apart from delivering food and fuel supplies.

Thanking him for his input, they returned to the ketch and sailed off up the coast towards Batrun.

John found himself wondering about the current mission, looking at Gabrielle relaxing on deck he worried about the possibility of things going wrong. What if she got hurt or was killed?

He shook his head and told himself to stop worrying. They were there to make enquiries not to take action, so it was no use shrinking at shadows. It did come home to him again how important Gabrielle was in his life. When he considered what they had been through already, he was appalled at the risks they had taken. With a wry grin he realised that risk had been part of their relationship. He was going to have to accept the fact that, having committed themselves to an 'interesting' life, they were just going to have to get used to it!

As he looked around the peaceful blue waters he sighed. It was difficult to imagine that there was another world of pain and anguish just over the horizon. The recent tragic history of the once ultra-civilised Lebanese was still fresh. The continuing operations by the radicals was still a major stumbling block to serious consideration of a peaceful regeneration.

They spotted ships during that day, a tanker heading south and several coasters used for trading back and forth to Cyprus and Egypt. Otherwise there was little to disturb the quiet passage of the ketch.

They encountered the Israelis 15 miles off the coast as they were coming abreast of Batrun. The two Ribs were motoring towards the shore at about ten knots, their twin outboards burbling quietly at the low speed. The twenty Shayetet Commandos seated on the air filled tubes were armed to the teeth with Uzis and grenades, faces streaked with black camouflage paint. The boats pulled alongside the *Altair*, one each side and their officer boarded, without waiting to be asked. He stood by the cockpit looking down the barrel of the H&K smg.

"Please, lower your gun. Sit down, and ask your men to stand off and wait for your instructions!" John's voice was calm and reasonable, but there was no doubt he meant every word.

The officer called to the two boats to stand off and wait. At least John presumed that was what he said, because the boats withdrew. The H&K was not visible from the boats. He was obviously uncomfortable with having been taken so easily.

John asked his name.

"Aaron Smith." He wasn't volunteering much.

John said. "Relax. You're among friends." He put the H&K down. "Since you seem to be heading for Batrun, I presume you are Israeli troops contemplating an insertion into the probable target of the training camp located on the east side of the bay at Batrun?"

Smith said nothing. So John continued.

"We are also en route to Batrun. Our task was to establish whether the camp is being used to train suicide bombers and obviously, if there was any way we could upset things, we would."

Smith still sat close mouthed, saying nothing,

"In the circumstances can I suggest we join forces in this case?

I think you will agree, the arrival of a yacht looks a lot more innocent, than two Rib raiders. It would permit an innocent approach to the area without causing alarm. Both Gabrielle and I are experienced at handling and using guns. If needed it's always useful to have a backup"

Smith spoke for the first time. His English was good though the accent was American, he spoke in an oddly formal way.

"I am sorry to have intruded the way I did. Your offer of help is appreciated, though I don't think my superiors would be happy with the idea of using foreign civilians in the circumstances. The idea of using your boat to approach without immediate detection is obviously a good one, and I must confess that was in my mind when I came to call." He had a wry smile as he spoke."We do not have many friends in this area and I'm afraid we have been more inclined to shoot first. If you are still willing, I would like to take up your offer."

He explained "In this area the terrorists have become more and more aware of our raids. They keep watch for sea raiders and this does make it more difficult." He thought for a moment. "If perhaps you could moor alongside the quay, it would make our job easier and place us at a much more advantageous spot for entering and leaving the camp. As you pointed out, it's located immediately east of the harbour. The beach on that side is used for simulated landings by many of the courses run by the camp. It is what, in fact, drew our attention to the camp in the first place."

John thought for a few minutes,

"Call the boats to close in and keep station on us. We will approach at twilight and the men can board. Leave a boatman to stay offshore with the Ribs, out of sight and range of the short range radar. It will be a squeeze, but the men would not have to put up with it for long.

When we come alongside, I will go ashore to show our papers. You and your men can climb ashore under the pier, out of general sight. The darkness should conceal you. We will stay overnight and leave in the morning. I presume you have an extraction plan? If there is a problem, call me on my mobile phone. It's not registered in my name and quite safe. If you need backup for any reason, we'll be here until 10.00 am tomorrow."

The uncomfortable proximity of so many sweating young men

and women lasted for two hours, as the *Altair* sailed into Batrun in the gathering dusk, and it was dark by the time they motored up to the quay on the east of the town. Gabrielle jumped ashore and moored the boat fore and aft. The darkness was relieved by two lamp standards, one on the end of the quay the other in the middle. The boat was between the lights, but shaded at the rear by a coffee stall normally open during daylight hours, but conveniently in darkness now. Under its shadow, the Commandos were able to debark without detection.

Clearance was accomplished without questions. His papers, already accepted by the authorities in Beirut, were passed without query, and he and Gabrielle went into town to find a restaurant for dinner.

They were both quiet whilst they ate. The food was good and, as good friends, they were both capable of sitting and enjoying each other's company without the need of conversation, but equally, both were aware of the feeling of suppressed excitement brought by being back in action.

Although not directly involved, they were close enough to stir the blood. On the way back to the boat they held hands and looked anxiously towards the eastern shore, to see if there were signs of the action that should be taking place.

At the boat John poured a glass of wine for them both. As he did he felt the boat move slightly, as if someone had quietly got on board. He put a finger to his lips for silence, opened the gun panel and retrieved a Glock from the locker. He closed the panel and poked his head through the hatch. He was in time to see the figure of a man hiding behind the cabin on the sea side of the boat. He slipped the gun under his shirt into the waistband of his trousers against his back, then stepped onto the deck and quietly spoke to the concealed man. "The fore hatch is open slide in through there while I distract anyone watching." He then stepped off the boat and checked the moorings fore and aft, using the torch that stood beside the main hatch. He waved the torch about checking the shadowed spots around the coffee bar, and then returned aboard.

In the main cabin Gabrielle was bandaging a flesh wound in the commando's arm.

"What happened?" the words came out more harshly than he intended.

"We were ambushed. I was tail-end Charlie and they closed

the trap too soon. There was nothing the Captain could do. They put down their arms and were all herded into a big hut with guards outside armed with AK 47's and Uzis, they were laughing at how easy it was. We were betrayed by one of our leaders." The young soldier was almost in tears.

"Can you show us where they're kept?" John asked. The soldier nodded. "Do they know about you?" The soldier shook his head, hesitated," I don't think so. I got this from the razor wire on my way out."

John looked at Gabrielle. She nodded, "If we act now we have a good chance of getting away with it."

The soldier looked astonished, "What do you mean. We have no men, no weapons.. .....Nothing."

John grinned and opened the gun panel. He took out the two H&K smg's and several spare magazines. He also took out the packets of charges and the other Glock which he threw to Gabrielle. While he fused the Semtex charges, she collected an H&K smg and two spare magazines. She checked it, cocked it and put the safety on. She then did the same with the Glock slipping it in the waistband at the back of her jeans. She collected a bunch of cable ties from a drawer and thrust them in her pocket. They each slipped the sheath of a Fairburn knife onto their belts. Then, turning to the soldier, John said, "Let's go!" It was an order not a request. "Mustn't keep them waiting too long!"

They filed out of the cabin. Under cover of the shadows, they slipped along the quay to the shore and made their way towards the camp on the eastern side of the bay.

The soldier led the way and as they reached the outer fence wire he swung down to the beach and walked along parallel to the fence. He stopped and went over to a spot where the sand and earth had been disturbed, he scraped away the loose sand under the wire. There was a break in the fence concealed by the sand. He cleared the gap and slithered through. John and Gabrielle followed.

The camp was quiet, but a guard alongside the first building was outlined against the window of what was obviously an office. Other buildings were silhouetted against the loom of light from the nearby town. The soldier indicated a figure visible in the faint light through the glass windows in the door. Signalling them to wait he crawled forward on his stomach, slinging his Uzi across his shoulder out of the way,

There was a thud and a faint whimper. Then the soldier called quietly and they joined him at the second building. They lay on the sand in the shelter of the hut wall, the sand sticking to their sweaty skin. The guard within the enclosed porch stirred, scraping his boot on the floor as he shifted his position.

From within came sounds of movement and voices. The soldier indicated the building and waited while John slowly got to his feet and peered through the glass panel on the door. There was a lobby inside partially lit by the glass panels of the interior door. He looked around and could see only one sentry inside. Handing Gabrielle his H&K he opened the door and slid in. As the sentry looked up he lifted his finger to his lips the international sign to be quiet. The puzzled guard rose to his feet to be met with the full force of John's straight fingers to his throat, closely followed by the Fairburn knife under the ribs. The sentry collapsed with a sigh, dead in John's open arms. He lowered the body to the floor and waved the others in.

Through the interior door it was possible to see a row of men sitting on the floor with hands on their heads. In front of them, was seated an Arab wearing a keffiyeh, the headdress made famous by Yasser Arafat, the Palestine leader. He was writing, while to one side, two others were holding Aaron Smith. A third beat him with cane lashing his back with vicious efficiency.

Two men armed with AK47s watched the seated prisoners. John pointed to the two armed men, and then to Gabrielle and the soldier. He indicated one each. They nodded and taking back his H&K from Gabrielle, he eased the door open quietly and they all stepped into the room.

The suppressed H&K and the soldier's suppressed Uzi each spat two bullets. The men with the AK47s dropped to the ground. John jumped in front of the table waving his smg at the man at the desk. Gabrielle shot the wielder of the cane and the soldier smashed one of the men holding his Officer with the short butt of the Uzi and shot the other man.

Time stood still. Then the man at the desk went for his gun. John shot him in the arm and the gun fell from his hand. The Israeli prisoners started to rise and a murmur went round the room John put his finger to his lips for silence. Well trained, they were immediately quiet. He spoke to Aaron

"Can you manage?" Aaron nodded and picked up the pistol belonging to one of his guards. He sent two of his men over to the door on the other side of the room. The bigger of the two gripped the handle and wrenched the door open. Inside was piled the soldier's equipment. The gear was handed round and the men assembled ready to move off. Aaron took the papers from the desk and shoved them down the front of his shirt, then turned to John.

"Do you know where the trainees are housed?" John shook his head.

"There are three cantonments on the south side of the camp allocated for the training and accommodation of the bombers. On this side is the training area for terrorists from all over the world.

John lifted his holdall containing the fused explosives. "I'll deal with the terrorists. You deal with the bombers," he raised his eyebrow in query? Aaron nodded. "O.K. set the time delay and meet back at the boat? Give it 30 minutes." Taking his soldier as guide, John and Gabrielle left the released Commandos and went out into the night once more.

The sentries stationed round the barrack were disposed of quietly, one at a time. The Israeli's were highly efficient and after the ambush, on their mettle.

John placed the small packets of Semtex around the building ensuring the timers were set.

When they were ready to leave, they left the camp by the main gate. The guards were disposed of before they knew what hit them, with well-placed shots from the silenced smg's.

By the time the explosions started, the last man was back at the boat. John radioed the Port Captain and said that in view of the explosions he did not wish to get involved and he was leaving immediately. The Port Captain having been awakened by the noise, quite understood and wished them a safe voyage.

While the *Altair* sailed south, Gabrielle attended the wounds on Aaron Smith's back. Apart from the cuts sustained by the soldier on the razor wire, and one or two other cuts and bruises, he was the only casualty.

John asked Aaron about the so-called betrayal by one of their own. Aaron just said, "I will deal with it," and tapped the papers now folded in his shirt pocket!

They made the rendezvous with the Ribs without a hitch, over

15 miles offshore.

Last to leave the yacht, Aaron Smith shook John's hand and kissed Gabrielle's.

"Thank you both for my life, and my men's lives. I will not forget. If you ever need us, just call." With that he jumped over to the Rib and they both roared off.

John watched the ribs roar off, then turned the *Altair* westwards once more and made for Cyprus.

Kelly phoned later that day, "I understand you have been busy, both of you!"

"What do you mean?" John asked.

"Only that you are now listed as honorary members of the Shayetet, Israeli Special Forces, both of you, and that the training base at Batrun has been completely destroyed, without loss. Whatever you did, it seems to have worked. So tell me about it someday. The bad news is, one or both of you may be targeted because you were in Marseille when everything was happening there, especially since you departed so promptly. It may have been enough to set the wolves loose. They could be on your trail so take care. Watch your back. Take no chances and if you need help, call!"

The harbour at Limassol is dominated by the Castle once occupied by Queen Berengaria of Navarre, wife of King Richard 1 of England. As the *Altair* slipped into her berth on the pontoon, the shadow of the castle covered the boat causing John to shiver. Perhaps it was an omen. He shrugged and concentrated on coming alongside without damaging anything. That night they dined out in style, mainly to celebrate completing a mission, perhaps rejoicing that they were still alive. They slept with weapons at hand that night.

The feeling of unease lasted for the entire stay on the island of Cyprus, and when they eventually left after a three day stay, there was a distinct feeling of relief for both of them. The pressure of events over the last few weeks had been building for them both, and it was not surprising that both would feel happier when they finally reached Barcelona and the base at Rosas. The fact that they had not planned their progress through the Mediterranean, and therefore no one else could do other than guess where they would be, finally dawned on them both, and they decided to continue and call in at Crete, an island neither had visited before.

The wind was right and the boat heeled to starboard with the pressure. At the speed they were making they would be in Crete in the next 12 hours. The sun shining on the blue sea tempted them to forget the warning from Kelly. Although they were not threatened during the passage they watched every boat sighted with extra care. They made for Aglos Nikolaos at the north east of Crete.

The picturesque little harbour was busy with boats of all shapes and sizes. Having starred in several movies and TV series, the port had acquired a popularity which necessitated the development carried out to accommodate all the extra holiday business that came with it. John could not help being a little uneasy at the hordes of holidaymakers.

The *Altair* was one among many moored to a pontoon busy with boat crews coming and going. The unease persisted and they cut their visit short. They left the famous harbour on the evening tide setting the boat on course for Barcelona.

Kelly had been in touch on the satellite phone asking them to call in if possible. They were sailing west along the Mediterranean anyway, since they intended spending time in Britain. The side trip to Barcelona, whilst slightly out of the way, was at least at the right end of the Mediterranean.

Happier away from land once more, they were both able to relax. And the next two days were spent in the sheer pleasure of each other's company.

John took the opportunity to speak seriously with Gabrielle.

Taking her hand in his he spoke. "Gabrielle, I know we have only been together for a short time. During that time a lot of things have happened to both of us. For me it has been one of the best times of my life, but I confess I do worry about you. You are young and have your whole life ahead. I worry that you may feel you should stay with me from some sort of feeling of loyalty or gratitude."

Gabrielle put her fingers against his lips to stop him saying more.

"Are you saying that you won't marry me?"

"But......"

Once again she hushed him with her fingers.

"You have been leading me on with no intention of making an honest woman of me. After all I've been to you? No. Don't speak.

Listen. You cannot get out of marrying me no matter what. I've invested a lot of time and trouble on catching you and if you think I'm going to let go now, you can forget it!"

He swept her up in his arms and crushed her against his chest.

"It's your funeral. On your head be it. If I must I must, and as soon as we get to England we'll get married!" He kissed her with a joy he could hardly contain.

At Barcelona the weather had become dull and the clouds threatening by the time the *Altair* nosed into her berth in the yacht harbour. To their surprise they were met by Mike and two troopers in plain clothes, who kept a wary eye all round as they made their way to the parked Suburban. The driver set the vehicle moving immediately after they had taken their seats.

"What's up, Mike?" Asked Gabrielle. "Why all the cloak and dagger?"

"Sorry, folks, I'm under strict orders to keep my mouth shut until we reach the office!"

The journey was silent from then on.

The base at Rosas had been developed since John and Gabrielle had departed on their cruise. The sheer size of the place was daunting. The office block rose three stories high beside a second block sited on the other side of the runway. There was a disposal area for several aircraft, and a C130 was just moving past the Gulfstream being towed back into a hanger. Other aircraft were to be seen within the hanger.

Seeing their interest, Mike said. "This is the commercial side of the business. We have two troops of mainly Special Forces from both sides of the Atlantic based in the underground complex below the offices. That's where we keep all the interesting stuff." At John's raised eyebrow, he continued, "Heavy weapons, light armoured vehicles etc."

When the vehicle drew up inside the underground garage, they went up immediately to the office suite occupied by Kelly and Paul.

The other board members were already seated round the table. The conversation stopped when they entered the room. It was not until the kissing and handshaking had been disposed of that they actually found out what the emergency was about.

"There has been a report of a breach of security. The word is that the Marseille mob has a photograph of one of the group that conducted the raids in Marseille. That's the reason I warned you whilst you were cruising in the area."

"One of the surveillance cameras was not completely destroyed and they have been able to extract a recognisable picture from the wreckage. It was not known who, so it was necessary to warn all the personnel involved in the raids."

Chapter Thirteen

Kelly shuffled through the papers on her desk. "Before I go any further I would like to introduce you to the latest recruit to our board. It became obvious that a US section would be called for, and we had already recruited an organisation known as Retreads Inc., a detective and security agency, comprising ex-agents from FBI, DEA and Treasury Departments: agents who left for the right reasons. The Retreads formed and became extremely successful because of their expertise. They are the nucleus of the US section. Former Special Services Major, Mark Foster, has been recruited to run the Troops with the back-up of Captain George Washington Harris, who is due here today for training."

"Michael Brooks has occupied a senior security position at the highest level in the US. He has agreed to join us and act as our US advisor on the board here in Spain." Kelly buzzed her Secretary and Michael came in and introduced himself.

The President of the United States of America had long been suspected of having a private special operation section, responsible to the President alone. The truth is that this organisation actually exists. Run under a complete blanket of silence the section was operated by Michael Brooks, a respected lawyer with a practice including 120 lawyers, and occupying its own building in downtown Washington.

The security surrounding the section was formidable, but with the changing of the President after an election, the incumbent was not always ready to accept the situation. It had become apparent that the new President was not happy with Michael Brooks in charge, a person he had not selected. The dissatisfaction had become more and more apparent, mainly manifested by the increasing interference of Henry Smith, former Deputy Head of the CIA and a close friend of the President, who made it obvious that he felt he should take over.

Despite the fact that he was not officially aware of the existence of the section, he seemed to be in the loop and informed of matters that were private between the President and Michael Brooks.

The problem was that Michael knew where the skeletons were buried. It was impossible to avoid it since it came with the job, which presumed, actually demanded, an intimate relationship with the President.

Because he knew what he did, and suspecting that he was about to be replaced, he pre-empted the inevitable and tendered his resignation direct to the President. Significantly Henry Smith was present in the Oval Office when he called in by appointment to see the President, an unprecedented and, to Michael, unforgivable, breach of trust and security.

From the Oval Office, Michael went direct to Dulles Airport to meet his wife and board the BA flight to London.

It had occurred to Michael that the only way he could be trusted to keep his mouth shut, was if it were closed permanently.

It was from London that Michael contacted his Executive law partner in Washington, and suggested the group make him an offer for his interest in the practice. He assured him that he would not be greedy. An offer over ten million was enough to clear his obligations and fund whatever form of retirement he and his wife Marion cared to follow. The business was worth well in excess of that figure and, as he suspected, his partners jumped at the offer. He left it with the Executive to arrange the formalities and set about arranging his plans for the future.

Some years earlier, a joint operation concerning the previous President and the Prime Minister of Great Britain had put Michael in contact with Kelly's husband. A friendship between the families had resulted and blossomed over the years and continued after Kelly's husband had died. Kelly was still Deputy Director of M16 when Michael resigned. Luckily he had informed her of what was happening, and which flight he and Marion were travelling on.

When he arrived in London, selected personnel were detailed to protect Mr and Mrs Brooks. The precaution had turned out to be necessary. Two attempts were made to cause accidents on the road from the airport to London. Both attempts had been foiled by the skilful driving of their escort. At least one of the would-be assassins died in the wreckage of his car. Michael and his wife had been accommodated in a safe house, whilst a message was passed to his successor.

The force of the message was emphasised by the inclusion of

some highly embarrassing information, which would be released in the event of any further attempt on the persons of Michael and Marion Brooks.

They had decided that their future would be more secure in Britain from now on, and it was from his UK residence that he was eventually recruited to join the board of TOT as the US representative for future operations. Michael took his place at the table, having been introduced all round.

Kelly addressed the board." Just now, we have another problem that has just come up." Kelly stopped and to the surprise of the group, tears glistened in her eyes. The reason for the tears was quite straightforward. Kelly's two godchildren had been abducted, abused, and murdered.

Their parents, Kelly's sister and brother-in-law, both forced to watch, had then also suffered gang rape and been left for dead. Her sister's husband had survived long enough to tell the horrific story before, mercifully, dying. The UN peace keeping force had identified the group who had carried out the crime, but, such are international politics, they could do nothing to punish the offenders, nor could they prevent subsequent atrocities. Though the abductions had been carried out in Austria, The kidnappers had crossed over from Slovenia and taken their victims back with them, to their base.

The murders had occurred there. The bodies of the victims had then been dumped back over the border, where they were found by a horrified holidaymaker and his family. Kelly told the story and left the board room to allow the board to discuss matters. As the door closed John looked at Gabrielle, the question in his eyes. She nodded and deferred their retirement once more.

Kelly stood at the window gazing down on the scene below. Paul entered the room and walked over to the solitary figure. He slipped his arms around her waist and held her close. She melted back against him pulling his arms tightly round her, tears ran down her cheeks unchecked. Paul knew there was nothing he could say, nor anything more he could do. So he just stood and held her shaking figure while she sobbed her heart out.

Kelly was calm and collected when she next went back to the board "I will not take part in any decision on this matter. I have too personal a stake in this." She sat silent listening to the discussion as the others made their decision.

Gabrielle spoke first. "I am ashamed of the reactions of the so-called civilized leaders at the UN. They seem to treat people like pawns in a game of chess. We are not subject to the same restrictions as the so-called peacekeepers. We started the company to combat lawbreaking that the authorities could not, or would not, act upon. Since these people cannot be brought to trial because of the letter of the law, I consider this is a situation that comes within our remit. I vote we bring them to justice in our own way!"

The former US security director, Michael Brooks, said "Have we the forces to deal with this matter?"

Paul assured the assembly that, having investigated the logistics involved, though the Slovenians had an advantage in numbers of at least two to one, the three troops under Alan Gilmore should be able to manage. The guerrillas were armed with AK 47's small arms, well supplied with shoulder fired rockets and anti tank missiles, mines of various types and transport, including two armoured cars stolen from Government forces during the turmoil following the death of Tito. The leader was a former officer in the Yugoslav army, a Major Kosky. He was known as Vlad, after Vlad the Impaler, presumably because of his ruthless slaughter of innocent civilians since the earlier turmoil of the break-up of Yugoslavia.

Paul continued, "We have already formulated a plan for this type of deployment that we think is adaptable to this situation. If we decide to go ahead and erase this blot on the landscape, we will refine things with the most up-to-date information, and should be ready to start things off in five days. That is Sunday."

The silence that followed was broken by John. "Casualties?"

"We estimate at least 10%. But the troops have all volunteered, including the troop under training."

Since all the men, including trainees, were ex-servicemen, it was valid to include the trainees in the assault group.

The discussion became general, even though the decision was already a foregone conclusion. The planning was passed back to Major Alan Gilmore, commander of the newly-formed company troops. His men would lead the assault. Mike, Paddy and John would comprise the intelligence section and the communications would be handled by Lieutenant Marie Cameron, with the assistance Sgt Charlie Harper, ex SAS signals.

Patsy, the Geek (Lt Patsy Gorman computer expert) set up a

programme to cover the area and intercept all internet and satellite communications. The C 130 would be armed with cluster bombs and the full attack set up for ground support. Six helicopters would carry the ground attack teams who would be air-dropped on the encampment itself. Located as it was in a village, long vacated by its original inhabitants, the clutch of houses in the little valley had once been a pretty mountain retreat for the population of 400 souls. Sadly most had since perished in the struggles, to and fro, of the various private armies that had infested the land for the past 20 years.

Satellite pictures revealed the gun posts on the roads in and out of the village. Concrete roadblocks were sited to force a vehicle to zigzag before it could enter the main street. The church bell tower, without its bell, was now another machine gun nest, gaps in the stonework filled with sandbags to protect the gunners.

The village hall was the main canteen, the kitchen staffed by the kidnapped womenfolk from several of the isolated farmsteads, as well as survivors taken in raids throughout the area. The officers of the group occupied the houses on the main street, once the homes of the wealthy locals. The mayoral residence was, of course, the quarters of Vlad himself, kept tidy and clean by Marianne Vladek, daughter of his former regimental commander, who had been personally disposed of by Vlad. He enjoyed keeping the girl to warm his bed and to look after his house. He expected her to watch as he entertained other women, in the bed he forced her to share. The occasional revolt from the girl amused him, and gave excuse for the exercise of his ingenuity in devising punishments, normally resulting in eventual rape in a frenzy of sexual arousal, leaving his victim a sobbing, bloody mess, on the floor. She would be expected to be cleaned up, with the place restored to its normal state by the morning regardless of her condition the night before. Vlad was not the patient or forgiving kind, and she lived only to get her revenge for her dead family and herself.

The once, highly-disciplined force had lost the sharp edge of efficiency that had once made them a crack front line unit. The casual savagery of the guerrilla life had made their discipline lax.

The helicopters left on Saturday morning. Listed as mercy flights, they landed for last minute maintenance at an army base in northern Italy. The assault group paid for, and had complete anonymity and refuelling facilities, at the section of the base on the private side of the landing strip. The C 130 joined the group that evening, landing and taxiing over to the parked helicopters. With a start time of 5.00am, the men prepared and rechecked their equipment ready for the following day. The intelligence group gathered with Major Gilmore, Captains Pete Maddox and David Cameron, and the surprise addition of Captain George Washington Harris, whose arrival at Rosas had coincided with the departure of the assault group.

John rose and spoke to the assembled men.

"As you all know, this operation is just as illegal in the eyes of the world as are the activities of Vlad and his men. If we are caught, expect rough treatment from UN forces. They may agree with what we are going to do, but that won't stop them arresting us if they can. I do not want to get into a fire fight with a bunch of Swedish Blue berets. All clear?"

The men nodded and grunted their agreement.

"Good luck, everyone. We are not looking for prisoners, but look out for the hostages who may be employed by the bandits as servants, and may be used as a shield"

The engines of the C130 roared as the plane took off, the helicopters were already gone, en route to the target. The rendezvous was twenty miles west of the target.

The helicopters started the final run to the village, following the valleys with their ground-hugging radar. All were fitted with low-noise rotors which reduced the normal racket, but did not eliminate it entirely. The C130 climbed up to over 10,000 feet becoming just another passing local transport.

At the village the initial approach was made stealthily, until the last minute when the force lifted over the last ridge to descend on the packed houses. The men abseiled from the helicopters onto their pre-planned objectives, the helicopters promptly adopted a defensive mode, circling around the village outskirts.

Divided into their squads, the men scattered through the village. The sound of their suppressed guns made soft, popping noises in the still-dark morning. The group assigned to the Mayor's house kicked the door in and shot the two-man guard before they could respond. Upstairs, Vlad leapt out of bed and picked up his automatic from the bedside table. He wrenched open the door and called down to the guards. "What the devil is going on out there?"

Receiving no reply, he assumed the guards had gone outside to see what was happening. He started down the stairs only to encounter the butt of the smg carried by Captain Peter Maddox who was leading the unit. Vlad stumbled back into the bedroom. Marianne Vladek was waiting for him with the sword bayonet in her hand. It was used by Vlad on people when on a raid, and incidentally for killing regimental commanders. She made no move toward him, so he assumed that she had armed herself in self defence. He turned to face Peter who was coming through the door.

The pain in his back was incredible. He screamed as another slash with the bayonet crossed the first wound. He collapsed to the floor sobbing in agony and saw Marianne standing over him in her nightdress, the bayonet was held in her right hand. In her left was a hammer that he used to smash peoples fingers one by one, one of his more innocent pastimes. "Noooooo…!" he cried and tried to lift his arm to stop the descending blow. His arm would not move, but he felt the impact of the hammer between his legs, smashing his genitals. His scream could be heard throughout the village. The bayonet ended his agony as it chopped his head off sending it rolling across the floor. Peter and his men stood, stunned at the ferocity of Marianne's attack. Then recovering, Peter sent the men to search through the house. They discovered four girls cowering in the cellar, and fetched them up, doing their best to reassure them that they were not about to be assaulted or killed..

Peter grabbed Marianne's arm. "Get dressed and look after these girls," he ordered. "Sergeant, stay with the ladies and keep them safe until the helicopters come back."

The Sergeant nodded and turned to see Marianne strip off her nightdress and pull on underwear, sweater and cargo pants. She spoke sharply to the girls and ordered them to sit on the bed. Obediently they sat, staring at the head of their erstwhile captor, as it lay on the floor in front of them.

The rest of the squad, under Peter, went down to the street and joined the gun battle with the machine gun in the church tower. The skirmish ended abruptly with the tower collapsing from a direct hit from one of the missiles fired from a circling helicopter. The surprise had been complete. The bandits had been mainly half drunk and occupied with some newly-taken women captives.

The troopers seeing the men raping ten year old girls, and their mothers showed no mercy. The women, when given the chance, tore their attackers to pieces using knives, scissors, saucepans and their bare hands.

They marshalled the women in the street outside the Mayor's house. Of the group, three had died during the initial attack at the hands of the men raping them. The remainder, twenty in all, were loaded into trucks and, with a trooper escort of six, were taken out of the village to a safe area for the next phase of the rescue operation.

The troopers had six casualties, two serious. They were evacuated immediately by helicopter. The total number of bandits killed was 82. None of them survived.

Having removed the contents of the file cabinets and safe, the last of the troopers were picked up by the remaining helicopters. The silent, deserted village lay stinking of blood and cordite. The bodies of the dead bandits had been left where they lay, until with a roar of engines the C130 swept over the little valley and the village disappeared under a shower of cluster ordnance. When the dust and flames had gone all that was left of the village was a heap of rubble. The signpost with the name had been buried in the debris.

The final phase of the operation came with the arrival of the two helicopters sent to collect the women who had been taken to safety from the village. Four of the women decided to stay and seek their families elsewhere in the hills. The others, including Marianne, boarded the helicopters and travelled to Rosas. The events of the day were reported through the UN publicity machine. It was referred to as yet another atrocity, and attributed to quarrelling warlords, though the public were not informed of the sheer ferocity of the attack which had destroyed the entire village. Nor were the actual attackers ever identified. The TOT group were well satisfied with both the result and the misinformation, happy to have the incident thus swept under the covers.

The wounded men were treated in the base hospital in Rosas. The two seriously wounded were flown out to a US hospital in the Gulfstream.

The officers of the unit met with the board members to debrief and discuss future plans.

G. W Harris was impressed with the dedication shared by the entire group. There was no feeling of 'goody two shoes' about these hard bitten men: just a determination that they would only deploy in a just cause. They all seemed genuinely of the same opinion, and, when he thought about it, so was he. He grinned wryly, 'Who am I, Superman?'

He looked around the group. All were casually dressed and all could pass for the sort of young people to be seen on the beaches of the world. Men and women, all fit, most pretty good-looking he noticed.

He was not the only coloured person there. Three other men and at least two women were also present. He was surprised to see Marianne Vladek among them, dressed in casual clothes like the others and looking none the worse for her ordeal, apart from the dark rings round her eyes to show for the privations of the past few weeks. He had last seen her rounding up the women in the Serbian village and chasing them onto the trucks. She must have asked to join the group. He couldn't help noticing she was a fine looking woman and, despite her recent ordeal and the tired lines around her eyes, she stood out in that room to the tall, black man from Washington.

John Murray stood up and called the group to order.

"Thank you all for a tight operation. I will take this opportunity to introduce an American colleague, Captain George Washington Harris, who took part in the operation despite having only arrived on the base one hour before we left. Stand up, Captain, please!"

The big American stood and looked around the room. His eyes met Marianne's, and he felt a thrill as she held his gaze coolly, and looked away.

Down in the basement bar that evening, whilst he was enjoying a quiet drink with Pete Maddox, an old friend from their Special Forces days, someone tapped his shoulder. He noticed Pete's grin and turned to find Marianne beside him.

Chapter Fourteen

"How do I get a drink here?" she said. "I have no money!" She shrugged. G W Harris stood and with that old fashioned courtesy, often found in American officers, invited her to sit on his own stool. "What can I get you, Ma'am?" he drawled.

"Scotch on the rocks would be great," she said with a small smile and sat on the stool. Pete waved and disappeared, leaving his stool vacant. George sat in his place and raised his beer to the lady, "Your good health, Ma'am" They drank and then, breaking the rather awkward silence, George asked. "What are you doing here in the group?"

"I asked to become a member. Although I am not a Special Services soldier, I was a Lieutenant in our army. I served in the line as well as being an Intelligence Officer in my father, General Vladek's Brigade. After my experiences with Vlad, I don't really feel able to return to civilian life, at least not just yet. I have been accepted in principle, but haven't yet been found a place suited to my particular expertise."

"What might that be?" George waited with interest to see how Marianne answered.

"Intelligence." She looked him straight in the eye. "My job in the army was in Intelligence. I am particularly good at interpreting information." The words were spoken without boasting, just a statement of fact.

George was impressed. There was more to this woman than her appearance. She had a type of honesty in her look and speech that he understood and responded to.

It was at that point that he consciously decided that he wanted to know this woman better,

He met her look. "If there is anything I can do to arrange it, I think there is a place that might be of interest to you, in Dearborn. We have plenty of people who are expert with the local population. But so many immigrants are coming into our country, legally and otherwise, that we have a real problem dealing with them. The completely different mindset of these Europeans in an increasing criminal population is causing us problems that I think you could help us solve. What do you think?"

He did not take his eyes from hers throughout his speech. She ducked her head and sipped her Scotch.

"I think I would like that."

"Only if you're sure you are fully recovered from what must have been a terrible ordeal. It would be foolish to get involved too soon."

"I have been lucky," she murmured. "The Doctor tells me that I have not been diseased from my stay with that man. Even though he was a pig, and he died squealing like a pig, he was a clean pig." The words were said with such feeling George felt a shiver run down his spine. He reached out and took her hand. She let him hold it for a moment then she squeezed it briefly and released it.

John, Kelly, Gabrielle and Paddy were sitting over coffee in the deserted lounge, it was late and the others had all retired to their various rooms and apartments; friends, because they now had accepted, over the past months, that they with Mike, had formed a bond of friendship; an empathy that none mentioned but all accepted.

The companionable silence was broken by Paddy who said, "Do you notice how all the events we have been involved with, except Slovenia, have been across the line normally drawn between criminal activity and terrorism? Including the Slovenia episode, all our operations have been justified. What is worrying me is that all our actions are reactive. We don't know who we are fighting. The people we're dealing with, gun running, drug smuggling and flesh trading all are carried on under the same roof. It's almost as if someone was directing these activities, from some central Headquarters. Do you think perhaps we are tackling things from the wrong end? Maybe we should be looking for some central body or organisation, rather than tackling individual limbs as we always seem to be doing!"

The silence that followed Paddy's words was electric. Everyone started to speak at once. They all stopped, and then started again. John held up his hand and pointed at Kelly. "You first!"

Kelly sat for a moment collecting her thoughts. "I think we all accept that in USA there is the Syndicate: Mob, Mafia, call it what you will, that seems to have such an organisation. But here, in Europe? I hadn't noticed, but I think you may have a point." She paused thoughtfully. "It's an area we should look at. Don't you think?" The others sat looking at each other for a few moments, then one by one they nodded.

John said, "It's probably worth sifting through the papers recovered from our various raids to see if any common links show up. After all, the memo that started this whole business was to Mathieu from USA." With a scarcely concealed yawn he rose to his feet. "I suggest we wait until tomorrow to look into it!" Gabrielle and Kelly also got up and the party broke up.

Eventually, Paddy stopped tossing and turning in her bed and got up. The night was cool and she found running round the perimeter fence relaxing. The regular padding of her feet, in rhythm helped her put her thoughts in order, and as she ran, the suggestion she had made earlier, kept turning over in her mind. When she got back to the office building, instead of going into the apartment block, she turned into the offices, punched in the entry code and went straight to the secure cage where the documents had been stored.

On top were the papers taken from the Slovenian base. With the thought that she had to start somewhere, she picked up the pile of documents and went through to the offices and dumped them on the desk. Over the next two hours she sorted through them. Many were in Slovenian, some German some English. The Slovenian she put to one side, the others she put into two piles and, starting with those in German, began to read. By the time the office staff appeared, the pile of papers had been reduced to just a few put aside for re-evaluation.

One of the German documents and two of the English had specific references of interest. The German paper was a note from an arms broker in Munich, and referred to an earlier transaction between the broker, a transport company and a shipping company with a familiar name. Estes Romande et Cie.

The papers written in English had additional intriguing information. Not only was the Marseille shipping company used for a shipment of anonymous livestock but there was another address of a company in Bulgaria. This was apparently an agency for livestock and medical supplies, a strange combination, and with the associated connection to Estes Romande et Cie, certainly worth a second look.

The transport company in both cases was the same: Bannington Transport, a subsidiary of Bannington Transport (UK), itself a subsidiary of COMCO Inc. Chicago USA.

The other two papers in English referred to shipments of hardware and jewellery to and from the Slovenian base. There were references to a Singapore address and links to an Iranian Company, with branches in Pakistan and Riyadh, Saudi Arabia. It was difficult to imagine why a Slovenian war lord would be interested in the movement of turquoise jewellery from Iran to Saudi!

Paddy put the papers in a folder for Kelly's attention and went to bed. The most puzzling question was why Slovenia at all. She had only looked at the Slovenian papers to eliminate them, and possibly to pick up any items of information on lost people who had disappeared during the tragic events following the breakup of Yugoslavia.

When Kelly appeared in the office that morning she found Paddy's folder and notes for her attention. As a result she brought Patsy, the Geek, into her office and gave her the key to the secure cage.

"Get your team to work on all the papers captured so far, especially those from Mathieu's office in Paris. I want you to go through them for addresses, contact details and any other links you think may be of interest. What we are looking for is a possible relationship between all the people involved. In addition I want you to liaise with our American friends on any mutual contacts that turn up. I see no reason why your hacker friend should not do a trawl for interesting contacts, especially in the transport contact files. Move into a spare office here. Get the place security checked and protected. Keep the keys yourself, except of course a copy for me. Any questions? Or suggestions?"

"Yes. Who can know about this?"

"Board members only." Kelly's reply was emphatic and brooked no exceptions. "If anyone shows any interest, I want to know. If you feel you are under surveillance in any way or are concerned with security at all, tell me!"

Lieutenant Patsy Gorman drew herself up to attention and nodded "Yes, Ma'am. I understand!" She turned and left the office, with a briskness not often seen in the normally laid-back computer specialist.

When the others appeared Kelly advised them of Paddy's findings and of her action in seconding Patsy to the task of researching the mass of material held in the secure cage.

Deferring their retirement once more seemed to be the right thing to do. When Kelly suggested John handle the setting up of the UK Base for TOT, whilst Bill Hamilton would be the obvious choice for operating the company once a UK Base was established. Because of his past associations as a management consultant and his British business experience, it seemed the natural thing to send John to England to set things up. John was agreeable because there was the question of Gabrielle's book which still awaited a publisher, if one could be found.

So John and Gabrielle left for London, armed with a healthy bank account and an introduction to a publisher, well known to Kelly for some years.

Douglas Stewart had been in publishing all his life. Now in his fifties he was Managing Director of Cardwell Press, one of the more respected publishers in London. He was also a member of the board of three charities concerned with the care and protection of the homeless. A tall, slim, distinguished man with silver hair, neatly cut close to his head, he wore Saville Row suits as if he had invented them. As Gabrielle and John came in, he rose from the chair behind the big walnut desk to greet them

When they were seated, he suggested coffee, and after the initial comments regarding their journey and the weather, he addressed Gabrielle.

"I am happy to say your book has been well received by my colleagues, and we expect to come to terms with your agent as soon as you advise us of his name."

"I'm afraid I don't have an agent as yet. I was rather hoping that we could deal direct with your company."

"We would be very happy to deal direct. I confess that agents can be helpful but they can also be a complete pain in the neck! If we can agree terms we would be pleased to represent you."

"I am willing to put myself in your hands in this matter. You come highly recommended, and I know nothing about the publishing business."

"Very well," Stewart said slowly. "Leave it with me and I will have an agreement drawn up by our lawyers, for your signature within the next few days. Now, if you would like to join me for lunch, there is a rather nice restaurant not far from here."

Later, over lunch, John mentioned a matter Gabrielle and he had discussed on the plane.

"Donald, I understand you are involved with several charities. I wonder if we could interest you in a matter that has come up recently?" He went on to explain about the current international traffic in girls and boys from the East European countries. "With the break-up of the East-European Bloc more and more entrepreneurs had been exploiting the ignorance and poverty of these countries. By luring their victims with promises and bribes, and in some cases abducting them from orphanages and children's homes, they trap them into a life of prostitution in the west.

"We've become aware of a considerable number of rescued women and girls and boys now being cared for by a lady of our acquaintance, staying in a castle in northern Spain at present. They have funding and are currently getting the castle adapted for effective use for the training and rehabilitation of the women and boys. But they really need an effective framework within which they can operate.

"It's not a matter of money. It's professional knowhow to look after them and get them back to the real world with the aftercare. That's the problem. Can you help?"

Stewart looked concerned. He looked at the pair of them. "I am not going to ask how you happen to be involved with this group of recovered women. I do understand the problem and I am aware that the situation exists. Here there are many girls and boys in the same situation. If money is no problem then there is one possible answer. Set up a charity. Buy or lease premises and staff them with experienced nurses and teachers. Leave the matter with me. Give me a contact and I'll see what I can do!"

John gave him Jeanne's number, and the conversation stuck to everyday subjects from there onward.

Recruitment of staff for the UK operations had already begun. The security group was in process of selection, though there were still premises to be found.

Going through his contacts book John looked up an old friend, Wally Peterson. Not only an electronics and electrical expert, Wally was somebody who could make things happen. He kept a close eye on the property market for personal reasons, as he put it. His son who was also his partner in the business, reckoned it was because he didn't trust banks. Property was his way of securing a pension.

He had not changed a bit. John introduced Gabrielle to Wally, a dapper, small, wiry man with a wrinkled, weathered face and trim, short greying hair, who immediately smiled as he took her hand. He was dressed in a well-cut sports jacket of subdued pattern and his slacks were immaculately creased. Brogues, well polished, completed the ensemble and he spoke in a soft voice tinged with a touch of the East-End of London as he confirmed what they were looking for.

After thinking for a few minutes, Wally came up with two properties he thought might be of use.

"I presume the reason you are not trolling round the estate agents, is that you are not seeking publicity?"

"I don't see any reason to advertise my interest if I can avoid it. What have you got in mind?"

"There's a place in High Wycombe, a former furniture factory site with a selection of existing buildings and planning permission for development. Price about £1million, but with the way things are, probably negotiable. I looked at it myself, but it was a little rich for my blood. The other is in the City Riverside area near the old Tate and Lyle refinery in Silvertown. Handy, for both London City Airport, and the Channel Tunnel, if needed."

The site at High Wycombe was located at the edge of the industrial area. It was surrounded by a chain link fence, with a sagging gate currently secured with padlock and chain.

Inside, the area was divided into three major buildings with concrete hard-standing between them. There were loading docks at two of the buildings. The third building was composed of offices and storerooms.

Despite having been vacant for five years there were no leaks, except where windows had been broken. The power supply was standard, industrial, three phase for the operation of machinery, and according to the details supplied, both power and water were readily available at the turn of a switch.

Wally mentioned that the Wycombe Air Park, the former Booker RAF base at Lane End, was just three miles outside the town. The airfield had a 735 meter asphalt runway, in addition to two of grass, with hangars and facilities for light aircraft and helicopters. The town had rail links to London, and the M40 between London and Oxford was part of the local infrastructure. Wally reeled off these details to John and Gabrielle as they followed him around the site.

They had already visited the Silvertown premises, but by comparison, High Wycombe was an obvious choice. Privacy was important and not really possible in the City conditions. The buildings here would require conversion not replacement, and it was immediately available.

There was a rear entrance to the site, obviously seldom used as the track leading out to the A40 was partially overgrown. John looked at Gabrielle, she nodded. "Wally, can you undertake the alterations needed discreetly?"

Wally nodded. "My oldest lad, Martin, (he's my partner now), has his own building firm, and I can handle the electrics. I presume, when you say discreet, you will also require electronic security, which I will also be happy to supply. I've just come across some state-of-the-art Japanese gear you wouldn't believe...."

John stopped him with a raised hand. "I'll confirm tomorrow. See what you can do with the price,"

On the way back to their hotel in London, as Gabrielle drove down the M40 John spoke to Kelly on his mobile giving her a rundown on the property and promising to fax the details from the hotel.

In the lounge John and Gabrielle were enjoying tea when they were interrupted by the waiter who gave them a note. Gabrielle opened and read the note. She passed it to John. The note said that Mr Arthur Wilson would appreciate their company at an informal reception at the Savoy, that evening. John looked up. Across the room was a Ministry messenger, a familiar sight at any of the government offices scattered around the Westminster area. He wrote 'yes' on the back of the note and signed it. He gave the note to the waiter and watched him deliver it to the messenger.

"I think Kelly's replacement wants to talk to us," he said. "I wonder if Arthur is any relation of Charles Wilson, our acquaintance from Marseille."

The lounge of the Savoy was an extremely civilised place to meet. The waiters were efficient and quiet and the hum of conversation restrained among the assembled guests. The uniformed messenger was present at the door. He immediately recognised the couple and escorted them to a private lounge, occupied by about a dozen men and women.

As John and Gabrielle entered they were met by a dapper young man who introduced himself as the deputy Director's PA. They were provided with champagne and escorted to a small group of people, including to their surprise Julian Ross, MP, renowned for his rabble-rousing style of rhetoric.

Ross was a young man possibly twenty-five to twenty-eight years old. He stood about five foot seven, with lank, black hair drooping over his right eye. He had a habit of flicking it back as he talked. In the opinion of many of his colleagues he had an inflated idea of his own importance that was not justified by his intellect. His public speaking persona displayed a certain charisma, though most of his meetings finished up with a punch-up of some sort. He was regarded by John as rather dangerous because of his disregard for the outcome of some of the more inflammatory comments he regularly made. Also because of the blatant untruths that appeared to be part of his regular discourse to the public.

Others in the party were Arthur Wilson, whom they had now established to be the brother of the late Charles, and Saud Ali, the hawk-faced black sheep of an Omani family, suspected of links with Al Qaeda. Unproven, but believed to be, one of the sponsors of the camp recently raided by John and Gabrielle with the Israeli Commandos. He looked at Gabrielle and raised an eyebrow. She smiled back and turned to acknowledge the introductions to the group.

Julian Ross immediately moved to her side and tried to monopolise her attention. His rather loud, aggressive voice rose above the murmur of conversation all around. Saud Ali asked John what business he was in, and on being told that John was a management consultant, lost interest. Arthur Wilson turned and asked John whether he was in London for good, or perhaps just passing through. John was non-committal and said, "We do enjoy the Savoy, but we were rather surprised to receive your invitation to this soiree. Why did you ask us?"

"I was under the impression that as a former member of MI-6 you might be interested in a little contract work for the department." John looked around. Saud Ali appeared suddenly so interested in the material of the tablecloth on the serving table covered with snacks, that he was obviously waiting to hear John's answer.

"I might be! Perhaps we could discuss it elsewhere."

"Of course," Wilson said hastily with a wave of his hand. "Though we are all friends here." In the trade, the word friends is used normally to describe members of a trusted group.

"At my hotel perhaps," John suggested and handed over one of the cards obtained from the Intercontinental in Park Lane.

"Tomorrow morning suit you?" At Wilson's nod John turned and slipped his arm through Gabrielle's, and steered her away from Ross who was beginning to become petulant at her lack of reaction to his charms. As they moved away, Ross turned to speak to the others in the group with a comment that almost sounded like 'tease'.

"What an unpleasant little toad." Gabrielle pulled no punches. "I could almost feel him mentally stripping off my clothes as we stood."

"Darling, look around the room. Apart from yourself and the rather striking lady speaking with the PA, I think all the other women present are actually available, if you take my meaning!"

She shivered. "I hadn't noticed, but I think you're right. Let's get out of here, now."

John caught the eye of the PA and indicated the door. The PA came over and escorted them out of the room,

"By the way, who was that young lady you were talking with when I so rudely interrupted you?" The young man blushed, "Oh. She is Sheila Davenport the MOD liaison officer, here for discussions. She is just leaving." As he spoke the door behind them opened and the lady came through.

"Oh. Miss Davenport. May I introduce Mr and Mrs Murray? You may have noticed he was with the deputy Director."

"How do you do, Miss Davenport? If you are leaving do you mind if we walk out with you?" Nodding to the young man, John and Gabrielle swept Sheila Davenport through the lobby and out into the summer sunshine.

Gabrielle commented on the outfit the other was wearing and

asked if she could recommend a hairdresser. Before she knew it the lady had been invited, and had accepted, their invitation to dinner that evening at Inn on the Park.

David O'Neil

Chapter Fifteen

The pleasant dining room in the hotel overlooked Hyde Park beyond Park Lane.

Sheila Davenport and Gabrielle managed to capture just about every male eye, and many of the female eyes between them. The focus of this attention seemed quite unaware of the effect they were having; and once seated, they carried on the conversation, started when they had met in the foyer. John seated himself and looked on with amusement. Gabrielle suddenly realised and looked at John,

"What?" she said,

"I have become the object of the envy of every other man in the room," he grinned. The two women looked at each other and burst out laughing. The atmosphere at the table immediately relaxed and the conversation flowed back and forth between the three, as if they were old friends. John quickly discovered that there was no love lost between the MOD and M1-6, in the person of Arthur Wilson. It appears the odious Saud Ali had been trying to arrange for licences to export arms that he was not legally permitted to purchase. Apparently Arthur Wilson was trying to influence the MOD to permit the purchase and export of the weaponry, using security considerations as an excuse.

Sheila said, "I am aware, John, that you are a friend of Kelly Martin. She has dropped out of sight since she left M1-6, but I have been friends with her since we attended Roedean together. I also know that she was railroaded out of her job by Arthur Wilson. If by any chance you are able to contact her, please tell her that the Coven still exists and would fully support any action she would like taken here in London."

John raised his right eyebrow questioningly.

"We girls have an intelligence system here in London, especially throughout the Civil Service. Very little passes us by. The chauvinism we encounter at high level has caused us to band together, to ensure they don't always get away with it. At present we have enough on the M1-6 directorate to dump them big time, though I hasten to say the Director is not crooked, just easily led. All Kelly has to do is say the word, and the Coven will go into action."

John stored that piece of information away for future reference, the beginning of an idea already beginning to take shape. Speaking to Wally the following day, John confirmed their interest in the High Wycombe site. He arranged for Wally to do the purchase as agent on behalf of Trans Ocean Trading and promised to be in touch about the modifications.

The deal was done at £780,000, and the deeds were signed within a week.

One of the benefits of having friends like Wally was trust, often lacking between owner and contractor. In this case there was no holding back. John and Wally knew each other well enough to believe what each had to say. Because of their dealings in the past, Wally realised the sort of security required in the world John lived in.

The planners in Rosas, having been provided with the site plans, geological survey, and soil samples would set out their requirements, with outline drawings of what was required. The rest would be up to Wally. He would produce detailed blueprints of the site layout, complete with the complex of underground accommodation. After visits by TOT experts and with the plans approved, Wally's son, Martin, would undertake the construction under the watchful eyes of his father.

The meeting between John and Arthur Wilson at the Inn on the Park, was not a success. The sort of vague fishing expedition undertaken by the deputy Director to sound out John's attitude to what could only be described as gun running, was not to John's taste and why Wilson had even suggested it, angered him. The appearance of Said Ali towards the end of their meeting was the last straw, causing John to request they leave the suite rather precipitously. He afterwards said to Gabrielle that he felt they had come on a fishing expedition rather than with a serious proposition and, had they not gone of their own accord, he would have thrown them out, physically, by himself.

Gabrielle did suggest that he had probably made an enemy for life, a very dangerous enemy. John just shrugged. "I have friends that thrive on enemies like that."

They returned to Rosas and reported the successful outcome of their visit and also their feelings regarding Wilson and the unpleasant Julian Ross. The base was a hive of activity and the expansion of the organisation was continuing rapidly. They needed another visit to London to follow up the work started on the base. And for Gabrielle, her book contract would be ready.

Kelly required a personal message to be delivered to her friend, Sheila Davenport, whilst Gabrielle intended to take Jeanne to meet Douglas Stewart about the plans for the new Charity. For John, a visit to Wally was imperative, with the added need to oversee the entry of the new UK Head of Station.

But it was three months before they had time to return to London. The High Wycombe project was up and running. The Trans Ocean division had already moved into their premises under the eagle eye of Bill Hamilton, whose contacts in the shipping world were already producing results. The works in the Secure Inc. building were progressing well.

When they had checked in to their hotel, John spoke to Wally Peterson about the High Wycombe Security premises, he was informed that the work was being performed as specified. The covert project was incomplete, but progressing well. The premises had been kept apart from the overt TOT premises, despite being within the site.

Secure Inc was trading from temporary premises as an across-the-board Security company, whose first customer was TOT, so the cover for the covert Security Section was in place.

Gabrielle had accompanied Jeanne to meet Douglas Stewart who had arranged for her contract to be signed. After signing she left the pair to get acquainted and discuss the practicalities of the new charity. She went to meet Sheila Davenport with messages from Kelly, and incidentally arranged to get together with her for a shopping expedition on the basis of the friendship established when they last met.

At High Wycombe, by using the private rear entrance and exit from the site, the desired separation between the overt and covert sections had been achieved.

At Wycombe Air Park the construction of a hangar had been commenced. In the interim, hangar space had been rented for the accommodation of the Cessna Caravan and the Bell 407 helicopter, assigned to the base initially.

The actual 'Secure Inc' premises awaited the arrival of the local Commander who had been interviewed by Alan Gilmore and on whose recommendation he had been originally been selected.

Colonel 'Mad Mike' Madden had been Commander of Airborne forces in Basra. He had made himself unpopular by speaking out against the entrenched notions of the British Government on the subject of the occupation of Iraq. Although not required to, he had resigned in disgust, quietly and without fuss. Alan Gilmore had dragged him out of his self-imposed retirement and, following a quiet discussion on the purpose and aims of the Secure Inc, Mad Mike had joined the club.

His arrival was anticipated next day. Although he had his own place in the country, quarters had been prepared for him at the depot. John had arranged his visit to the site to coincide with the Colonel's takeover. Secure Inc (UK), as the UK section was named, had been provided with a skeleton staff already in situ, including the Colonel's former batman, who had gladly come out of his early retirement to resume looking after his former C.O, who was divorced. The other staff already billeted in the premises, included admin and maintenance who were working to prepare for the reception of the influx of troopers and others who would complete the complement of the British base.

Back at their hotel suite, with Gabrielle's book due to be released at the beginning of the month, Douglas Stewart was well pleased. He was already talking about a follow up. Now her contract had been signed, the arrangements had already been made for a book-signing at Waterstone's.

Douglas Stewart had registered an application for a new Trust called 'Homelass', to accommodate and rehabilitate women and young men recovered from the vast network of vice operations throughout Europe.

Jeanne Ascher and Douglas, after their meeting, had nominated the Spanish castle already in use as their first Haven under the supervision of Jeanne Ascher who had largely funded the project anyway. The building had been restored using voluntary help from both the Troopers of the Rosas command and in many cases, the inmates themselves.

The hotel suite was quiet after the busy day, but there was no time for an early night. Room Service provided a buffet, and the senior staff of the Trans Ocean Trading's operation came and were introduced by Bill Hamilton, the new Managing Director of the UK division. The company had been in business now for two weeks in the UK and the signs were good. Hamilton's contacts within British business were paying off. The covert operation was just opening its doors. It was presented as a Security division, utilising the extra building on the High Wycombe premises. This added authenticity to the use of the extensive uniformed security operated from the site, and provided a cover for the other operatives based in the building.

Following the reception, the suite was visited by Michael Brooks, who had been inspecting the proposed premises of the charity 'Homelass' in London. He had been asked to assist in the expansion of the charity into the United States, where the exploitation of the wetback population, had created a similar need. At the same time he had been in touch with some former colleagues who were unhappy with the way things were going on the political front. There were influences around in Government circles, that suggested payoffs and favours were being traded for protection of assets that would normally be vulnerable to prosecution. The American agents had been hearing that the home administration was being penetrated by similar subtle methods, and organised crime was benefitting accordingly.

The young Member of Parliament, Julian Ross, was making a name for himself by calling for reforms of the police and the duties of the armed forces. Despite being a member of the Liberal/Democratic Party, his detractors placed him somewhere left of Mao Tse Tung. There was no doubting his popular appeal and this popularity was giving authority to many of the ineffectual policies being undertaken by the police, in direct opposition to many of the tried methods being discarded with almost indecent haste in the name of modern politics.

Wherever he appeared to speak, a large following always gathered, and trouble had broken out on several occasions. Michael was of the opinion that the two factors were linked. John respected Michael's opinion and told him of his own meeting with Ross and his personal opinion of the man. The more they talked about it the more they tended to agree. At John's suggestion Michael would produce an intelligence brief for the USA while John would create one in the UK.

The following day at High Wycombe he welcomed Colonel 'Mad Mike' Madden DSO, to his new position.

The premises were impressive. After the tour, at a meeting of the senior staff, John raised the question of the first task to be undertaken. The intelligence section of the UK unit consisted of two officers. One, a former Special Branch Detective Inspector, Bob Pullman, the other a petite, little woman named Gaynor Jones, a feisty, 30 year old Londoner of Jamaican parents; who had, against all odds, risen to the rank of Sergeant in the Intelligence Corps. In the end the odds won and she left in disgust. She was recruited whilst working for a detective agency in the East End of London.

She hadn't decided whether she liked Bob Pullman or not. Bob was 40 and a divorcee. His career had been distinguished by a series of brilliant investigative coups that had not endeared him to his superiors, or his juniors for that matter. In the end he found working in the current environment called for him to question the principles of the people he worked for. The result was he took early retirement. He had recruited Gaynor himself. The intelligence community was a close knit one and her reputation preceded her.

They listened to the briefing by John and while Gaynor took notes. Bill just listened. He had the sort of mind that forgot nothing he heard.

John's review of the information given him by Michael Brooks, struck a familiar chord with both the operatives. The general unease of the situation was obvious to most sensible people. They undertook the brief with an enthusiasm that was reflected throughout the new organisation. When John left the Security section he was pleased with the way things were progressing, and happy with the choice of Mad Mike as boss.

The meeting was discreet and the people attending made every effort to ensure that there would be no record of what transpired. Of course several records were kept. Briefcases with conveniently installed recorders, and the usual array of recording pens, watches, and other paraphernalia that can record, allegedly without detection, were all used. All were useless, since the room had been especially set up for complete electronic suppression. No recorders or other electronics would produce intelligible sounds after being operated in the room.

It was perhaps as well since the assembly comprised a mix of politicians, senior business men, major criminals, and several members of the most wanted terrorist organisations in the world. No question of patriotism was allowed to interfere with the single purpose of the group. Money and power transcended all.

The subject of the meeting was control of the economic and political resources of the World. There was no Fu Manchu figure looming in the background. In this meeting what you see is what you get. This was a group of pragmatic, ruthless, business men for whom there was only one goal:- Gain, in its many shapes and forms.

At this meeting the subject of the replacement of the President of the United States was top of the agenda. The board member of COMCO detailed the arrangements made to replace him with the Vice President who was much more persuadable. The meeting gave its approval.

The subject of France was raised to a murmur of argument over what had gone wrong with the local arrangements in the Paris branch. How it was possible for the agent there, Mathieu, to be compromised and killed, with enormous loss of product and capital. The suggestion was, based on the reports of the assaults on the Paris warehouse divisions, that it could have been undercover operations of the French Special Forces. This idea was immediately dismissed by one of the French members present who stated categorically that he would have been informed had this been the case. Even if he had been bypassed, by now he would know if any such operation had been carried out. Whilst the Paris organisation was once more in control under the leadership of Jean Barat, there was much to be done before the full recovery of the European Division would be complete.

The conclusion of the meeting was that it seemed some other organisation was interfering, with the intention of taking over. Instructions were issued for counter intelligence to be initiated to find out who they were, and how they could be eliminated forthwith.

There were politicians from many of the major countries in the world, each determined to take control of their own government and, if possible, as many other governments as they could manage. It was no surprise that the British MP, Julian Ross, was present, though it would have surprised the Director of MI-6 to see his deputy, Arthur Wilson, there. Henry Smith was also present with another senior member of the secret community, the current Deputy Director of the CIA. Several Congress men and women had taken their seats beside Europeans of different nationalities and Arab and far eastern nationals of various shades and sex.

The last speaker was a respected member of one of the largest criminal families in the western world.

His comments were terse and to the point. "My people are looking for this outfit, whoever they are. Your own governments and organisations must do their part. It is possible as we ourselves have proved, to run a big operation without the public catching on. These guys must be doing the same. They must be stopped or we will all go down."

Back in Rosas the enquiries into the world-wide crime and terrorism organisation were indicating the probability of it being well-established. Evidence of links between widely diverse groups had been confirmed. Based originally on the documents found in the early raids in Europe, the collection of addresses and links had been followed up, since John and Gabrielle left for England. It was now highly probable that there was an international accord working between widely varied organisations, which had no apparent common links.

Patsy faced the assembled company, armed with her laptop and a projection screen on which was displayed a map of the world. Peter Davis sat toying with the mouse to his desk top computer. The swiftly changing stream of information would have been confusing to an onlooker unaware of the object of his search, but whatever was happening, Peter seemed quite pleased with the results.

Patsy spoke. The assembly listened with serious attention as she laid out the parameters of her research, and the results achieved. The locations were all highlighted on the world map. The countries involved were all subjects included in the dossier created from the documents recovered so far. The indications were that the extent of the criminal infiltration was even greater than originally thought.

Peter printed off the results of his current research and handed it to Patsy. Her face paled.

"Aral Adamski, President of the Ukraine has just been assassinated and Georgi Zukhov has declared a State of Emergency." The news was bad. The dead President had been a target for the hard liners of the Russian Federation for the last few years. Ever since he had swept to power with popular support from the anti-communist majority in the Ukraine, his rise had been bitterly opposed by the minority population of Russians living in the territory. Russia herself had used this population as an excuse to interfere in the internal affairs of the Ukraine wherever they could. The separation of Ukraine from its former links to Russia had been greeted as a triumph by the Ukraine people and the Western world. The current attempts of the Russian Government to re-establish its dominance over its former territories had led to condemnation all over the world. The battered visage of the assassinated President was attributed to an earlier attempt to remove him from the political scene, by his enemies from the extreme left, led by Georgi Zukhov, who was in process of carrying out a coup. With the country in the distressed state of disarray, the chances were good that he would succeed.

The group received the news with dismay. Adamski had been a light in the darkness of the former Soviet Union. He was regarded as a voice against the descent into criminality, which had so swiftly overtaken the other countries of the former Communist bloc. The financial effect of the Russian disintegration was being felt throughout the world, intruding into all aspects of everyday life, from sport to utilities, manufacturing to drugs, and money laundering to prostitution. Murder to settle disputes had become commonplace.

Patsy rapped the table and drew attention back to her presentation.

"The conclusion reached by us is that the criminal organisations have banded together to suborn Governments, elect their own candidates and otherwise gain control of the very forces created to eliminate them. Recommended action is to continue to destroy the criminal's ability to create wealth, by eliminating the financial basis of the political nominees. The public would have the chance to regain control of their Governments, and return to a state where law and order prevailed once more. Of supreme importance is the maintenance of the Secure. Inc, armed units, at an increased manning level, plus the absolute stress on the secrecy of our organisation identity."

She stopped and sat down. Her audience applauded her effort, and surged to their feet to question Patsy and Peter on details of the presentation. At the later board meeting plans were discussed to enlarge the Troop force and spread the net of agents wider, to gather the information necessary to hit hard and fast at the nexus of the problem.

In the USA Mark Foster had been immersed in the investigation of the interface of crime and politics. With the return of Captain Harris, he acquired assistance in the form of Marianne Vladek, who had been provided with a Green Card through the good offices of Michael Brooks, who still had plenty of friends in the US administration. Her usefulness became immediately apparent when reading the brief. Though she knew no one involved, her uncluttered viewpoint was a godsend. The politics of her own country, as seen through her father's eyes as well as her own, were no different to those of every other country in the world. The main object was, as much power as possible whilst parting with as little as possible.

Having been given a list of criminal names and political movers and shakers, she sat down almost immediately at her computer and went to work. As Mark Foster told Kelly when he made his regular contact. "Marianne is a natural for this sort of work. Her instincts lead her to connections others just don't see."

Marianne set up home in the secure section apartments to start with. It was convenient for work and it had a complete military set up including a pistol and a rifle firing range. She used both regularly, attaining marksman qualifications in both disciplines. The Master Sgt in charge of the unit rated her 'best pistol shot' at all aspects of the course.

Her friendship with George Washington Harris progressed. Taking things unhurriedly and recognising that there was plenty of time for them. Both thought they already knew where their relationship would end. Both were willing to wait for Marianne to recover from the trauma in Slovenia, and for George finally to accept that he had met the woman with whom he would be sharing the rest of his life.

Chapter Sixteen

The research had thrown up several instances where Government agencies had been using private contractors for work formerly done exclusively by secure agency staff. Whilst it was not critical in many cases, in some it entailed access to information way beyond the contractor's level. There was evidence that, with so much work being factored in this way, many of the contractors were being regarded in the same light as Government agents. The consequential dispersal of information was disastrous.. Though no one was willing to admit it, information was being used to bypass security barriers and defeat anti-crime operations.

One company stood out as a major contractor for the CIA and, occasionally, for the Drug Enforcement Administration (DEA). Over years they had earned millions in fees for a series of jobs apparently completed for CIA targets. Called Reagents Inc., this was an allusion to the fact that many of their employees like those of Retreads Inc were ex-government agents. Unlike Retreads however, a remarkable number of the Reagents employees had left their government employment hurriedly, or had actually been dismissed for misconduct.

Marianne's research was aimed at the origins and background of Reagents Inc. She was interested in COMCO, who is the main investor, and listed as a founding shareholder. A major player in many and diverse companies, some involved in risk specialities, armoured trucks, agency work, and private security. Others ranged from one of the biggest transport companies in the world, to security, investments, insurance and banking. Marianne's concern was the origin of the finance used to back this conglomerate. She concentrated on the origins of the people behind the company, and behind Reagents. There she hit a wall. It was beyond her computer expertise to penetrate further into the background of the financial providers of COMCO. Luckily she knew someone who could help.

The call to Rosas came at midday. Patsy, the Geek, was just considering the prospect of lunch. Marianne sounded tired. "Patsy," she said crisply, "a company called COMCO worries me. They seem to be involved in all sorts of business and I need to find out more about them. Can you or Peter help?"

"Leave it with me, Marianne. I'll get Peter on to it as soon as I can. I'll get back to you when I've got something for you."

Intrigued Patsy swung into action. She put Peter on to COMCO and he started the initial search. She herself recalled the information about COMCO that came in at the time of the creation of Trans-Ocean. The founding of the business had been obtained at the expense of the COMCO organisation.

Between Patsy and Peter they spent four hours finding out just what sort of security surrounded COMCO. Peter had several suggestions for Marianne to search in associated sites. He included a backdoor into CIA, giving specific instructions for penetrating their records. Now both of the experts set to and invaded cyberspace in search of COMCO.

Peter's hacking expertise came to the fore, though it took time, since they needed to infiltrate without being discovered. By five o'clock they had broken through. COMCO appeared to be funded by the crime syndicates, and was the main channel for laundered money.

The discovery of these facts was by illegal means. The information could be funnelled to the US Treasury, but it would have to be very carefully presented. Currently it was not a viable option. There were too many other projects on the table.

Marianne passed the news on to Mark Foster at 9 am the following day. He sat back in his chair and began to rethink the whole project. Knowing that organised crime was involved in the work of the CIA, something that had been often suggested but never proved, was a whole new ball game.

"I suggest that we work on the US end of the problem. Would it be possible for Rosas to strip COMCO of their assets at their end?"

At this suggestion, Peter Davis, a broad grin on his face, said, "Leave it with me!" He was in his element and immediately started to construct a programme to allow secret access to the COMCO bank accounts.

A major effect of the burgeoning influence of control exerted over the public by Governments was the arrogance of authority. This in turn created an answering contempt, reflected in the criminal fraternity, who found it increasingly easy to bypass legal barriers and influence both law officers and the public. The law officers had themselves become cynical following the lead of their superiors. Now more gullible and controllable than ever, the public were kept ignorant, as their freedoms became increasingly restricted by stealthy legislation.

Jokes about 1984 were longer funny!

The job Peter undertook was simplified because his victims had become so accustomed to getting their own way. It had never been considered that anyone would risk the wrath of the crime lords by actually stealing from them!

Over the next few days, Peter worked almost non-stop on the project. Every time he thought he was breaking through, another wall would intrude. Finally he broke through a wall to discover no more walls, He was free to surf the company records and accounts at will.

He called Patsy with the news and for advice. She gathered up Kelly, John, and Michael who was visiting Rosas as a board member of TOT. They joined Peter in the computer room.

"How do we stand at the moment?" she asked.

"I've installed a backdoor and come out," Peter replied. "I didn't want to fumble around like an amateur. I'm not accustomed to robbing banks, on or off a computer!"

Michael suggested that an appropriate deduction would be a donation to the TOT war chest. At the same time it might be an idea to benefit the Homelass charity, and perhaps a selection of other charities deserving donations, particularly those who help the victims of crime.

Peter mentioned the size of the funds lying in the COMCO accounts.

There was a stunned silence as the enormous scale of the undertaking dawned on them. The account was divided into two separate sections: one, obviously used for current money movements, had a balance of $32,395,780, the other, apparently a deposit account, contained a balance of $7 billion. The market value of COMCO currently stood at a respectable $12 billion.

Kelly spoke. "I'm going to get Mark Foster in on this." She picked up her mobile and called Paddy O'Hara. "Paddy, call Mark Foster. Tell him to drag his sorry ass over here. He can hire a Lear jet if necessary, but, whatever else, tell him I want him here yesterday. We need to deal with the mess he has dumped on us." To the others she said, "Sleep on this. We'll sort it out when Mark arrives, in the morning!"

Paddy and Mark walked into the boardroom together, the others had gathered when the Lear arrived. All sat around the table. Patsy and Peter sat beside the laptop that was hooked up to the internet.

Kelly turned to Mark and said, "Sorry to call you here at such short notice...."

He held his hand up, stopping her in mid stride. "Drag your sorry ass over here! What's that all about?"

The entire group rocked with laughter. Kelly looked at Paddy sitting happily next to Mark. "I thought it important for you to be here to take part in this discussion. Since the lady to your left was looking more and more depressed, and this meeting was urgent, I thought I would get you in a hurry and incidentally lift the world from her shoulders!"

Mark looked around at Paddy.

Paddy blushed!

The group discussed the movement of the funds; first the method, then the amounts and finally the beneficiaries. Michael's suggestion of funding the TOT Security division was accepted unanimously, also the enhancement the Homelass funds, to build shelters in more countries for the increasing number of girls and boys in need of help. The disposition of the remaining monies could be deferred to another time. The immediate requirement was to clear the account of all funds to some safe haven. It was decided to lodge the funds in a Cayman Island Bank. What was proposed was: shifting the money from the present bank to Switzerland via electronic transfer and from there to an assortment of companies that would survive for one day only. Then to other bank accounts,..... At this point the group gave up, establishing only that the funds would be secure, and available when needed. Reagents Inc would not cease operating, as some of the associated companies within the group owned by COMCO were only there to launder funds. Consequently they were not designed to trade at a genuine profit. They would suffer, even possibly have to close down.

The electronic transfers were carried out then and there. With the push of a button $7 billion fled across the Atlantic, to disappear into the financial wilderness. $20,000,000 from the current account followed the route but finished up in the TOT account. The remaining $12,000,000 went into the accounts of the TOT organisation, and the Homelass charity fund. Their final act was to close both sections of the account, requesting that all trace of the accounts be removed from the bank's records.

"And that will give them a serious headache!" Peter Davis remarked.

The headquarters of one of the world's largest shipping and trading companies occupied the top twenty floors of the sixty story skyscraper, standing in its own grounds on the east side of Chicago, overlooking Lake Michigan.

The upper floors were all carpeted in fine loom and the furniture was modern but comfortable. Wherever possible the individual offices were placed in the outer walls to take advantage of the natural light, and senior executives were placed where the view across the Lake and the City was regarded as superior.

The penthouse suite was occupied by the Chairman's office, and the boardroom. There was an outside patio, reception area, and a swimming pool with changing rooms at the far end of the roof.

The Chief Executive Officer and his operations staff worked ten floors below on the 50th floor. The headquarters of the subsidiary companies were located on the lower floors of the building, and no particular connection was advertised linking these operations as part of the actual conglomerate, to which they all belonged.

The main function of the company seemed to be the transport sector. Bannington International was the prime operator in this business occupying two completed floors, dedicated to the collection and distribution of goods worldwide, through local subsidiary companies.

The security company, Reagents Inc., was on the ground floor and its uniformed division was responsible for the building security, and consultancy and detective work, including anti-espionage and the provision of mercenary forces the world over.

It was the mercenaries who were particularly in demand by the CIA, for operations in South America and Africa. They were used in cases where the official forces would be an embarrassment, because of the many restrictions on their activities.

The international nature of the organisation and the specific facilities entailed in the goods traffic worldwide allowed the company to move cargo of questionable nature on their own transport, more simply than if employing others.

It was this facility, and the worldwide links enjoyed by the company, that attracted the attention of the crime syndicates.

Taking advantage of a recession in the transport industry at a time where major expansion was needed, the money men moved in, buying up shares and injecting capital for rebuilding and expanding facilities. The head office building was just such an investment, and the construction of the building had included several modifications which the building inspectors would not have passed.

The sub-basement was not there, according to the plans. Being at least one of the illegal additions made to the original building. The complete extra floor, inserted by saving six inches from the ceiling heights of the floors from 20 through 50, allowed the installation of the sub-rosa section of COMCO premises, without the apparent knowledge of the overt business surrounding it.

The impact of the raid on the finances of the company was felt initially on 24A, the floor that didn't exist. Here the money laundry service was operated by the syndicate's staff. Money from a whole range of criminal activities was gathered and fed into the system through dummy companies, adding to the legitimate income of the companies that could support and cover the extra funds.

The loss of virtually the entire current capital of the group was shocking and nearly disastrous. Only swift action using incoming cash flow made it possible to keep the legitimate businesses afloat.

The enquiry was run parallel to the reorganisation of the entire computer programme, involving a new system of firewalls and anti-spy software to protect the assets.

It was a tribute to the skills of Peter Davis and Patsy, the Geek, that the trapdoor they inserted was not discovered.

The main result was that the commercial directorate of the

main board of COMCO at last became aware of the nature of the sub-rosa business, up to now only suspected of being conducted under their noses.

Whilst it did not sit well with the Chairman and commercial directors there was little they could do about it. The rewards for their silence and cooperation were so huge, they found it convenient to turn a blind eye to the whole matter. As far as the company was concerned, the result of the disclosure was the discovery that many of their business experts operated at a much more efficient level, unfettered by regard for ethics, or interference from law officers.

All this widened the scope of activity for the group. The use of political means to gain commercial ends had long been a tool of the trade in the world. COMCO had taken the system further. By owning the political scene, they could initiate and protect business that in other circumstances would be illegal. This also simplified the movement of arms in the weapons trade and people in the vice industry. Transferring people across borders with government help was simple, and the risk of unannounced raids was eliminated.

The interference in the previously unknown operation in France and the elimination of the French agent, Mathieu, had been a severe blow, as the French operation had been pivotal in the European distribution and collection system.

The journey back to Dearborn was interesting thought Mark. He looked across the cabin at Paddy who was dozing in one of the facing seats. Both were conscious of the electricity that existed between them, though neither had openly acknowledged it. Looking at her now he could not believe how lucky he had been, meeting Paddy as he had. She was quite beautiful in that dazzling dark-haired, blue-eyed Irish way. Mark's experience of relationships had been limited by his career path, which had taken him all over the world. Women had been a passing phase in his life. He had never been in one place long enough to build a lasting relationship. Paddy had been posted to Dearborn to help in the setting up the team for the collection and collation of intelligence, so things could well get interesting.

When they landed at Detroit Airport it was early afternoon, and the party went straight to the TOT site. This gave Mark the opportunity to pick up the threads of what had been going on while he had been away. For Paddy it was a chance to settle in to her quarters in the accommodation block.

Mark had only been back at his desk thirty minutes when he looked up to see Paddy as she checked in to start work. She was showered, changed and ready for work, so he stopped what he was doing and took her on a tour of the site, introducing her to the team leaders. She knew George Washington Harris of course, and had heard of, though not met, Captain Clark Kent, Ex-Delta Force, codename Superman. He was 5ft 9ins of medium build, though very fit and toned. Tangled blond hair gave him the look of a Californian beach bum. Only when you looked at his eyes, grey-blue like arctic ice, did the steel show through the casual exterior.

Marianne greeted her with a hug and a kiss on both cheeks, and then got back to work on her computer. "How is the Reagent job going?" Mark thought for a moment, then replied. "Thus far there are no signs of the financial losses that CONCO have suffered. It seems that, while the final transfers were taking place, an extra $5 million was deposited just before the account was closed. It was picked up with the rest and transferred to the security account. They decided to add it to the funds allocated for communications between our branches, and buy another C130 and another Gulfstream. Both aircraft are available for immediate delivery, so the plane that brought us over is now stationed here. The crew will stay here until we have hired local replacements. They will then fly the new aircraft back to Spain."

At a briefing session with the Secure Inc personnel in Dearborn, Paddy was able to establish that several of the former agents had knowledge of members of the Reagent team. She instructed them to give as much background information as possible to Marianne, to help compile as complete a dossier as possible.

Her main theme however was to accentuate the intelligence aspect of their work, a change from the past. They were now working with an enforcement section, not expected to act on their own. She took the opportunity to stress that the Secure Inc group was in being to fill in the cracks missed by the Government agencies. What they were not formed to do was to act for any selfish or commercial motive. The team assembled for the briefing consisted of a mix of men and women aged between 30-50 years. Up to now they had been split into working units based on pairs.

Three teams of two were controlled by a senior agent, who was paired with his or her own partner, who in turn had their own three teams of two. As of now, effectively, Paddy was the agent in charge.

Following the briefing, she set up in her own office and from there, arranged to interview each team individually.

Chapter Seventeen

John and Gabrielle were seriously contemplating a relaxed honeymoon after their efforts of the last few weeks. There was little to keep them back. With the expanded staff of the company all involved in the various aspects of the current investigations, they were left with little to do except stand by and watch the specialists work.

Kelly was now involved in segregating the overt and covert sections of the company. Bill Hamilton was in line to take over the Trans Ocean directorship as International controller. The immediate success of the London division was a tribute to his expertise and enterprise.

Whilst he was aware of the existence of the security section, he was only informed of its purpose as a traditional security company, operated on a strictly, separate basis by Kelly Martin. She, however, retained an overall interest as President of the Trans Ocean Associates, the holding company for both organisations.

Having discussed the matter with Kelly, John and Gabrielle took leave of absence for an extended period of up to a year. In Kelly's opinion, by that time the company should have made a significant impact on the international crime and political scene.

Two days later the pair lay on loungers by the pool at the villa they had rented in Harris in the Hebrides. Outside the double-glazed windows the sun shone in a clear blue sky. The controlled temperature within the conservatory was a pleasant 72 degrees Fahrenheit, though outside it was just over 60 with a gusty breeze lifting small white caps from the blue waters of the Atlantic. It hadn't been a difficult decision for either of them. Both had had enough of the high temperatures of the Mediterranean area, for a while at least. John had longed for the chance to walk the hills of Scotland and Gabrielle was quite willing to visit the land of her forebears. The rather gothic house they had found on the west coast of Harris had all they could wish for. The enclosed pool, overlooking the sea where they currently lay, was long enough at 40 feet to allow for proper swimming. The ground floor of the house had a large lounge and dining room, both overlooking the ocean, a gun room and kitchen and utility room. Upstairs there was a billiard room with full-sized table as well as four bedrooms, two of which were en-suite, the other two sharing a bathroom between them. The annex behind the house contained the quarters for the staff who came with the house: a cook/housekeeper, housemaid and butler, and a stable lad who looked after the horses housed in the stables behind the annex.

With the house came the freedom of the estate lands, over 1000 acres of hill and glen along the shores of the Atlantic. Taran House had been built by a Yorkshire mill owner, whose early life and struggles in the Bradford area had, in later life, encouraged him to get away when he could and walk the high hills of the fells in Cumbria and hills in Scotland. The location of Taran House, in the shadow of Taran Mor was the result of his love of the hills and a late acquired love of sailing. The mooring and landing stage on the shore of Loch Crabhadall at the foot of the hill below the house were still available, though the helicopter pad on the foreshore received more regular use nowadays.

Both of John's daughters had been to stay with them. Thankfully they had both taken to Gabrielle immediately. The two weeks of their stay had been a success, especially for granddaughter, Gracie, who had entranced John and Gabrielle, as she had already captivated her aunt. Surrounded by adoring adults she had the best time of all.

John raised himself from the lounger and stood for a few moments by the pool edge. In the eyes of Gabrielle he looked pretty good, he was tanned and smooth muscled, tapering from broad shoulders to a slim waist. The action of the past few weeks had trimmed off any excess fat, leaving a fitter, healthier version of the man she had fallen in love with. Still quite acceptable, she thought. He dived into the water and swam lazily up and down the pool a few times before hauling himself out of the water. He picked up the towel from his seat and started drying himself off.

"Come on, lazybones. Drag yourself off that chair and get dressed. It's time to take a ride along the shore."

Willie, the stable lad, had the two horses saddled and ready to go by the time they got down to the courtyard. They mounted and set out at a walk along the shoreline, dipping in and out of the water. John encouraged the horse into a canter and Gabrielle followed, both laughing as the spray spattered them.

The man on the hill watched through powerful field glasses tracking the two riders along the water's edge. He picked up the satellite phone beside him and punched in a number. The voice that answered asked a question. The watcher grunted in reply. The voice reacted angrily. The watcher said. "You want it. Do it yourself." And he switched the phone off. Wrapping the aerial up he replaced the phone and dish in their sockets within the case and closed it. He then put the glasses in their leather case and, carrying the two cases, descended through the heather to the track at the foot of the hill. The Range Rover was parked facing down the track towards the paved road to Tarbert. He climbed in and drove off at a sedate speed looking forward to the comfort of a hot bath and a dram before dinner. He was furious with his employer. Having been asked to find and report the whereabouts of the two people at Taran House, he was not going to be pushed into an action that would make him a murderer, as well as probably also making him a target, because of what he knew. A chill ran down his spine, as it occurred to him, that, after the phone call he had made, he was already a target. He knew too much. He calmed down, it would be necessary to disappear fast, but not before he had a word with the people at the house. At the Tarbert Hotel he rang the number of Taran House. The butler informed him that the gentleman was dressing and unable to take the call. The watcher said very slowly and clearly, not at all impressed by the butler's supercilious manner. "Get your boss to the phone. Now!"

Abashed, the butler said, "Hold on, please," and went to get John.

"What's up?" John asked, wondering what it was that couldn't wait. A cultured voice at the other end of the phone spoke. "There is a foreigner, sounded French, wants you and your pretty lady dead, today."

"Who are you?" John said. "What do you know about this?"

"I was watching you from the hillside as you rode along the shore. When I reported to my employer he told me to shoot you both and he would see me looked after. I'm not a fool. I'm out of here and, if you have any sense so will you be." The phone went down with a click as the caller rang off.

John turned to the butler. "Do you know where the call came from?"

"I think it was from one of the hotels in Tarbert. We always have a sort of hum on the line from there."

"Do you think you could find out for me? It's quite important."

"Very good, sir. Will you be dining tonight?"

"I'm afraid not. In fact we have to leave early. Could you get the car brought round?"

John ran up stairs and called Gabrielle to pack, He explained about the call as he threw things into his suitcase. By the time they had finished, the butler had the name of the caller and his room number at the Tarbert Hotel. He thrust the piece of paper into John's hand as he opened the car door for them. John thrust a bundle of notes into his hand. "Thanks for everything!" He said. And they left.

The Tarbert Hotel was lively when John and Gabrielle went in. He enquired at the reception desk for Mr Jones in room 14, only to be told that Mr Jones had checked out, half an hour ago.

As they drove onto the ferry to Skye, John rang Mad Mike at High Wycombe and told him what had happened. "By the time you get to Skye, I'll have the Cessna at Skye airport waiting for you. You can't miss the airport it's off the road to Kyleakin and it is signposted. Don't stop for anything until you get there. From Uig its no more than three quarters of an hour by road.

The Cessna sat on the single runway of Skye airport, its engines still running as the Range Rover drew up alongside the open passenger door. The man waiting by the door came over, opened the car door and spoke to John. "I must run the tracer over the car and your luggage before you board the plane." John nodded and stood while the tracer was passed over his body. Gabrielle went through the same process and then handed over her handbag for similar treatment,

They found the bug under the rear bumper of the Rover. John and Gabrielle boarded the plane leaving the other man with the car. There was going to be an interesting chase for the trackers before they finally caught up with the Rover.

The Cessna flew to Cork where, after a second scan of their bags and bodies, they drove off in a hire car into the wilds of Ireland to continue their holiday.

The Rover drove onto the mainland via the bridge and headed north towards Achnasheen. It was met at Strathcarron at the top end of the Loch, by the Secure group who had maintained contact throughout the drive. The ambush was carefully set up at the hotel which was closed. The Rover was parked out of immediate sight.

The group was equipped with an interesting assembly of electronic gear which included a tracer that locked onto the signal produced by the bug on the Rover and so were able to monitor the progress of the tracking party right up to the hotel door.

The Ford Galaxy people-carrier disgorged six men all in ski masks and armed with Uzi smg's. They assembled in a group beside the vehicle. The sound of the ambush party cocking their H&K smg's drew the instant attention of the newcomers.

"Place your weapons on the ground one at a time, here under the light." As the voice spoke, a blinding floodlight illuminated the area. Obediently, the six men laid their guns in a row on the ground. They were then lined up and searched, producing a further haul of weaponry. Within the empty hotel building, masks removed, the men were individually interrogated.

Gaynor Jones spoke to the leader of the trackers, her voice calm, her tone measured and reasonable. "I'll ask you again. Who sent you?"

The man sneered. "And I'll tell you again. Fuck off, bitch!" Gaynor looked at him calmly.

"Is that your last word?" The man spat on the floor.

"Take him out and shoot him." Gaynor's voice was calm. "Take his flak jacket off first. It could be useful."

Two troopers grabbed the man under the arms and lifted him out of the chair and stripped off the slim flak jacket.

"Make sure the others see him shot. It will probably encourage them to talk."

The man struggled and said, "Come off it. You can't shoot me."

"Sorry. I thought you intended shooting me and my men. Why can't I shoot you? You haven't given me any reason not to: no information, nothing!"

The man's shoulders slumped. As the two troopers turned him

towards the door he called.

"All right, I'll talk. What you want to know?"

Gaynor signed to the men to put the man back in the chair..

"Who are you, and where are you from?"

The questions were answered promptly He was Robin Court from Wandsworth, London, and then it all came out. Employed by Reagents (UK) Ltd, he was called to back up an operation set up by the French branch. The team were all members of the firm. Every man was an ex-agent or soldier, from the ranks of the many mercenary groups disbanded in recent years.

The UK branch of Reagents was headed by an American, Charles Scott, who operated out of a disused warehouse in Whitechapel. Their main function was as heavy mob, on contract to the London mobsters.

"What was your task today?" Gaynor was particularly interested in the answer.

The man looked about furtively and almost in a whisper said, "Take the man and woman and deliver them to an address in Shettleston in Glasgow. We were then to wait, in case there were any disposals to be arranged."

"Disposals?"

"You know what I mean, the concrete shrouds, the cement swim fins. I don't have to explain it to you!"

"I see," Gaynor looked at the pad in front of her. She carefully inserted a full stop after a sentence. "Take him back to the others and bring in the party leader."

"I've told you. I'm the leader of this mob. The rest of them couldn't lead a dog for a walk, let alone command an exercise like this!"

"Take him out." She said "I'm not interested in the kind of bullshit he's been feeding me. Shoot him first, then shoot the others one by one, until we find the boss."

"I told you. I am the boss. That bunch of tossers does as they're told."

Gaynor looked at him.

"Alright. I've done my best. I was told to kill them both. Make it look like a suicide pact, but just make sure they are dead. The order came from France, a bloke called Jean Barat, some wheel in the French Mafia. We've had men watching London Airport for weeks waiting for the target to appear. The instructions were to make sure the girl died first, in front of the bloke. When they arrived at the Airport, my man stuck the bug under the bumper of the Rover. We had a spotter out on Harris within hours of them arriving. We were just waiting for the right moment, when the spotter let us down and tipped off the target."

"Take him to the others." The anger was just discernable in Gaynor's voice. "Send Jock in."

Jock was a former SAS Sergeant, originally a member of the HLI.

"Jock, where is the most remote place in Scotland?"

"I would think that one of the uninhabited Islands off the west coast would qualify!"

"Could this lot survive there?"

"Maybe!"

"Naked?"

"I could."

"Strip them and dump them!"

"Yes, Ma'am." Jock left with a grin on his face.

Gaynor picked up the phone.

The deaths of John and Gabrielle Murray were reported in the Daily Telegraph and the Scottish Daily Mail. The story of the tragic, double suicide appeared and the story was picked up by 'Paris Soire', since it involved a former resident of France.

Jean Barat was reading the account with satisfaction as he travelled in his car from Paris to the chateau of his deceased boss, Mathieu. He was well pleased with life. The chateau had come complete with Mathieu's girlfriend, a cause of considerable envy in the past. Barat had returned to Paris just before the death of the Boss. Despite the wound incurred at the Marseille warehouse raid, he had been in time to seize control over the heads of several other claimants. He was a feared member of the organisation and had little difficulty in taking up the reins of leadership in the Paris area.

Whilst curious about the lack of information from the London contractors, he intended checking with them when he returned to the office the following day. He would not permit work to intrude with his home life unless it was vital.

The car swept into the drive through the ornate gates of the chateau.

Just around the bend of the drive a garbage truck stood, engine running, blocking the drive completely. The chauffeur beeped the horn impatiently. The garbage truck started to reverse, The horn beeped without effect, so the car was put into reverse as the swearing chauffeur tried to get out of the way of the truck. Behind the car another garbage truck appeared, reversing towards them. Trapped between the trucks, the car began to crumple in response to the pressure from both ends. Barat tried to open the door but, already distorted, the door was jammed in the frame. The windows cracked and shattered, but the apertures were already closing up too small for the man to get through.

The pressure eased as the vehicle behind the car drove out of the drive, leaving the helpless car and contents being pushed backwards through the gates once more. Outside a breakdown vehicle was attached to the battered car and it was hoisted to the platform of the truck. Ignoring the cries of the trapped men, the driver secured the vehicle in place, climbed into the cab and drove off.

At the scrap yard, Jean Barat was able to follow the progress of his execution in minute detail. The crane that lifted the car from the breakdown truck, lowering it into the gaping maw of the crusher, and the glimpse of the smug look on the face of his carefully selected second-in-command, were the last things Jean Barat saw. The jaws of the crusher clamped down on the crumpled car, reducing it and its human contents to a metre square block of scrap metal.

Chapter Eighteen

The newspaper that Jean Barat had been reading formed part of the block of scrap. Etienne Farmer, the new Boss of the Paris region would not have been interested anyway. He had never heard of John and Gabrielle Murray.

A report on Scottish news mentioned the discovery of the bodies of six men washed up on the shore near Ballantrae in the south of Scotland's west coast. They were believed to be those of crew members of a Belarus fishing boat lost at sea several weeks before. The condition of the bodies was such that, without DNA comparison, proper identification could not be confirmed. Unfortunately, the authorities in Belarus were not in a position to provide the information. The inquest returned a verdict of accidental death of unknown seamen.

To John and Gabrielle, the chance to start a new life was almost irresistible. They hated parting with the *Altair*. The boat had been part of their lives together for several months and of John's life for several years. Unfortunately, as Gaynor pointed out, it was also known to be theirs and was therefore a security risk they could not afford. Changing their name was more emotive and they compromised by only changing their surname.

John and Gabrielle Graham landed in Boston with brand new passports, suitably aged of course. The nationality was still British, though the US residence formalities were all complied with, to go with their US address in San Francisco.

They had through tickets via Detroit, but were breaking their journey in Boston to 'chill out' as Gabrielle put it, and gather a few history points in the cradle of modern America. For five days the couple relaxed and toured the area, playing the traditional tourists. The USS Constitution, afloat in the harbour was of particular interest to them both. The Holiday Inn, at Salem surpassed all expectation. Sadly, to no avail. By the fourth day neither could face the thought of another happy excursion. They boarded their flight to

Detroit with a mutual sigh of relief.

Marianne met them at the airport, and drove them smoothly and swiftly to Dearborn in her Saab saloon, chatting all the way about the progress they were making in the US branch of Trans Ocean Trading.

The premises off Michigan Avenue were impressive. The main buildings, once part of a major, car manufacturing plant, had been discretely modified for the use as part of the TOT Distribution and Shipping network. The whole site was ringed by a high security fence, standard for these types of premises, not only in the US but becoming necessary now on a worldwide basis. The armed and uniformed First Safety security at the gates and patrolling the fences were also now a normal sight and provided the perfect cover for the covert security unit quartered within the area.

After a brief check of ID at the gates, Marianne drove the Saab round to the entrance of the security building which operated in the US as First Safety. The big FS logo on a blue shield was emblazoned on the glass doors. The reception desk in the hallway had security screens with microphone and speaker systems installed. A security guard in uniform took their bags and led the way through a double door behind the desk.

The doors closed with a sigh and the carpeted corridor with offices leading off on both sides gave the impression of an exclusive hotel. At the bank of elevators at the intersection with another similar corridor, their uniformed escort put down their bags, saluted and returned to the entrance hall.

The elevator door opened, and a man stepped out to retrieve their cases and ushered them into the quietly humming interior of the elevator. The smooth surge of power swiftly took them to the top floor of the building. John noticed the button used by the attendant was marked Presidential Suite. Marianne led them into the suite located on the roof of the building.

The morning sun lit the room through the big patio windows. The view extended across the river to Windsor, on the Canadian side. Lake St Clair, to the East glinted like a sheet of silver and there was a slight haze already forming over the city of Detroit. The breakfast tray was placed on the patio table by the maid. John could see the steam rising from the coffee pot and he called Gabrielle to hurry while it was still hot. The voice from the shower told him to go ahead. She would be with him in one minute flat.

There were few things in life that could equal the pleasure of a leisurely breakfast facing a beautiful woman. John's mood was relaxed as he enjoyed the moment.

"I feel better now," he commented.

"I always knew that you would be happy as long as someone fed you regularly!" Gabrielle smiled as she teased him about his enjoyment of food.

"What are we doing today? Do you know?"

"I suppose we will be expected to visit the troops downstairs. I notice there is a briefing folder on the table in the lounge. Perhaps if we read it we might find a few hints inside!" John's dry remarks on the silent service within the Presidential Suite, which they had learned they were occupying, reflected his mild discomfort at what he considered to be typical American overkill in the hospitality department.

Gabrielle laughed delightedly at his comment.

"When will you learn 'different strokes for different folks'? The American way is not the British way. We are two people divided by our common language. Make no mistake. So just sit back and enjoy it!"

Mark Foster greeted them like old friends, complementing Gabrielle on her hairstyle and dress, as he seated them both in his comfortable office one floor below their suite.

The briefing notes had been a general background of the current US scene, detailing the spread of the agency's influence throughout the country. It also listed the contracts currently being serviced by the uniformed division, and the general work undertaken by the Retreads in covert activities.

John was disconcerted to notice that, on the rather bare walls of the office, was a framed picture of Gabrielle himself and Michael Ascher, taken at Rosas, on their first visit to the site. The picture was titled typically, 'Our Founders'. The other picture, hanging next to theirs, was of Kelly, entitled 'Our International President.'

Returning his attention to Mark's remarks, John was pleased to hear that the COMCO operation had taken the huge loss of funds badly. Several of their financial staff had been removed, some terminally, as he euphemistically put it. The accounts had been completely reorganized using state of the art programming. Peter Davis had already begun inserting his own little spy into the works, to allow the regular monitoring of all COMCO money transactions for the foreseeable future. He had recommended that they defer any further transfers until there is more money in the till. In addition he wanted them to become complacent about their security once more.

The results of the transfers of money from COMCO had funded the purchase of aircraft and other tactical equipment, together with the provision of accommodation for the security companies designated as 'First Safety Inc', that constituted the backbone of the anti-crime division of TOT.

Mark continued with his update of the company progress. TOT itself had benefited from the acquisition of top transport and shipping staff. In the UK Bill Hamilton had recruited a first class team whose qualifications had drawn in business from many of the companies that would normally have been their main competition. They had also acquired, by merger, two of their rivals whose backing had transpired to be from doubtful sources. The loss of the operating capital in both cases had resulted in their inability to service contracts. Only the timely intervention of TOT had saved them from the hands of the receiver. The rest followed on naturally. TOT was now the third largest shipping company in Britain.

Mark was interrupted by Marianne, who knocked and came in with two envelopes. "I thought I should bring these in. They have just arrived from Rosas." She passed the envelopes to John and Gabrielle.

"Excuse us, please," John said, as they opened the envelopes. As he scanned his letter John gasped. He dropped it on the desk and turned to Gabrielle, who looked equally shocked.

"What's up?" Mark asked. John waved to him to read the letter. It was from Kelly

Dear John,

We have just issued our first year results for the TOT and ancillary companies, created by Michael Ascher, yourself and Gabrielle.

As the major shareholder, your proportion of the first half year dividend is based on your 40% shareholding, the others on their equal 30% share.

The actual dividend declared for this period has been better than anticipated. I am pleased to report that the combined effect of trading and acquisitions has resulted in major profit taking, and consequently healthy dividends.

The current value of the shares, initially quoted at $1.00 on Nasdeq, is $240.00 per share, your shareholding, of 40.000 shares, is currently valued at $9,600,000. Your dividend for the half year stands at $22.00 per share, a total of $880,000, which sum has been credited to your account at Barclays Bank International in the Cayman Islands.

Hope I am the bearer of good news. Speak to me when you get the chance,

Regards

Kelly

Mrs K. Martin

President Trans Ocean Trading Inc.

The silence was broken by Gabrielle, "I didn't know there was that much money in shares."

John had recovered by then and reread the letter. He whistled. "Someone said 'crime doesn't pay'. I don't know who it was, but whoever said it wasn't sitting where I'm sitting at the moment."

Mark spoke quietly. "John, Gabrielle, whatever you may feel about it you must look around us here in this building. All this came about through you and your determination not to be pushed around by a bunch of crooks.

"You both stuck your necks on the line and invited them to chop them off. Neither of you gave up nor did you baulk at taking risks that the average person would happily have refused to take. For Pete's sake. Remember that the Israeli Commando forces have appointed you honorary members of their elite forces. I know of no other civilian or foreigner to be accorded that honour.

"Please. Everyone in the company is aware of the contribution made by you two. You are an inspiration to us all.

John found the comments extremely embarrassing. Mark's comment overstated the part he had played in the establishment of the company. But he recalled Gabrielle's remark that very morning, and decided he would just have to live with it.

Mark had gone onto another subject, while John had been lost in thought,

"I was about to pass on a message from Head Office about your boat the *Altair*. She has been stripped and refitted and is currently being used by the sail training association of Great Britain.

The replacement *Orion* is fitted out and awaiting your collection at the Benicia Marina in Richmond, San Francisco. I believe your house is in that area, so it should be convenient for you to pick it up, or keep it there if you want to!"

John and Gabrielle were taken aback, it had not occurred to them to think of what they would do with the *Altair*, though they had realised and agreed they could not keep her. Everything seemed to be happening around them, pieces slotting into place without any effort on their part.

John thanked Mark for his consideration on their behalf and admitted that they had not even thought about disposing of the *Altair*. Mark pointed out that, since they were officially dead, someone had to deal with things. Kelly had passed the job over to Bill Hamilton who had arranged everything with the help of Douglas Stewart.

Chapter Nineteen

The house found for them was in a new development in Jetty Drive, overlooking San Francisco Bay, just a few minutes' walk from the marina where their new boat awaited them. Living in the United States had taken some getting used to, both John and Gabrielle were taking things slowly.

The boat provided to replace the beloved *Altair* was a sixty-three foot Dutch, steel-built ketch. It lay alongside the outer pontoon of the Marina, white hull protected from the abrasive effects of the timber dock by clean, white fenders. The raised, central deckhouse, containing the controls and the navigation equipment, stood out above the sweet sweep of the main deck. Over the past few days they had provisioned the boat for an extended cruise. The charts were updated and a complete set for the west coast of the United States stowed in the chart locker. Gas and fuel were all topped up ready and their crew was standing-by with his kitbag.

The lean, young Chinese/American was waiting for permission to come aboard. Having been given the nod, he threw his kitbag onto the deck and loosed the fore mooring. Gabrielle slipped the aft rope and coiled the rope down on the aft deck. John eased the throttle forward and the boat moved smoothly away from the pontoon. As the others lifted the fenders and stowed them, he steered the big ketch through the harbour entrance into San Francisco Bay, pointing down past Angel Island towards Alcatraz.

Peter Chang, student at UCLA, currently on a gap year from his Philosophy studies, lifted the fore hatch and dropped his kitbag onto the bunk below. Then he moved to the mainmast and commenced hauling the mainsail up to the masthead. Gabrielle released the sheets for the roller-reefed foresail and then hoisted the mizzen sail, hauling it snug as John cut off the Perkins diesel engine. He allowed the head to fall off until the setting of the fore jib and the mainsail had been accomplished. Then he brought the boat up into the wind, adjusted the course to clear Alcatraz, and pointed towards the Golden Gate and the magnificent bridge spanning the strait.

The boat had a positive feel and answered quickly, requiring little effort to maintain the course. The GPS, projected on the LED display, showed the coastlines and the track of the *Orion* as she made her way through the narrows to the Pacific Ocean.

A large motor yacht, radiating pop music, passed them as they started to make the turn southwards for her first port of call over 300 miles south at Catalina Island. The yacht, John noted was named *Boomerang*. It had been widely publicised when it had been chartered by one of the current favourites of the Pop industry, one Jared Baer, almost as well known for his carousing as his music. His preference for young girls had on occasion led to brushes with the law from which he had only managed to escape by the hasty provision of money to the offended parties. John had little doubt the occupants of the *Boomerang* were the usual collection of hangers-on and groupies that habitually gathered round pop figures. He handed the wheel over to Peter and joined Gabrielle in the lounge below for lunch. Gabrielle took a plate of sandwiches up to Peter with a mug of coffee and left the young man to enjoy the thrill of controlling the elegant ketch through the blue Pacific waves.

They spotted the *Boomerang* again anchored in the Santa Cruz Channel, between the islands of Santa Rosa and Santa Cruz, midday on the third day of their cruise. Judging from the noise, the operators of the yacht had no respect for the hearing of their passengers. As they sailed past the channel John saw three people on the deck of the yacht, two men chasing a woman, their calls and shouts rising above the heavy pound of rock music shattering the peace of the otherwise quiet area.

The *Boomerang* appeared once more whilst they were anchored at Two Harbours, Santa Catalina. John and Gabrielle were ashore picking up fresh provisions for the onward journey. Peter was checking the engine oil levels and making sure the wind generator and self-steering were useable. Although Peter was a philosophy student his father ran an electrical/electronics business in Los Angeles and Peter's pre-college years had been spent servicing everything from echo sounders to TVs, wiring premises and repairing radios. He had been hired because of his cheerful personality and sailing experience. His background was a bonus.

Gabrielle pointed out the 'Gin Palace' as she had dubbed it, as they went into the Harbour Restaurant for lunch. John looked at the vessel moored offshore noting the tender racing towards the jetty.

"Let's have lunch and get out of here. I've suddenly lost interest in this place."

Like most of the waterfront eating places, the seafood was great and John's mood was mellowed somewhat by the time they left the restaurant. There was no sign of the shore party from the 'Gin Palace' as they returned to the quay, and collected the tender to go back to their boat.

On board Peter had not only serviced the mechanical gear, but he had also tidied the main cabin, pumped the bilges, replaced a broken bulb in the starboard navigation light, and retuned the radar which had been ghosting at the 15 mile range. As they boarded he had hot coffee waiting, and was on hand to haul in the provisions as John passed them up into the boat.

While John attached the sling shackles for the davit, Gabrielle put the provisions away. Between them, Peter and John handled the davit manually, swinging the tender onto its chocks on the aft cabin roof.

They ate on board that night. The setting was fabulous, worthy of inclusion in a Hollywood epic. They watched the sunset over the Pacific while the water moved, just a gentle lift of the almost flat-calm sea. The faint touch of breeze was just enough to keep the residue of the daytime's heat to a bearable level. They sat quietly until the night fell cloaking the scene. Peter left them to go and take practice star sights with the sextant. John and Gabrielle sat holding hands under the canopy of stars.

The following day they motored over to the harbour quay and touched shore to lodge their course plans with the Coastguard. Then swinging away from the quay, John and Peter set the sails whilst Gabrielle steered the boat under power out of Two Harbours and set sail along the coast of Baja California bound for Mazatalan.

With the prospect of a lengthy voyage ahead they arranged a loose rota to keep watch. Had it been a deep water trip, they could have set the self-steering and depended on the radar warning, but running down the Baja California coast was such a busy route, that it would have been foolish to depend on electronics in the circumstances.

Gabrielle came out of the cabin with a steaming cup of coffee in her hand. "I've come to keep you company," she said, nestling down in the circle of John's arm. She passed the coffee over to him after taking a sip herself, snuggled down beside him and almost immediately fell asleep. John took a sip of the coffee, grinned ruefully at his 'company' and returned to his regular survey of the ocean ahead of the *Orion*.

When Peter came up to relieve him, he shook Gabrielle awake and chased her down to the cabin. Then he handed over to Peter, reminding him of the course, to keep a good lookout, and to call if anything worried him. Finally he went below, leaving Peter with the boat and the night.

The current flows southwards along the shores of Baja California and Mexico. The *Orion* was making good time under sail, making good an average of 9-10 sea miles each hour. They had passed the lights of San Diego in the evening and the town of Ensenada in the early morning. John had estimated a voyage of perhaps ten days, and, provided they did not get bad weather, they had a good chance of achieving it.

It was during the fourth night after leaving Santa Catalina that they became aware of the *Boomerang* once more. Having eaten, they were all relaxing in the deck saloon, with a glass of wine. The roar of powerful engines gradually drew closer from astern, then the doppler effect made it obvious that they had been overtaken and the power boat had passed. It was just possible to catch a glimpse of the name on her stern as the big ketch reared and tossed in the wash created by the passing boat.

"Bugger!" John's comment was the result of his spilling wine as he coped with the gyrations of the sudden disturbance in the waters. The lights of the speeding cruiser were still visible when they heard the shots, several, probably fired from an automatic, then two more. But this time the deeper boom of the gunfire made it likely that a shotgun had joined the party.

The boat ahead had stopped and it lay rocking on the Pacific swell. A second boat seemed to be in the water, and this boat, driven by what sounded like a powerful outboard, roared away from the, now drifting, motor yacht in the direction of the coast of Mexico.

As the *Orion* approached it was possible to make out figures sprawled on the sundeck. John went below to the lounge of the ketch and retrieved two of the Glock automatics stored in the arms locker behind the settee. Gabrielle called up the *Boomerang* on the VHF radio without result.

John said, "I'll go and have a look. See what's going on!"

"Be careful, John." She was busy checking the Glock John had passed over to her. Her skill with the weapon caused Peter's eyes to blink.

"Shall I call the Coastguard?" he asked. John gave it some thought, then shook his head.

"I would rather not, until we know what has happened. Gabrielle, watch out for the return of the outboard. It may have gone for help, but I doubt it."

Chapter Twenty

The ketch closed the gap between the vessels. As she came alongside John jumped over to the other boat and the ketch drew clear.

On the yacht John checked the bodies sprawled on deck, only to find that they were all dead. Judging by their dress they were all crew members. Cautiously he entered the deck saloon, gun ready. The sheer luxury of the fittings was impressive The girl lying on the settee in her bikini spoilt the effect. Her blood had splattered the white upholstery and her posture made her look like a discarded rag doll. She was dead. John explored further through the door into the central dining saloon. Here two more bodies lay, a girl and a man, John became aware of a tapping sound that seemed to be coming from the bridge deck, up the stairway at the far end of the dining saloon. He climbed the steps with care to make no sound.

As his eyes cleared the deck level he almost toppled back into the saloon. A pair of unseeing blue eyes looked directly at him from the body lying on the deck behind the steering wheel, from the four stripes on the man's epaulettes, John judged he had been the Captain of the *Boomerang*.

The tapping seemed to come from the deck locker on the starboard side of the wheelhouse. John approached it with care. He lifted the hasp and flung the lid of the locker back. The figure inside moaned and tried to stand up. The shotgun clattered to the deck beside the locker. John kicked it away. The girl in the locker tried to stand once more. This time she managed to get out of the locker and lean against the chart table, using it for support.

"I heard the engine of the outboard and guessed they had gone. But the locker lid had dropped on my head and knocked me dizzy. When I tried to get out, the lid wouldn't move. It must have locked itself. I was trapped in there." The voice was low and melodic. She was dressed in jeans and a sweater. On her feet were deck shoes and, though she was a shapely good-looking woman, John could not see her as one of the guests on this yacht.

"Who are you?" He asked. What are you doing on this yacht?"

She looked at him with disturbingly steady, blue eyes. "I am the first mate of this craft. The skipper is my husband….." Her voice trailed off as she noticed the dead man by the steering wheel,

"Oh no…!" The distress in her voice was real, John decided. He reached out in time to catch her as she stumbled towards the corpse of her husband.

John called the *Orion* on the VHF and asked them to come alongside. He dropped the fenders over the side, took the rope from Gabrielle and secured it to a forward cleat. Peter jumped across at the stern and tied up there. Turning to come forward he nearly stumbled over one of the dead crew members. He looked, promptly turned and was sick over the side. After a few moments he gingerly stepped past the dead man and came forward to the deck saloon, trying to avoid looking at the other bodies on the way. The girl's body in the saloon nearly caused another bout of sickness. But he managed to hold back and made it to the wheelhouse. The body of the skipper still lay on the floor of the wheelhouse, but mercifully covered now with a sheet.

The first mate turned out to be Moira Sherman, now widow, of Los Angeles, qualified offshore skipper for sport and private craft up 120ft length. She and her husband made a comfortable living from the charter of their 98ft Dutch-built, steel motor yacht. The crew were extra staff hired for this cruise by the charterer, Jared Baer, the stalwart of the music industry. The cruise was laid on to entertain a record producer and three women, probably hookers, at least one of whom lay dead in the saloon.

"What caused the shooting?" Gabrielle asked.

"I'm not sure. One minute we were running smoothly south. The next minute the throttles were wide open and there was a row going on in the saloon. I came up on deck. I had been supervising food for supper. I caught a glimpse of your boat as we passed. By the time I made it to the bridge the shouting had stopped. The boat had stopped as Bill, my husband shut the throttles. It was then that I heard the outboard motor of the rib that had come alongside.

"I think some men had boarded us. There was some shooting, so I ran to the locker to get the shotgun we keep handy. I turned back having checked it was loaded. A man came up the bridge stair shooting. I shot him. Since I was not braced properly I stumbled and fell into the open locker. I started to get up. Another man appeared with a machine pistol so I shot him, and fell back in the locker again. I banged my head this time and the lid came down and locked. You know the rest."

"Where has the pop star gone?"

"I caught a glimpse of Jared Baer and Marco Palermo getting onto the Rib during the confusion."

John decided to get the bodies moved onto the aft deck of the yacht to make it easier to move about. Gabrielle called the Coastguard on the emergency channel and let them know what had happened. Since they were currently on the high seas, and both boats were American registered, they sent the nearest cutter to their location. They told them not to move the bodies until the cutter arrived.

The four of them crossed over to the *Orion* and waited for the cutter to arrive.

The figure of Lt. Commander Robert Burke, fully erect, reached the height of John's ear. In sharply-pressed khaki's and white topped cap, he was the model of a Coastguard officer. He stood feet apart at ease, rocking back and forth heel to toe, as he listened to the story of events detailed by John.

He interrupted him abruptly. "What part did you play in this business?"

"We came to the aid of the *Boomerang* when we saw her drifting. We had heard shots, and we heard the sound of the outboard that left the scene as we were approaching. I then released Mrs Sherman from the bridge locker, and secured the boat to ours."

"Very good, Mr/ Graham," Burke was brusque almost to the point of rudeness. "I'll take it from here!"

He turned to Moira and commenced to question her about the activity on the boat prior to the shooting. His manner to Moira was just as abrupt as it had been to John. It was not long before Moira was beginning to look upset. John looked at Gabrielle and raised his eyebrow. She nodded.

John walked over to Moira, took her arm and passed her over to Gabrielle.

Burke exploded. "What do you think you're doing? " He blared, grabbing John's arm.

John plucked the Coastguard officer's hand from his arm and spoke quietly to him.

"Touch me again and I will flatten you." The Petty Officer standing by the cabin door tried to hide a smile. "Furthermore!" continued John. "I would remind you that the woman you are addressing has just had her husband shot to death almost in front of her. Speak to her like that again and I will throw you off this boat. You are here at my invitation, on my deck. If I have to put up with you posturing and playing detective any more, I might just send you back to your ship under escort!"

At this the P.O. had to turn away to hide his grin at his officer's discomfort. The crew of the cutter would love the story about Lt Commander Burke's put down. Since he had assumed command two weeks ago, the little man had not endeared himself to his crew. The man concerned was almost purple in the face, at being told off like a naughty boy.

"How dare you," he got out, before finding himself lifted up and carried to the rail where he was deposited on the thwart of the motor boat alongside the *Orion*. He teetered for a moment getting his balance and then stepped down into the boat.

"You haven't heard the end of this," he shouted, beside himself with rage.

"You were warned!" John said. Then, ignoring him, he went below and sent a fax of his statement and that of Moira, Gabrielle and Peter, to Coastguard H.Q. in San Diego. He also sent a copy to Dearborn, just in case.

To his surprise the Dearborn fax brought an almost immediate reply from Marianne. The short message was simple. 'Rough Records' is a subsidiary of Archer Communications, a major player in COMCO set up. 'Sat/comm.' follows.

The Coastguard H.Q. at San Diego came back by radio to John on *Orion*, thanking him for his action and requesting his co-operation in clearing up the scene of the crime. The Captain in command of the San Diego base spoke directly to John with respect.

"Sir, I understand you are an experienced former police officer with the authority to act on behalf of the United States Government, issued by the State Department. I have instructed Lt. Commander Burke to place himself under your orders in all matters relating to this investigation. If you have no objection, he will report to you for orders!"

John imagined the reactions of Lt. Commander Burke who

would, no doubt have a fit and protest his orders. John shrugged and accepted his suggestion to take over, with the thought, *'Shit happens'.*

The bodies were removed to the cutter and several of the crew helped clean up the mess on *Boomerang*. Enquiries into the present whereabouts of Jared Baer and Mario Palermo had established that they had been put ashore by the rib on the Baja Californian coast. Neither had been injured, apart from a few cuts and bruises. No explanations were given and neither man was prepared to comment at present.

John read the report with disbelief. The fax from the Coast-guard in San Diego paraphrased the Mexican authorities report on the matter. No mention of the men and girls killed or of the two missing girls.

The *Boomerang* had turned back in company with the *Orion* to San Diego. John and Gabrielle decided to postpone their holiday cruise to support Moira Sherman and see her safely back to the United States. At the moment the two craft were sailing in convoy, the four sharing the task of crewing between them. Currently John and Moira were manning the motor yacht. John used the opportunity to find out a little more about the charter by Jared Baer.

"It was not actually arranged by Jared himself. His agent, Claude Richter, arranged it two months ago. The final arrangements were made last week and the crew were recruited at that time by the client. He apparently wanted his own people looking after him Our regular staff was miffed at not being wanted. Jared Baer was quite a favourite of the younger members we keep on call.

"As it happened the people they hired were not particularly good at their jobs. The reason I was in the galley when it all went wrong, was because the 'so-called' cook was useless."

"Do you think they were chosen for another reason perhaps?" John asked.

"They looked more like bodyguards than servants, in my opinion."

John rubbed his chin, rasping the 24 hour growth he had acquired. "Why would they need bodyguards? Was there any sign of drugs on board?"

Moira laughed, "You must be joking. Of course there were drugs on board. This was supposed to be a pleasure cruise. Drugs, plus women, plus booze - just your usual music industry junket."

"I was wondering if the drugs element was perhaps a little more important to this crew than the leisure activities. I was trying to think of a reason for the massacre, and also why Jared and Mario survived without a scratch. I am beginning to wonder also, if you were intended to survive."

Moira shivered. "I'm beginning to think it was lucky the locker lid shut when it did!"

John could not lose the feeling that there was something wrong about the whole business. His sense of unease was not helped by the feeling that he had missed something.

"What happened to the luggage? Did it go with the rib raiders?"

"I don't know. I didn't think of it with all that was going on. You could check the master stateroom. It was placed there when they came aboard. They always kept the cabin locked and only their own staff went in or out. I must confess I haven't even looked in there since we sailed."

"Do you have a spare key?"

"Try the key locker on the port side of the lounge bulkhead."

John found the locker and located a key with the tag marked 'master'.

Below, the door to the master suite was still locked. When John opened it, he detected a musty smell as if wet clothes had been left too long. The room was nicely proportioned with king-sized bed and double wardrobes each side of the room. The bed was unmade. John went first to the bed and threw back the clothes to reveal a large damp patch, the cause of the musty smell. He went to the wardrobes next, flinging open the doors and revealing clothing hanging in both. Suitcases were on the shelves above the hanging rails. The suitcases, when pulled down, were empty. He piled them on the bed. Behind the clothes in the left hand wardrobe was a panel concealing the safe used for the convenience of the wealthy clientele. John slid the panel open, and examined the safe. The door was not quite closed. Using his penknife, he carefully opened the door wide. Within the safe it was apparent whoever had last opened it had been in a hurry. The left hand, bottom drawer was not quite closed. Again John opened the drawer fully with the knife, revealing the remaining contents, a small packet of papers crammed at the back of the drawer. The other drawer was still closed firmly; the knife came into play once more, prising the drawer open to reveal paper money crammed into the drawer, filling it completely. Thousands of dollars, John guessed, without touching it. Elsewhere in the safe there was the residue of white powder. John guessed cocaine.

On the bridge once more, John told Moira what he had found. She thought for a moment, then.

"What about the drawers under the bed?"

Down below once more John stood back in amazement. The drawer from the right side of the bed lay on the floor, in it was a neat row of Ingram smg's with a block of loaded magazines at one end. There were fifty units in all and they smelled of the cosmoline with which they had been protected. He went to the other side of the bed and removed the other drawer which was empty.

The port of departure had been San Francisco, but the bulk of the luggage had come aboard, as far as Moira could remember, at Catalina. It had been loaded from a small boat in the evening of their arrival at the Island. The bags had been delivered by A/C Carriers, otherwise known as Archer Communications, of Los Angeles.

On the satellite phone to Dearborn later, John was able to confirm the connection between Rough Records Inc. and the COMCO organisation. When he told Mark about the guns and money found on the *Boomerang,* Mark responded by saying that the goods would be collected at San Diego by TOT by arrangement, on this occasion, with the Department of Homeland Security. The authorities had been advised of the guns. TOT wanted to follow the trail of the guns to their source, if possible. That could only be done if the secret of its discovery was kept.

Moira had been kept in the picture to some extent by John, though he had not told her of the existence of TOT, merely that the goods were being lifted by Homeland Security.

Chapter Twenty-one

At San Diego the transfer of weapons was undertaken under the cover of forensic examination and subsequent cleanup. Over a two-day period the boat went from bloody mess to sparkling clean, with the quiet removal of the loot undertaken piecemeal during the night.

Moira arranged for the funeral of her husband, and John saw to the transfer of the rest of the bodies to police custody. The arrangements for the transfer of ownership of *Boomerang* to Moira's name were a formality only. Bill's life insurance covered the cost of securing the house they shared and the final payments on the boat. Since the charter had been prepaid for a four week period, Moira had time and the finance to arrange the legal matters arising from the attack. John and Gabrielle returned to San Francisco in *Orion* and met Moira in time to attend the funeral and see that all business matters had been settled and her affairs in order.

Attempts to contact the pop singer and his manager got nowhere. The agent, Claude Richter, would only confirm that the errant pair were still in Mexico and had not said when they would return. He did promise to let John know when they did come back, however.

Jared Baer and Marco Palermo were currently keeping a low profile in Mexico, despite repeated phone calls from Jared's agent asking him to return to fulfil commitments. Neither man was prepared to take the risk. They were totally obsessed with their fear of being charged with the murders of the ship's crew. It was going to take considerable persuasion to get them back over the border.

It later came to light that they had both been devastated by the bloody murder of the crew of the *Boomerang*. When they had made arrangements for the delivery of a supply of cocaine, neither was prepared for the arrival of the local, drug importation boss. Some glitch in communication had resulted in the message going to the main man in the area, rather than the street source that they had anticipated. Marco had not mentioned the guns he was taking for delivery to interested parties in Mazatalan. The money was for a little private enterprise to set up a channel for supplies, of whatever was in demand in the States from time to time. The arrival of the drug lord was bad luck.

Not surprisingly he had reacted at having his time wasted. It had only needed the intervention of one of the bodyguards at the wrong moment to start the ball rolling. The mad chatter of the sub-machine guns had seemed to go on forever.

When the noise had stopped, Jared Baer had lifted his head from where he had buried it in his crossed arms. The smell of blood and cordite nearly caused him to vomit. As he looked around at the carnage he spun round and was sick over the side. He was grabbed and thrust down into the Rib that had brought the drug lord and his men. Marco was pushed down beside him. The boat took off with a roar and sped to the coast a few miles away to the east. The yacht was left behind rocking, without power, drifting with its dead crew.

Ashore the two Americans had been just dumped on the beach. The boat withdrew and motored off with their captors, leaving them both shocked and terrified. After a few minutes Jared walked up the beach to the small village beside the bay. Marco pulled his cell phone from his pocket and called Chicago. After a short discussion, he cut off the call and walked up to join Jared.

Moira remained composed throughout the funeral. The few people present reflected the fact that both she and her husband had been orphaned at an early age. Only her sister Carol was there from family. Younger than Moira, she was a Marine officer stationed at San Diego. The medals indicated the fact that she had served in Iraq and in Afghanistan. The Purple Heart advertised that she had been wounded in the process and the Bronze Star indicated her courage under fire.

In the hotel after the burial, they all sat quietly drinking in the rather awkward manner that seems always to accompany these occasions. Eventually Moira broke the silence. "I'm dammed if Bill would have put up with this. He was a great guy and I loved him in my own way. We looked after each other. Only this time I didn't quite manage it. I'm not going to live the rest of my life paying for it. From here on the business is going to be Sherman and Mears. Carol is on termination leave now and joining me in partnership to carry on running the *Boomerang*, and any other craft we may get hold of."

"Here's to Sherman and Mears." Gabrielle raised her glass and John and Carol joined in. Once the ice was broken, the conversation became general and John found himself discussing the future of the charter company with Moira. It seemed that they would need to expand, if they were going to survive in the extremely competitive world that was the charter business. That required money, which could be difficult, as banks were still wary of lending money to women, especially in a business that was traditionally male dominated.

John was interested. "How much do you need, and I don't mean minimum. Think best scenario, and what sort of share offer would you be prepared to make a lender?"

"Whoa. I didn't mention shares in the business. I'd be looking for $750,000, but I'm not interested in share allocations!"

"A bank might play that game, but a private lender would need more than just hardware collateral. Think about it, the wrong turn and the collateral is piled up on a rock, or worse sunk without trace. On the other hand, a financial business partner takes part of the risk as a shareholder and, with the right person, part of the future expansion, if and when it happens."

"You sound as if you have someone in mind?" Moira said curiously.

"In fact I have," John said. "Why not us?" John grinned indicating Gabrielle and himself.

"We could raise the money, and help with the running of the business. Both Gabrielle and I hold international yacht master certificates and can handle deliveries and charters if necessary. We live in San Francisco, and, as of now, we have nothing to do!"

Moira sat back and looked steadily at John. She called the other two over. When they were all four gathered close enough to hear without being overheard, she told Carol and Gabrielle what John had suggested. Sitting back she looked for their reactions.

Gabrielle looked at John. "What a great idea," she said delightedly. "I was worried about what we were going to do for the next fifty years!"

They all laughed at this. Carol leaned forward and said, "I'm not the expert here. Give me an M-16 carbine or an Ingram and I know just what to do. I can sail a sailboat and run a rigid raider, or a ships boat, but I'm a novice at business. I need to be trained to run an oceangoing yacht, power or sail. I'm in your hands. If it's O.K. with Moira, its O.K. with me."

In Mexico the two Americans boarded the train for Tijuana. As it drew out of the station Marco said to Jared , "Don't forget, it was a raid. We knew nothing. We were taken close to the beach and we managed to roll over the side. We guessed the crooks would not make a big thing out of it, since we were close to the shore and there were people watching the boat from the beach.

We didn't know the killers, nor did we expect them to attack the boat. The whole business was arranged just to scare the shit out of you, to make sure you did what you are told, without argument, in future. You got the message?"

A very quiet, chastened Jared Baer arrived back in the United States. There was no big reception committee. It was without doubt one of the most discreet interviews ever given by the pop star of the year. The quiet admission was that the abduction that had cost several lives. It had spared the lives of Marco and himself, and was published in the Chicago Tribune, on the thirtieth page. It hardly made a mention in the Pop magazines. Jared returned to his career as a singer and produced a series of hit records for his record company. Privately he was seething over the way the Company had framed him to secure his cooperation. For the next several months he would be seeking some way of getting out of the trap he had been pushed into.

Chapter Twenty-two

The signboard said, 'Sherman, Mears and Graham'. Yacht charter. Sales and deliveries. It was new and it stood over the gate of the boatyard on the Richmond waterfront. Three months after the funeral, the work of building up the business had progressed to the point where the inventory now comprised, not only the *Boomerang*, but also *Waterwitch* (60ft steel, 8 berth ketch), and *Polynesia* (90ft steel hull motor cruiser), currently lying offshore in the basin. Gabrielle was cruising with a family in *Waterwitch*, north round Vancouver Island for two more weeks. *Boomerang* was in the Hawaiian Islands with Moira and a bunch of high school girls having a reunion, 20 years after leaving high school.

John was on board *Polynesia* preparing for a charter to Acapulco with a party of Rotarians, a month of booze and fun with middle-aged businessmen and their companions.

The cell phone played its merry tune. John cursed and plucked it from his belt and spoke. "Yes!" Carol spoke at the other end, "John, the group are arriving and hopefully they will be sober by the time they board. There is one person you will have to watch. Can you come ashore and meet them, but see me first?"

"What's up?" John said.

"One of the Rotarians is as genuine as a three dollar note. My guess he is a hitman for the mob."

"Why do think he's a hitman?" John was interested and intrigued that she should know what a hitman for the mob looked like.

"As soon as I saw him, I knew he was a killer. Remember I've killed myself. I know what a killer is like: the body language, you know."

"What about the mob?" John persisted.

"Just a feeling, that's all. He fits the pattern, and he worries me."

"I'll look them over and we'll see what I think, O.K.?"

In the visitor's lounge, the group was sitting around enjoying a welcoming drink. Eight men and six women at present, two more would join in San Diego. John looked at the group amused at Carol's description of the Mafia hit man. He held out his hand to greet Captain GW Harris. "Rotarians, I understand?" he laughed. "Carol had you pegged hit man for the Mafia, definitely killer material!"

GW grinned "We needed some sort of cover and this is the USA. Do you know all the other guys?"

Looking round the room John noticed three of the girls, all ex-marines, and nodded to several of the other men whom he knew. He turned round to meet the woman who had just come in from the rest rooms and found himself enveloped in Marianne's arms, and firmly kissed on each cheek.

"Lovely to see you, John. It's been too long. Where is the beautiful Gabrielle? You look good, so fit, so young. This life obviously agrees with you."

"All right. What is this all about? He noticed Carol chatting with the three ex-marines. "Well. Come on. Tell me what's happening!"

"We have a special job on for Michael Brooks. The word is his old boss is travelling to San Diego and taking a side trip to Tijuana to meet the Mexican version. The President has not made many friends since he came to the White House and he has upset a lot of powerful people. The guy who took over from Michael has a lot of friends in the Mob. He is also close to the vice-President, who also has strange friends, and would probably be a lot more amenable to suggestions. Security in the Tijuana area is going to be tricky, so we are the best insurance he could come up with."

"I thought the present man was a pal of Henry whatsisname, who took over from Michael."

"It seems they had a falling out over the amount of information leaking from the White House since Michael left. Henry is very much under suspicion. In addition a lot of familiar faces have disappeared and been replaced by Reagent Inc personnel. The two people in San Diego are following the group with Press credentials as cover."

John brought the 80ft *Polynesia* in to touch the jetty. He had a crew of five on board, including Carol as mate. She had now qualified on paper as Watch Officer. Full status took another three months under supervision. She worked well with the youngsters comprising the other members of the crew, all students from the local University on summer break.

The group boarded while John held the boat against the fender on the jetty with the bow and stern thrusters. The group's luggage had already been transferred to *Polly* as she was already called, by the base crew. Over in the boatyard Brian Ascher, Michael's young brother, watched the easy handling of the boat with satisfaction. As a design engineer Brian had participated in the specific funnel design of the bow and stern thrusters on *Polly*. Watching them in action gave him a real feeling of accomplishment. He turned back to his assistant, the workshop manager of the boatyard, and returned to their earlier discussion over the modifications to *Boomerang* which were scheduled on her return at the end of next week.

Mary Slessor was the workshop manager and deputy yard manager. She was a shipwright who had served her apprenticeship building trawlers in Bangor, Maine, and her high standards of workmanship had earned her the current job in the yard. Now in her 50's she was widowed. Her husband had a disagreement with an Atlantic storm, 25 years ago. She had moved to San Francisco to be near her two sons, who had both become computer engineers, working with Michael Ascher's organisation.

When the yard she was working for had folded, she looked for another job and heard, through her sons, that a new company had bought the Richmond site. So she came along to see. After three months working in the friendly atmosphere of the yard, she was well satisfied with her choice of job. She and Brian had an empathy not often found between people of such different age and background.

Brian, at thirty, was the youngest of the Ascher family. A welcomed afterthought of his parents, he had been thoroughly spoiled by his older brother and his parents. Despite all, he had studied hard to get his qualifications, and turned out to be a talented, good-looking young man, fond of fast cars and long legged-blonds. Nearly married twice, he was glad he had not succumbed. having met Carol Mears, who—whilst being long legged—was no blond. He had decided, come what may, he would marry her. His only problem was prising her away from her work long enough to let her know what he had in mind.

The *Polly* swept out of the marina area into the Bay, the

powerful engines driving her round between Angel Island and Alcatraz heading for the bridge and the open Pacific. With Carol at the helm the big motor yacht made a fine sight to the watchers on the shore. Her clean lines and raked upper works gave her the look of speed reflected in her performance. The group of aerials arrayed around the control area signified the state-of-the-art electronic communication and navigation equipment with which she had been fitted. Her previous owner would not have recognised her in her present form.

Below, the group assembled in the main lounge, the stewards making sure everyone had drinks and snacks before they retired to give them privacy. G.W. Harris stood and called for quiet. He then introduced John, ensuring that they understood that John was secure to share all information and available for consultation and advice. Also that he was the man pictured on the wall of their depot in Dearborn, founder member of the company, and privy to all its secrets. He then ran over the outline of the programme to be followed en route to San Diego. This was mainly concerned with the study of locations and sites in and around the San Diego/Tijuana area.

John would provide up-to-date weather forecasts from the satellite, on a daily basis. They were all warned not to discuss what they were doing with the other crew members.

As they approached the roadstead off San Diego, dusk was falling at the end of the second day at sea. The *Polly* had averaged over twelve knots continuously since leaving San Francisco. John and Carol were delighted with her performance knowing that the engines had been cruising at an economic speed the whole way and the top speed, in excess of twenty knots, was obviously achievable. For her first voyage with SMG charters she was right up to specification. The tender was lowered and the first group went ashore to scout the scene. Carol had been let into the secret of the special fittings in the ship: the armoury, located in the engine room within the auxiliary fuel tank and a second GPS located within the locker with the drop-back panel beside the helm.

Because Carol knew the three female marines and two of the men it would have been very difficult to keep it from her anyway. John briefed her personally, stressing that there was no need to tell Moira unless it was unavoidable.

The shore party spread out to their various, assigned tasks locating the sites on the Presidential agenda and checking, discreetly to see that proper arrangements had been made. From the initial investigation it seemed that all had been done correctly.

In fact one of the advance party of Secret Service men was known to one of the TOT agents. He was able to confirm that the normal protection team was being supported by the White House special agency, which was going to supply protection over the border in Tijuana, leaving the regular security to concentrate in the US. The report said the Secret Service was uneasy about the whole business. They had advised the President that they were responsible for his protection; also, that they were the experts. Using the alternative agency for the Mexican excursion was not a safe option.

The President had evidently made his decision on the advice of Henry Smith, and would not be persuaded.

As a result of the findings of the scouting party, GW decided to concentrate on the Tijuana side of the border, and placed his troops accordingly. The gaudily-dressed group went ashore and raised a little dust, as any self-respecting Rotarians on an outing should. They collected the other two who had been in the City for the last week and partied, apparently a little too well, for most of the evening. On the boat GW de-briefed the two agents. He learned that the precautions taken on the Mexican side of the border did not include any Mexican Government agents at all. Their offer of local knowledge and assistance had been rudely rejected.

Chapter Twenty-three

In the circumstances, George's senior agent had privately arranged with the Mexican security chief to cover the visit with discretion. Using the cover of forged Secret Service credentials, he had pointed out to the very angry senior Security officer that if anything happened to the President while he was in Mexico all hell would break loose. And the fact that he had been warned off by the protection detail would be no excuse.

The Presidential detail was scheduled to arrive in two days time, which did not give the team much time to establish themselves in Tijuana. However by the time the big entourage of the Presidential party arrived in San Diego, the team was in place. The weapons were loaded into the yacht tender as it sailed down coast to Rosarito. Some of the party went ashore and arranged a fish fry on the beach that night, and under cover of the hi-jinks, the weapons were smuggled ashore. The hire car driven down from Tijuana collected the guns and took them back for distribution to the agents in place. The fish fry party consisted of the youngsters of the crew plus Carol.

John stayed on the Polly as caretaker and backup if needed. He also monitored the radio frequencies, using the scanner installed in the radio equipment on the boat.

The visit to San Diego was a great success. The official ball held in the City Hall was a sparkling affair, attended by all the local dignitaries as well as the President of Mexico and his lady. The security was tight but there were no incidents.

The senior agent for Presidential security was seriously worried by the President's decision to allow his cross-border safety to be in the hands of his own private agency. He was baffled by the insistence of Henry Smith that his men have the chance to show that they were capable of covering the President securely. In view of the popularity of the President with the general public it had not seemed to be too much of a problem, except....?

The letter had been routed through several countries before

reaching the Secret Service. Tracing its origin was apparently pointless to the point of impossibility. The content of the letter was clear and chilling. The writer had reason to believe that the entire charade of the President's protection below the border was a set up to remove him from office. Two scenarios were suggested: either the President would be assassinated, or an attempt would be staged which would be foiled by his loyal escorts who would emerge in shining armour having demonstrated their efficiency as protectors. The money was on the assassination plot in view of the current attitude of the President to the big business interests who were pressurising the Government for more freedom of action with government contracts.

The Secret Service was in a bind. Henry Smith had dismissed the letter as the usual lunatic ramblings that occurred whenever the President made a move, despite the fact that the letter had borne all the elements of a seriously professional hand. The suggestion that Smith's men might be plotting to betray the President he dismissed as ludicrous, and got away with it.

Nevertheless, the Secret Service did initiate enquiries into the background of the agents assigned to the cross border detail, so far without result.

It was with serious misgivings that the agent in charge of the protection detail contemplated the next two days. A proposal that his men act as back-up to the protection squad was dismissed impatiently by the President, who considered the whole business an unnecessary waste of time and resources. He forbade any further mention of the matter. What the President did not know was that the extra protection that would be normally provided by the Mexican Authorities had been dismissed on the orders of his personal security detail

The programme for the following day included a parade through San Diego with both Presidents sharing an open limousine (shades of Dallas John thought), followed by an afternoon visit to a children's hospital, by the US President and his lady. Upon the transit of the border in the early evening, the party would be met once more by the Mexican President and his wife. At this point the protection detail would take over from the Secret Service party. The entire entourage would travel in open carriages to the Viceroy's Palace where the President and his Lady with his aides would be entertained. The party would stay overnight in apartments in the Palace and return over the border the following day. They would be back at City Hall by eleven o'clock for a farewell lunch before departing in Air Force One for Washington.

GW's First Safety agents were assigned to shadow the presidential protection agents on the Mexican side.

As a result of the problems of close supervision in the circumstances, GW decided air cover, not helicopter, would be a good idea if it could be arranged. He contacted John who managed to arrange for an aircraft particularly well suited to the task.

The Otter aircraft used by the border patrol was a familiar sight along the length of the land border of the southern United States. Obtaining one could have been difficult, but, as it happened, a new model still under test, was being flown on location trials over the desert region of Southern California. Michael Ascher had a good relationship with the manufacturers through supplying the fly-by-wire software for the new model. He persuaded the test team that a trial in real time of a real situation could be useful in the fine tuning of the software. The addition of the sniper and various other items of manpower and equipment were just for authenticity. It was with relief that George heard the distinctive sound heralding the arrival on station of the oddly configured aircraft that could hover by turning its wings with oversized propellers vertical. On the ground, George opened his laptop and captured the view projected from the Otter. The rooftops of the buildings along the route were in view and the crowds in the streets made it difficult, though not impossible, for the First Safety operatives to be located. He spoke over the circuit ordering the group to switch on their personal IFF signals and was impressed at the effectiveness if the system. Every operative was highlighted on the computer screen showing up as a blinking light in the throng lining the Presidential Route.

The sun sank below the western horizon and the evening shadows lengthened. The picture on the screen changed as the system altered to take advantage of the ambient light. That now came mainly from the street lights and the shop front lighting, causing patterns of different shades to confuse, to some extent, the picture received.

It was just a glimpse seen in the corner of his eye that warned GW that something had changed. On the top of one of the tower blocks a figure had appeared. To the skilled eye of the ex-Delta officer the setting up of the sniper point was obvious. Roof cover was normal in protection routines so he was not surprised at the figure appearing. He was surprised at the timing. Normally the set up would have been well in advance of the critical time. Leaving it this late was odd. Also he realised the sniper was too far away to be covering the route specifically, and he was lining up in the wrong direction. He followed the sightline of the sniper and a chill ran up his spine. This was a set-up. On a roof overlooking the Presidential route there was another sniper, just as carefully lining up his sights on the street below.

The entourage had reached the international border, and the Mexican President was welcoming the US President and his Lady. GW issued his instructions to the airborne sniper. At the same time, he called a two-man team to mount the roof of the building, a shopping Mall standing beside the Ave Paseo de los Heroes and take out the sniper setting up there.

He watched the drama develop on the computer screen. The first sniper suddenly staggered and then dropped to the roof where he began sliding down the shallow slope, his clothing caught on a projection, and the body stopped just short of the roof edge. It made no further movement.

George called all agents on the circuit. "It's time to remove all opposition agents. I repeat remove all of your targets, now!" On receipt of their orders the First Safety team moved in and quietly began to secure the protection team from their positions in the crowd. As each agent was arrested they were secured with flexi-cuffs and steered into a warehouse behind the row of buildings along the street. No effort was made to do other than disarm and secure the people in order to remove their threat to the President. They accounted for all the street agents leaving only the bodyguards and the snipers.

Two agents went up to the roof where the shot sniper still lay. They carefully roped themselves and retrieved the body confirming that the woman was dead She was later identified as an army-trained sniper, who had been discharged when it became apparent that she had a taste for killing that amounted to hunger. The army psychologist had decided that she was a threat to her fellow troops and discharged her.

On the roof of the Mall the two agents edged through a door at the far end of the roof. They both dropped down and crawled towards the sniper who was now lying prone, lining up his sights on various points in his view. The rifle was mounted on a bipod and the barrel projected slightly through the gap left for drainage in the low wall surrounding the roof. This allowed him about 120 degrees swing from side to side, ample scope for his purpose. The voice from the Otter reported that though first sniper had been neutralised, there was another nest spotted further down the route with the possibility of another trap situation. GW swung the cursor to the new location. This time the place was suitable for an assassination shot or a neutralising shot. He ordered the Otter to sweep the area for more snipers, and reassigned two more agents to attend the third sniper.

On the roof of the Mall, Carol Mears lined her sights on the prone figure on the roof edge.
"Drop the rifle!" She spoke clearly and crisply. The figure jerked and looked around. "The rifle, drop it!" The order was explicit and the sniper carefully laid the rifle down. "Move back away from the gun and spread your arms and legs out!" The figure did as it was told. Carol stood keeping the silenced Glock lined up on the recumbent sniper. Her partner stood back keeping a close eye out for trouble.
Carol waved her partner forward and they changed roles. Carl Betts was a former G-Man and knew the routine. He approached the figure and holstering his gun he lifted the left hand and snapped on the handcuff, following through quickly with the right hand cuff. He then ran his hands expertly across the back, down the sides and between the legs of the prone figure. Then he lifted the shoulder of the figure and ran his hand down his front. He did the same the other side, then turned the man over. Carol looked down the sights of the rifle noting that it was a target Springfield .308, with sniper sight and a ten-shot magazine. It was lined up on the other side of the street, out of the sightline of the vehicles still passing below. She reported back immediately. "This is not the kill weapon. This is a clean-up gun. The assassin must be on the street!" Looking through the sights she tried to spot the gunman, but failed initially. Then, as she swung the rifle, she saw a man standing still among the surging crowd. He had a slightly elevated position, like many others

standing on a box or some such to get a better view.

"I think I see him," she said calmly. "He could just be watching but I have the feeling." She broke off still studying the man as she spoke. The man moved to stretch himself and she caught a glimpse of a weapon, looked like an smg hanging beneath his colourful shirt. He turned and looked down the street as the crowd stirred. The carriages were coming, Carol watched as the man's hand gripped the pistol grip of the weapon.

"We don't have anyone near," GW said. "Can you deal with it?"

"Suppose I am wrong?" Carol was calm but worried.

"It's your call I'm afraid. I'll back you whatever!"

Carol loaded a cartridge into the breach and checked the safety catch then settled down as if she was on the range at Annapolis. Carl called out.

"What's happening?"

"I think I can see the assassin down below. I may have to take him out." Her voice was steady. "You O.K. there?"

"Sure. I'm O.K. I've locked this guy to the railing." He came to her side and looked down. "Is that the guy, with the red floral shirt?"

"Yes, he has an smg under his shirt. Do you know him?"

"I certainly do, his name is Miguel Jones, wanted for murder and assault in three states, been on the run for the last year."

The agents assigned to the third sniper did not have an easy task. The man was on the roof of a locked building which stood isolated on a site back from the main street about 50 yards. It was surrounded by a chain link fence surmounted by dagger wire. They made a lengthy detour to reach the back of the building which was at a different level to the front. They cut the wire and squeezed through keeping low, staying out of line of sight of the sniper who they could see silhouetted against the sky from their position. The noise of the crowd on the street covered the sounds they made lowering the fire escape. They climbed the ladder carefully taking particular precautions when they reached the edge of the roof.

Access to the higher section of the roof was through a closed door. The stairs upwards could be seen through the window beside the door. The door was unlocked.

"Escape route," ex-marine Charlotte Green whispered to her companion Robert Sikorsky, nickname 'Igor'. They entered, carefully negotiating the trip wire strung across the bottom step The stairs led to a vestibule with a window and a door opening onto the flat roof. The window faced the other way and Igor immediately examined it to see if it could be opened quietly, without success.

At the door Charlie—as she was known—was trying to see through the key hole. Igor passed over his spy scope, a slender tube, key size, that allowed the keyhole to be used as a viewpoint. By passing the scope through the keyhole, the area beyond could be seen rather as a spy hole in a hotel door allowed the outside view to be seen. Charlie grinned her thanks and inserted the spy scope and looked through.

The sniper was busy laying out a sheet on the concrete, beside him the sniper rifle had been assembled and was resting on its bipod. A small pad was already in place to allow the snipers elbows to rest comfortably protected from the rough concrete.

She tried the door. Like the first it was unlocked. The sniper was now looking at the progress of the Presidential party. With great care Charlie inched the door open. It made no sound. She noticed the oil and realised the hinges and lock had been treated with WD40 to allow them to be opened and operated quietly. Creeping on the balls of her feet Charlie approached the sniper. She got within ten feet before the figure swung round in alarm. Charlie's gun was up and aimed at the middle of the snipers body.

"Stay still!" She ordered. "Raise your hands and step forward!"

The sniper stepped back, probably in surprise. He reached for the gun strapped to his waist and started to lift it into line. The man suddenly realised he had stepped back too far and Charlie saw the look of horror on his face as he toppled back over the edge of the roof on the long drop to the ground. She put her gun away and grabbed the sniper rifle before turning back to the door. Igor opened the door and they ran down to the lower roof, across the flat area to the fire escape. They cleared the building seconds before the police arrived. They watched from within the crowd as they milled around the dead body on the ground.

The crowd swayed forward as the carriages came near. The

assassin moved, pushing people aside with the barrel of his gun. They fell back when they saw the weapon. He raised the gun toward the Presidential carriage. The bodyguard fell sideways leaving the two Presidents exposed. As Jones raised the gun a hole appeared in his forehead, and the back of his head exploded over the people nearby. The bodyguard, seeing what happened lifted his automatic and pointed it at the President. Before he could fire, another bullet took him in the shoulder throwing him down in the street, gun flying out of his hand. The Presidents, both appalled at what was happening, just sat rooted to their seats. There was nothing else they could do.

Then two Holiday-garbed figures appeared beside the coach, mounted the step at either side, and drew weapons, turning outwards scanning the crowd. The nearest to the US President said in Spanish. "Please, gentlemen, keep low until we get to the Camino Real. He shouted to the coach driver who was sitting frozen with shock in the driving seat, "Get those horses moving." The driver whipped up the horses and the carriage leaped forward down the street, breaking into a gallop throwing the passengers about and nearly causing the agents to fall off the steps.

The Mexican Security took over the protection of the two Presidents quickly, reinforced by the Secret Service for the remainder of the visit. The agents who had carried out the rescue operation melted back into the crowd as the carriage reached its destination.

Over the next few days the scandal of the protection debacle was studied. The mystery of the rescuing party went unsolved. The credit for the foiled attempt went to the Mexican Security services, though the Chief Security officer in the Mexican Service was aware that the real credit belonged to the mysterious agents who had stepped in and covered matters before they could get out of hand. Not surprisingly, he kept his thoughts to himself.

In a quiet reshuffle, the President's personal security advisor resigned from his post to be replaced by the former deputy Director of the FBI. Several members of the security detail were replaced, and things gradually returned to normal.

The Otter performed so well the Secure Inc board decided there was a need for an aircraft of that particular design. So they bought one. On the *Polly* the group reassembled for debriefing and John threw a party for the successful agents. The crew members having returned from the fish fry party at Rosarito threw themselves into the job and produced the food and even managed a disco for the group to dance the night away.

George Washington Harris spoke to John about Marianne. "I would like to ask her out, but I'm afraid she will not be interested in me."

John eyed the big ex-Delta Officer gravely, but with some amusement. "Are you serious about this? I mean have you thought about what this might entail. Remember she has been through a lot and I would not like to see her hurt anymore!"

George drew himself up and gritted his teeth. John realised he might have gone too far.

He said soothingly, "Just kidding. Come on, George, everyone saw the way you looked at each other from the moment you first met!"

"That was six months ago. Things change." GW looked glum, rather like a small boy who was facing a beating when he got home.

"There is only one way you are going to find out whether she's interested or not. Ask her...Ask her... Now!" John spoke sharply and GW looked shocked for a minute,

"Right, I will!" He straightened up and walked over to Marianne and asked her to dance. She nodded and rose to her feet. They danced over to the double doors leading out to the promenade deck. John watched them disappear. "About time too!" he said aloud, and oblivious to the astonished looks of the people standing beside him, he strode off to talk to Igor beside the bar.

The yell could probably have been heard in San Diego despite the fact that they were now moored over half a mile offshore. Everything stopped: the dancing and the talking. Everyone looked at the doorway. GW and Marianne entered together holding hands, looking round in astonishment at the attention they were getting.

"What?" GW said lifting his shoulders.

"You did it!" John said.

GWs face broke out into a broad grin. "You bet your life I did. She said 'yes'!" He put his arm round Marianne and hugged her close, an attention she returned with interest.

"I thought I was going to have to ask him myself," she said blushing. "But he managed it in the end, all by himself!" The assembly cheered, and the party went on until dawn.

The cruise back to the base at Richmond was conducted, in all ways, like the pleasure cruise it was supposed to be. The crew worked hard to ensure the party had a good time and there was no doubt they succeeded.

By the time the boat had been moored and valeted for the next hire, John estimated that the bonus he paid his young crew was well earned. The farewells to the departing troopers were heartfelt. John could not help feeling a slight twinge of regret that he was not going back to join them in their active status.

Over the next few months the business progressed happily for the partnership. As the year passed John handed more and more of the work over to the safe hands of Moira, Carol and Brian. He and Gabrielle enjoyed more time together and both were delighted when they discovered Gabrielle was pregnant. The company had expanded its yacht brokerage to the extent that John and Gabrielle had concentrated more on the delivery of boats rather than the charter business.

The call from Kelly came at a convenient time for them both and the opportunity for a holiday was taken with delight.

The TOT Citation picked them up at San Francisco Airport and carried them in comfort to Detroit where they were joined by Mark Foster and Paddy O'Hara for the transatlantic flight.

In Rosas the others waited to greet them with open arms, for the first complete reunion in the two years that the company had been in operation.

The base at Rosas had acquired a feeling of permanence. The newness had worn off and there was a more comfortable feeling in the quarters and restaurants. John and Gabrielle settled quickly into their apartment and prepared for the reception laid on for the evening.

There was a knock on the door while they were relaxing with a glass of wine prior to dressing for the occasion. John opened the door to Mike and Paul who came in and greeted them. They sat down and chatted bringing each other up to date with the events since they had last met.

After a period of catching up, Mike got serious. "Something

has come up."

"Well, that's a conversation stopper if ever I heard one," John remarked. "Just what is this 'something'?"

"COMCO! We seem to have reached a point where either we sort them out, or we go under!"

Mike's expression was grave as he sipped his wine.

"Things are that serious then?" Gabrielle asked gravely.

"Kelly is quite worried about the situation. Michael and Jeanne are joining us this evening, so it looks like tomorrows' meeting will be pretty intense." Paul grinned. "It seems we have to face up to something we knew would happen at sometime or other. Better now when we've managed to get properly organised, rather than earlier when we would have been a sitting duck for their big guns. There is a move afoot for the Americans to start a programme of de-militarisation. Apparently a current bill is being discussed to pass several military functions over to civilian contract"

"I have been reading something of the sort in the US papers, but how will that affect us?" John asked.

"I think Kelly will have to tell you about that tomorrow," Mike said. "I'm not sure myself!"

The evening sun was still shining when the reception began. The main reception hall gradually filled with the staff and their partners from both TOT Commercial and the First Safety Inc, loosely referred to as the 'Underworld' because of their subterranean headquarters.

Chapter Twenty-four

The reception group comprised Kelly who was dressed in a stunning, yellow sheath dress. Next to her, John in his dinner jacket, and Gabrielle, her hair natural blond once more and her tanned skin set off by her electric blue gown. Michael, in white tuxedo, stood with Jeanne dressed in a scarlet gown that set off her dark hair and flashing, black eyes.

Jeanne Ascher had become a regular visitor to the Spanish headquarters because of her association with the Homelass charity, headquartered in the Castillo Toro, located just 39 miles away in the foothills of the Pyrenees. The charity had expanded considerably through the rescue efforts of the Secure Inc teams.

The group received the invited guests as they entered the hall for the celebrations.

It would have been difficult for anyone to be aware of the tension behind many of the guests' smiling faces. Bill Hamilton had successfully fought off several attempts of the COMCO group to take over his operation in High Wycombe. Secure Inc had also felt the impact of the heavy hand of the COMCO security consultants over the past few months.

Colonel Mike Madden was arrayed in his full regimental dress. He made a dashing target for some of the more mature, single women present Without doubt the star of the single ladies' evening was Paul, elegantly arrayed in a midnight blue tuxedo, with his world weary charm. Sadly for the lonely ladies, he only had eyes for Kelly, whom he escorted with tact and discretion throughout the evening.

The senior security personnel, many in regimentals though most in evening dress of some sort or other, did circulate and the single ladies found plenty of company among their ranks.

Douglas Stewart, invited by Gabrielle was astonished at the size and scope of the TOT Group. He was, of course aware that the reports of the death of Gabrielle and John were false and for reasons of security. He had also been told of the part played by the security company in the recovery of the young men and women helped by the Homelass charity. But he had no idea of the international strength of the company. In Jeanne Ascher he had found a serious colleague who had been involved in the care of the girls from the beginning. Between them they were planning major expansion of the charity to include a larger part of the world.

The evening ended in the apartment used by John and Gabrielle, sitting around with Paddy, Mike, Paul, Kelly and Remy. He had returned from a detachment to Ukraine in time to join them, swapping stories and enjoying the company of each other after the lengthy separation since they last met.

It was difficult to avoid the topic uppermost in most people's minds, but to do her credit Kelly forbade any reference to business until the meeting next day. Paul opened more champagne and the party continued until the early hours of the morning.

They assembled in the board room at 2 pm, seating themselves around the table.

The tension in the room was evident. Kelly came in accompanied by Paul. They seated themselves side by side at the head of the table placing their notes in front of the screen located in front of each of the seats.

The group sat silent, waiting. Paul rose to his feet and spoke.

"Thank you all for coming. This meeting is at the turning point for the company. Time has now caught up with us. Up to now we have dictated our own progress. To the rest of the world we are a company that has come out of nowhere and established a marker for all our competitors to aim for.

The biggest problem for Trans Ocean comes from COMCO. It appears that they are beginning to focus on us as their main competition. I don't think they know that we have been the opposition they have been encountering on the criminal-political front. The Security division has been enjoying great success everywhere it is operating. As you now know we have decided to keep the title Secure Inc. All local branches retain their existing First Safety Inc titles but the holding company will be administered under the title Secure. The corporate names used individually will all be standardised in whichever language is appropriate to the country concerned.

To return to our greatest problem at the moment, the topic is COMCO!" Paul sat down with the murmur of the group's approval for his effort in his ears.

Kelly spoke next. She basically directed the group to look at the information being posted on their screens, while she spoke.

"In the light of the US government's move to place elements of the military support services in the hands of private contractors, bids have been placed by several companies for the services to be thus dispersed.

"COMCO, in a race for position in the world market, has bid for the contract to operate the entire shipping requirement for the US army. If they succeed in obtaining this contract, they will have control of every sub-contractor currently involved in the movement of goods for the Army. At present, not only would this put many of the small contractors out of business, it would also cause Trans Ocean to lose a high proportion of the work they had gained in the US.

"The conclusion from this information is that the COMCO group has found a way to influence the Senate Committee to put the entire transport and travel arrangements into the hands of a single company. The company will be required to demonstrate, in open session, their ability to honour the contract. At this stage there is the possibility that they may fail to produce the assets required, though it is unlikely in the circumstances. This is not a move you would make without nailing the basic components beforehand.

"Their security division is their weak point. We have now obtained evidence of their complicity in the attempted assassination of the President at the Mexican Border. This may be enough to upset their proposal. But I think we are going to need positive action to be sure they do not succeed. They have plenty of Senators on the payroll and if they can steer the vote in the right direction they will."

Kelly sat. "Has anyone any suggestions please?"

"Have we any friends at the table, I seem to remember Michael saying there were several Senators and Congressmen who were opposed to privatisation of the services for the armed forces. Can't we get them mobilised in opposition?" John looked at Michael Brooks.

Michael Brooks spoke. "The Senate and Congress are both run on a basis of checks and balances. By the time this gets to the enquiry stage they have already sorted out the opposition. In effect, unless something comes up at the enquiry, this should go through. As I see it we have two chances: first, to prove COMCO cannot be depended upon to perform, to show that they are cheating in some way, or to demonstrate their disloyalty to the United States."

Paddy spoke up, "We have proof that they have been supplying arms to the Taliban in Afghanistan and that they have supplied fissionable material to Iran."

"Sorry, Paddy. That won't work. They can claim that the end users deceived them and illegally supplied the weapons and plutonium."

Mark Foster interjected, "But what about the documents we captured from Slovenia, and some of the Marseilles material. Is there nothing among them we could use? If I remember correctly, Paddy was combing them for useful information. Is there nothing there of use even if only as a starting point?"

Kelly spoke once more, "We did think of that and Paddy is digging at the moment to see if there is anything she may have missed. If anything shows up it will display on the screen."

Mike Ross asked. "Can we do anything with our computer interface?" He referred to the back door inserted by Peter Davis after the COMCO computer reorganisation.

"Once again we need to walk warily. We must never let them know that we are in their system. To answer your question we can access their money movement records, but we can't disclose the irregularities without exposing ourselves." Kelly was firm. "Can I just suggest you go away and concentrate on what positive action we can take, and reconvene tomorrow morning?"

The group broke up and drifted out of the room.

Over the next three days plans were drawn up for the battle for survival against COMCO. It's present composition of a collection of companies included communications, trucking, banking and shipping. With branches throughout the world, the conglomerate owned six hundred companies and turned over in excess of $4 billion annually. Their security operation, 'Reagents Inc', had expanded to take in some very questionable organisations throughout the European Community. In some of the South American countries they were represented by outright terrorist gangs.

At Rosas the board split up into three main groups: action, commercial and subversive. The action group comprised Colonel Mad Mike Madden in charge, with Alan Gilmore and Mark Foster in support. Commerce was left to the direction of Kelly Martin, supported by Bill Hamilton. The subversive group was headed by Michael Brooks with the active help of Patsy, the Geek, and Peter Davis. He also had the direct support of Retreads Inc. who were the basis of Secure Inc.

Meanwhile John and Gabrielle, with Michael and Jeanne Ascher gathered to discuss what they might do themselves.

"I have spoken to Wally Peterson in London," John said. "I have suggested he might like to join the club in our little battle against the opposition. I have explained the consequences of failure. He appears to regard the whole business as a challenge to his expertise and an insult to the profession that he follows."

Gabrielle said. "Whatever we do, we must make sure we don't clash with the others. Perhaps we should make sure that our actions are cleared with whoever is operating in the UK field."

Michael offered to start his company team working on specific projects whenever called. His understanding of the problems they faced was re-assuring. It made him particularly well equipped to undertake the tasks being tackled today.

John went to see Michael Brooks and suggested that, with the co-operation of Bob Pullman and Gaynor Jones, Gabrielle and he would like to tackle the British end of the task, pointing out that his own past experience in the UK and his contacts, still extant, he could make a difference.

Michael Brooks was only too pleased to give them the problem of UK. It gave him the chance to concentrate on the biggest, to his mind, problem of them all; the USA. So it was arranged.

Jeanne Ascher had a base in London for her charity work with Homelass. Douglas Stewart had found the charming Georgian house in Overton Gardens, Knightsbridge, which had plenty of room for John and Gabrielle to stay while in London. Jeanne was delighted with the company since, though Michael accompanied her as much as possible, he still needed to keep up with the ever-changing requirements of the electronics market in the US. They moved in, taking over the basement of the house which was already fitted out as a one bedroom flat. The house had a lift to service all four floors. The attic had also been converted before the house had been reverted to a single dwelling, when the Aschers purchased it.

John got in touch with Wally and his enterprising son, Martin, the all-rounder. They assembled in the lounge of 822 Overton Square to formulate a plan of action and identify targets. Although the British scene was not as high profile as the US, John was convinced the loss of the UK connection would damage COMCO badly. The links to the European setup had been apparent when the business of Mathieu had been undertaken. The group still felt the attempt on the lives of John and Gabrielle by the Reagents team required a suitable answer.

The COMCO Transport group was represented by Bannington Transport (UK), operating from depots throughout the country, delivering and collecting goods from across Europe, and parcel deliveries on a break-bulk basis combined with local distribution. They also had a high speed, package delivery, rivalling DHL, though not yet in the same league. The other company was Reagents Ltd.

The discussion included, of course, the rather unpleasant Mr Arthur Wilson and his associate Said Ali, with the rather nasty piece of work, Julian Ross MP.

Wally had actually already started a sting in respect of the MP and his Parliamentary agent. The backing provided by Reagents Inc had so far kept the more extreme deeds of the pair out of the limelight. But Wally, having bugged the car and the house occupied by the MP had sufficient dirt on the pair to make their removal from the public scene of positive benefit to the nation at large.

They discussed the scam that Wally had already set up. The beauty of the set-up was its simplicity. If everything went wrong, there was nothing to link it with anyone else. The main reflection would be on the security of Reagent's cover. It involved the exploitation of Ross's involvement in making money to fund his lavish lifestyle.

Two main sources of income were; the provision of drugs to his circle of friends, a nice little earner that netted him a higher income than his Parliamentary pay; the other was his particular joy:

the collection and provision of girls and boys for the London porn market, ranging from prostitution to skinflicks, to the blackmail business that transpired from his provision of companions to his colleagues and friends.

Wally had laid on a significant lure, a secret society party, set up in the famous Hellfire Caves in West Wycombe, to celebrate the re-creation of the Hellfire Club. This was a once popular diversion set up by Sir Francis Dashwood, for the benefit of his friends and hangers-on, in the caves on his estate. The parties were renowned for their lascivious content involving group sex and drug taking. It was just the thing for Mr Ross to enjoy, and profit from.

The idea for the party was floated because a new club of the same name, had just been opened in the East End of London. The suggestion for the party in the Hellfire Caves had been from a planted remark, to one of Julian Ross's friends.

He, of course, saw the possibilities for profit and fun, took the idea over, and organised the party himself. The secrecy did require Ross to bring the girls personally and arrange for the supply of booze and drugs to be available at the same time.

The services of Bob Pullman had been requisitioned to make sure the right group of police officers was in the right place at the right time. The weak point was in the pick-up from Ross's source, the tracker on his Range Rover indicated a warehouse in the south of London, operated strangely enough by Bannington Transport as a distribution depot. Martin, Wally's son, the builder, had friends in the area and they were willing to keep an eye on things.

The French Manager of the warehouse was not popular locally, because he had not made any effort to extend the entente cordiale in the immediate area. The security at the warehouse was very tight. Most of the open warehouse jobs were performed by local men, but none of the 'bond' or secure room positions had been given to locals. All had gone to French or American people. It was suspected that people were brought in from the continent in trucks. But the offloading was obviously carried out in the closed, bond section where there was certainly room. It was guessed that the initial grooming of the girls would probably have been done in Europe, but that the final touches would be added in the London depot.

As a start Wally's plan was accepted as it stood. Nobody could find any faults with it though they all accepted that things can go wrong whatever provisions you make.

The big move would be the attempt to remove the COMCO presence from the UK scene. The removal of Arthur Wilson would be a good start, as he did supply protection and cover for the organisation involved in the drug and weapons trading. If Wally's project worked it would make a big dent in Wilson's power base.

The present location of Said Ali was unknown, but the word was out and eyes were open all over town through Wally's network, and with the Coven who had been contacted by John when he returned to London.

Before leaving, Wally screened the entire house for bugs. It came out clear. He left a scanner with John for regular use.

The next day they contacted Sheila Davenport and met for lunch in Fortnum's. They chatted amicably over the meal, very much old friends getting together. When they left the restaurant conversation became much more intense. John said, "When we last met you suggested you were in a position to dump Wilson any time you liked. Is that still possible?"

"Who takes over if Wilson goes?" Gabrielle asked.

"Either, myself or Charlie Watts, a protégée of Kelly's." Sheila said. "Probably me, but whatever happens there'll be a sympathetic ear at M1-6, and that's the main thing!"

"What have you got to do to dispose of him?" John was curious.

"He has had his hand in the cookie jar, as my American friends would say. In fact he has lifted so much that the fact that the money has been used by known criminals can only increase the prison sentence he would be expected to serve: not that he will ever go to prison, nor will he go to trial. He will just be quietly retired."

"I see, "John said quietly. They parted with the imminent dismissal of Arthur Wilson arranged.

When they got home that night Gabrielle said to John. "You are going to kill him, aren't you?"

John thought of the drugs being imported by the Wilson set-up, and the ruin and degradation that they were involved in. "Yes!" he said simply. Gabrielle nodded and said no more.

There was little to be done until the Hellfire club scam had been completed in two weeks. John went to High Wycombe to confer with Bob Pullman, leaving Gabrielle and Jeanne arranging a shopping spree in the West End.

At Wycombe, John and Bob Pullman were able to start formulating a strategy to put the Bannington Transport on the back foot. The local depot was in the Industrial Estate, well protected by Reagent security men. John intended having a look around inside to see if the local warehouse was being used illegally for drug or weapon storage.

They devised a simple plan. Run a truck into the front gate. While the distraction was at its height John would get over the back fence and hopefully enter the premises and take a look around. If there was anything interesting there, he would call Bob on his mobile phone and Bob could bring the cavalry. That way there would be no chance of disposing of the evidence before a raid could be mounted.

David O'Neil

Chapter Twenty-five

And so the first victory of the campaign for the clean-up of the UK was achieved. They never realised that John had been inside the warehouse. He had walked out with the searchers of the police party wearing white overalls and carrying a small black case.

As planned, the truck had crashed into the main gate of the compound having burst the near front tyre at exactly the right time. The professional stunt man driving was very good at his job. When he emerged from the cab he had blood on his face but only a small wound to account for it.

The attention of the security within the compound was distracted enough for John to get over the wire and into the compound without detection. He ran over to the building and walked down to the Judas door in the big side door of the warehouse. As he entered he saw the other people within all looking toward the front of the building where the crash had occurred. He walked over to a rack where there was a clipboard lying and collected it. With his head down studying the board, he walked to the entrance of the secure area. At the door the guard, who was peering towards the front door, asked what was going on. John thrust his driving licence at the guard and said some idiot has bashed into the front gate. The guard hardly glanced at the licence pushed before him and waved him through. John entered the secure area and looked around. There were three people visible in the 640 sq metre area. The place was divided into lanes with goods piled in orderly rows, and stacked in places 20 ft high. There were several forklifts stationed around the aisles though none was in motion at the time. He strolled round to an empty aisle and along to the end, out of sight of the other people there. He started examining the cases nearest to him: straightforward goods in transit, nothing at all suspicious here. He went on to the very rear wall of the building scanning boxes as he walked. He became aware of something remarkable. The boxes he was now passing were immaculate, despite labels that indicated they had, in some cases, travelled from the other side of the world, the wood smooth and undamaged; after a lengthy voyage half way round the world, some from multiple places, all in pristine condition!

He examined one of the boxes closely and found it was not a box at all. It was a panel made to look like a stack of boxes. Had the maker been a little more careful and dirtied the timber to make them look travelled, he would have missed it.

He found the joint where there was a concealed hinge. Following round the outline he found the door, if that was what it was. At that moment voices warned John that someone was coming. He looked around. There was nowhere to hide. Looking up he saw, on the left side of the aisle there were proper boxes. Without thinking he grabbed the top of the nearest box and hauled himself up, then the next and finally the top box. He was still not out of sight when two men came round the corner deep in conversation. John froze. The men had not noticed him above their eye line. The first man reached the door opposite and pushed firmly halfway up the door which sprang open. The men walked through, leaving the door open. The false wall was too high for John to see over from his present position so he climbed up to the box on top of the next stack and looked into the concealed area. 'Bingo,' he thought. Inside the closed area were stacks of ammunition boxes beside stacks of weapon boxes. There were shoulder fired missiles, a row of mortars with boxes of bombs standing beside them. The two men left the area still deep in conversation, closing the door behind them. When they were gone John descended to the floor once more and entered the closed area, pushing the door as he had seen the man push it. Inside he confirmed the inventory of arms and ammunition. He searched the whole area carefully seeking another way out. As far as he could see there was none. He did notice that the empty 19 meter container had a sink and toilet installed and the door locked from the outside only, possibly a holding pen for smuggled people.

He pulled out his mobile phone and pressed the speed dial to Bob Pullman. He answered immediately. John gave the codeword. "Bingo. Back of the secure area, aisle four on the right, six boxes back from the corner" and rang off.

The sound of a police siren warned John that the cavalry had arrived. Loud voices could be heard approaching through the door of the secure area. The voices neared the aisle where John was crouched. As they turned down aisle four John came from aisle three and joined the group. When the party reached the spot John had designated, the senior police officer ordered the warehouse staff to remove the fourth box. Of course it could not be moved and the door was discovered.

The discovery of the arms and ammunition was greeted by silence on the part of the warehouse staff and a raised eyebrow on the part of the senior police officer. The police photographer was called in to photograph the weapons in situ, and the forklifts were requisitioned to remove the goods from the premises. The transit documents for all the goods in the secure section were requisitioned and the paperwork for the transport of the weapons was demanded, though not forthcoming. When the police party started to mill about in the area John slipped on the white coat he had concealed in his small black case. He left the premises by just walking out of the front door.

The subsequent closure and investigation of the company by Special Branch, followed by the close attentions of the Fraud Squad, made the operation of the company impossible. To add to the troubles for COMCO, the security firm Reagents Ltd., was under scrutiny for the improper conduct of their staff.

The second part of the exercise swung into motion two weeks later:-

The limousine, carrying Julian Ross and his agent to the gathering at the Hellfire Caves, was stretch. It was needed as the car had ten people scattered round the twelve seats. With Ross and Ken Travers his agent, were five girls and a boy, all of whom were woozy with the effects of tranquillisers.

Julian looked over the group and selected a likely-looking teenage, blond who looked interesting, reached out and pulled her on to his lap, The boy tried to rouse himself in obvious protest. Julian ignored him while he sat and ran his hands over the small breasts of the blond. He dropped his hand to her leg and lifted her skirt, sliding his fingers up to the white lace edged knickers. Running his fingers over the girl's mound, he sighed and put her back onto her seat, promising himself a further investigation later. The car bumped over the rougher ground at the churchyard location of the cave entrance. With Travers he urged the group out of the limo, and with the help of the burly minder stationed at the entrance, ushered them into the caves.

Once inside they were taken into an annex to the main cave where they were given clothes to wear, consisting mainly of a white sheet and nothing else. In the main room Julian and Ken were greeted by the assembly with raucous shouts from the already half-drunk occupants.

The men and women within were all dressed loosely in the Roman-style togas and simple white sheets that concealed little of the bodies beneath. Some of the people were already clutched together, groping and kissing with abandon. Julian and his companion went into another annex where they stripped and changed, returning to join the party in the main cave.

Julian carried the bag of cocaine into the middle of the room and poured it on to the centre of the low table arranged especially for it.

The group of police officers especially selected by Bob Pullman's former colleague, D/Supt Peter West, closed the circle around the Hellfire Caves. One by one they collected the ring of Reagent minders. Disarming them and passing them back to the waiting police vans.

The vans moved out, to be replaced by more vehicles, lined up and ready to receive the main reason for the ambush.

Inside the caves the group of youngsters brought by Julian had been paraded into the main cave. They were more nearly alert now, and their protests merely inflamed the lusts of the assembled crowd.

Julian claimed the blond girl once more, and was not surprised to see Ken claim the boy. In the noise being created by the chatter and music the protests of the girl and boy were ignored. The boy seemed more concerned with protecting the girl than himself. Ken hit him smartly to keep him in order, but the boy struggled, wriggled out of Ken's arms and plunged at Julian who was busy pulling the sheet that covered the blond girl. The boy got to Julian, who looked up in surprise. His surprise changed to anger and he lifted one hand to hit the boy. The girl jerked his other arm struggling to get away. The boy took the opportunity to attack. He grabbed Julian and bit the side of his neck over the carotid artery. Julian screamed, the cry cutting through the noise of the party, creating a sudden silence in the room. He frantically tried to tear the boy away from his neck, but the boy clenched his teeth tighter. Julian screamed again and suddenly the boy was thrown off spitting out the piece of flesh from Ross's neck, leaving Julian clutching the savage wound. He removed his hand from the wound and looked at his bloodstained fingers in horror. The wound was deep. Suddenly the thin, weakened wall of his carotid artery broke and a six foot spurt of crimson gushed from his neck to splatter the people around him. Those nearest shrank back appalled, and condemned him to death. Their presence stopped the only person who could have saved him. Ken Travis, his agent and a trained nurse, watched helplessly unable to reach his boss because of the packed crowd. The boy had been ignored in the panic of Julian's death. He and his sister, the blond, had dashed into the outer annexe where they were getting dressed when Travis found them. They were dragged into the centre of the cave whilst the group decided what to do with them.

A trial was arranged, and it was whilst the judge was being selected, that the police party joined the group. The batons came into play immediately. When the chastened party were properly subdued, the body of Julian Ross was bagged. Of the people arrested, there were three MPs, and several senior civil servants from the Home and Foreign Offices. The police refused to allow any of the party to dress. They were placed directly into the police vans, and taken by arrangement, to West End Central police station for charging.

The clothing from the changing room was all collected, sorted and searched, disclosing all sorts of interesting finds including several memory sticks of information illegally copied, an offence under the Official Secrets Act.

The results of the sting were impressive. The bulk of the people concerned may not have been charged with anything, but none of them survived in positions of trust. The mass resignation of so many would normally have caused raised eyebrows in the press. With commendable discretion the Civil Service closed ranks and kept the whole thing under wraps, releasing the final few personnel in dribs and drabs over a period of time, to save their departure from causing comment.

The last casualty in the British debacle was the deputy Director of MI-6. Arthur Wilson. His demise had been stage managed by Sheila Davenport personally, with the delicacy of a surgeon. The Director was not famed for his brains or his tact, and so, when the first hints were given like bait to lead him to the right conclusion, he snapped them up avidly.

There was an inevitable build from step to step. How did Arthur Wilson gather the information with which he blighted the prospects of Kelly Martin? Why did he not advise the Director of the reason for his support of Said Ali in his attempts to obtain weapons for supply to terrorist organisations?

His belated story of an attempted sting to follow the weapons to their destination fell on deaf ears. Documents supplied by the Coven testified to his further efforts to cover up shortcomings in equipment supplied to British Forces overseas, and the subsequent supply of the equipment concerned to units facing the British's own men.

The final blow came from evidence of his close association with Julian Ross, the disgraced, deceased, former MP. There was ample evidence to charge Wilson with several offences that would result in him never leaving prison alive. The ways of the service could not permit the washing of its dirty linen in public, so Arthur Wilson was permitted to resign.

As he left the building for the last time Arthur Wilson turned and looked back with a sneer at the building that had housed him for a major part of his life. He was unaware of the presence of the small Asian man wandering along the road aimlessly. Wilson waved at a taxi but it ignored him. He started walking west along the riverside swinging his umbrella jauntily, deciding where he would spend the next part of his life. The sharp blow on his leg caused him to stop and look down to see what had caused it. As he bent over, the Asian took advantage of his momentary distraction to nudge the bent figure further into the direction of the pavement edge, causing him to stumble into the path of a speeding van. The body of Arthur Wilson was flung into the air by the force of the impact. He had time to know that his retirement package was complete, before blackness.

The item was short and succinct. The accidental death was announced of the deputy Director of MI6 who was struck by a passing vehicle when he stumbled and lost his balance crossing the road outside the South Bank Offices of MI-6. Mr Wilson was a bachelor without any surviving family. The vehicle had not stopped.

David O'Neil

Chapter Twenty-five

The United States of America has for years been regarded as a place where everything is available, provided you have the money. Comments, like knowing the cost of everything and the value of nothing, are used to refer to the nation as a whole, but like all generalisations, it was not a true picture.

The cynics may delight in castigating the security services, seeing conspiracies in all directions, but those who really are aware of what goes on have a different opinion. Michael Brooks had been part of that world for many years. He was aware of the shortcomings of the system, and had nearly fallen victim to it on more than one occasion. Now his brief was to protect the system and this he was determined to do.

COMCO's hold on the government contract was by no means as secure as it had once been. This latest attempt to grasp the big prize would make its position much more secure and give it the opportunity to garner profit from sources hitherto beyond its current scope.

Now, there is nowhere a more puritanical body than the US Senate when faced with corruption in a public enquiry. That was the aim of Michael Brooks.

Stage one of the new assault on COMCO was the cleaning out of their bank account once more. Peter Davis had arranged matters differently this time. Working in conjunction with Patsy, the Geek, instead of the direct removal of funds, they had devised a scheme to rob Peter to pay Paul. It was a basically simple plan, When Peter took a half million from the current account. Patsy immediately transferred a like amount in from one of the several ancillary accounts. Peter's half million would be placed in a holding account. He then removed one million from the current account, which Patsy replaced with a half million. The instantaneous transfers were repeated with increasing sums until the holding account was standing at $50,000,000. At that point the holding account was cleared. The current account was still in funds, though some of the outlying accounts were looking a little sad.

This operation was continued over three days, by which time the intruders had stripped the finances of the company for the second time. The financial raid netted in excess of $2 billion, still in limbo travelling the electronic highways of the international money markets. The real effect of this operation, apart from funding the fight against the criminal organisation, forced the use of unlaundered cash by the COMCO group.

As Patsy, the Geek, explained to Michael Brooks, "This time they know that they have been ripped off and they will move heaven and earth to try to find who has arranged it. We have to make sure that if we are caught, it has been worth it!"

Of the branches of COMCO throughout the country the major depots were located in New York, Los Angeles and Chicago.

The US of team of Secure Inc., had, of course, managed to prevent the assassination of the President. Unfortunately though the President was aware that the attempt had taken place, and who was responsible for his security at the time, he was not convinced that the agency carrying out the operation was part of the attempt. He had more or less accepted that it was the work of an individual team, possibly funded by one of the many enemies currently to be found throughout the world. The popularity of the United States at present was at a low ebb and the brief sympathy following the events of 9/11 was no longer to be felt. Thus Reagents Inc. was just a part of the COMCO group, not regarded as a danger to the security of the country.

The Secure Inc agents had been collating evidence for some time on the deficiencies, and the actual treason, of the Reagent group. The CIA and DEA had both been involved in cover-ups caused by using Reagents to conceal their part in certain, unattributed operations. This did not make it any easier to obtain the proof. None of the agencies employed wished to reveal their mistakes by publicising their failures.

On the transport front things were a little more hopeful. Several men had been inserted in key positions in the transport system. Promising information was beginning to filter back to the investigating team, in spite of the operators tightening up their security in expectation of receiving the transportation and distribution contract for the US Army.

Michael Brooks was in consultation with John in UK and Mark Foster in Dearborn, over the video link. While he suspected the trucking company would be keeping a low profile during the run up to the Senate enquiry, he also realised that the driving force of COMCO was greed. Despite the losses the company had suffered, he could not believe that they would cease operations. Two areas produced the big money needed to replace the lost funds: drugs and weapons.

Informed opinion within TOT was that the financial losses experienced by COMCO had caused the formerly covert presence of the criminal elements in the company to raise their profile and take more control of everyday operation.

The previous success of the group had been possible because it had been run by professionals: experts, who had expanded the business using strictly business methods, which, while by no means always ethical, were still within the bounds of legality. With the increasing interest of the criminal elements on the board the company profile was changing. The descent into criminality was becoming more and more obvious to the watchers from Trans Ocean Trading.

The everyday operations of running drugs over the border, and bringing in illegal immigrants were still occurring. Secure Inc agents in the border area were keeping an especially sharp eye out for smuggling operations. All their contacts were being encouraged to produce information.

The results so far were disappointing. It seemed as if they had either slowed down or stopped all movements' of illicit goods. There were still people demanding drugs, still prostitutes on the streets and still workers needed for the truck farms of Southern California. The supplies for all these things had to stop whilst the company found out what was going on.

The temporary cancellation of the cross-border traffic caused problems for the watchers too. The expected proof of illegal operations was not, at the moment, forthcoming.

At a meeting in the COMCO Headquarters in Chicago, Marcello De Angelis CEO, was not happy. The smartly dressed man seated across the desk was the main object of his anger.

"Explain to me now. How, after all the expense and bullshit we had over this sort of thing two years ago, how did it happen again?"

"We have no idea at present. Whoever did it is an expert!"

"You are supposed to be an expert. How could you let this happen?"

The man spread his hands and shrugged his shoulders. He was terrified.

De Angelis looked over to the man leaning on the wall in the corner of the office. A nod and the man tapped the terrified accountant on the shoulder, causing him to jump.

"Out!" the man said, and the accountant hurriedly got up and gladly left the office. He called into his office, picked up his coat and briefcase and went home. On the way he decided, he wanted no more of this job. It had been good to start with. The money was fabulous, but after the first financial adjustments it had all begun to get difficult.

The second loss was too much. He feared for his life. It wasn't his fault. He had done nothing wrong. He set the financial policies. Someone else carried out the work. He wasn't a computer expert. That was a young man's job.

He drove back to his apartment and gathered the bags that he had kept packed ever since the first money loss. The most important bag contained not only his laptop computer with the company accounts, but also two DVDs with copies of all the transactions over the last year. In his car as he drove down through Illinois to the Michigan border, Barry Rodgers, erstwhile accountant for the biggest corporation in the shipping industry of America, became the most wanted man in America.

At 55 years, Barry had a lot of life behind him, but he was hoping to have a lot of life ahead of him. If he stayed with the company, he felt his chances were slim.

The road was long and straight and it suddenly occurred to him that his car was not only known but also tagged in case of theft, standard procedure with this type of Mercedes. He had to dispose of it quickly, but how, where? He looked at the Satnav. The next town had an airfield, mainly for private and local traffic. It would have to do.

Another idea came to mind. He thought about it while he negotiated the turn off the I-90 to the little town of Marshall, Michigan. The airport at Brooks Field was just outside the town to the south.

Barry stopped in the car park in the centre of town. Collecting his bags he stepped out of the car and locked it. Looking around to see he was not observed, he placed the key in the exhaust pipe and walked away. In the train station he placed his bags in a locker and found a payphone. Using his phone credit card he called the local Mercedes agent in Battle Creek. Giving them the car registration number and location, he asked them to collect the car and deliver it to the COMCO Headquarters in Chicago. He paid for the service with his company credit card. Then he went round all four banks and withdrew cash from each one collecting forty thousand dollars in all, which he packed into a brief case purchased at the local Woolworths.

He collected his bags and called the air charter company at Brooks Field. Still using the company credit card he ordered a plane to take him to Detroit the next morning. Still on the phone he booked a room for the night at the Hampton Inn, once again paying with the company card.

He boarded the Chicago train westbound to South Bend where he left the train and took a taxi to the Marriot Hotel. The taxi dropped him off outside the hotel and he paid the driver with a $20.00 bill, to include the tip. When the cab drove off he entered the hotel and left his bags with the concierge while he had dinner in the restaurant. When he collected his bags from the concierge he caught a taxi to town. On the way he changed his mind and went to the airport, arriving just in time to walk on to the late Delta flight to Atlanta. In the toilet of the aircraft he carefully shredded the credit cards in the name of Barry Rodgers, both company and personal. He realised that he had burned his boats. They would never let him live if they caught him now. So he had to find a way to protect himself.

Chapter Twenty-six

Elsewhere the movement of arms and ammunition was a multi-million dollar enterprise. It could not be stopped overnight.

The British raid had provided information on the international organisation, though without implicating the USA specifically. A particular idiosyncrasy of the United States Senate is that the evidence given to them was only taken seriously if it affected the United States specifically. With a case based on direct wrongdoing in America, the British evidence would be taken into account. On its own it would not be enough.

After two weeks with nothing, the breakthrough came. A container of equipment for the oil pipeline in Alaska had been tagged and searched discreetly. It was found to contain explosives, mace and containers of Sarin nerve gas. In addition there were Russian AK47's and the ammunition to go with them.

The on-shipment of these goods was to Seattle for consignment to Anchorage, Alaska. The Indonesian cargo ship scheduled to pick up the consignment was on the list held by US Customs as suspect.

Michael Brooks sat in the office of Victor Bonetti waiting for the man to return. The gum-chewing receptionist propped her leg on the desk and started painting her toenails through the gap in her open-toed shoes. The operation entailed the display of her stocking clad legs all the way up to her short skirt. The fact that she was showing all this off to a complete stranger caused her no apparent embarrassment. Michael did notice her glance sideways at him as she adjusted her position.

He grinned and picked up the paper and started to read the article on the front page.

The phone rang. The receptionist picked it up on the third ring. "Yeah!" She said round her wad of gum. She listened for a moment, and then jerked her head at Michael." Go in." She put the phone down and swung her legs off the desk with a flourish, grinned at him, turned to her computer screen and began typing.

Michael silently applauded the show and entered the office. The man at the desk was smartly dressed and had the untypical look of a lawyer in a Brooke's Brother's suit, white shirt and subdued grey/blue tie, neat gold cuff links, and carefully arranged hair dark, with a touch of grey. The voice matched the appearance. "How can I help you, councillor?"

"I have a problem with a transport company that is involved in treason against the United States. The cargo being shipped is capable of killing thousands of people. But the real problem is not this current cargo. It's the possibility that the company concerned is in a position to take over the entire transport and travel arrangements for the US Army."

"What do you want me to do about it?"

"I want you to monitor this cargo throughout its journey across the country. If it stops for any reason I want to know about it. If it is opened at any time I want to be told, and if anyone takes anything from the container I want to know! Why do I want this? I am a patriot. I don't have a problem with private enterprise unless it allows foreigners to hurt this country. Anyone who smuggles weapons to terrorists is a traitor as far as I am concerned. I came to you because you are the boss of the Truckers' Union and I have no doubts about your loyalty to the United States."

Michael had done his homework. The man before him was an ex-Marine, a Captain with the Silver Star awarded for bravery in the Gulf War.

Victor Bonetti looked at Michael steadily for a few minutes. "You're talking about COMCO United Trucking, I presume?"

"Exactly, we caught their British company with their pants down, but that's in England. To stop them we'll need to get something on them here!"

Bonetti pressed a button on his desk. The door opened and the receptionist came in, still looking gorgeous but without the gum. "Sarah, please take Mr Brooks for lunch, while I make some arrangements. Be back by 2.00 pm!"

"Certainly, Sir." The cultured voice was a surprise to Michael who rose, shook the outstretched hand offered to him by Bonetti, and followed the elegant back of Sarah out of the office.

Lunch was interesting. Elsewhere in the same building they sat in a small dining room overlooking the dock area. They were served with a seafood cocktail, followed by a fillet mignon, medium rare, with crème brulee to follow. There was a fine Margaux to accompany the steak. The coffee to follow was a perfect finish to an excellent meal.

The conversation was interesting too. Sarah was a graduate of Vassar, and daughter of one of Michael's former partners from the law firm he had once headed. Far from being the rather sluttish person she had played initially in the office, she was cultured and erudite. Playing the dumb broad was an act to protect her boss from unwanted visitors. She had recognised Michael the moment he walked in and took great delight in playing her role for his benefit. Michael was amused, especially when he thought of what her father's reaction to the scene would have been. Her father had always struck Michael as being a pompous ass.

Back at the office they were met by Victor and another man, introduced as Ben Speight. Ben would be the liaison between the Union and Secure Inc. He would co-ordinate surveillance of the cargo throughout its transit from Baltimore to Seattle. United Trucking was not popular with the independent truckers throughout the country. The bully boy tactics employed to grab business had put several small companies out of business. Ben was confident that liaison could be arranged with the Secure Inc bases throughout the country. He had contacted several of his contacts across the country to ensure the container was not lost en route. Meanwhile Secure Inc swung into action with chase cars and ambush groups situated strategically across the country.

Michael did not mention that the surveillance was being maintained by Secure Inc as well as the Union men. The main concern was that, in its journey cross-country, the container would be emptied of its lethal contents, for use in the United States.

George Washington Harris was on the move with two helicopter teams of troopers, first to Columbus, Ohio, to a small private landing field, awaiting the arrival of the truck after its first 400 miles. The helicopters were refuelled immediately so that they were available for instant take-off if required. The company had men out watching and quietly enquiring of local contacts for any clue about the possible fate of the container, or at least its contents. The whole organisation was committed to the task of taking the COMCO operation out of the field. Known COMCO agents were being shadowed wherever possible. Working on the principle that the container might indeed be destined for onward shipment to Alaska, it still begged the question:- what possible use would anyone in Alaska have for Sarin? It was in fact consigned to an obscure oil field support company based out on the tundra, supposedly exploring for a suitable location for a minor field storage site.

A report came in while they were still listening to the departure schedule from the agents based at Wheeling, on the Ohio River. There was a gathering group of survivalists so-called, assembling at a service area next to the Highway, on the western side of the city. They had forklifts and four box vans parked. Also it appeared they had biohazard suits which made the agents believe there was a link between the gathering and the container passing through.

An urgent amendment to the message came in within minutes of the original. The personnel were not ordinary survivalists. They all appeared to be of Middle Eastern origin. The word was sent to Michael Brooks who was co-ordinating the operation from Dearborn.

In accordance with orders, GW Harris took the entire force at his command to Wheeling, the journey taking just over an hour due to the detour needed to avoid early detection by the target force. He deployed his men in loose formation in the woods behind the service area and sent scouts to establish the situation before he moved in. Master Sergeant Wally Walker edged forward to the low growth beside the service area, cursing the litter of plastic bags and bottles lying around on the ground. He indicated to Trooper Pete Collins to move further round to cover the area shielded by one of the box trucks parked in the area, whispering into the communication bead, telling him to keep his head down and report what he could see.

GWs communicator buzzed quietly. He answered, then acknowledged the message and passed his orders to the other men in his party. Then he slowly rose to his feet and crept forward to the truck. There was no one in the cab. He opened the door carefully and climbed in. Crawling across the seat keeping his head low, he peered out of the corner of the side window. There were about twenty men scattered around the area. The entrance was blocked with flashing barriers normally used for road works. Most of the men were wearing high visibility clothing generally worn by road maintenance staff. Two yellow forklifts were parked next to their carrier on the far side of the area. There were trees growing, partly obscuring the view of the highway, though the noise of passing traffic and glimpses of vehicles could be seen through the trees.

Four of the men were grouped together talking earnestly. The biggest of the four stepped back and threw his hands up in disgust. He turned away and called to several of the others scattered about the area. As they gathered around him he spoke with great emphasis. The group broke up and started to load up the forklifts. The other three men started to shout. They rushed over to the forklifts and pulled the men moving them away. There was more shouting. And angry voices and suddenly the shooting started. The big man shot two of the men who were stopping his men moving the forklifts. Answering shots began to hit others and suddenly everyone was shooting. In less than three minutes there was no one left standing.

George Washington Harris looked on in amazement. He spoke to his men to keep out of it, stay back, in fact, to withdraw for the moment. When the shooting stopped George slid out of the cab of the lorry, and reached for his cell phone. He called 911 and reported the shooting without giving his name.

In a small office in the tower block that was the headquarters of COMCO in New York, a group of four men discussed the problem of moving a container from Baltimore to Seattle.

The smartly dressed man at the head of the table raised the question they were all thinking about. "What the hell is going on with this container? We have passed dozens of similar parcels through, without trouble. So what's different about this one?"

The equally well-dressed man named Cameron-Smith, thought for a few moments before replying. "For some reason word has got out to the lunatic fringe that the container has serious goodies on board."

The heavyset man in the off-the-shelf sports-jacket and button down shirt, Kempinski by name, one time trucker and enforcer for the Union, put his thoughts in. "We've had a leak somewhere in the shipping office. I am working on it, but it will take time!"

The last of the four listened and, when they all looked at him, he shrugged his Armani clad shoulders. "My guys are out there doing their jobs. But we have a problem from another source. I've been getting vibes about another outfit, maybe in the same business, which is butting into our turf and getting jobs that Reagents should be getting. This, added to the competition from Trans Ocean in the shipping field, is causing some anxiety in the boardroom. As you may know we are bidding for the contract to carry the US Army. We don't need problems now so let's keep this under wraps. Just now the container is only someone's goods being carried by us as common carriers. Let's keep it that way. Any sign of problems, change the route. Let's avoid difficulties all the way to Seattle."

Kempinski lifted his hand. "Did no one tell you? The container is shipped and owned by our COMCO subsidiary Carr, Armitage Et Cie, of Toulon, and the contents are listed as Eco survey equipment. If anyone opens that container it could be disastrous for the company and the people involved. There is a consignment of Sarin in there. Opened wrongly, or carelessly not only the guys on the spot but also anyone downwind for possibly several miles will die. Within a city area we could be talking thousands!"

"If the word gets out, every nut case and crazy outfit in the country will be after that container. And the word is apparently out. So what can we do about it? Somehow we have to take the pressure off!"

The four sat in silence. Kempinski got to his feet and walked to the side table. "Coffee, anyone?"

Cameron–Smith sat in his office several floors below the meeting room, a plan evolving in the back of his mind. Supposing the container was hi-jacked by his own men, or at least under their supervision. It could be quietly disposed of without any repercussions. The more he thought about it the better the plan sounded. He wondered if he should discuss this with the other three. Perhaps not, he decided. The suit at the top of the table would probably chicken out, though Kempinski would go for it. He picked up the phone and called Kempinski, putting the suggestion to him. As he thought the big ex-trucker took up the idea straight away, and from his experience was able to suggest a possible site for the hijack. He arranged to meet outside the office in a quiet corner of the diner down by the fish market.

The first suggestion by Kempinski, Wheeling, West Virginia, Cameron-Smith discarded immediately. He passed on the information from the evening news of the gun battle at the service area there. He then asked what route the truck was taking. On learning it was passing through Des Moines and Council Bluffs, suggested somewhere between the two. He pointed out there were airfields at both places for the advance placement of men and the distance involved near 800 miles approx 24 hours driving time, if the two man team kept going. Cameron-Smith realised they would need time to set up ambush.

If the drivers had been arranged by Reagents there would have been no problem, but these men were straight truckers used by Bannington's United Trucking. They would have to be disposed of. He explained that they would need another truck and container to replace the hi-jacked set.

Kempinski pulled out his cell phone and punched in a number. He growled instructions to whoever answered, and nodded to Cameron-Smith. The truck and trailer with container would be on its way to Des Moines from Chicago within 30 minutes. It would park at Des Moines and wait instructions. He passed over a business card with a call sign written on the back. The card belonged to Kempinski. The call sign was the truck driver's CB handle.

The two men separated amicably and Cameron-Smith called his agent in Des Moines, and instructed him to locate the best spot for intercepting the target truck. He then rang Chicago office and ordered an assault group to be prepared for his collection by 8.00 am next morning. He would collect them at the Gary, Chicago airport. The equipment needed should be loaded into a parcel van and driven directly into the C130 that would be at the airport waiting. Make sure the van had a CB radio.

The arrival at the airport at Gary went without a hitch. The C130 was on the apron ramp down waiting, when the parcel van arrived. The driver drove straight up the ramp which immediately started closing. Inside the aircraft a big man with a webbing gun belt strapped round his waist, stood waiting. He gathered the men from the van into a group, and hooked them up to headphones. His brief was short and succinct. Lift the truck and bring the container to the plane, sending the decoy truck onwards to Seattle. Deliver the container by plane. Having completed the brief the big man settled down to sleep for the rest of the short flight to Des Moines.

At Davenport a truck waited. The container had the same markings as the target vehicle. It was awaiting the call from the raiding party to come forward and take over from the target truck.

The shadowing team watched the switch take place. To their surprise the team of men who took over the container were all dark skinned and very professional. They then followed the goods to the airport at Des Moines. It was an inspiration that caused the pursuit team to blow two of the starboard tyres on the C130, making it impossible for it to take off. This did give them time to arrange to shadow the C130 when it resumed its flight.

When the C 130 took off certain things had happened. The loadmaster was no longer the big man who was on board when it left Gary. His replacement was a small busy man, whose orders were obeyed without question.

Chapter Twenty-seven

The tracking team from Secure Inc had been observing the progress of the target truck and so far they had watched it make two deliveries, carefully photographed, one at Danville, the other just outside Peoria. Both deliveries consisted of guns and ammunition only. The Sarin remained in the vehicle. The deliveries confirmed the theory that the container was never intended for delivery to Alaska with its current cargo. The only question was where would the Sarin be dropped off?

Under the command of George Washington Harris, the troop withdrew to the helicopters and moved on to Des Moines, Iowa to wait for the next move.

The truck moved down the highway smoothly. There was little heavy traffic to slow it down. The trail car was in fact at least half a mile back, though the lead car was only three hundred yards in front, at the moment apparently held back by a support truck in front of both of them.

This truck was fitted out as a control room with full communications and video and radar coverage of the target and the surrounding area. It was the communication truck that picked up the intercepting vehicle first.

G. W. Harris was in the air flying west from Wheeling. The news services were full of the shootout at Wheeling, but GW was unhappy about the progress so far. Accordingly he refuelled and continued with both helicopters as soon as he could. When the warning of the interceptor came in from the communication truck, the helicopter was seven minutes away from the scene. With the truck and helicopters closing all the time, it was soon possible for George to scan the area for the interception.

The suspect vehicle picked out by the radar was what looked like an off-road vehicle and trailer it was packed with several men and weapons. The target truck pulled up at Danville and unloaded part of the cargo into the trailer. Money changed hands and both vehicles departed in their own directions. GW sent instructions to the other helicopter crew to resume shadowing the truck to cover the next delivery if necessary.

While the trailing team and helicopter continued to follow the target truck. George and his men followed the off-road vehicle. They came up to the destination near Tuscola. They landed just over a mile away behind the low hills in the area. George and his team took to the woods and skirmished down to the small farm where the target vehicle had been parked. They lay in cover watching the movements of the group of men and women at the farm.

There were ten people in all, four women and six men. It was possible to see them when they sat down to eat. The loaded trailer was still outside. The troopers approached the house carefully keeping low, trying to keep below the level of the windows. The trailer was unhitched by two of them, who unlocked the brake and rolled it away from the house while the other troops waited, holding their breath, until the trailer was out of sight of the house. The two men returned and joined their comrades.

On GWs signal they entered the house, front and rear, guns up and ready. The surprise was complete. The people sitting round the table eating had no chance to react.

The leader of the group turned to the sergeant. "What the hell you doin' bringing a nigger in here. This is my house and I don't allow any trash here without my permission." He rose to his full height of 6ft 7inches towering over the sergeant's 5ft.10inches. The sergeant hit him in the belly with the butt of his SMG, causing him to double up with a gasp.

"Sit down, redneck!" the sergeant said quietly. He wasn't impressed. He turned to GW, saluted and said, "Sir, what are your orders? Sir."

GW grinned. The sergeant was rubbing it in. "Disarm this bunch and carry on as instructed, Sergeant."

The sergeant stamped his boots together and saluted smartly. Then spun around and ordered the men to carry on.

The men proceeded to disarm the men at the table. The women could have been a problem but the two women troopers managed efficiently, recovering guns from the women, including one from a holster located on the inside leg of one young girl. Talking later between themselves, the searchers admitted they had never seen a holster like that before. They both thought it would be quite uncomfortable, but a good place to hide a weapon from male searchers.

Having disarmed the prisoners, GW questioned the people individually and managed to discover that the guns had been purchased by arrangement with their regular supplier. A man from Chicago, named Chapel who gave the itinerary of the truck and had the driver briefed.

Interestingly the arrangements had been made over a month ago. The goods had been removed from the rear of the truck as if already arranged in its delivery order! It took three hours to question them all and it wasn't until they got to the last prisoner that the really interesting discovery was made.

The last man was the big loud mouth who had called GW a nigger. His attitude was surly when he was finally brought forward. Despite his manner it was obvious he was genuine in his loyalty to the United States. Having served in Vietnam his anti-negro attitude was largely bluff to impress the others. In fact as he admitted privately, he had served with Afro-Americans in 'Nam and had no real problems with them. He apologised to GW. On a hunch GW mentioned that the arms suppliers also were supplying Muslim extremists in the United States, who were openly boasting of their joy at the bombing of the World Trade Centre, and the 9/11 air strikes.

The man, who called himself Bart, on hearing this, gave vent to his feelings on the subject which were not really printable. He gave a complete rundown on the whole system of supply through which he obtained his material. It turned out that it was regulated from a Chicago phone number, connected to a man named Chapel. An interesting thing came out when he remembered an occasion when he realised that the number they used was obviously being switched through another switchboard. On an earlier occasion the call had been answered by an operator who said "Good morning Co"………. The phone then clicked onto the familiar line used by Chapel. He now noticed the click on every call they made.

GW had an idea. "Call up this Chapel guy. Tell him you've been hijacked by a bunch of Feds, who seemed to know everything."

Bart looked at him. "You must be crazy. They'll find you and kill you all!"

GW grinned. "That would be a first," he said. "Let's do it!"

Bart shrugged his shoulders and picked up the phone, GW put his hand on the phone stopping the action while he said to the sergeant, "Tape it!"

The sergeant produced a small plug that he clamped to the phone, the other end of the wire plugged into the hand Satnav. "O.K. go now."

Bart carried on dialling the number. GW put the extension phone to his ear and was able to hear the phone being picked up.

"Chapel!"

"Hi, Mr Chapel," Bart sounded pissed." Some son of a bitch has been talking. I've just been ripped off by a bunch of Feds. They took everything!"

"Feds, how do you know they were Feds? Did they show I.D.? Where are you calling from? Are you in jail?"

"Naw, they didn't arrest us. They just took all our weapons and said they would deal with us some other time."

"What are you? Stupid? Feds would have arrested you. They must be private. You've been hi-jacked."

"So how did they know where to come? Someone has been talking. My people are all clean. What about yours? Who else knew about this place?"

"No one here knows where your place is. Not even I know. So the leak is not from this end!"

"Then they must have followed us from the delivery. Who else knows about the deliveries? These guys were ready with all the firepower they needed. They had to know in advance where the pick-up was. So who knew?" Bart was convincing and the anger in his voice was genuine.

Chapel didn't answer for a few moments, then he said, "Leave it with me. I'll ask around, and come back to you. If this is from my end, I'll replace the weapons."

The sergeant nodded at GW, and GW nodded to Bart. He said. "O.K. I'll wait to hear from you." and put the phone down.

GW said. "Where?"

The Sergeant replied, "Chicago" and he read off the address of a building in the City Centre.

GW spoke to Bart carefully. "You have done a service for your country. I will remember it when I report on this incident. However if I find out that you have warned anyone about this, I will come back and personally cause you pain and grief. Do you understand?"

Bart looked belligerently back at GW. "I made a deal. I keep my word. No one here will talk, but I promise you, if you come back here with anything less than the United States Army, I will cause you pain and grief, buster!"

The troupe left the clearing, towing the trailer of weapons. At the helicopter, leaving two men to drive the vehicle, GW and the remainder of the troopers boarded and took off to connect up with the other helicopter, shadowing the truck.

The information passed to the Dearborn office was processed. The address was verified as that of the COMCO HQ in Chicago. The calls were being diverted to a smaller office downtown where the distribution was co-ordinated throughout the mid-west region. This was through a company called Tempo Trading, who acted as a call centre for several different operations, all of whom were owned by the same company.

The Secure Inc office in Dearborn arranged a quiet visit. Little information was found but a complete list of staff was copied with addresses and surveillance was arranged for the man identified as Chapel, though that was not the name on the door of his apartment.

Barry Rodgers relaxed for the first time in days. The California sunset laid a bleeding line along the horizon. He sipped wine from his glass of Zinfandel, from the vineyard not 50 miles from where he sat. The beachfront apartment was a property that had belonged to his deceased ex-wife. It had not been transferred to his name when he had inherited it. He smiled wryly. He hadn't wanted a divorce. It had been her idea. They had both made wills when they married over twenty years ago in the expectation that they would have a family. It had been the sensible thing to do. Sadly they discovered that they could not have children. He always thought that that was the reason she eventually left him. The real tragedy was, that while she was returning from her visit to Vegas with her divorce in her hand, a dump truck from a building site just south of Barstow lost its brakes and crushed her Jaguar beneath its six foot tyres.

She had not changed her will, so it all reverted to Barry: two houses, this apartment in Redwood City and a sizeable fortune in bonds and stocks.

Barry realised that there was no way he could continue to use his own name. He was studying the information on the disks scrolling through the index of files to see if there was anything he could use to cover his tracks. It was a curious coincidence that he recognised the name Michael Brooks, apparently a one-time target, whose name for some reason had been removed from the hit list. That was part of a three-month recording that Barry had made to prove, if necessary, systematic illegal activity. The brief resume of the career of Michael Brooks included, with the original hit order mentioned, his link with the protection of the President. His later connection with Trans Ocean Trading International was noted, with the address, in Rosas, of the company HQ. The hit was postponed not actually cancelled, which indicated that Brooks was still listed as a threat.

In his position as senior accountant Barry was well aware of the threat Trans Ocean posed to the legitimate operation of COMCO. It persuaded him to take the risk of contacting Michael Brooks, for help and possibly protection.

The email addressed to Michael was forwarded to Dearborn from Rosas. The phone number was for a payphone in Eureka in Northern California at 12.00 pm local time, for the following day. The message merely said, 'I believe you wish to speak to me.' The message was unsigned.

If for no other reason than curiosity, Michael decided to call the number. As insurance he called John Murray, explained about the message, and asked if he could be at Eureka at the time to keep an eye on things: perhaps identify the person on the end of the phone.

At Richmond, John was free at the time and decided to drive up to Eureka, taking Carol with him. Gabrielle was now six months pregnant and spending most of her time working in the office with Brian Ascher at the yard. She was avoiding the effort involved in sailing for the sake of the baby. Carol had been recruited on a part-time basis, to operate in Gabrielle's place if required.

John and Carol arrived in Eureka at 10 am. There was a hint of rain in the air as they drove into the centre of the small town. They identified the public phone which was located outside the sport hall.

There was a cafe on the other side of the street, so John settled down at a table where he could keep watch while Carol strolled across to the phone, the end in the row of phones. She picked up the handset and slipped the tiny microphone behind the board on which the phone was mounted.

"Can you hear me, John?" She said.

Across the road John nodded, without looking at her. Carol put the handset back, strolled over to the café and joined John at his table.

Barry arrived at the phone ten minutes before the appointed time. He drove up in a hired Mercedes and parked at an empty meter. He looked around the area seeking a familiar face, and found none. He himself was no longer the neat accountant of three weeks ago. His hair was now longer and wilder. The moustache altered the shape of his face and the golden tan was in sharp contrast to the pale, sickly skin that had been the price of his job as accountant at COMCO. Now dressed in a sports shirt and tan chinos, he was not the man who had left Chicago. At the sound of the phone ringing he lifted the receiver and listened. John heard him answer.

"Yes, I thought you might be interested in the record of the last two years trading of a company you may know of."

Brooks answer could not be heard.

Barry Rodgers continued. "COMCO," he said. "I am in need of a safe place to stay. The company will know now that I have escaped and they will be looking for me." There was a note of panic in his voice.

John's cell phone rang. "John, collect the man on the phone, discreetly!"

John nodded to Carol, and she crossed the road to the area beside the phones. As she neared the man, a Crown Victoria saloon car drew up with a squeal of tyres.

Things happened fast. Barry dropped the phone and turned to run. Two men got out of the car and drawing guns grabbed at him. John left the café at a run across the road. Carol kicked the nearest man in the back. He collapsed in agony to the ground, dropping his gun. The second man started to turn lifting his gun. John struck him with a straight arm punch to the throat. He dropped, gagging to the ground.

Barry stood, stunned by the speed of events. John took him by the arm to his car. Carol ran to their car and drove off, followed by Barry and John in Barry's Mercedes.

"What was that all about?" John asked him.

Barry did not answer. He just sat frozen to his seat, saying nothing.

John explained quietly that Barry was safe now, under the protection of Secure Inc who would keep him safe in their Headquarters in Dearborn. There they would consider the possibility of either relocating him in Europe or if he wished elsewhere in the world, but first to Dearborn to debrief.

They drove to Barry's house and collected all his belongings. From there they drove to San Francisco's International Airport, where the Gulfstream collected them and took them to Dearborn, and the haven of TOT Headquarters.

The evidence given by Barry to the Michigan State Attorney was critical to the case against COMCO. The continued operation of the company, after the disclosures and prior to the Senate Committee hearing, indicated that the money laundering aspects of the company were still in full operation, albeit temporarily.

In the circumstances it became a race between the State Prosecutor and the final closing down of the COMCO operation. The Trans Ocean analysts decided that the only reason the company continued to function was to launder money already within the system. That money would only be legally available if a prosecution was mounted whilst the company was still trading. The alternative would be the illegal draining of the company funds by Peter Davis.

Chapter Twenty-eight

The C130 flew direct to Seattle. The transfer of the goods from the truck had been observed and GW and his crew were able to be at Seattle by the time the C130 arrived. The crew within the big transport drove out in the van that had been carried from Chicago. Their leader exchanged the necessary paperwork with the handling agents without comment.

As they left the airport the shadowing group followed in a three-car trail party. As GW expected the destination of the van was the waterfront, what he didn't expect was that the van would evade the trail party. One minute it was there then it was gone. The worry was that the content of the van was suspected to include highly lethal materials. Since their only clue was the link to the Indonesian freighter, GW made for the docks.

The van appeared in the view of car three. The trail group had split-up to cover as much of the docks as possible. It was pure luck that the van was spotted. The ship they were contacting was in fact a 120 foot motor yacht moored alongside in the inner yacht marina. It seemed the story of the Indonesian freighter was part of the fog of misdirection that had surrounded this particular exercise. The call came from car three to GW in car one. "Keep them in sight and we'll join you shortly. Do not let them spot you. Car two you're with us."

He moved along the quay to a point where he could observe the movements on the deck of the big black yacht. With his binoculars he could see the men unloading the van very carefully. Suddenly all the men ran onto the ship. Two men dressed in protective gear lumbered down the gangway and onto the quayside. One climbed onto the van and the other stationed himself at the rear of the van, to receive the case and support it until his companion dismounted and took the other end. Between them they carried the case carefully on board the moored craft.

Within the political establishment of Washington, rumours

travel fast. COMCO was in trouble. Documents had come to light showing that the company had been involved in criminal activities. As yet no hard facts had been published but it was only a matter of time before all would be revealed.

Surprisingly one of the sources of information seemed to be the White House.

Following the investigation into the debacle over the protection of the President, the Secret Service had revealed that several of the people detailed to the assignment for the over the border task, had been found to be criminals. At least one had attempted to shoot the President personally. The evidence of the President himself was taken in this instance. It had been revealed that the men concerned had been supplied and bonded by Reagents Inc, a subsidiary of COMCO who was applying for the exclusive transport contract for the US Army.

The Washington Post headlined the dismissal of the application and the recommendation that COMCO and its subsidiaries be removed from the list of favoured tender companies.

In Dearborn Michael Brooks, visiting the US headquarters to co-ordinate the fight against COMCO, spoke to Rosas, passing on the good news to Kelly. He stressed that while the victory was significant, the battle was not over.

There was a sombre silence as the members of the Executive Board of Directors of COMCO gathered. The previous meeting of the full board had been to discuss the final details of the takeover of the transport for the US Army. At the time it had been a foregone conclusion. All the signals had been set and the right people greased. There had been no way it could go wrong. The Chairman had already decided where and when he would retire, and also with whom.

Among the group seated around the 30ft table were some of the finest legal brains in the country. Four men were rated as the most successful lobbyists on Capitol Hill. In terms of sheer business skill the board could not be faulted. As the Chairman looked around his eye rested on the group of smoothly attired men seated halfway down the table. The financial basis of the company was firmly centred on funds provided by this group. They contributed nothing to the trading operation but the capital came from them. The Chairman had not enquired about the source of their funds, merely used them.

Whilst not involving itself in the major operations of COMCO, they had been involved in many of its minor businesses. Through the unions and by employing their own nominees they actually controlled a large part of the company.

At the grass roots of the organisation was the basis of their drug distribution operation, smuggling immigrants over the borders and gun running. Money laundering was simplified because of the wide variety of businesses operated. The security operation was particularly useful because the accounting was fogged by the number of off-the-books payments needed to maintain defences against industrial espionage. This had been particularly necessary following the cash raid by unknown persons on the two occasions in the recent past.

This meeting had been called by the Chairman because of the debacle over the disastrous outcome of the US Army bid. The findings of the Senate Committee, supposedly 80% in favour of COMCO's application, had made it clear that the recent events involving the Group worldwide had decided the Committee to reject their proposed takeover of the Army movement control. Additionally they removed COMCO from the list of preferred bidders for Government contracts, until further notice. In effect, a complete disaster that had cost the company three million in sweeteners alone, and a total loss in business terms of over one billion dollars.

The Chairman opened the meeting, calling on the company accountants to report the current financial status of COMCO International.

The report was only half delivered when one of the group of money men broke in. Standing up, he said. "Let's just cut the bullshit! We got screwed over the Army deal. At the moment we've got to fall back on regular business. I vote we lay low for a while until things cool off. Then we can decide where we'll go from there. This board meeting is pointless unless there is a positive proposal for immediate action. If there are no suggestions then I vote we close the book for just now, and meet next month when we have all had time to cool off and perhaps come up with suggestions for future business."

There was a deathly silence. Such an outburst was unheard of at this level. The assembled directors looked to the Chairman for guidance.

The Chairman laughed. "Just what gives you the impression that we will still be trading next month? Have you any real idea what rejection by the Government means to a company of our stature? To trade in the markets at the level we occupy we have to depend on our name. Credit is trust, and we have effectively lost the trust of the Government.

"As we are all aware trust is easily obtained. But once lost, it's almost impossible to regain. All major companies work to be listed as preferred bidders: not so that they can trade with or for the Government, though that can be a bonus, but to establish a base line of credit for trade in general. Up until now we could be trusted. Now we can't. It's as simple as that!"

The Chairman's comments were received in silence. The professionals on the board knew exactly what the Chairman meant. Most were considering how they could sever their connections with COMCO without too much publicity and with the minimum losses.

The accountant rose to his feet once more. "My recommendation would be for the urgent trading down of the whole COMCO group. Separate the various divisions and re-establish those profitable ones in new ownership and allow them to trade at their own level. The discredited companies should be stripped and closed. The holding company, COMCO, must be dismantled and if necessary a new holding company created and allowed eventually to replace COMCO." He sat down amid a murmur of comments as the others thought over the suggestions.

The Chairman called for a vote. The accountant's suggestions were accepted and the meeting adjourned for lunch.

The group of moneymen gathered in the board room after the others had left,

"This was a sweet operation while it lasted," the man who had risen and spoken earlier commented.

"I need this company to wash money. We cannot allow the company to close for at least six months We have too much riding on it. It's going to take that long to set up something new. If we have another bank raid like the last, we are all dead. If the present money set up is closed, we will have shown the bosses that we are not amateurs." The other four men looked apprehensive. Noticing their look, the speaker continued, "Whatever we do, the company must keep trading at high level for the next six months agreed?" He looked at the others, and one by one they nodded.

The afternoon session was short. The Chairman opened the meeting with his resignation. He was followed by several of the others. The remaining directors were told by the leading money man that the new Chairman would join the reconstituted board within a week. Meanwhile the company would continue operations as before. The protests of the dissenting Directors were stilled when they read the obituary of the former Company Accountant.

In Seattle the tension was rising. The group with GW were all skilled at silent assault. Dressed as they were in their black coveralls, they boarded the moored yacht in twos and overpowered the two watchers on deck. Sending men to cover the other entrances, GW cautiously went down the companionway followed by four of his men. Finding the door where voices could be heard he put his hand on the handle. With the next man covering him he pushed the door open and stepped inside.

The room was obviously a saloon with a long table down the centre. The seven men at the table were taken completely by surprise. Two reached for weapons and died then and there from bullets from GW and his partner. The others all raised their hands. GW called in two more of the men from the passage outside. While the three others disarmed and bound the men round the table, he went to examine the pile of weapons and explosives piled at the end of the saloon.

There was no sign of the case so carefully carried aboard by the two men in protective gear.

"Where is the other case?" He asked the seated men. They all looked at him with blank faces. One of GW's men asked the question in Arabic. It was obvious that his words were recognised, but still nobody answered.

The door opened once more and one of the deck watchers came in. He whispered to GW. "Stay with this lot." He indicated two of his men. "If they move shoot them."

The others left with him as he followed the newcomer up on deck and along to the door marked engine room.

Through the door the hot breath of the idling engine greeted the men, They quickly closed the door before decending the stair toward the increasing noise of the engine room space.

As they reached the deck below, the big twin diesels hid most of the rest of the compartment. GW went low to peer past the nearest engine to see what was beyond.

In the space at the rear of the room there were the two people in protective clothing. They had opened the case and were removing green bottles from the moulded packing within the box. Beside the nearest was an open suitcase with wadding in the bottom. Placing the bottles carefully in the case side by side with wadding between them, it was apparent after the seventh bottle that there were no more to pack. The two exchanged looks. In the packing case were eight moulded places, but there were only seven bottles to be found. Shrugging he placing the packing round the seven already transferred. Then he closed the suitcase, and shut the locks.

Both stood up and with sighs of relief and pulled off the heavy gear, revealing a man and a woman, both sweating heavily.

The woman spoke raising her voice above the noise from the engine. "It should be enough, but I don't like to be screwed. They cost enough as it is."

The man said "We can deal with them afterwards. At least we know who they are."

She nodded thoughtfully in agreement, and stiffened as she felt the touch if the gun barrel in her back."Don't even think about it" said the quiet voice in her ear. "Now carefully put your guns on the floor. Gently now. GW gave them no leeway the two were ruthlessly searched and their hands bound with plasticuffs. It had been obvious to GW that they had been unaware of missing canister of Sarin gas. So he made no attempt to question them here, deciding to leave it to the experts at Dearborn.

The suitcase of Sarin was carried up to the main deck where GW called up extra transport. He then assembled the entire party on the quayside. If anyone saw them they did not attempt to interfere as the prisoners and the ordinance were loaded and driven off.

In the Captain's cabin on the boat, the papers for the port authorities were found. The small safe was unlocked by a specialist ex-SAS trooper on attachment. Trooper William Bond, known as Dublo was a specialist at many things, among them safes and doors. He studied the safe for a few moments, then reached into his pocket and removed a small piece of what appeared to be plasticine. This he kneaded and warmed in his hands. He broke it into two and attached one piece to each of the hinges. Taking a small spool of wire from another pocket he set it down, while he removed a flat box from another pocket. About the size of a cigarette box, from it came two small alloy tubes. He replaced the box then attached the tubes in series to the wire on the reel. To his fascinated audience he said "Please leave the room, chaps. This can cause some disturbance." Reluctantly the observers left the cabin while Dublo finished his preparation by inserting the two tubes into the plastic blobs on the hinges. He left the cabin walking backward unreeling the wire. Once outside behind the steel bulkhead he unlatched the separator on one end of the reel revealing a press button. "Stand by for the bang," he said before pressing the button. The bang through the half closed cabin door was disappointingly dull, a thud rather than anything else.

The result was pleasing. The door of the safe was looking drunk, sagging from the hinge side outward. Dublo reached out a gloved hand and pulled it easily away from its seating, revealing the contents of the safe untouched within.

Apart from money there was little else to show for the effort, though one document was of interest, the bill of sale for the boat. It was made out to the accountant, Barry Rogers, as a private sale.

The only other document was in Arabic. The other British trooper attached to the group was also ex-SAS. His name was Amir Khan, known as Abdul. His expert qualifications was a knowledge of Hindi, Urdu, Tamil and several other dialects of India, Iran and Iraq. He studied the document carefully. "These are instructions for blowing up the boat when the task has been accomplished; no refererence to what the task is, just a list of locations in the boat and suggestions where it should be destroyed for maximun effect if the chance arises. Boss, I think we have won a boat. What shall we do with it?"

George Washington Harris grinned. "Why do I get the idea that you fancy a cruise in the sun? On your way, Abdul, there's more work to do. To Dublo he said, "Take a quick look round the boat for demo charges etc. Take it easy and make sure. I'll see what the Boss says about disposing of this gin palace."

There were dues paid for a three-day stay for the boat which carried the name *Amun Ra* registered in Bermuda. The original name according to the bill of sale, was *Carolina Lady*.

She was described as pale grey with white superstucture, a far cry from the rather drab, black overall of her present outer décor.

On deck once more, GW passed on the news about the boat. The reply, after a half hour delay, was that the boat was at the company's disposal and that a passage crew would arrive in the morning to transfer her to San Francisco for overhaul and refurbishment. The passage crew would be led by Carol Mears and they should be there by 11am. They would arrange the handover at that time.

Chapter Twenty nine

Whilst it was not written in stone, one of the regular commitments of the incumbent President was to support of the annual St Patrick's Day rally in New York City. The preparations for the occasion were elaborate and detailed.

For the Secret Service, it was one of several nightmares that they had to deal with annually. If the weather was good it was possible that the President would accompany the Mayor of New York in the drive through the streets as part of the parade of pipe bands, floats and societies, that marked the culmination of the festivities on this favourite Saint's Day.

The group of Provisional IRA that had been involved in collecting for the cause at the time of the Easter Agreement was still living in New York. Perhaps they feared to return to Ireland or maybe they were too accustomed to the rather less inhibited, living conditions they enjoyed in the USA.

The cell had been tempted to join the criminal fraternity in the city. They had existed thus far on the contributions of the faithful. The signing of the Easter Agreement and the dissolution of the Irish protest organisations had meant that the contributions had dried up and the easy living was no more.

Henry Smith, former head of the President's personal Security Agency, was no longer persona grata at the White House. That did not mean his sources of information had dried up. The movements of the President were supposedly kept secret wherever possible. But to someone who had been in the inner circle there were ways of finding out. He had the motivation. The scheme that went so disastrously wrong in Mexico was still extant. Knowing the contract still existed, Henry Smith still needed the pension that the removal of the President would earn. With the help of the skilled assassins of the former IRA he felt it would be a reasonable possibility.

The canister of Sarin gas had been a windfall. The stealing of the case had been easy for him. The money would come in useful.

Removing one of the canisters from the case had been a spur of the moment decision.

The terrorists plan for the use of the Sarin a pointless waste of time. For anyone to believe the San Diego Naval Base, the target they had selected, would be so easily accessed, was to his mind not only stupid, it was suicidal. The threat of the use of the Sarin may well have got the men in, but the chances of ever getting out were non-existent. Lifting one of the bottles of Sarin had been sensible. After all they were going to waste anyway.

He was not entirely satisfied with the IRA as his helpers in the current engagement. The fact that their co-operation had been purchased with cash, or the promise of cash, was not as reassuring as it should be. There was no problem with loyalties. To a man they blamed the US President for his part in the Easter Agreement. They were happy to exact a little revenge for that alone. His main problem was one that many had experienced before when dealing with the IRA. They listened to the orders, and only sometimes obeyed them. That was the problem!

Because of the simplicity of the plan Henry felt it would be difficult for even the most stupid to get it wrong. The Mayor's limousine was booked into the garage for service and valeting. It would be kept in the garage until 17th when it was needed to carry the Mayor and the President to take part in the parade.

During that period the bottle would be fitted to the chassis of the car. A small hole would be drilled in the floor to allow the gas to be injected into the car. It would fill the passenger compartment but would not affect the driver who would be protected by the glass screen. The plan was that the raising of the screen would trigger the gas release. This was particularly important as the driver would be Henry Smith himself, suitably disguised of course.

It was a position that he particularly cherished. It was his plan that had gone awry in Mexico, and he had not forgiven the President for sacking him after the abortive assassination attempt.

The three major members of the IRA cell had taken the job from an intermediary, a man known to them and obviously known to the principle, Smith. Whilst they were quite happy to undertake the work, there was no way they would complete the contract without knowing who set it up.

One of the reasons they were all still alive was the care they took over each operation they undertook.

In this case the three, Patrick O'Neill, Michael Heggarty and Peter Mahon, gathered at O'Neill's apartment to discuss the project.

"Have we decided yet who is going to do the work of fitting the gas bottle?" Peter asked.

"Would you stop talking about specifics, Peter. Just remember. You never know if there is a listener!" Patrick sounded annoyed.

"Ach. This is not Armagh, Patrick. We don't have the scum breathing down our necks here in the land of the free."

Patrick grasped Peter by the lapels of his jacket and thrust his face to within six inches of Peter's.

"If you don't learn that we are always liable to be watched, you will be the death of us all one day!" He spat the words out forcefully, and let Peter's jacket loose. Peter fell back looking shocked.

Heggarty intervened,

"Calm down both of you. We'll get nowhere fighting amongst ourselves. Let's get our priorities in order. I, for one, want to know who is in charge of this little operation? So I think we'd be better concentrating on that."

The angry Patrick cooled off and Peter sat down, relieved that the atmosphere had calmed down.

Of the three, Peter was the weakest, normally content to follow the others. In Northern Ireland he had been the brother of one of the heroes, and he had been taken on and looked after for that reason. It hadn't stopped the fear he experienced every day, year after year, the terror of being targeted by the SAS or the Proddies.

As part of the US fund raising group he had started to feel safe for the first time in years. Certainly the money for the contract was attractive, but he had got used to not looking over his shoulder all the time. Now because of the contract it seemed the fear was going to start all over again.

Heggarty had several girl friends and lived in an 'Apartment Hotel' in Queens. Patrick's apartment was also in Queens, located nearby. Peter lived in Greenwich Village with his girlfriend. He had considered getting a job, and even moving to the west coast to get away from the pressure of being with his two companions who were a continual reminder of the 'Cause' that neither could ever forget.

Revenge and getting back to home ground, suitably rich of course, seemed to be all they ever bothered about. Peter shuddered at the thought of returning to the narrow streets and the harsh accents of his home. Here he was comfortable with the laid back attitudes and the company of people who talked of other things, smoked a little grass to chill out and enjoyed life.

He was brought back to reality to see both of the others were looking at him,

"What?" he said. "Did I miss something?"

"Oh. Go and make coffee!" Patrick said in disgust. Peter gladly departed for the kitchen and put the pot on.

In the apartment next door the Homeland Security Agent came in and closed the door quietly. He took off his coat and turned the heating on. His task today was simple, the same every day. 'Come to the apartment, check that the tape was running properly, pick up the used tape and see that the replacement had loaded properly'. The automatic system was virtually foolproof, but the boss always said 'better safe than sorry!' So every day George Blake came to the apartment and performed the tasks laid down.

Of late he had begun listening to see if anything interesting was going on. He flipped the switch to hear what was happening next door. The harsh Irish voices came through the loudspeakers. He left the sound on while he made instant coffee in the little kitchen. As he walked back through the door to the lounge he caught the word 'parade'. He listened and he heard the word 'contract', followed by the admonition to shut up from another speaker. "I told you before we don't know who could be listening." Another voice spoke. "Have you decided who will fix the car? Remember the glass screen must be airtight!" The first voice broke in once more. "For Christ's sake, will you both shut up. The place to talk about this is elsewhere. The contract needs just five men. We'll talk about things when we get them together at O'Malley's." The reference was to an Irish Pub, well known to the agent as a meeting place for the old IRA,on the run and staying in New York.

George had heard enough. He collected the tapes, including the current one. Having manually changed and updated the recorder, he left for the office and reported to his boss.

A lot has been written about coincidence. When it happens at the right time in the right place, quite rightly, it's worth double checking.

Captain Pete Maddox was in New York on his way to

Dearborn. He was taking a couple of days off to relax before reporting to Mark Foster on temporary assignment. Sightseeing in New York on a sunny day was a pleasant occupation that was spoiled by the sight of Patrick O'Neill, Michael Heggarty and Peter Mahon talking on the corner of the street. Pete was dressed in a black, hip-length coat and hair in need of cutting. In addition he was wearing wraparound Raybans in the March sunshine, so it was highly unlikely that he would be recognised. Especially since, when he had last seen the trio, he was in uniform overalls with cammy cream on his face looking along the barrel of a pump action Winchester.

He watched the group talking, noticing that Peter Mahon was looking uncomfortable to say the least. When they split up, Patrick and Michael going one way and Peter the other, he followed Peter north along Broadway towards Greenwich Village. Pete swiftly caught up with Peter and taking his arm he murmured in his ear. " I have a Glock in your ribs." The nudge of his knuckle was enough to convince the thoroughly frightened Peter. Pete firmly steered him into his hotel, through the lobby and into the elevator. Once there he removed his glasses, and said in a friendly voice. "What a pleasant surprise. I did not think we would ever meet again, and here we are." The elevator stopped and he pushed the cowed man out into the hall and along to his room.

He sat Peter down into a chair and sat himself, still smiling in the chair opposite.

"Well now, Peter, it must be five years since we last spoke. How time does fly. Tell me all about yourself. What are you doing in New York, and with such exalted company too?"

"Now, Mr Maddox. You have no right to make me come here I am a law abiding citizen and I have my rights you know!" He sounded hurt and indignant.

"How can you think I would make you come here? I just invited an old friend up to my room for a chat, and perhaps a drink." Pete was all smiles. "Now tell me what were you doing with Patrick O'Neill and Michael Heggarty?"

"Nothing. I just happened to see them on the street and I stopped to pass the time of day."

"Those two would only be in your company if there was something planned. So you might as well just tell me before it gets painful." Pete's soft voice hardened with the last comment Peter shivered.

In Belfast Peter Mahon has been persuaded to assist the security services in their battle with the IRA, later the Provisional IRA. His identity was protected and he survived without being found out, largely because as Pete's informant, no one else knew he existed. He made a last try to convince Pete that nothing was going on, before he caved in and told Pete everything. "Please, Mr Maddox, if I'm found out they won't just kill me. They'll kill by girlfriend here, and my mum in Ireland. You know what they're like."

Pete thought for a while. "O.K. we'll arrange to meet again uptown. Find out all you can about the hit and call my cell number. He gave it to Peter. If it works out well, I'll arrange to send you and your girlfriend to California with a new identity!"

"Really. You would do that?" Peter could not believe his ears. It was what he had prayed for over the last three years. Being involved with the other two had made it seem impossible,

"I'll do my best. I really don't like what they have agreed to do this time. This country has been good for us all. But they don't seem to care about that. As far as they are concerned the President dared to poke his nose into Ireland and for that he must pay."

Peter gave Pete his address and telephone number in the Village. "Please don't talk posh if you ring up. If someone else answers the phone it'll give the game away."

They agreed and Peter left the room to a worried Pete Maddox.

His first thought was to contact Mark Foster, but he could not use the phone. He was aware that the use of certain words triggered an alert to Homeland Security and, though they may come into things at some time, he did not think now was the time. He realised that he had the answer in his luggage, his satellite phone was encrypted with a scrambler.

He picked up his bag, unpacked the modem and plugged it in to the wall socket. The call went through within seconds. Mark listened to what he had to say and confirmed he should stay in New York until the situation was resolved. He told Pete that GW Harris would contact him in the City and that he would have a full team with him if required. Meanwhile, sit tight and well done.

Out on Broadway once more Pete located a souvenir store and bought a programme of events for the upcoming parade.

At Homeland Security George Blake spoke to the agent in charge of the New York office. He had made his report based on what he had heard personally and had given the tapes in to be analysed by the specialists. Meanwhile, George was having a problem convincing the boss that there was a serious threat from the IRA team in New York. He suggested that the surveillance had been put in place for the purpose of keeping an eye on what had always been recognised as a security risk. Now the expense has been justified. The trouble was that George was having problems getting his boss to take action.

The agent in charge had reached his position by keeping his nose clean. Making waves was not his style of operation. The surveillance had been mounted on orders from above, and until they spoke he would do nothing.

George was frustrated, and he confided his frustrations to his wife. Her reaction was not helpful. She herself had been lobbying for George to retire and join her brother's car hire company where he could earn good money without the risk to life and limb entailed with being a special agent for Homeland Security.

Elsewhere in America the doors were closing on the group directly involved in the movement of the Sarin gas. The Chicago executive was being questioned mercilessly by the FBI, who were determined to take the entire team of people involved to the Grand Jury.

For the first time in this case the FBI had the chance to seize the records of the shipping company and start digging, connecting the links in the chain from first dispatch to delivery. With each new discovery, the executives concerned came under specific scrutiny. For their efforts, and despite the intervention of a team of high-powered lawyers, several members of the senior executive of COMCO were due to enjoy a sojourn in Leavenworth as guests of their government.

There were no hints as to the disappearance of the last bottle of Sarin gas, though an in-depth investigation of the entire delivery from collection in Europe to its eventual destination was underway.

The survival group, who had received the delivery of arms interrupted by GW and his team, received a call from the FBI.

Having been alerted by GW on the subject, Bart had given the agent full details of his collection of the small arms the group had purchased. Without mentioning the identity of the group he had complained bitterly about being hi-jacked. The details of the phone contact in Chicago tied in nicely with the information already in FBI hands.

The west coast of America was a congenial place to live, but it must be said the rather bland climate had begun to pall on both John and Gabrielle. The baby, Ilona, was a happy, healthy child and the delight of their lives, but both realised that they were missing Europe. The financial situation was healthy. Apart from the charter company the private fortunes of both had been accumulating steadily. Trans Ocean Trading was now a market leader in the transport business, and since both were millionaires, money was really no object.

The charter operation was now secure by reputation, and the guiding hand of Brian Ascher had ensured the future of the company. His pursuit of Carol was being continually interrupted by her popularity as a charter skipper. But on the whole the company was a happy place to be.

It was therefore without guilt the Graham/Murray family decided to return to visit the Rosas base, with a view to finding a home in Europe.

Chapter Thirty

Henry Smith was not a happy man. Despite all his efforts to keep the plan for the St Patrick's Day Parade just between Patrick O'Neill and himself it now seemed that he had already discussed matters with two other IRA men. He was aware that the men had a part in the scheme but that made no difference. They did not need to know yet.

Although the car was already in the garage, it was too early to fit the gas bottle. There was the risk of the set up being discovered. The actual fitting need not be done until the last minute. This did not stop them making sure of the seal round the window between driver and passenger. Nor would it prevent the fitting of the trigger switch to open the gas bottle when the window sealed. So far none of this work had been done.

The mechanic allocated for this task had not shown up for the job. When Henry had spoken to his go-between on the subject he had been told that the IRA team would have it done when it was needed, not before. It was because of this that Henry decided to contact the leader Patrick O'Neill direct. He needed to follow the process all the way through to be assured that all went well and up to specification.

Patrick O'Neill was giving his orders to Peter Mahon and Heggarty when the phone rang. The voice at the other end spoke introducing Henry Smith, and then passed the phone to Henry. He gave Patrick his orders and indicated that he wanted them carried out immediately.

Patrick grunted agreement several times then put the phone down.

"Did you hear all that?" he asked. When the other two nodded, he said, "Well, now you can forget it. That eejit seems to think he knows it all. He'll soon learn! So, Peter, have the mechanic do the work on the car window. Make sure he knows to disconnect the release on the rear locks."

Peter nodded and sat back relieved that he had a simple task to perform.

Patrick turned to Michael Heggarty. "I'll need you to go and find out who this Henry Smith is. I'm not happy working for a man I cannot identify. Take a camera and get a picture, and everything else you can gather. Let's have an idea of who is paying the bills here."

The three men discussed the orders. Patrick was contemptuous of the manner with which the plan had been arranged. "This guy is an idiot. His plan stinks. If he wants to hit the President, all he needs is a decent gun and we could have done the job for him without all this nonsense."

Michael pointed out that the whole idea of killing the President in public was to make a point. "It's obvious", he said. "Why else would he go to the trouble to steal a bottle of Sarin gas to do the job, and why include the Mayor of New York in the hit?"

Peter got up and went to the kitchen and made coffee.

"What do you say, Peter?" Patrick's question was as usual sarcastic. He didn't expect a reply and was surprised when Peter spoke.

"I've looked at the instructions and I think it's a good plan. It pays well, and we come out clean. Smith does the dirty work. We stay out of the frame. In fact it would be a good idea for us all to be in California for Saint Patrick's Day. What's wrong with that?" Peter looked at the two men who were both looking at him open-mouthed.

"Something I said?" He looked back at them surprised.

Patrick looked at Michael, shrugged his shoulders and took the coffee handed to him by Peter.

"I suppose your right," he said grudgingly. "Looking at it that way does make sense,.... Though," he hesitated, "I think I'd rather go to Las Vegas. I've always wanted to give that place a try!" To the surprise of the other two men, he grinned. "O.K. we'll do it the way its laid out. Then we'll split up and get lost for a while until the heat dies down."

They sat down and worked on the mechanics of the set-up. While Peter arranged for the modification of the car, Michael went to research Henry Smith and Patrick went off to make the rest of the arrangements for the big day.

Pete Maddox opened the door to Peter Mahon and waved him to a seat. "What's happening in the big wide world outside?" he asked.

Mahon looked thoughtful, then. "I can give you the whole thing, but before I do I want something back!"

"And what might that be?" Pete asked, wondering how much money Mahon wanted.

"I want Pat, Mike and me left right out of it. We are being used as a working party: nothing to do with the hit. I want us all to have a chance to get away from this life."

"I can't promise anything, you know that. All I can do is try and keep you all out of it. My advice to you all would be to get away before the parade. If possible leave the night before at least. The people I'm with are interested in real threats. If we get the planning team and the trigger, it could be enough. Now, what's the score?"

Peter looked at Pete and decided that he could trust him. So he detailed the plan. When he finished, he said, "If you could warn the President in advance, the whole thing would go away."

"Only until the next time!" Pete put in, "When we may not have a friendly face among the planners."

There was a silence while both relaxed with their thoughts. After a few minutes Pete resumed.

"What do you plan on doing when this is over? Do you intend to continue running with Pat and Mike?"

"Not if I can help it." Peter's reply was heartfelt. "I've had enough of the running and hiding, never knowing where the next threat is coming from, nor whether the next meal will be in prison or hell. No, I've had it big time. This is it, the last time, for me and my lady. It's time for a proper job, coming home nights to a real life and perhaps even kids."

After Peter Mahon left, Pete marshalled his thoughts. Then reached for his satphone and punched the speed dial to connect with Mark Foster in Dearborn.

GW liked New York. He had for some years made a point of visiting the city whenever he returned to the US from overseas duty. There was an atmosphere about the place that excited him and whenever he came it was like a new beginning. This time the order, diverting his troop following the incident at Seattle, came out of the blue. The order to liaise with Pete Maddox was a pleasant surprise.

He and Pete had operated together in the past, even before the raid on Vlad's headquarters where he had met Marianne for the first time.

It was an even bigger surprise to discover that the co-ordinator of this operation was Marianne, who had established herself and her laptop in the apartment owned by Michael Ascher on Park Avenue overlooking Central Park. GW found accommodation for his troop in the other four apartments occupying the rest of the top floor of the apartment building.

Michael and Jeanne had decided to convert the entire floor to make one apartment. That was before the kidnapping in France. With the establishment of the Trans Ocean/Secure companies they had decided to shelve the conversion and make the building available when and if required.

GW and Marianne had reached an understanding that would result in marriage, but not yet. They shared a small apartment in the HQ accommodation in Dearborn. Now here in New York, GW was at last able to show her the city he loved and hoped to move to when the time came settle down. It has to be said that since meeting Marianne, he was beginning to think the time had arrived.

Pete was in the apartment chatting to Marianne when GW came in. After the reunion had been celebrated appropriately with coffee and cake, the three were able to sit and plan how they would tackle the latest threat.

Ideally they would stop the car before the President entered it. The main problem was the Secret Service responsible for the security of the President. Obviously they could not warn them too much in advance. The Secret Service would change the routine and ruin the chance of arresting the assassination team. They had a free hand to deal with this operation. Mark Foster did not want to clutter the scene with too many people, and he had a true leader's talent for delegation. With the confidence of the Boss behind them the team was able to make their plans on the spot.

Peter Mahon kept the team up to date with the progress of the preparation of the Mayoral limousine. His participation was no longer unwilling. Now his lady was established in Carmel in a house overlooking the beach, he was feeling more secure than he had felt for years.

The latest news gave the team real hope of a safe option if any delay occurred. The Sarin bottle had been delivered for fitting to the car. GW had obtained a replica painted and marked to replace the deadly gas with a mild soporific. The bottle was identified with a small mark on the base so that mistakes would not be made.

The name, Henry Smith, had meant nothing to the team, until the link was made by Michael Brooks who had seen the photographs of the man provided by Peter Mahon. The man had been located and was under observation as they sat. They had studied the brief on the man. In the opinion of Michael Brooks, Smith had become obsessed with the assassination of the President. The fact that a man, who had for years obtained whatever he was after by wheeling and dealing, now wished to take a physical part in a project, indicated a personal interest in the outcome.

Henry Smith attended the garage where the limousine was being serviced to fit the gas bottle himself. It was with some amusement that the man shadowing Smith observed him donning a gas mask as he fitted the bottle to the underside of the vehicle. Had the bottle leaked the mask would have been useless as a defence from the Sarin gas, since it only needed to touch the skin to take effect.

The replacement bottle was fitted the same night. The original Sarin bottle was sent for careful analysis before disposal.

With his part of the action done, Peter Mahon said goodbye to Patrick and Michael and boarded the United Airlines flight for San Francisco and his new life in California.

Patrick and Michael having seen the plane off, returned to the apartment, where Patrick agreed that he had never intended leaving New York. Michael smiled wryly at Patrick.

"You know that the plan is blown, don't you?"

"The lad was never cut out for the life as I'm sure you know. His brother was a different breed." He sighed. "Now, there was a real soldier. Anyway I've had it. I can't face the thought of sitting by the fire talking old times with a bunch of ex-hard men. The eejit arranging this hit is so bloody clever he will balls the whole thing up, for sure. So it crossed my mind that I could step in and tidy things up. I don't like the President. He's an interfering bastard, and

I have no objection to wiping out a few scuffers on the way. So it's me for the street in the morning, and to hell with the lot of them!"

Michael listened to the man with a small smile on his face. "It's been too long since we had a good scrap. D'ye think New York's finest would be up to it?"

"Well, they are supposed to be mostly Irish, so it should be a fair match!" Patrick opened a bottle of Bushmills and poured two glasses. "To the Cause."He touched Michael's glass with his own and they downed their drinks in one.

Chapter Thirty one

The 17th of March and a street decked with green. In New York there are few events undertaken with more trouble than the celebration of St Patrick's Day. The Tartan Day celebrations of the Scottish links with New York are a respectable worthy effort. But nothing has been able to upstage the tribute to what was once the major part of the population of the City: the central feature of the celebration as always, the 'Grand Parade' through the streets.

Floats, pipe bands, the groups representing the various societies, balloons and ticker tape add up to a glorious public display of nostalgia. Then the siege of the many Irish pubs and bars where the Guinness flows like the Liffey in Dublin.

Of course there are fights and, for the cops of New York, the annual nightmare of parade security is followed by the annual nightmare of the evening. The night becomes a cacophony of sirens of the police cars and ambulances.

This year it was going to be different. This year, to add to their troubles, the President was going to celebrate his Irish heritage along with the Mayor of New York, who happened to be Jewish, though today he would be as Irish as the rest.

Henry Smith came to the garage to collect the Mayor's limo. He looked under the body of the car to confirm the gas bottle was in position. Reassured by the glint of the green paint, he smiled smugly at the thought that the colour was appropriate to the day. Then he opened the driver's door and got in. He wore dark glasses. Luckily, though it was cold, the sun was bright and it already glinted off the cars and the puddles where the streets had been washed. The switch to open the circuit to link the screen to the tap on the gas bottle was next to the gear shift. Even when it was switched on it would not operate the tap until the screen was up and sealed.

He looked forward to telling that self-righteous idiot of a President exactly what was happening as he watched him die.

He had no particular problem with the Mayor. It was his tough luck that he was going to be there in the wrong place at the wrong time. As the car moved off, Patrick O'Neill and Michael Heggarty came out from the garage and stood watching the disappearing vehicle as it turned the first corner on its stately progress to the City Hall.

With a nod the two men climbed into a panel van marked with the city maintenance colours. They drove off down the street in the opposite direction.

In the world of the terrorist, one of the most insidious of glitches is that which can arise out of exclusivity. It is, on occasion, not a problem when one organisation communicates its intention to another on the grounds of mutual benefit. Where the problem does arise is when security rears its head, and the secrecy surrounding the job is such that the hit is only known to the assassins.

Here in New York on the day of the big parade, no less than four assassination plots were lined up, two by separate Middle East groups, one by Henry Smith, and finally the intrepid Irish, in the form of Patrick O'Neill and Michael Heggarty.

The FBI had tabs on the two Middle Eastern groups. Secure Inc, represented by Pete Maddox had Henry Smith covered, but possible interference from Homeland Security was anticipated.

The wild card that no one had anticipated was the IRA team:- Pat and Mike, armed with Armalite rifles loose in the City with no supervision and suicidal tendencies.

The plan for the Mayoral car was to hijack it before Henry Smith released the gas. The screen that was intended to release the gas when it closed had been sabotaged by the simple expedient of placing small stoppers at either end of the screen to prevent it closing properly. If something did go wrong the gas itself would be quite harmless, just a little soporific.

The car was bulletproof. This was general knowledge. The Secret Service had arranged for a decoy car, if needed, to stand in for the Mayor and the President.

The van with the city insignia progressed along the route of the parade as if inspecting for faults in the arrangements. It stopped several times and once Patrick got out, wearing a hard hat to look at some feature.

The progress of the vehicle was followed on the CCTV cameras from the traffic coordination centre. It was here that the inevitable question was asked. "Who ordered that last run through?" The chief traffic coordinator threw the question to the room. No one answered. "Come on. Someone must have." Still no answer. The Chief picked up the direct line to the Police Chief.

"Harry! We've got a maverick cruising the route in a city vehicle. He's on 5th Avenue heading for Times Square. On the cameras the police patrol car appeared from a cross street and blipped his siren, and flashed his roof lights. The panel van took off and swerved round the corner into 42nd Street past the bus depot with the police unit following. Two more police units appeared in front of the van blocking its way down the Street. The van spun in a handbrake turn and passed the pursuing car back to 5th Avenue.

Henry Smith stepped out of the car and opened the rear door for the Mayor.

"Where the hell is George?" the Mayor asked.

"He called in sick this morning, sir, so I stood in for him."

"Who the hell are you?"

"I'm Henry, sir, from the transport office, pulled in at the last minute to substitute for George."

"Well, let's get the show on the road!" The Mayor was fed up. He didn't want to be here anyway.

"The President, Sir?" Henry reminded the Mayor.

"Oh, we pick him up outside Bloomingdales. Weren't you briefed?"

"Sorry, sir. Of course. I had forgotten."

The limo drew up in front of the famous store in time to collect the President who came through the swing doors shaking hands with the store manager. Smith held the back door open while the President seated himself beside the Mayor. He ran round to the driver's door and set off at a sedate pace up 5th Avenue towards Times Square.

His first inkling that something was wrong came when he tried to close the glass screen to cut off contact with the passengers in the rear of the car. Despite several attempts the screen would not close properly. He was forced to stop as the procession allowed other floats to join in from 42nd Street

He looked up at the screen and noticed the wedge in the

channel on the other side of the car. As he began to reach across to remove it, there was a rapping on the glass. The Mayor told him to lower the glass as there was no reason for it to be used.

Henry lowered the glass, and resigned himself to waiting until the end of the parade and taking his chances at that time.

Elsewhere in the City, Pat and Mike were rapidly being overcome with clouds of teargas. As the gas took effect Pat blazed away in desperation, with the Armalite on full automatic. He changed magazines with practiced ease, inserted a 24 round stick into the receiver and cocked the lock. As he lifted the gun, two bullets from a cop's Glock ended the life of the career killer.

Michael, already wounded with a bullet in the stomach, turned his rifle to put it into his mouth. Before he could fire, the rifle was removed. He lashed out to try and recover the gun, only to have his hands cuffed and feel himself being lifted onto a gurney before he lost consciousness. When he woke in hospital he was looking into the cold, blue eyes of the cop beside his bed.

The police authorities in Belfast, Ireland, received the news of the demise of Patrick O'Neill and the arrest of Michael Heggarty, with quiet satisfaction. They made no comment about the absence of Peter Mahon. He was never regarded as a major threat anyway!

As the limousine drew up outside the Yankee Stadium, Henry was getting desperate. So far he had had no chance to remove the wedges from the window channel. He had no idea that they had been deliberately placed there. His only thought was that they had been left in after the window switch had been fitted. Whilst he roundly cursed the so-called experts who had fitted the car, he had no idea that his scheme had been discovered.

While his two passengers were inside the stadium, Henry removed the two wedges from the channel and breathed a sigh of relief. Now he could operate the window properly and carry out his own private execution without interruption.

The rally within the stadium was as long-winded and chilly as it always was. When the last pipe band marched through the exit doors, the Mayor and the President were swiftly bundled into their limousine and, with the heaters going, the car set out back to the Mayor's mansion. The Mayor reached forward and lifted two champagne flutes from the cabinet and from the fridge, a chilled bottle which he opened expertly. He filled the two glasses and handing one to the President, he lifted his own and toasted his companion.

"I'll be honest, Mr President. I always regarded you as a bit of a wimp. But I'll tell you: seeing you stand there today, telling that bunch of mad Irishmen that it was time they grew up, put their toys away and started to concentrate on the new country instead of the old..... I gotta hand it to you. You've got guts, and that crowd knew it. I drink your health, Mr President!"

He clinked the glass against that of the President and drank the wine.

Henry once again pressed the button to close the screen and give the passengers privacy. But once more the Mayor stopped him. When the screen continued to rise he threw his coat over the screen to stop it rising. "I said, keep the goddam screen down!" He turned to the President, "I'm sorry, sir. I hate the damn screen. It makes me feel I'm suffocating so I only have it up if something really special comes up. Do you mind?"

"No problem, Mr Mayor. I kinda agree with you. Keep it open by all means."

In the driving seat Henry was almost in tears. What was up with people these days? Why couldn't they just do what was expected of them? He had a good plan. Why should it go so wrong? They would be back at the Mansion soon, and the chance would be gone. The passengers were deep in conversation. He cautiously slid the coat from the screen making it possible for the screen to be closed. He carefully slid the screen higher and higher until, as he drew into the driveway of the Mayoral mansion, the screen seated itself with a sigh.

Henry sat in his seat waiting for the few moments necessary to finish the two men off. He felt tired, it had been an exhausting day. In his rear view mirror he watched the two passengers slump back with eyes closed. Then he felt a sharp pain in his chest, Like his passengers he fell back, eyes closing.

The waiting Secret Service men opened the doors of the car and helped the President and the Mayor out of the car. Both perked up within moments. They looked at the driver still slumped over the wheel. The President said, "Is that who I think it is?"

The Secret service man said "Henry Smith, Sir. Once Director of the Presidential Security Bureau."

"Is he all right? He looks unwell!"

"I'm afraid he passed away. Looks like a heart attack to me. Please leave it with me, sir. We will take you back to your hotel when you are ready."

The Mayor took the President by the arm and led him into the house for a late supper and a nightcap with their wives, who were already within.

Chapter Thirty two

The old harbour was built in the bay formed largely by a cove in the otherwise unbroken wall of cliff running along the coast in this region of the Golfo de Rosas. The village was clinging to the narrow strip of land lining the wall of the cove, mainly fisherman's cottages. On a strip where the land widened stood the Castillo. The 16th Century construction had survived war and revolution and now it presented its battered face to the 21st Century, sadly unloved, but still substantially complete. It had its own quay and there were the partial remains of a boathouse. It only needed tender, loving care to be restored to its late 18th Century glory.

John and Gabrielle discovered the village and the castle whilst exploring the coast from the Rosas base. The cleaner in their apartment on the base had mentioned the village and the Castillo. Last owned in the 19th Century by a French family, the whole building had been abandoned thirty years ago by the caretakers. A telephone call to the Alcade in Rosas quickly established that the Castillo Dorado was currently the property of the state. The keys were, of course, available for the visitors to examine the building at their leisure. After searching down the coast for several days the couple decided to pick up the keys and look at the castle. They did not anticipate that the place would be suitable, but they had an afternoon free.

Driving down into the old village of Rosas, it was a surprise for them both to realise they were passing from one age to another. Despite the signs of modernity, TV aerials, modern cars and smart clothes, the buildings and café's seemed to breathe the past. Their first view of the Castillo caused John to stop the car in the nearest parking spot and get out. Gabrielle followed and took his hand as they stood spellbound by the sight of the old building standing against the cliff in the afternoon sun.

They were both entranced. John broke the spell and they walked forward to the iron gates, standing between twin towers in the unbroken wall, tied into the cliff on both sides. The big padlock submitted to the key from the bunch supplied by the Mayor's office in Rosas.

They crossed the cobblestones of the courtyard to the main door of the building. The shutters over the windows in the entrance hall made the place seem gloomy after the glare of the sun outside. But when John threw the shutters back the dusty sunlight streamed in to disclose the patterned moulded ceiling and panelled walls. The broad stairs rose directly opposite the front door and there were reception rooms off to both sides. They walked through the ground floor, the door under the stairs leading to the kitchen and scullery, with further rooms for the servants behind, built into the face of the cliff.

Upstairs, there were several bedrooms, all with windows overlooking the sea. The curtain wall was low enough to allow the view.

A further stair gave to three more rooms and a terrace, with an embrasured wall, the cannon mounted on slides and rusted in place. Two outer stairs on either side led to a high terrace, where the flagpole leaned drunkenly against the cliff face.

John and Gabrielle descended to the ground floor and took the side door to the boathouse and quay. The steps descended beneath the shelter of the boathouse roof to the quay where the waters of the Mediterranean washed the face of the cut stone blocks. The gates at the seaward end of the dock were battered and partly broken, though they still offered some protection from the weather. On closer examination it was obvious that they had been constructed to seal the dock to allow the water to be pumped out to allow the dock to be used as a dry dock. The couple stood on the dock side by side. They turned to face each other. Both had a look of sheer joy on their faces.

"Oh, yes, John. This is the place!" She buried her face in his chest.

"Of course. You see it too." John said. He lifted the cell phone from his pocket, and one-handed pressed the speed dial number for their Spanish lawyer. "Castillo Dorado, buy it!" he said and closed the phone.

The working party had done wonders. The entrance hall had been cleared and the stone floor tiles scrubbed and polished, the panelling had been rubbed down and polished. The stairway was now carpeted. The balusters and banisters were gleaming and the shuttered windows had been curtained with tasteful drapes.

Upstairs, all the bedrooms had dressing rooms, a relic of the early 20th Century. These had been turned into en-suite bathrooms, making the castle visitor friendly. The complete rewiring of the building had been accomplished with minimum damage and disruption. Even the servants' quarters had been fitted to modern hotel standard.

The housewarming was held in the two large reception rooms and allowed to flow through the entrance hall between.

Wally Peterson stood talking to John as they enjoyed a quiet moment outside the French windows of the drawing room.

"I'm pleased with the way the alarm system has been fitted. There are no obvious connectors etc., to muck up the décor!"

John nodded." Your lad did a wonderful job on the restoration."

"We were both surprised and impressed by the local craftsmen here. The lad has taken six of them back to UK to do some special restoration work on a stately home in Kent. At UK rates the boys reckon to make enough money on the job to give them a good living here for some time."

"The Alcade was delighted you used the locals here. It made it much easier to put the purchase through, and with the local servants, we seem to have the whole village on our side. The main thing is that Gabrielle and I are delighted with the place. By the way I was told to remind you that you are welcome here anytime. If we are away, to use the house. If we are full up, use the guest house by the gate."

Wally looked around to make sure nobody was near. "Have you looked in the secret passage and rooms yet?"

"Not yet, after this is all over we'll take a proper look. So far I've only had time to see the main passage. There is obviously much more to explore."

John went back in to his other guests while Wally drifted off to look over the grounds, just in case.

The passage had been driven straight into the cliff face behind Castillo Dorado. The entrance was located behind the fireplace in the drawing room that overlooked the sea on the left hand side of the great stairway. When Wally had been checking the stone work to ensure the chimney was safe to use, he had pushed one of the finely cut slabs that made up the back wall of the great fireplace which was big enough to stand in. The slab had moved. So Wally had pushed and the entry had opened on beautifully crafted pivots making room for a man to step through comfortably. Wally had fetched the torch he had been using to examine the chimney and shone it through the entrance revealing the passage stretching away into the rock. Before closing the door he had checked the mechanism from inside, before hastily closing the door to ensure that the entry was still concealed.

When he spoke to John that evening he explained that, since he suffered from claustrophobia, he did not investigate further.

It was several days after the housewarming party before John had the time and the inclination to explore the secret passage found by Wally. Gabrielle and the baby, Ilona, were visiting John's daughter, Sally, and her family; combining the visit with discussions with Douglas Stewart over her new book.

Following the instructions given by Wally, John found and pressed the slab. The entrance slowly pivoted revealing a dark passage beyond. Checking his torch, John stepped into the passage and stood looking at the beautifully crafted stonework that formed the first few feet of the secret area. The stonework was jointed to the bare rock. A fault in the cliff face had been widened and chiselled to create a tunnel. Immediately to the left and right of the entry were rooms that had once been occupied. At this point the entry closed behind him shocking him momentarily. He examined the controls on the inside of the door and found the lever that opened the door once more. He also found the simple, locking bar which would prevent anyone opening the door from the other side.

Ensuring the door operated by testing the mechanism a few times, John allowed it to close by inertia as it was designed. He then turned and examined the two rooms in detail. The left hand room had a stone platform at the far side which was probably used as a bed. A cut-out section of the wall had two books and a few pieces of paper. A quill and a pot of dried-out ink also lay there in some dust, though not an excessive amount. He decided to investigate later and turned to the room on the right which was, by contrast, full of interesting-looking bits and pieces, worthy of proper investigation later. One item that particularly caught his eye was the sword which lay naked beside its scabbard on the wooden sideboard against the wall.

When he picked it up it seemed to nestle in his hand as if it belonged. Lifting it immediately demonstrated the balance of the beautiful weapon. With a silent promise, John laid the sword down once more and turned down the passage to explore further.

The way followed the fault in a series of curves, the rough rock trimmed where necessary to make passage easy. About ten metres along there was another room, obviously a store room still piled with anonymous boxes and furniture. Beyond the passage was blocked by what looked like solid rock. On close examination however John found there was another lever in a fault to one side. A piece of rock was lying on the floor, and when John picked it up, he realised it fitted into the fault concealing the handle within.

A pull on the lever caused a groaning noise. With a little help from John's shoulder the door opened. Once again created by an expert, the door merely needed the dust to be cleared away to operate as other one had, also closing by inertia. The door led outside behind a natural slab that concealed it from direct view. The outside area was around the cliff from the Castillo and under the shelter of the overhang of the cliff above. What looked like an animal path meandered off through the scattered rock partially covering the area, The path disappeared round the face of the cliff.

John sat on a smooth rock realising as he did, that the rock had been placed by others and used as a seat in the past. He ran his hand over the surface wondering who else had sat like this gazing out over the sea.

He rose and returned to the secret complex, carefully closing the door behind him. Leaving the store room for the moment he went back to the first room and started to examine the contents.

The books were all old: possibly a first edition of Don Quixote, a book of prayers in Latin, and what looked like a diary with entries in copperplate handwriting in French, but not modern French.

He put it to one side and looked at the papers. The first was unfolded and the paper brittle: a note written in what looked like the same beautiful copperplate. It translated:-

Castillo Dorado
21st September 1697
My Love,

If you are reading this letter then I will probably be dead. You know I will come for you as soon as I can, but if you have needed to enter our secret place then the Moors have conquered and our home has fallen.

There are provisions for many months if needed, but if you take care and choose your time, escape, using the boat at the foot of the cliff, should be possible. Look after the children and assure them I love them. Hoping we meet again in the life hereafter,

> *All my love,*
> *Michel*

John picked up a second paper, of different texture to the first note and written in a different hand.

To whoever finds this note:-

I, Madame Jeanne de Borlaine do will all the contents of this secret place, to whoever finds it.

Having lost my beloved husband and my two wonderful children. I no longer wish to live without them. I shall take a last walk ere I take my last sleep, praying to rejoin my family in the hereafter.

> *Pray for me,*
> *Jeanne de Borlaine*
> *January 1698*

John sat in silence for several minutes before rising and examining more closely the platform bed in the corner of the room. Beneath the top cover on the bed, what he had taken to be a heap of clothes was in fact the remains, well preserved in the dry atmosphere, of a lady in a long dress, obviously very old, untouched for centuries. A cup lay beside the body and a small bottle stood beside the wall.

He thought of the events that had brought him to this point in his life: the loss of his wife, not forgotten but no longer the sharp ache it once was: his new family and this wonderful home that was the scene of this earlier love story

The boat that they found housed in the cave at the foot of the cliff still sat in its cradle. The combination of the sun's warmth through the cave mouth, and the dampness of the sea washing the lower reaches of the cave had combined to preserve the 40 foot, carvel built boat. The mast lay on its chocks though the sails had disintegrated many years ago. The oars lay behind the thwarts still ready for use, and the dismounted rudder was laid beside the hull on blocks, the bronze pintles waiting to be dropped into the bronze rings projecting from the stern of the boat.

John and Gabrielle decided that the boat should be left in place, and arranged for it to be checked and repaired, in situ if necessary. It would be sailed for the first time in nearly three hundred years at the celebrations for the little village's 250 year birthday celebrations.

The departure of the two experts from the Victoria and Albert Museum followed the clearing out of the secret rooms and passage. They used Martin, Wally's son, sworn to secrecy, with John helping with the heavy lifting. Most of the items found had gone to the V&A though some went to the Louvre and other items to the Prado. No disclosure was made of the discovery of the secret passage. The sword, found in the right hand room on his first exploration now cleaned and restored to its former glory was the main feature on the wall of what was now John's study.

The whole complex of the secret passage and rooms was now lit by electricity and running water had been installed. Simple furniture had been fitted and communication established with the outside world including, on the insistence of Kelly Martin, a direct line to Rosas in case of emergency.

The secret of the complex was known only to the four of them, Wally and Martin, his son, John and Gabrielle.

The enquiries into the origins of the de Borlaine family revealed that the Comte de Borlaine and his family had been reported lost at sea in 1696, during a storm in the Mediterranean. The Comte and his Jeanne, with their two children, had sailed from Marseille with their possessions to the colonies in India. The ship was presumed lost when planks from the ship's boat were found washed up on the coast of Mallorca, two weeks after the ship had sailed, nothing further had been heard of the ship or the family. The de Borlaine name disappeared during the French Revolution, their family home in Gascony being destroyed during the early riots of the period.

How they came to Castillo Dorado and why, remains a mystery. The diary of Jeanne, found by John, included only vague references to the years before 1698, no specific comment on how or why they came to Spain. Nor was there reference to the enemy (Moorish Pirates?) that caused the lady and her children to shelter in the secret rooms.

John and Gabrielle settled down in their first permanent home, the Castillo and the area surrounding it being in all ways perfect for their requirements. The local people were friendly and the ability to step onto the *Orion* from their own private quay and sail away at will was joy to them both. They entertained both the local friends and the many friends encountered through the establishment of TOT international.

Michael and Jeanne came regularly and spoiled Ilona, who wrapped them round her little finger. Michael had stood as Godfather, alongside Kelly as Godmother, so both John and Gabrielle felt the future of their daughter was assured whatever happened.

They sat together on the stone seat looking out over the sea at the descending sun. The water rippled and shimmered in the evening light. The red ball seemed to drop quite sharply for the last few minutes of its path and the velvety dusk swiftly changed to night drawing a curtain over the view. John put his arm round Gabrielle. They rose and slowly walked back through the secret passage to the lounge,

"Do you realise that since you thumbed a lift on the *Aimee Bretonne*. Life has been one long series of alarms and excursions from our first meeting until now. This is the first peaceful moment we've shared since we met."

Gabrielle hugged him,

"That's life. Exciting isn't it?"

The End

www.ingramcontent.com/pod-product-compliance
Lightning Source LLC
Chambersburg PA
CBHW051540260626
47170CB00003B/1023